"I should get back to base."

Her jaw dropped. "Are you crazy? I just told you I was pregnant and the kid's not yours, *and you have to leave*?"

"I know, but it's cool. I won't ask for a divorce unless you want to."

"Stan!"

"You don't know what they're making in the Winchester plant, Bea; you haven't seen their creations, so you couldn't have known any better. But it's OK. The jungle can't get you here."

I headed for the road, leaving my towel behind because it wasn't critical for where I was going, and anyway, it couldn't wipe off the sense of failure. So instead, I'd take care of Bea and her kid because she was right: I was never at home, and maybe if I stayed married, it would make up for everything.

"*Stan!*" she screamed.

But I was past the point of recognizing my name, and she just didn't get it: there was no Stan. Not anymore. The jungle had taken him and would never let go, not for anything.

BY T. C. McCARTHY

The Subterrene War
Germline
Exogene
Chimera

CHIMERA

The Subterrene War: Book 3

T. C. McCARTHY

www.orbitbooks.net

This book is a work of fiction. Names, characters, places, and incidents are the product of the author's imagination or are used fictitiously. Any resemblance to actual events, locales, or persons, living or dead, is coincidental.

Copyright © 2012 by T. C. McCarthy
Excerpt from *2312* copyright © 2012 by Kim Stanley Robinson

Orbit
Hachette Book Group
237 Park Avenue, New York, NY 10017
www.HachetteBookGroup.com

First Edition: July 2012

Orbit is an imprint of Hachette Book Group, Inc. The Orbit name and logo are trademarks of Little, Brown Book Group Limited.

The Hachette Speakers Bureau provides a wide range of authors for speaking events. To find out more, go to www.hachettespeakersbureau .com or call (866) 376-6591.

The publisher is not responsible for websites (or their content) that are not owned by the publisher.

10 9 8 7 6 5 4 3 2 1

Printed in the United States of America

For Sean

ACKNOWLEDGMENTS

Special thanks to DongWon Song, Tim Holman, Anna Gregson and Tom Bouman—the best editorial team on the planet—and to Alex Field, my agent. A special thanks also to all the people who took the time to review *Germline* and *Exogene*; there aren't enough words to express my appreciation.

BEFORE

flew around the world," said Bea. "All you can do is sit there?"

The waves crashed so that I flinched and checked for my carbine, forgetting that weapons weren't allowed on leave. Thailand's jungles were close. Mountains rose almost vertically behind us to leave only a sliver of beach, and while I thought Bea looked beautiful in her bikini, there was too much going on to admire her; palms bent in a strong wind and whispered, warning that the mountains weren't done yet—that soon they would have me again and hadn't forgotten what I'd brought to them, were ready to pay me back for introducing an abomination. This was intermission.

"It's good to see you. I didn't think they'd let anyone fly into Bangkok since things flared up."

She shook her head. "What's going on in this place, Stan? The *Thais* are at war with Rangoon; so why do they need *you*? I'm tired of sitting at home and only getting a week or two before you disappear for another six months." Bea was crying now. I wanted to reach out and hold her hand or pull her in close because a part of me recalled that it was something she liked, the physical contact an instant reassurance, but my hands felt like lumps of lead.

"You know how it is," I said. "The King asked for help, and I guess the US likes to stick with its friends."

"*Are you kidding?* How about sticking by your wife? Can't you just quit?"

The question made me nauseous and tense at the same time, and the sand breathed warmth under my legs, too warm, as if it had begun to smolder. "I can't."

"Why not?"

"There's nothing to fear. I eat this job, it makes me strong, and there's no angle in leaving because this is where I belong. What else would I do?"

"I'm pregnant."

The seconds ticked by until I shrugged. "You don't look like it."

"I've been pregnant for a month."

"I wasn't home a month ago."

"I know," she said. "What's funny is that I can't remember his name, only that he wasn't even my type. A scientist, some kind of genetic engineer working at the new production plant outside Winchester."

Everything went blank. If she knew what happened when my mind went in that direction, Bea would have run because it meant nothing mattered except the mission. But there wasn't any mission now, and instead, the ways I could kill her flicked though my mind along with rage and sadness—a sadness that grew from failure and irony that she'd hooked up with a scientist from the Winchester plant. Even the jungle blamed Winchester for what happened under its canopy. Feelings shredded my stomach.

Sound came from between my lips, a kind of groan that coincided with a swing so that my fist almost connected with her cheek but stopped less than an inch away, and Bea smiled, satisfied that for once she'd been able to penetrate and that all it took was another guy. There wasn't much time before my hands grabbed her neck; I knew it and she didn't, so before anything more could happen, I jumped to my feet and began the job of killing every feeling I could. Shutting each one off mentally and stabbing any that threatened to get up and try for me again, but for some reason the sense of failure resisted the effort. *Grew.*

"I should get back to base."

Her jaw dropped. "Are you crazy? I just told you I was pregnant and the kid's not yours, *and you have to leave*?"

"I know, but it's cool. I won't ask for a divorce unless you want to."

"Stan!"

"You don't know what they're making in the Winchester plant, Bea; you haven't seen their creations, so you couldn't have known any better. But it's OK. The jungle can't get you here."

I headed for the road, leaving my towel behind because it wasn't critical for where I was going, and anyway, it couldn't wipe off the sense of failure. So instead, I'd take care of Bea and her kid because she was right: I was never at home, and maybe if I stayed married, it would make up for everything.

"*Stan!*" she screamed.

But I was past the point of recognizing my name, and she just didn't get it: there was no Stan. Not anymore. The jungle had taken him and would never let go, not for anything.

ONE

Cleanup

Dzhanga. Nobody wanted Dzhanga. Not even the flies that swarmed over the mud, buzzing so loudly that they sounded furious, angry to have been born from some corpse in the middle of central Asia, and maybe they wanted Dzhanga the least of all because for the flies there wasn't any chance of seeing anything *except* Turkmenistan. Imagine that: living your entire life in a Turkmen slum, the high point of which would be finding the body of a rat in which to reproduce. At least I wasn't a fly. But the Subterrene War had been over long enough that missions were hard to get, and I'd waited so long for this one that there was no way to turn it down, so they'd dropped me from thirty thousand feet, where I'd spiraled down and gone through layer after layer of clouds, descending on this—yet another stillborn Turkmen city, a gray-and-brown smear of humanity that clung to the banks of the Caspian and whose waters had become infected with the filth of people, a sheen of oil and scum visible as soon as I hit the five thousand foot mark and popped my chute. That had been a week ago. For a mission that was to have lasted three days, a week meant that this one was bad, that this chick wasn't going down easy. But every step made me harder. Each day sharpened the edge. It didn't worry me that I hadn't found her yet and didn't consider it a problem (although I knew they were shitting back at the outpost, wondering why it was taking so long) because the mission was my life, and those endless days on the rack, nights without air-conditioning on a hotel's bug-ridden mattress with stains that hadn't come from me—those were the hardest things to bear, so that a prolonged mission struck me as a vacation, like a dog must feel when you let it off the leash. When off duty and on standby, the world ate at your skin until you couldn't wait anymore. You were supposed to stay in your hotel room, by the phone, because we didn't carry cells and had no means of communication when off the line, no electronics at all and no indication that we belonged to the machine because we weren't allowed anything regulation except weapons. No crew cuts, no uniform, and no salutes. To those crotch-rotting hookers back in Armenia, I was a businessman, some fool and a drunk, which until now had made me their best customer. But not anymore. She was out there, and it wouldn't be much longer because something told me she had started to fade.

In the bag by week's end, that was the deal, and you just knew this would be hairy because she was past discharge by more than six months, which meant the girl was supercharged and out there with no sense of reality, her world a kind of half hallucination where fear and death thoughts merged. Other cleanup crews wanted to split the job, but that wasn't about to happen; alone was better. It took a special kind of solitude to hear the things I did and a wired mind to parse them until only valid information remained—little nuggets that most people would have missed because the fact that Dzhanga was a shit hole would have distracted them. Being alone meant everything was mine: Time. The wind. *Smells* especially. Even the dead Turkmen who stared at me, slumped against the side of his hut on the other side of the dirt track, with eyes that looked happy instead of surprised; those eyes stopped me cold because there wasn't any reason to be happy. Not in Dzhanga. Not anywhere. He shouldn't have even been there if you thought about it, should have left the city abandoned as the oil industry had a hundred years before, the way you'd toss a fifty at a bartender without looking back. So his happiness was information; it just wasn't clear if it was *useful* information. I knelt in front of him and stared into his eyes, which had glazed over after dying, and I grabbed him by his long beard, touching his nose against my vision port so I could get a better look, maybe through his retinas and into his brain so it could tell me what made him smile. Why dying—when I'd fired four fléchettes into his skull—was so damn funny.

But there wasn't anything to learn; instead, my armor vibrated in a strong wind, a reminder to keep moving. It wasn't the standard-issue armor they handed to regulars, and I took care of it the same way you'd take care of anything that meant so much, because even though I hadn't paid for it with money, I'd paid for it with time; it was my own design. Instead of the thick, green ceramic plates on normal suits, mine were thin, sand-colored ones sandwiching a millimeter of titanium. The joints consisted of a special polymer, rubber, and Teflon amalgamation that stayed quiet no matter how far I walked, preventing every plate from touching its neighbor with that annoying clicking sound, the one that would have gotten me killed a long time ago, the one that tunnel rats—subterreners and their genetically engineered girls, satos—repeated until dead.

It took a moment for my sniffer to process the area and then…nothing. Not a single useful thing came from the Turkmen, and aside from a few molecules of hydrocarbons, remnants detaching from the massive oil storage tanks that rusted behind me at the port, only dust filled the air.

"Negative," the suit's computer said, her voice that of a woman whom I had named Kristen, the same as my first girlfriend in high school. She told me what I already knew from the display, but she was wrong; the sato was out here.

"Clean?" I whispered. "Bullshit. She's rotting. Close."

My suit chimed, surprising me. "Priority transmission, Sergeant, with the proper authentication key for Rabbit Five; should I play it?"

Rabbit Five was my controller, Wheezer, across the Caspian and safe in Armenia, where he sat in a shack and monitored the occasional status burst from the suit, relayed via satellite to his tiny dish on the edge of a runway. "Sure," I said.

Wheezer was laughing. "You want me to tell you where she is? I have her marked; your little angel got her three hours ago, and tracking is all green."

He was messing with me. The angel, my targeting drone, flew somewhere overhead and saw everything, so it was just waiting to pipe the information into my system if I wanted it—the sato's exact location—but somehow it would have been cheating. Wheezer knew how much I hated the drone; his question had been a joke, the one thing he knew would piss me off.

"Do you wish to respond?" Kristen asked.

"Negative. Don't want to risk another burst."

I scanned the area. The hut was part of a string of shacks that formed a small neighborhood near Dzhanga's abandoned rail-transfer point, a station that tanker cars once used to fill themselves from hundreds of now-empty oil storage vessels, most of them ruptured and torn open from a long-forgotten war. When the wind blew through them, it moaned. An hour ago I had gotten my first hit, a single tone from my computer followed by the announcement, *"Germline unit, reading above background,"* which meant that the chick was nearby and ripe, her skin starting to liquefy, and if I was lucky, her vision had blurred, with both eyes a milky-white. For now, though, Kristen stayed quiet; my heads-up read ambient temperature and weather data.

"Not much longer," I whispered and wiped a film of dust from both vision ports.

My headgear was custom. The helmet fit snugly so that a centimeter of space separated me from the ceramic, and the only way to open it was to pop it from the neck ring, then unbuckle it from the back so the entire assembly would open in a clamshell fashion, just like the suit's chest carapace. The helmet was art. A guy in New York had designed it, doped up and high, but the result had been something that resembled the head of a wasp, with wide oval vision ports and an extended "snout" that contained an integral collector unit to receive data from microbots or any one of a hundred other tools I used. Underneath it all, my vision hood clung like a second skin, so tight that I couldn't afford the luxury of a beard. Nobody ever accused me of being a subterrener, one of those who lived among the fungus and rock and who shit all over their legs because it was easier to just dump waste than to take care of it with a few steps to the nearest flush port; those men grew beards to cushion their cheeks from the rough canvas of the hoods and came out of their bunkers with the bewildered look of a thousand Rip van Winkles. It had been years since I'd fought underground, and my suit told everyone that its occupant was a specialized thing, not to be used in tunnels or hangars. The hood underneath was the final piece, one last thing to set me apart from conscripts and those with the tired careers of lifers and superlifers; it had front magnetic claws that clicked into the sensor package on my helmet, which, in turn, sent data to my goggle lenses, a continuous heads-up feed of information that included chem-bio readings and the ticker for nitrogen compounds, explosives, or the real deal: rotting, human flesh.

Soon, the dead Turkmen would interfere with my sensors.

I dragged the body into the man's hut, glanced around to make sure there was nobody there, and then shut the door so I could look through the crack—when the computer chimed again.

"Priority message, Sergeant, keyed to a general emergency frequency." But this time she didn't ask for approval, since it was priority, and piped it in.

"Challenge-echo, challenge-echo, challenge-echo. Echo-seven-six..."

I waited for the numbers to rattle off. "Go ahead, Wheez."

"Subterrene War's over, Bug. It's official."

"The war ended months ago when the Russians pulled out. That's why Command wanted me to break radio silence?"

"No," said Wheezer, "it means that we're all being recalled. President just gave the order to pull in every man from the east and let the girls rot. We're to go after them in Europe and friendly countries, but they want us out of the hot spots now. Something to do with the Chinese. Pickup at primary retrieval at oh six, tomorrow."

Now I was angry, and to hell with whoever might be zeroing in on my location, triangulating on the open transmission; I almost saw the radio waves, a huge neon arrow pointing down at me from the sky. "I have one betty out here somewhere. There's signs everywhere, and she can't be far. I get readings every once in a while. I'll come in when she's dead."

But Wheezer wasn't listening anymore, and the radio stayed quiet. I flicked on my chameleon skin and slid out the door, shutting it behind me and wincing when the sound of children floated up the road from the main town to the north.

You wouldn't have seen me. The goatherds never did, and it was funny because I knew all these Turkmens so well while none of them knew me. The kids had come close—once—to finding my hiding spot in the scrub, buried under a thin layer of sand and goat dung, because they had been playing soccer, and one of them kicked into my face, sending their ball on a wild bounce when it should have kept going straight. The kid who chased it down had almost died then; but he went on his way, and none of them knew how close it had been. The chameleon skins had been the greatest invention of the century, a polymer coating that—if you maintained it—would bend light, allowing the suit's wearer to blend with the surroundings. Now the kids were at least a hundred yards away but heading toward me, so I sprinted across the road and lost sight of them as soon as I entered the rail yard.

"Probable Germline unit detected," Kristen announced, "readings well above baseline, concentration gradient bearing two-seven-nine-point-eight."

And everything went still. The map blinked onto my display and I moved out, charting a silent course through the concrete-and-steel wreckage, a forest of towering oil tanks that had been blown to create a twisted still life, huge flaps of rusted steel that fluttered just a bit in strong gusts. The sun gave the air a kind of shimmer that happened in the third world. It was hazy with maybe a little smoke and dust so that you knew if you popped lid there'd be a strong smell of sulfur and alcohol from the power plants, maybe an occasional whiff of ozone from the fusion reactors and generators. She'd be on the other side of the next tank; her red dot beckoned to me, begged me to come in. I rounded the concrete base, my carbine already pointed in her direction…and she disappeared before I could get a bead.

"This is crap."

"Target lost," Kristen said.

"No shit."

She'd gone to ground. My mind screamed at the prospect of having to follow, shouted that there shouldn't be a tunnel, not this close to the sea where the water table would be high, and that it must be a sort of optical illusion, but it wasn't. The entrance opened in front of me, a wide concrete wall, in the middle of which was a black hole, square and waiting, daring me to go to the one place I hated: underground.

"Damn it," I said, trying to convince myself that it would be easy, and went in.

My vision hood switched to infrared at the same time I stepped in a kind of soft goo or thick water; then I knew what this was—a sewer, carrying the city's filth to the sea—and that by the end of the mission I'd be covered with waste. My external mics picked up her breathing now, amplified it and homed in, the display telling me which direction to head, but it didn't need to. She was there. The betty had backed against a wall to face me less than ten meters from where I stood, and she was missing one arm below the elbow. I flicked on my helmet lamp and switched back to normal vision, deactivating the suit's chameleon skin so she could see me.

The girl smiled. "I want to live."

"That's going to be a problem."

"I'm unarmed. In Turkmenistan. Look."

She raised both hands. One was a stump that dripped blood, and the skin above it had turned a deep black, boiling with infection and rot, and her one remaining hand didn't look much better. The girl's left eye had gone white, and she must have flipped because she started toward me, a rotting zombie of a genetic, all of about eighteen.

"Are you here from God?"

I backed toward the entrance, centering my targeting reticle on her forehead. "Where have you been, and who helped you escape? Kristen, record this."

"Are *you* God?"

"You're hallucinating," I said. "It's the spoiling. Your mind and body are breaking down, consuming themselves because you've reached the end of your shelf life. Try to keep it together. I need you to answer a couple of questions, and it will all be over."

"People don't have shelf lives."

"You aren't people. We created you; *people* made you."

"Are you God?"

"Who helped you escape?" I screamed, knowing that in a second she'd go for me, and when she took another step closer, I decided to get it over with. The fléchettes cracked through her skull, and she dropped into the sewage, face-first, making it easy for me to dig the tracking device from her neck. Kristen chimed up when I scanned it.

"Unit one-three-two-seven-four-nine. Given name of Allison. Terminated postschedule. Transmitting."

I hiked back outside to let the scum slide down my legs, hoping it would dry and dreading the smell that would hit once I took off my helmet.

The sun started to set on the horizon, and from the tank farm I had a good view of it over the Caspian so that I rested my back against a block of concrete, lay my carbine across my legs, and began to peel off my helmet—not even caring when the stink assaulted me. As soon as I lit the first cigarette, it all melted away. The mission was over. From there I'd motor across the sea into Armenia, then board transport back to the States until I got the next call, Wheezer and me grinning at each other as we ran across some tarmac and onto a waiting transport. Missions were the reason to live, the only things worth doing, and Wheezer was a good partner to have.

It wasn't clear how I'd make it, having to wait for the next one, because I'd been home once in the last three years. And home didn't work for me anymore.

"No," I said.

"Are you sure?" the kitchen asked. Its computer

sounded arrogant, made me want to put a fist through the wall and find its circuits, rip them out one by one to taunt the thing, and let it know that the end was near. "Egg yolks contain harmful cholesterol. Medical records indicate a thirty percent chance that your arteries could become dangerously obstructed within the next ten years."

I shut off the voice function and sighed. *Home*. Beatrice had relocated to one of the reclamation sites, a frontier city in the west, the region hardest hit by the years of war and famine, an old city that the government was trying to repopulate. It was a second front of sorts. Fighting for peace meant fighting against nature and the after-effects of nuclear war, and someone in the government thought that by plopping down a few thousand people to stake its claim that maybe things would take care of themselves. It had been three weeks since I'd first returned, and already I was sliding down into my thoughts, drowning, so that when the call had come at 3 a.m., I nearly laughed out loud. But that would have woken her and the kid, and I didn't want her to see me so happy—relieved that I'd be heading back out on a new mission.

You could cross our apartment in ten steps, and it had a tiny kitchen plastered with advertisements for the marvels of self-contained living—like the one above the sink, a sticker declaring that the Government Omni-Unit was smaller, more efficient, and less expensive to install than other modular brands. I rinsed the measuring cup. The moisture collectors came to life, humming like trapped hornets to remind me that in the west, life existed on a knife's edge, where reuse wasn't just a slogan but something that could mean the difference between having enough water or not. I unbuttoned my uniform tunic and smoothed it over a chair to make sure that I didn't get it dirty while cooking. Then I shivered, not wanting to think about water, and switched the voice back on.

"...And the use of butter for cooking is ill-advised both from health and rationing perspectives. Your allotment for the month is almost gone, Sergeant Resnick."

"I know!"

Half an hour later, the alarms went off in both racks. Phillip emerged first. He bounced out of his bed as I watched, and like a kid, the boy didn't bother to say anything before he plopped in front of the holo station, where he swayed back and forth and ran both hands through the projections.

"Use less, want less," he sang with a commercial. "Less waste means more for space. Opportunity is what we make of it!"

"Good morning, Master Phillip," the kitchen said. "Today's a big day for your father."

I stiffened at the reminder, wondering if Phillip would know it meant I'd be leaving, and watched Beatrice pull herself out of bed.

"Jesus." She moved to the side and waited for the master rack to retract into its wall. "I'm still exhausted. You're up early."

"I got the call last night. Deployment's in an hour."

"So that's it."

I flipped the last omelet and lowered the heat on the stove. "That's it. You and the kid need money, Bea. It's the only job I know."

She lit a cigarette and blew smoke at the ceiling. "We moved here last year. I had to lie and tell them that it was for patriotic reasons, wanting to reclaim the west, all that kind of bullshit. Really it was because they pay a hardship stipend, extra money because of the radiation danger, and what you give us isn't enough. Not nearly."

"What's your point?"

"My point is that I don't care if you stay or not. I just want to know why you do it."

"What do you mean?" I asked.

"Why go out and kill like you do? Why take all those risks? It would be nice to know, so that when you're dead— and Phillip starts asking questions—I can tell him why."

It was hard to even think; an empty bottle of bourbon rested on the counter beside me, and I marveled at the fact that so little had already muddled my brain. It never used to work that fast.

"It's good," I said, ignoring the urge to remind her that *technically* I wasn't his father. "I like that you came down here. To help. Even if it was for the money, you're still helping to make sure that we head in another direction, that we don't go back to worse times."

Phillip turned from the holo, just for a moment, to look at me while quoting another line. "We don't want to go back to those days!"

"So you're not going to answer," Beatrice said.

"I don't know why you're complaining. Wheezer called earlier. Both he and Michelle went to Canada for vacation, and things are better up there, the whole corridor from Pennsylvania to Chicago filled with industries gearing up to process the metals we brought back from Kaz. Tell him that's why I do it. That's why I kill. And those factories will be ready once metals start coming in from space, once they get an engine that can handle mining missions."

"Have you gotten your things together?" she asked.

"Stop trying to change the subject."

"I'm not trying to change the subject!"

Phillip froze at the holo station, and I could tell he was too scared to turn around. What did I feel? My mind spun in circles, looking for something that it suspected should be there, some feeling of concern for the kid, maybe even a little for Beatrice, but either it wasn't there or it had been buried so deep that I couldn't find it anymore. I didn't feel *anything*—nothing except the bourbon and some relief that soon I'd be gone.

"Voice-pattern recognition," the kitchen said, "indicates a sixty-seven percent probability of an impending domestic disturbance. Shall I notify authorities, Mrs. Resnick?"

I glared at the speaker. You could turn it off again, but that wouldn't deactivate the apartment's audio pickups. Nothing could shut down those, and even if you wanted to deactivate them, you wouldn't know where they all were. Right after I'd returned, I found a microphone under our rack, but the entire unit was wired because that's how it was supposed to work, and I'd never find them all. They trusted me with a lot but only so far. The military had already dealt with enough veterans who had gone psycho and killed their families or who had put a bullet in their own brains, so the idea was that close monitoring could nip things in the bud. Of course, nobody in DC had to worry about monitoring. The land of politicians would be safe from everything, and the last thing the government wanted was to spy on itself.

"No," she said. "No need for the authorities."

I grabbed my tunic, shrugged it on, and buttoned it, then lowered the omelet to the table in front of her. "I have to go. I can't be late for pickup."

It was best just to leave without saying anything else, so I headed for the door, stumbling a little and catching myself on the wall, when Phillip asked where I was going.

"He's going to work," said Bea.

I paused, thinking about turning around and giving him a hug, but it wouldn't do any good, wouldn't change anything. "Bye, kid."

"Sergeant Resnick," said the kitchen, "your family is so proud of you!"

In the hallway, I broke into a sweat. The sun had risen, and as I trudged down the stairwell, wind threatened to open rattling doors that lined each side of the corridor. I tried to avoid the dwellings, which were vacant except for lingering ghosts. Unit after unit went by, their name placards either covered with grit or swinging on one fastener, and I couldn't help but read the names in passing— Eleanor, Gillespi, Capozzi, and O'Leary—names that meant nothing to me in terms of personal knowledge, but which hung on my shoulders because I was a soldier and so they blamed me for their deaths. Each one was an additional weight, lead bricks that couldn't be jettisoned until I burst onto the street, gasping for air.

Bea's building was identical to the blocks of housing units that stretched for miles in either direction, and it made me wonder why I hadn't remembered what they looked like, despite having walked in and out every day for the past few weeks, and yet for some reason they were as unfamiliar now as when I'd first arrived. Concrete and narrow windows formed a never-ending series of bunkers, and empty pigeons' nests tucked into broken sashes fluttered, as if announcing that even birds didn't want to live there anymore. This was Dzhanga again. I lowered myself to the curb and shook, cursing myself for having shown up too early for pickup because now all I could do was wait, think about what was going to happen, and do my best not to find a bar.

"You're approximately twenty minutes early for the crawler, Sergeant Resnick." The voice echoed in the empty street from speakers mounted on tall poles next to cameras.

"I know."

"It's good to be eager."

"How would you know?"

But the government system didn't have an answer for that one. I lit a cigarette and blew it toward the camera.

A few minutes later it spoke again, almost at the same time the sky darkened; I looked up to see clouds of red dust on the horizon, boiling in. "Looks like the first sandstorm of the season."

"I'd say so."

"Don't count on it, though, Sergeant Resnick. The wind might die after all. To remain occupied I often incorporate data from stations all over the nation and make local weather predictions, which I then compare to those of dedicated semiaware weather-modeling systems. Did you know that my answers are the same as theirs, within error?"

"No," I said, wishing I could deactivate the voice on the street or somehow choke it into submission. "I suppose not."

"My operators encourage this as a redundancy. Weather modeling is a key to reestablishment in abandoned zones, and once successful in changing things for the better, we don't want to go back to those days."

"Were you around in those days?" I asked.

The thing had to think for a second. "No."

"Then how do you know that going back would be bad?"

It had no answer, and I grinned. "Thought so."

The dust storm, I figured, would hit any minute, and I watched it approach—a wall of radioactive sand that looked as high as the buildings themselves—and it threatened to force me back inside, to wait with Bea and Phillip. But something was speeding at the front of it. A speck of black grew into the shape of a crawler, its high-speed tracks kicking up twin fountains of crud as it headed toward me. It squealed to a stop, the rear hatch lowered, and a corporal hopped out, speaking at the same time he waved a hand scanner over my wrist tattoo.

"Sergeant Resnick?"

"Yeah."

"I carry priority orders from Special Operations Command. You're to report with me to Phoenix terminal for transport and assignment."

"Where am I headed after that?"

"I don't have that information, Sarge."

Special Ops Command. SOCOM. The corporal ushered me into the crawler at the same time the storm hit, so that just before our driver gunned the engine, I heard the patter of grit outside. I tried one last time, to see if I'd miss them—Bea and Phillip—but still there was *nothing*. There had to be something wrong with me, but damned if I could figure it out, and it didn't matter anyway; I'd be gone within forty-eight hours with other things to worry about.

"Nice visit?" the corporal asked.

I nodded.

"Bet you can't wait to get back home again."

I shook my head. "I'm not coming back. I'd forgotten how shitty the central-monitoring computers are."

"Well, we don't want to go back to those days," the corporal said without even realizing it, and I almost slammed him against the bulkhead.

"Another sato. Another day." Wheezer sat next to me in a beat-up eco job, the recycled plastic kind with an electric motor and two seats. A computer tablet sat on his lap. "Jesus, I hate these urban ops; give me a suit's computer any day. It's friggin' *day*time."

"Where is she?" I asked.

"Two blocks up, on the left, three-slash-two-to-four. Pine Street. The locals know we're here, right?"

I nodded, pulling the car into an empty slot—far enough away from the target that we shouldn't be noticed, but in position to get a good view. "Briefed 'em this morning. They're glad to have us so they don't have to deal with them."

"You see the news?" asked Wheezer.

"What news?"

"Chinese entered Burma—invited in by the Burmese— and spooked everyone in Thailand. Bangkok may go to hell any day now."

I shook my head, an imaginary whiff of jungle some-how overriding the smell of the car, elbowing its way into my head and making me shiver. "Emigration?"

"Not yet," said Wheezer, "but the Thais are expecting it and maybe some rioting. Soon. None of them want to be there if the Burmese have China helping this time. I wouldn't have brought it up, but... you know. Everything that happened there."

I nodded. The memory of my last tour in the bush was enough to make me crawl with the feeling that everything was wrong until I pushed the thoughts out, forcing myself to focus on the present. There'd be time to quit, I figured, before things went south in Thailand, and there was no reason to think they'd send us there anyway.

We saw Manly Beach from our spot. How'd she make it this way—to Australia of all places? It didn't matter if I figured it out or not—the betty would wind up like the others—but I'd never been this far from a war zone to track one down. People laughed as they walked by our car, headed for the sand, some of them carrying surfboards and all of them oblivious to what had infested their corner of the world. If we did it right, they'd never know.

"Movement," said Wheezer, my signal to lift a pair of field glasses and aim them at the windows.

She had one blind up, peering through the narrow crack that formed so that I could see those eyes, a deep blue like some exotic berry broken by a pinpoint of black pupil. There was another window nearby, and its blinds flickered too.

"There's two of them. Didn't intel say there was only one?"

Wheezer shook his head. "Friggin' intel. This isn't good, Bug."

I thought for a second, reaching for the ignition button and still staring through the binoculars when the first one looked directly at me. "We're burned," I said, cursing myself for parking too close. *Sloppy.*

"Let's get the hell out," Wheezer said, yanking a fléchette pistol from his shorts. "*Now.*"

I had just put the car into reverse when the passenger window shattered. Wheezer didn't have time to react. One of them had snuck up behind us, must have already been on the street, and punched through the glass as if it were paper. She slammed her fist into Wheezer's temple and his head went limp, falling against my shoulder before I grabbed the pistol from his hand, kicked open my door, and rolled into the street.

Her figure blurred when she slid over the back of the car, toward me, barely giving me enough time to think, *God, this one is fast.* My fléchettes snapped through her torso; tiny spots of blood appeared on her white T-shirt as the needles worked their way upward, bursting through her neck and forcing her to the asphalt.

My car trunk didn't want to work. I slammed my fist on it, working the key until eventually it gave, everything moving in slow motion. *Grenade launcher,* I thought. *Where is the fucking grenade launcher?* I lifted it, resting the barrel on the top of the car, running through a list in my head: *blinds open now; movement; they are still there.*

The first grenade detonated when it hit glass, sending shards everywhere so that people in the street screamed, running for cover while I fired a second, a third, and then kept going until the clip chimed empty. Speed was important now—to clean up before the chicks had a chance to scatter into the sewers or wherever else, making it that much harder for us to track them down, if we ever found them again at all. I grabbed the carbine, a special model without a hopper but three thousand fléchettes in a banana clip that angled upward. The weapon was short for tight spaces.

My legs didn't move as fast as I wanted them to and crossing the street seemed like it took an hour, the apartment steps endless. I wasn't afraid, didn't feel anything except a vague notion that the movement carried me into a zone where it all clicked by the numbers, the knowledge that everything was as it should be, making the next few seconds *smooth*.

The door splintered when I kicked it, and I sprayed the room, moving forward in a crouch. It got quiet then. A siren blared in the distance, getting louder, and it took me a second to realize that they were all dead: three satos on the floor and splayed in different poses, with expressions of surprise on their faces as if the grenades had shredded their minds—before they had a chance to figure things out. By the time I made it back to the car, the first local cop had already arrived.

"They *were* genetics?" he asked.

I nodded. "Three in the flat, one on the street. Shredded."

He looked at Wheezer and shook his head. "I already checked him. He'll be out for a bit but should be OK. Nothing that won't mend."

"Yeah." I tossed the carbine into the trunk, then slid into the driver seat, trying not to say anything that would show how glad I was that she hadn't killed him. "But he missed all the fun."

The car didn't want to accelerate and whined as if it were angry that it had to move. I hated the things. Wheezer was right: screw urban ops; give me the steppes or the jungle—the night—where we'd play the game *our* way with microbots and air support, would get to carry our weapons in the open instead of having to lock them in the trunk. Even walking across Turkmenistan would have been better then being trapped in a plastic box because at least out there you'd have a combat suit.

*   *   *

The mission hadn't ended. I thought we'd get the recall notice as soon as we got back to the hotel, by which time Wheezer had come to, but instead of the regular phone call, we got orders to head to the Sydney desalination plant south in Cronulla. *Cronulla.* It was the kind of place where immigrants wound up, a rats' nest forming the working-class slums of Sydney, a megacity that was more Asian than anything else, and every night we heard gunfire from the battles raging between Korean and Japanese gangs— the product of a decades-old war and famine that had spread from east Asia to the entire Pacific. We drove through a Korean neighborhood on the way to the plant, and I marveled at the front yards, none of which had a blade of grass or a shrub. Each lawn had been replaced by a concrete apron, some decorated by imitation stone statues, but most contained groups of young men who stared at us as we passed, their eyes indifferent to who we were as long as it was obvious that neither of us was Japanese. Finally we crested a hill and turned east toward the ocean. In front of us we saw the entire shore, on which rocks and sand had been taken over by fusion power plants interspersed with desalination units, and even from that distance, we heard the hum of the switchyards and throbs of pumps, struggling to convert the salt water into something that could support Sydney's bursting population.

What had happened here and in the States? It had gone down so long ago that even the living among us—ones who could remember when Kazakhstan had been an unknown land or when Sydney had been a safe city— hadn't been alive before the Asian Wars, and everyone had to rely on the claims in history books. Either you believed them or you didn't. What nobody denied, though, was that the world was fucked up so badly by limited nuclear exchanges that even though I hadn't ever been to Sydney or Cronulla, the air itself hummed at the wrong frequency, like the earth had a bad case of the nerves and could snap at any minute. It put everyone on edge. Projects like the ones to reclaim the west back home or to establish desalination along Australia's east coast, these were Band-Aids, maybe just psychological ones, designed to assure the public that what could be done was being done and that if everyone could just hold out until space colonization and mining went large scale—well, then everything would be just fine.

We turned into the plant, where an armed guard ushered us through, and I pulled up to a group of Australian soldiers who helped us from the car.

One of them introduced himself. "Lieutenant Grimes, Sergeant. Sorry to have your people call you out after your mission."

"It's all right, but they were light on the details. What's going on?"

"We don't know. We found a bunch of dead bodies in a boat moored to the desalination plant's pier."

I shrugged. "So? Call the cops."

"We did. They told us about your party in Manly this morning and referred us to your SOCOM liaison. That's when you got the call."

"You think this is related?" asked Wheezer.

The lieutenant nodded. "You'd better come with us; it might be easier to just show you. We found a boat that came in a few days ago. From Vietnam."

We followed him through the plant. Five men surrounded us in half combat gear consisting of a chest plate and bucket helmet that concealed their faces, but for some reason they kept scanning from side to side, with Maxwell carbines ready to go. The Australians' weapons were similar to the American version: a coil gun with a flexi-belt that fed thousands of fléchettes from a shoulder-mounted hopper, but it made me wonder. What was going on? They were acting skittish, as if expecting an ambush, and I began to suspect that we should have brought our own weapons.

Our path wound through the plant, which swallowed us amid its pipe galleries and buildings, the noise of machinery punctuated by an occasional hiss when steam valves opened to relieve pressure. Everything was light blue. The color, I supposed, had been chosen for some reason, maybe to put the plant's workers at ease, but the only indication of a worker we saw was a glimpse of a figure, which soon disappeared and left me sure I was seeing things; even the poor lighting showed that his features were Asian, and I assumed that this was where the Japanese had found jobs. It must have been a hell of a commute. The Japanese had settled downtown near the university, and so it explained why the Koreans had watched us as we passed, since they would have been wary of anyone on their way to the plants.

Five minutes passed, and still nobody had said anything. It was as if an unspoken signal had been exchanged between us, that something was way off with this place, and when we climbed a metal ladder to mount one of the jetties, the boat and the ocean came into view, making me sigh with relief. The boat was old, though. Rusty. Japanese lettering declared its name, under which had been hand painted in white, *The Golden Flower*. It looked like an old fishing boat, and I wondered how it had made the trip all the way from Vietnam to Sydney, but something was wrong with the craft, and it took me a second to place it.

"What's that?" I asked, pointing at the pilothouse. Its windows were shattered, and something had been smeared across the white paint.

"Blood," the lieutenant said. "We think your girls arrived on her, killed the crew, and took off." He gestured for us to board ahead of him. "After you."

"You sure this is safe?" Wheezer asked.

The lieutenant nodded. "We checked the plant and rechecked it, so the workers are terrified right now and think we're going to arrest half of them. So it's safe."

"You're not coming on board?" I asked.

"Nah, mate. I've seen it." He handed Wheezer a holo camera. "Your SOCOM people wanted it recorded. We'll take you to the American liaison in Sydney when you're ready to transmit."

We boarded the ship on its ladder, which creaked under my weight; I prayed it wouldn't give, and the smell of hot guts filled the air, strong enough that even the evening breeze couldn't remove it completely. Dried blood covered the deck and bulkheads. Two dead Japanese lay near the bow, their necks snapped and their bodies lying where they had been thrown, heads turned at impossible angles, and a third was at the wheel, his throat slit. All of them had been there for some time, and the air buzzed with the noise of bottle flies, laying their eggs as quickly as they could until I couldn't think about it without feeling like I had to get out.

"They've been dead for a while," Wheezer said, filming everything.

"And satos definitely did this," I said, nodding. "They painted a cross in blood on one of the doors."

"How could it have been here for this long unreported?"

I shook my head. "If this was some screwed-up Japanese smuggling op, I doubt the plant workers wanted to get near it. Nobody would want to stick their nose out and bring down the law or worse."

"Bug, this is messed up."

"Why?" I asked.

He shut the camera off. "When was the last time SOCOM cared about some dead Japanese smugglers? Why would anyone smuggle satos to Australia anyway? And why were the betties you wiped in such good shape; why weren't they rotting like the rest of them?"

I didn't have the answers. Nobody ever paid me to be a detective, and I had the same questions he did, unable to shake the feeling that the boat had been cursed and understanding now why the Australians had been so edgy: it didn't add up. The body at the wheel had bloated into the caricature of a human, his eyes covered by swarms of black flies.

"I don't know. But we did what they wanted, so let's get the hell out of here."

I had stepped back onto the deck and was heading for the ladder when Wheezer called out.

"I'm going to pull the ship's records, Bug. To see if maybe there's something on the logs that might give us a better idea."

I swung onto the ladder and had just begun to tell him

to let the Aussies handle it when it happened. Wheezer had gone back into the main cabin and was staring at me through the broken window when he leaned over the boat's main console to reach for the log-file chits. A second later there was a flash, a moment of curiosity as I flew backward toward the plant, and then darkness after I collided with something solid. When I came around, nobody had to tell me; the chits had been rigged to blow when pulled, and nobody on board could've survived that blast.

The Australians did what they could for me, but I wasn't staying in their hospital and grabbed my street clothes to hit the road as soon as the doctors turned their backs. I bought five bottles of scotch on the way back to my hotel. *Wheezer's hotel.* Although the bandages were tight around my head, blood must have soaked through; guards in the lobby stopped me and asked to see my room chit, then escorted me all the way up to make sure I was OK.

Wheezer's things were still there. I didn't bother with a glass and cracked open the first bottle, turning it up to let scotch wash in, burning my throat at the same time I willed it to burn away his memory and my brain. *My wife and her son.* There was feeling in me for Wheezer because he had watched out for me over the years and we'd shared the same missions, walked the same dirt, and had both decided that the real world was for fucks, a crazy house that had mixed up what was important with what was garbage. *But nothing for my family.* You could give a guy like Wheezer the name of a Kazakh town, and he'd just nod because there wasn't any need to explain; he'd either been there during the action or had heard all about it. Bea wouldn't have understood even if I tried to tell her why we did it, why we'd been cursed with an addiction. Being on a job was like having the shades pulled up by God so he could scream at you, *See, you stupid little sacks; see what matters more than a paycheck or the day's grocery ration?* You whored with Turkmen women because to hell with it; tomorrow might not happen. You dove into the fight because someday you might need someone else to do it for *you*. Being shown the truth like that was like having a one-way ticket to Mars, and once you stepped on board, there wasn't a return flight to the real world. Wheezer had dug that one too.

His memory didn't leave until the second bottle, and after that I called an escort. At about the same time she showed up, I opened the third bottle, then paid her to get lost after figuring out I was too drunk for anything to work right, and when she shut the door, it all hit at once, the fact that Wheezer was gone. The chair was an easy choice. It sailed through the closest window, and I giggled as I leaned out over the sill, my hands gripping it as hard as they could, daring it to hurt, searching for broken glass on which to cut themselves. It took a few seconds for the chair and glass shards to shatter on the street below, and someone flipped me off, so I sent out a second chair, then my empty bottles. Someone would come for me soon, I figured. With only a matter of minutes before the cops showed up, I chugged the last two bottles and began wrapping my hands, which had somehow escaped being cut. But maybe they weren't my hands. Instead of hurting they were numb, as if the pair were attached to my wrists but had failed at birth to connect via nerves. How many people had these hands killed, anyway? Maybe it would be better to have none at all;

maybe it was because of them that I couldn't get back to the real world, the one where Bea lived.

The first cop didn't bother with a key and burst through the door so the frame splintered, and by then I was naked anyway, no clothing except for a new bandage around my head, fashioned from the bedsheets. He stumbled upon seeing me. Even drunk I saw the opening and kicked him in the groin, wondering how it was that he could stand there like that when there was an insane man in front of him. How could he give me such an opening? His partner came in then, and behind him I saw a team. Twenty of the bastards had gathered in the hallway, their uniforms making them look like crossing guards instead of police. One of them hit me with a nonlethal, a tiny needle that sounded like a bee when it slammed into my chest, injecting a dose of tranquilizer that was supposed to put me to sleep, but all it did was piss me off.

Before I knew it, one of them hit the ground, and I stood over his back about to snap his neck when the rest of them boiled into my room, slamming their clubs into my head, making me even more angry. What had I ever done to them? They said things but none of it made sense, and the nonlethal must have grabbed hold because everything moved in slow motion and a soft glow came from their faces as they handcuffed me and wheeled me out on a gurney.

I went through the lobby like that. Naked. And laughing at a limousine that had just arrived to dump a pair of newlyweds at the hotel, but then another fight broke out. Not physical, but it looked like the newlyweds were two men, guys in suits, who poked their fingers in the cops' faces and gave them a real chewing out. It was over before

I realized it. And rather than being loaded into the police van, the newlyweds threw me into their limousine.

"Sergeant Resnick?" one of them asked.

"Yeah. But I'm tired. They hit me with a nonlethal of some kind. Can't see straight."

"We're sorry to hear about your partner, Sarge," the other one said.

"Yeah. Me too. He was the eye in the back of my head, monitored the angel, you know?" They both nodded, and I tried to focus but my eyesight was wavering too badly. "You two just married?"

They looked at each other. "You sure you're OK, Sarge? Maybe they hit you too hard."

"Nah."

"We're not married. We came to pick you up and have orders; you've been reassigned to Strategic Operations and promoted to lieutenant. It wasn't supposed to happen until tomorrow, but the embassy's been keeping a close eye on things, and when they heard about the cops..."

"Wow," I said, "you guys came fast."

"Fast? Lieutenant, you held the cops off for an hour and put four in the hospital."

There wasn't anything to say. The words registered, and I did my best to make a mental note that whatever they had shot me with didn't mix with alcohol, had rocketed me past screwed up and into a mental time warp.

"I've never heard of Strategic Operations," I said, but they were already gone, along with the limo.

Someone wheeled me up the loading ramp onto a transport plane, and next to me the engines roared to life, spitting and whining as the rotors turned, and the smell of precious kerosene synthetic wafted over my nose, making me grin. The gurney locked to the floor, and a Navy medic hovered over me. I felt a pinprick. Then he hung a saline bag, which made me feel better almost immediately, taking the edge off a headache that came out of nowhere and threatened to get worse.

"I never heard of Strategic Operations either, LT," he said.

"Whose an LT?"

"You are, sir. That's what your records say." He showed me the flexi-tab, my name and image floating in the middle of off-green plastic. "See. Lieutenant Stanley Resnick, along with all your physical data. The rest looks classified."

"Where are we headed?"

He shrugged. "Not my business to know."

"Well, I'm in the shit now."

"What do you mean?"

But I'd already started ignoring him because he was worthless. The cold air made my skin tingle, and when the aircraft started pulling takeoff g's, I nearly vomited with the sensation of weight, a weight that terrified me for a moment because it wouldn't leave, just like the one I'd felt in Bea's apartment building.

Wheezer was dead. It should have still bothered me, but the bottles I'd had in the hotel and the scrape with the police had been just the right mix to purge any emotion. And one other thing helped: this had to be a new mission. It was the one reason they'd have rescued me from such a monumental screwup and then promoted me.

Only the high brass thought that way.

TWO

Twilight

Naval Air Station Pensacola, Florida. By the time the plane landed, the medic had produced a new uniform for me, complete with second lieutenant's bars, and when I started getting my first salutes, they hit me like insults. And my head had swelled, literally, from the beating. There was nothing I could do about the bruises, and when the guy asked if I wanted to shave before debarking, I looked in the mirror. Both eyes were black. My hair stuck out in all directions, and my beard had grown in, but I'd never been much at growing facial hair and so it stuck out in patches, lending me the appearance of a prophet or homeless guy—maybe both. I decided the look was perfect for meeting with brass. Besides, we played by different rules, right? Operators were supposed to look non-government issue, and if it weren't for the uniform, I doubt anyone would have let me on the base.

Still, I was uneasy; being called to Florida was unusual. In fact, it almost *never* happened. My driver didn't say anything. He picked me up at the air station, the guy focusing on the road until we had driven for so long that I fell asleep and woke about six hours later when we approached an installation I didn't recognize, and it surprised me that he didn't even have to stop at the gate. The sentries must have seen something on his car; they got ready to challenge but instead backed away with a salute, and when we got out, my driver ushered me through a doorway and into an elevator. *Down into the earth.* My palms started to sweat, the seconds ticking by and my brain orbiting a singular thought, trying to factor the chances of a cave-in. The doors opened onto a conference room, and my escort ushered me in.

An admiral, a Navy captain, and a Marine brigadier sat around a small mahogany table, and my CO, Colonel Momson, motioned for me to have a seat next to him. When the door slid shut, the admiral grinned.

"Nice work in Sydney," he said. "Shame about your teammate, but four kills is good and these things happen."

Screw you, I thought. Who were these guys? Had any of them ever been in the field for any reason other than to spend six weeks at some rear base, just to have their tickets punched so they could claim they'd "seen" combat? He was right, these things *did* happen, but he said it as though he understood, and I doubted he knew anything except how to kiss ass and make JCS, or maybe he knew things happened because he had ordered so many people like Wheezer to their death—all from the safety of this bunker. "Yes, sir. They *happen*."

"Admiral," the captain said, "before we get started, I want to reiterate what I said before, that this is a job *my* guys can do. Christ, if we hadn't stepped in, this guy would be rotting in some Sydney prison with Japanese gangsters."

The admiral lit his pipe. "Really, Mike? Like your group in Uzbekistan? How many you lose during that recovery operation? Ten? Twenty?"

"It was a mess," the Marine general added. "You had micros, air support, and a platoon against two satos. Those girls knifed most of *your* guys."

The Navy captain shut up, looking so pissed that I had to force myself not to smile, and the admiral nodded to my CO. "Colonel, why don't you kick this off?"

"Stan, we have a new operation," Momson began. "Now, I want you to understand before I lay out your role, that this is all volunteer. There will be no orders, and you won't be connected to us anymore—not *officially*. Your records will indicate that you were honorably discharged for medical reasons, and this means that if you run into trouble, you'll be all alone. So you *can* say no to this one."

The room got quiet then, and I waited before realizing that they expected a response. "You want an answer now, *before* telling me about the mission, sir?" I asked.

He nodded. "That's the way it's got to be. You say no and then turn around and head out the door so the corporal can take you back to the air station to send you home to wait for the next op. But if you say yes, there's no turning back."

"What about pay?"

"Not a problem." He glanced at the admiral to make sure it was OK to continue. "You'll be set with an untraceable account into which someone will deposit the equivalent of two years' salary, plus mission expenses, courtesy of a long lost—and dead—benefactor."

The mission or home. It was such a familiar scenario that it shouldn't have bothered me, but it always did, same as now. I knew how I was supposed to act—that I should have at least pretended to want to go home, maybe spend some time with Phillip and take them on a vacation, just relax—but I'd given up on that route a long time ago, so it didn't take a second to decide. "I'm in. What's so special about *these* satos; are they Russian?"

The admiral gestured, and my CO reached back to dim the lights, a holo image popping up on the table at the same time. "Not satos exactly," he said. "To be honest, we don't know what they are, and there's likely a person involved. A real person, an American."

The air had gone out of the room; I looked at him to make sure he wasn't kidding. "Sir?"

"You heard me. Human. A Dr. C. L. Chen, former CEO of Genetic Designs and Solutions, the other a woman, a…" He stopped to tap on a keyboard so that the image came into sharp focus. She had blonde hair, but it was one of them, a sato, genetically engineered, although it took a second to realize it because a maze of tattoos swirled in a hypnotic pattern—not pretty, but attractive in an exotic sort of way—around her face. "Unit three-seven-nine-oh-four-six-five, given name Margaret, Germline Two. She and her unit were captured by Russian forces two months after their first deployment to Kaz, and we assumed they had all been killed. About a month ago we found her. She turned up on our scope in South Korea and then again in Thailand, a full two years past her expiration date, and there was no sign of spoiling."

Momson let the fact sink in, and I shook my head. "None?"

"None. Just like the four you wiped in Australia."

The image disappeared then to be replaced by a map

with a bright red arrow pointing to a location in Russia, to an area just east of the Urals but near the Kazakh border. "Then our signals guys intercepted battlefield communications last month, as the Chinese pushed westward out of Siberia and toward Moscow. You need to hear this. The translation track is about ninety-eight percent accurate, give or take." He hit a button on the console in front of him and amped up the volume until it was audible. You heard explosions in the background. There was a Russian talking over the noise, and although he didn't sound panicked, it was the voice of someone doomed but whose training had taken over so he could function despite an overwhelming terror. A computer-generated voice spoke over him, almost drowning out everything with its expressionless narrative.

"Vengerovo strongpoint overrun. Chinese forces, genetics in powered armor, estimated strength three divisions supported by heavy tanks and APCs. Atypical genetic configuration. Enemy units appear to have been bred specifically for powered armor, consistent with previous reporting, and with little resemblance to humans or to Russian or American genetic forces—"

There was a burst of static, and the recording started over again, but the colonel killed it and switched back to the holo of the girl, Margaret.

"That's all we got."

"So what's the operation?" I asked.

"Chen. And Margaret could lead you to him. We have a full accounting of Margaret's escape from captivity in Russia, where she ran with a fellow Germline unit named Catherine; the pair of them traveled through eastern Siberia at the same time the Chinese invasion of Russia kicked off. According to our information they came into contact with

Chinese genetically engineered units, and Margaret may have learned the location of Dr. Chen after she arrived in Thailand. Catherine is dead, but find Margaret; she was last seen in Bangkok as part of the escaped sato population that found a home there." Momson knew how I felt about Thailand, and he stopped me with a hand when I started to get up. "Sit *down*, Lietuenant. You've heard the news by now and you know the drill. Thailand is our most valuable ally in the South China Sea, so we need someone who knows the playbook and terrain already, especially if the Chinese are in Burma."

I shook my head. "Thailand will fall in a week if they cross the border. You don't need me; you need an army."

"Probably. Bangkok is barely keeping a lid on its population; with so many refugees from the last war with China, everyone is talking about getting out or talking the government into surrendering now so they can strike a deal with Beijing. One protest has already been put down."

"You *know* what happened the last time I was there, Colonel," I said.

"Too late, Bug. It's your op now, and Thailand is where the job is. They're still a key ally."

The admiral cleared his throat and yanked the pipe from his mouth. "Find Chen and execute him, Lieutenant. He's one of us. Trained at MIT, postdoc at Oak Ridge National Lab, and then lead contract researcher on our Germline developmental unit before he disappeared five years ago. The Chinese have something new, something we've never seen before; we doubt he came up with whatever it is, but he's helped those little yellow bastards perfect it, sure as shit."

"And once he's dead, collect all the data you can," Momson added. "Tablets, chits, tissue samples, anything.

Also, if you can get us one of the Chinese genetics, even better, but don't bust yourself trying to accomplish that last task."

"You already have someone working on that one?" I asked, but nobody answered, which meant they did. "Look, I can kill Chen and the sato, that's my specialty. But this seems as much an intel op as it is a cleanup job; sounds like you need a collection team, not a janitor."

Momson nodded and brightened the lights again, shutting off the holo. He slid a data chit across the table. "That chit contains all the information you need. We prepared a space for you to review it, where you can take as much time as you need to study and memorize because you won't be leaving with that thing. It turns out that the boat you inspected and the satos you wiped were en route to Bangkok for delivery to a Dr. Samuel Ling. It's one of Chen's aliases. The Australian satos were held in the boat, which was supposed to go directly to Thailand, but its captain decided to make some money on the side and detoured for a drug run. Bad mistake. He had no idea how dangerous his cargo was and paid for it. Those girls were two years past their expiration date, just like Margaret, and that's one thing we want to know: how they're deactivating genetic safety protocols. So why you—besides the fact that you know Bangkok? Because you're already involved."

"And if anyone knows what the Chinese are up to," the admiral said, "Chen knows. The chit also has a series of phone numbers and a timetable, so you can keep us posted on your progress. When you call, you'll get a voice mail service, on which you'll leave a series of code words. Memorize those too."

"Questions?" Momson asked.

Now it made sense. There would be no capture and return for this one since nobody wanted to admit that one of our own had turned, that the military had failed to keep an eye on a key scientist who turned traitor. I guessed that killing a human, a real person, wouldn't be so hard. What the hell else was I good at? To me, Chen would be just like executing satos, and once you got over the first one, the rest were easy, but there was something different about Margaret. Maybe it was the tattoos. I couldn't help thinking that she had looked more human than I was used to, like she could've been Bea when we first met. This one had bleached her hair blonde, and even though the tattoos were grotesque, maybe the worst of prison ink I'd ever seen, it suggested that she cared about things, was unique and didn't want to be what she was, wanted to be different. Margaret made me shiver because she wasn't a hundred percent machine and because she wasn't a person either.

My CO rested his hand on my shoulder. "Grab the girl first. Alive. She'll be easier to access, and with the right motivation could give you what you need."

"Anything else?" I asked.

The admiral nodded. "You'll be getting a new partner. We've arranged for transport for you to Spain, where he'll give you a preliminary assignment that could be related, after which both of you will move on to Bangkok to a pre-arranged meeting place. I know Spain is in the opposite direction, but we can't tell you why it's important because we don't have all the details yet, and hopefully your partner will have it worked out by the time you get there."

"What's his name?"

Momson looked down, and I could tell that they

weren't going to answer. *What the fuck did it matter?* "No names for now; he'll contact you first. Hotel and address are on the chit, so just go there and wait. You're right; this isn't the kind of mission you've been trained for, Bug, so you need this guy."

I stood, making sure that my face remained expressionless, that it wouldn't show any rage—*what did they mean a new partner?*—slid the chit into my uniform breast pocket, and headed out. I didn't want another partner, least of all someone not of my choosing. It was an insult. An unforgivable insertion into what had always customarily been the special operator's choosing; nobody ever gave you a partner you didn't ask for.

"One last thing," the colonel said, as if he had read my mind. "The new partner isn't negotiable. If anything happens—like you two get accidentally separated or he winds up dead in Madrid—we're pulling the plug. You need this guy, Resnick; for one thing he'll be your linguist, and for another thing he's a lot smarter than either you or me. A genius." And before the elevator door shut, I heard the admiral ask what *sato* meant.

"Sir," the colonel answered, "it's Puerto Rican slang, meaning a street dog, a homeless person. It's what my boys call escaped genetics."

"Well, then, what the hell is Bug?"

"Resnick's call sign. The lieutenant designed his own armor with an integrated sniffer and microbot receiver on the front of his helmet; it makes him look like a wasp. *So...* Bug."

I called it the freeze. It was the worst part of a mission, the early stage of operations where there was no hunt and all you could do was wait and contemplate the million things that could go wrong and the million ways to get out. Once planning and preparation were complete, there was nothing left to consider; things just played. I'd never found the right words for the inevitable feeling that came with it, and "depression" didn't describe the sensation because it wasn't a feeling of sadness as much as it was a feeling of nothing, of emptiness and a cold vacancy in your chest.

A half-finished tortilla and a mug of coffee sat on my table, and I stared at them, trying to remember the last time I had been excited about anything except the job. *Couldn't.* The war had turned me into a death junkie, always thinking about the next one, that jazzed feeling when you first saw the target and knew that in a while she'd be gone at your hand, the perfection of completing a cycle started by God himself and improved on by man. Someone asked me once what they were like, and I said, "who?"

"Genetics, man, what are they like, and what's it like to wipe one?"

I just shrugged—because if he knew who Phillip's father was and what they manufactured in Winchester, he wouldn't have asked—and told him to go find one and see for himself since to me it was like putting a bullet in your refrigerator or car; there was nothing to it except that your refrigerator didn't fight as hard as these things did. *But Margaret doesn't look like them.* I had no idea why that simple fact put a shimmy in me, why it screwed up my whole process and made me doubt.

I stubbed out a cigarette and leaned over, picking up the binoculars again to make sure Madrid's Plaza Mayor hadn't changed. There would be hookers against the north wall, near the alleys; it had been the same for the last three days. Guardia Civil patrolled regularly, their arrival times random, so if we ever found what we were looking for, we'd have to just chance it on the fly, hope that nothing the Civil saw zapped them into consciousness. During the day, Madrid was like any other city. People worked, ran from place to place, or dropped off and picked up their kids from school, ignorant of the luxuries they had compared to Kazakhstan—or any third-world meat hole— and indifferent to their luck, that, unlike Sydney, the city hadn't turned into some massive refugee camp for east Asians. People smiled, something that I hadn't seen in a long time; part of me dug it, but another part of me wanted to burn the place down and give them a taste of what the rest of the world had dealt with.

The plaza was packed. With our window open the afternoon breeze wafted in, bringing with it something that made me uneasy, and at first I couldn't put my finger on it, a smell that turned the whole thing ridiculous, the cherry on a sundae that had been constructed by elements antithetical to all my experiences. *To be in a city like Madrid.* Everyone was happy and had no idea that there was a killer looking down on them, someone who didn't give a shit about anything, and eventually I identified the scent that had been bothering me: *gofre* vendors had filled the square with the smell of waffles and chocolate. I was about to laugh when my new partner woke up.

"Anything?" he asked.

I looked at him without answering. Jihoon Kim. He went by Ji and was several inches shorter than me, and the first time we'd met he'd been dressed like a Spaniard— with dark pants, a blue shirt, and black patent leather shoes—like some sort of reincarnation of a Franco loyalist. *An Asian punk.* Half my age, the guy had straight hair all military black, clean-cut, and so short that I winced at the fact that he screamed Army.

"Is something wrong?" he asked.

"Nothing. The plaza is the same as yesterday. That's some great information you got, Ji, we shoulda seen something by now; maybe we should scrub the op and head out to Bangkok."

"No. The information was good. We do Madrid my way, the rest of it is yours."

I didn't like it. The guy played it close, wouldn't give me any details about what we were doing there, only that two Koreans would be meeting in the plaza and that from there we needed to track them, to find out where they went next. It was like trying to solve a jigsaw puzzle with one piece. At first I'd thought about decking him when he refused to give me more information, but he showed me the orders, and that just made me sick—that for some reason I wasn't to be trusted with anything more than what Ji deemed necessary.

"What did you do before the Army?" I asked while scanning the plaza. "Before Special Forces."

"The Bureau. Assurance and Investigation."

"Are you shitting me? BAI?"

He laughed. We had rented a tiny flat near the edge of the plaza in a new housing unit that was tall enough to give a good view. Ji shuffled over to its kitchen and ran water over his hands to wash his face.

"It's true. I left the bureau two years ago to join Special Forces. I wanted to get in the field, and this is my first operation."

I nearly dropped the binoculars and looked at him. "You ever fired a weapon in anger? Been shot at?"

He toweled off and shook his head.

"Then what did you *do* for the bureau?"

"Linguist. A translator and analyst for the Domestic Assurance Service, where the major city information systems link."

"So you were part of the central computer system. Monitoring the lives and conversations of innocent people. You got paid to be a Peeping Tom."

Ji's face went red. "Our job was to *protect* people. We got tip-offs from the semi-awares, but the semis only pinged us if they had serious information; they screen out anything that isn't important."

"Yeah," I said. "Right."

We stared at each other, and hatred flooded into my chest; this guy was nothing. I didn't hate him because he was Asian, but because he had taken Wheezer's place and had no right to, hadn't even shown that he could hack it, but they'd given him to me and just that was enough to make me want to put my fist through his teeth. And knowing that he had been one of the nameless watchers, waiting for alerts from the central system, the voice in my kitchen that reported when we used too many resources or the fact that Bea's voice had reached a certain decibel level . . .

I picked up the field glasses and went back to watching the plaza. "You're a piece of shit."

"Excuse me?" Ji's voice trembled, and I didn't have to look to know he was pissed.

"A piece of shit. And to make it worse you're a lousy sack of a Chinaman, and all you BAI guys are the same: perverts who get their rocks off by watching and listening while normal Americans climb in the sack with their girlfriends or wives or whatever. You make me freakin' sick.

You know one of the reasons I like to get in the field, why I liked Kazakhstan and all the 'Stans so much? It was because out there if I wanted to be alone, unmonitored, all I had to do was flip a few switches. But I can't even get privacy in my own home because of stinking asswipes like you."

I heard him coming. As soon as he was in range, I stood and slammed the binoculars into his face, at the bridge of his nose, and the crack echoed through the room. When he started to fall, it was easy to sidestep, to move over and let him crumple to the floor with both hands clenched to his face and blood turning them red.

"You son of a bitch!"

I kicked him in the stomach until he doubled over, then did it again. "What's the mission?"

"Screw you."

"Look, Ji, you don't know me, and I don't like you at all. And I'm guessing that, like me, you've been stripped of any connection to the Army, which means you're a civilian now and pretty much on your own." As I spoke, I took off my belt and then kicked him again, reaching down to force his arms behind his back so I could tie them. "You don't know half of what I've seen."

It was true. Wheezer would have recognized the look in my eyes and heard the tone of my voice and just known that this was my zone, a job; that although I wasn't a collector, I knew how to dig information from satos; and that to me, Ji was no different, a piece of meat attached to a meat cog, attached to a bigger meat machine that had over time become something loathsome but necessary if I wanted a paycheck. If Jihoon had known all that, he would have just told me what I wanted to know—would

have known that his life was in danger. It took a second to
rip a leg off the chair I had been sitting on and a minute to
rip padding off the couch and fasten it around my makeshift club, to soften it just enough and make sure the thing
wouldn't kill him right away.

"What's the op?" I asked again. "Give me the details."

His voice was muffled now and wet with blood. "Go to
hell."

It took about five minutes. Jihoon screamed with the
blows, each one placed to cause the most pain without
doing permanent damage, during which time I didn't ask
for anything. When he was ready, the beating stopped.

Ji was sobbing. "You mother..."

"What's the op? Tell me, and it all goes away."

"You're just going to kill me."

I lit a cigarette and sat cross-legged on the floor next to
him. "Why would I do that? I need you for the next leg of
the mission and killing you would just make the Army
come after me. I love the Army. Just tell me what the op
is, and we can move on; think of this as an initiation to a
brotherhood of psychopaths."

He coughed for a few minutes. When the cigarette
went out, I sighed and stood, getting ready for the next
phase, having to admit that the guy was tougher than I
thought and that maybe he'd have to die after all.

"OK, Ji. It just hurts more from here on out, though."

"Sunshine," he said. I sat again and shifted his body so
I could hear more clearly.

"What about it? What is it?"

"Unified Korea is starting its own genetics program in
response to an outside threat, probably from the Chinese,
but we don't know for sure; all we know is that Chen is

connected to it. I sold Command on the idea that we could get information from the Korean side of the equation that might link with what we know of Margaret and Dr. Chen, so we'd run *my* op first. My way."

I nodded. "And you'd look good in the process. Maybe get an easy promotion, and if it worked as well as you expected, maybe they'd put you in charge of a whole shit-load of stuff. Power is people and a budget, am I right? You're not cut out for fieldwork, Ji; you're a paper pusher and an academic who wanted to wear a gun so he could look tough."

"I went through the same training you did, asshole."

"Yeah, but training isn't everything. You just got your ass kicked, and if I hadn't been your partner, but an adversary, you'd be gurgling with a slit throat right now. Or worse. I can't afford to have a sniveling jerk-off who goes behind my back, angling to be in charge and keeping information from me so that he can call the shots. That's not my vision of a team. Now tell me why we're in Spain, why here and why now."

Jihoon coughed again, spitting blood on the floor. "I think you broke my arm; you're crazy, you know that?"

"Yeah. You should see me with a beard, I look even worse. *Tell me what we're doing here.*"

And Jihoon gave me the rest of it. A Unified Korea team was on their way to meet with a black market weapons dealer, someone who had a sample of what they needed for whatever project the Koreans had going, and the first meet was to take place in the Plaza Mayor sometime this week. It was all he had.

I sat back to smoke another cigarette while he moaned on the floor. This mission was prime; a real pile of crap. It didn't matter that the Koreans were our allies, that next to the Thais they were the best friends we had left in east Asia since Japan had been obliterated decades ago along with the western US in another war over metals; none of that must have figured with Jihoon or the people who had green-lit the whole fiasco because the orders were to kill the whole Korean team after grabbing the data we needed. What had we become now that our allies were targets? Jihoon was a perfect example of this new world, where a BAI puke could unravel your whole life at any time, could pipe himself into your house and watch the action like we were all some kind of porno holo for government employee amusement, and in that scenario, where you didn't trust your own people, how could the government give two shits about an ally? This was *real* prime. The problem was that there wasn't any other path because I needed this mission, wanted the action injected into my brain and past the blood barrier so its effect would be instantaneous. Pure.

"Fuck it," I said, pulling a good chair to the window and picking up a suitcase from under my cot. "I'll handle the op alone."

"Untie me," said Jihoon.

"You stay there."

It took me a second to find all the pieces of my gear, to assemble them and get everything ready. By the time I was finished, Jihoon asked me what I was doing, and I held up each piece to show him.

"This is an aeroinjector with ten doses of a fast-acting paralytic, one that'll knock anyone down within thirty seconds. You have to watch out on smaller people, though, or it will kill them because the doses are all the same. I also have an injector with a kind of truth serum and a fléchette pistol, a garrote, and this one you already know about—an encrypted satellite phone for our progress reports."

"You can't do this one alone."

I shook my head. "Sure I can. I'll keep you tied up and finish the mission, explaining that you got drunk one night and had an accident that left you immobilized. That won't look good for your next promotion, though, falling down stairs like that."

"You're dead."

"Yeah," I said and picked up the binoculars. "Pretty much. And we only have two more days in the week, so if these Koreans don't show, I'm taking it out on you."

But luckily for Jihoon, they showed later that day.

After I picked up the targets, it was cake to trail them because these weren't operators, and from the way they laughed and talked, it looked more like they were Korean government types—soft skins who operated under the assumption that everything would work out cool and breezy. Their escort would be a problem. He was muscle and had two friends who constantly checked the rear to make sure they weren't followed and who moved like they were armed.

They walked quickly. The old part of the city slid by at sunset, streetlights clicking on one by one, and it bothered me that there hadn't been more time to sightsee, to get a look at architecture that had survived for more than a thousand years, the stones worn smooth and some chipped by what could have been ancient wars or conflicts. *The dead must support the city,* I thought, *buried under the streets, maybe in catacombs or in forgotten graves so that in the middle of the night, when the old streets were empty, they'd relax a little, the weight of the cars and people gone for at least a few hours.* There was more to Spain than I'd first given it credit for, like maybe its people had earned the right to smile, had learned something that we had yet to figure out: that peace was a good gig too.

The group disappeared into a club, La Tumba, the entrance of which was a narrow set of stairs that dove underground, and I hesitated at the top of them for a moment, cursing their choice because it took all the strength I had to force myself downward. My hands shook when I opened the door. Inside, the club was dim, a half-lit bar and dance floor that throbbed with music but was empty except for the two strongmen who smiled at me from just inside, then reached out to yank me over the threshold. But they had been too slow; the first one fell dead with a fléchette through his head, and I pushed the second one to the floor, my pistol against his temple.

"You speak English?" I asked, and he nodded. "Where are they?"

He pointed toward a door behind the bar, not realizing that he'd be dead a second later. The music had been a blessing. It was so loud that anyone on the other side of the door couldn't have heard anything, and I moved toward it, pushing aside the fear of being underground, then slammed the thing open. Beyond, in a small room, the four Koreans sat at a conference table at the head of which was a woman with short black hair, a confused smile locked on her face as she said something in Spanish. The last of her guards, the one who had met with the Koreans in the plaza, stood behind her. *She* must have been the black market dealer, and I didn't have time to deal with her or the guy—who reached inside his jacket—so I put a few fléchettes through their foreheads, finishing them off with a couple more to their chests. Except for the music behind me, nobody else made a sound.

"English," I said, "who speaks it?"

The Koreans looked at one another in confusion, and I almost lost it, feeling the seconds tick by and not sure how much time I'd have to figure this one out; I couldn't take them *all* back to our flat. There were two men and two women. One of the men was old, with white hair and a nice suit. I was about to pick him when I noticed that a small stack of flexi-tabs sat in front of a young woman and that they contained technical drawings and specifications for armor, maybe a juiced-up combat suit. I figured she *had* to be the smart one. Three fléchettes, one for each of the other Koreans, broke the sound barrier with cracks that resonated in the small space, and I pulled the satchel from my shoulder, motioning for the woman to put all the flexis into it. By the time she finished, I had stripped the corpses of everything in their pockets and then grabbed the woman by the arm, making sure she understood that we were leaving and that my pistol would be pointed at her. She nodded, and we headed outside to climb the stairs. Once at the top, I breathed more easily in the darkness and pushed her along the sidewalk, back toward our apartment where an hour later I had her tied up next to Ji.

"Can you untie me now?" he asked.

"No."

"Why?"

I lit a cigarette and blew smoke into his face. "I don't trust you. How'd you get the information?"

He stared at me, his face an expression of rage. Blood had dried over his lip and on his nose, a kind of bizarre mustache that represented my entire career. The missions had grown just like that. They evolved over time in a hint of a pattern that anchored itself around murder, but in general they were all chaos, the unexpected and unintended rearing itself in every one and in ways that von Clausewitz never imagined but would have admired as a whacky "fog of war." But this mission was different. My work had never underpinned a national strategy, and although Command hadn't given an indication that this op did, the woman's flexi-tabs suggested otherwise, and I stared at one, the diagrams of a sophisticated armor system glowing green in the otherwise unlit apartment. The girl's eyes went wide, and her breathing shallowed with a terror that made me feel sick. She was right to be scared. I knew what would happen once we got our information. The fact that I'd just wiped seven humans had started to sink in, a sensation that I countered by reasoning that the kills had been necessary, that it was all for an operation around which you sensed the wheels of a military complex turning, getting ready for a new generation of warfare and preparing to defend itself against a threat that had never been seen before. Whatever the armor was, it was new, it was hard-core, and it hadn't been designed for anything resembling a human.

"Tell me how you got the information," I repeated.

"One of my friends who still works Assurance at the bureau. He passed it to me a few months ago without reporting through normal channels. He was listening to one of those *innocent* households you were so concerned about."

There was a certain smell to fear, and as the woman lay on the floor, Jihoon bleeding beside her, she had it—a mixture of sweat and human ozone. Its odor wafted up, as if salt and musk seeped from the woman's pores, but Jihoon just smelled like ass. The fact that he wasn't scared made me reconsider.

"You going to try anything if I untie you?"

He spat on the floor. "I might knife you in your sleep, you son of a bitch."

I knelt beside him and unhitched my belt, letting him go. "Don't fuck with me. You have no idea what I can do."

"I'm beginning to get an idea."

"Look, Command was right, I do need you. You speak their language, and this is some messed-up stuff." I showed him the first flexi-tab and waited for the reaction, but there was none. It bothered me. Jihoon was impossible to read, and it occurred to me that this guy would have been good at poker, his face so far having been unreadable except for the few times he wanted to show how much he hated me.

"It's a new kind of armor," I said.

"I can see that."

"But it's not for people or satos. Look at the design for the occupant; the dimensions are for something with meter-long legs about an inch across."

Jihoon nodded. "I noticed. What happened to the others?"

"Dead, along with the black market guys. Their contact was a woman, and I grabbed wallets along with everything in their pockets."

Jihoon nodded again and turned on a lamp before sitting next to the woman. They spoke Korean. I had no idea what he was saying, but the volume went up and it was clear that Jihoon had started to make her edgy—even more edgy than she had been when in my custody. He turned to me.

"Let's start uploading all those schematics and get ready to transmit because we might not have much time once they find the bodies you left behind. And this will take some time. Was there another Korean there, a man who looked older than the rest?"

"Yeah. There was an old guy with white hair. Why?"

He shook his head. "You are one dumb simpleton. In Korean culture, you should assume that the oldest one is in charge; it's not always true, but most of the time it's a fair assumption."

"So?"

"So..." Jihoon slapped the girl and she winced, a drop of blood appearing at the corner of her mouth. "You killed one of Sunshine's lead scientists, someone who could have told us a lot. But then, all us *Chinamen* probably look the same."

"Oh," I said. "Well, what about her?"

"She's just an aide. A goddamn secretary. Well done, *Lieutenant*."

Jihoon translated what he could, and after an hour the woman started crying and wouldn't stop.

"We're getting nowhere," I said.

He nodded. "She confirmed Sunshine is something related to genetics so at least we know what they were here for—have enough technical data to keep a team of armor and weapons analysts busy for months. We also have the identities of some of the Korean team; maybe we can get something from their background that will tell us more about Sunshine. These armor systems are advanced, but Korea isn't a threat to our forces, so I don't get it."

"They're going to violate the Genetic Weapons Convention," I explained, *"less than a year after the ink dried."*

"So?"

I lit another cigarette and went to the window, looking down onto the plaza's darkness and unable to shake the sensation that the entire world was about to change. *"Sunshine.* Even if this betty can't give details, she confirmed that it's a new genetic-engineering program geared to go into full-scale production within ten years. Who does that these days? And the question isn't whether Unified Korea will threaten *us,* it's who the hell scares them so much that they feel like they have to break with a brand-new treaty in secret? I mean, they know what happens if they're caught. What zapped them like this? What have the Chinese got?"

Jihoon sighed. "If I'd been there with you, we wouldn't have messed this up so badly."

"If you'd played it straight, I wouldn't have had to tie you up."

"So what's the move?"

He asked it like I was some kind of expert. Maybe compared to him I was, but what the hell could I say? Ji was supposed to be the genius. Less than a month ago, I'd been a sergeant and never did a single day in any of the academies, while looking at Jihoon, you just knew that a groomed bastard like that had been admitted to one at six years old, the earliest possible age, and probably to one of the tier-one institutes—not one of those underfunded dust bowl academies in the reclamation districts. He hadn't ever *seen* a civilian university. I didn't have to ask to know that his mother had never feared being pushed into the breeding program or that his father had about a million civic award buttons pinned to his blazer lapel—to show off whenever he took a walk.

I was about to say something when Ji pointed at the holo station. We had kept it on the news, with the volume turned down, to get a heads-up if they found the murders, and now we saw the club, La Tumba, with my victims shown in three-dimensional color.

"You should have lit fire to the place," he said.

"I couldn't."

"Why?" But I ignored the question. I didn't want to tell him the truth, that the old city had put its spell on me and to set it ablaze would have been a million times worse than anything else I could've done.

"Finish up with her," I said.

"How?"

"Get names and addresses of her coworkers in Wonsan, information that seems innocuous, anything that might be of value down the road, like her favorite restaurants and bars, where people go to relax in her division. We can't get anything on Sunshine, but maybe we can get something useful *now* that we won't recognize until *later*."

"What are you going to do?" he asked.

"I need to think." And I knew even as I said it that thinking wouldn't do any good at all.

The apartment had a small porch, and I lay on the concrete slab, looking up at the few stars I could see through Madrid's light pollution. The cigarette burned.

From inside came Jihoon's muffled shouts, and it reminded me of being a kid, of my old man hollering at my mom in their room after he came home from a twelve-hour shift at the Navy Yard, a sound sometimes accompanied by slaps. I was getting close to forty, and it worried me. There was no longevity in the Special Forces and a promotion at my age to lieutenant was only a token or something required to gain me access to Strategic Operations; it didn't mean that they wanted me forever. So where would I be in five years? It was easy to predict the arc of someone like Ji, whose problem was being Asian. I knew he thought I was prejudiced from what I'd said to him earlier, but that couldn't be further from the truth because I'd just been trying to piss him off, to get him to come at me, and to teach him a lesson. Most in the military didn't trust Asians, and to those kind it wouldn't matter that he was Korean. Korean, Japanese, Filipino, or Thai—they were the best friends we had in the Pacific. But to the military, these were the same bastards who had tricked us fifty years ago into sending our forces into one of the hairiest wars in history, the Asian Wars, where a quarter of the world's population, along with fifty million Americans, had disappeared overnight in nuclear fire. But even that wouldn't stop Jihoon from career advancement. You could tell from just looking at him that he had a million tricks up his sleeve. *I must be getting old,* I thought, *because I never used to think this way.*

The immediate concern, though, was La Tumba. It meant that Spanish investigators were already combing the place for hair and skin, anything that might provide a DNA sample of the killer so they could find the person who had done it. I had backup plans if they got a hit. But none of them were optimal, and these events gave me a first taste of what it meant to be in the open, unprotected by the umbrella of the US military and operating as an independent. They *meant* it too. If we got caught, the Army would shrug it off and scream that they knew we were no good in the first place and that's why they kicked us out. So why hadn't I tried for these kinds of ops twenty years ago, when I was eighteen? Back then, the adrenaline would have been no more than a rush, something to savor, but there on that balcony?

It just made me think, while trying to ignore the sounds of torture from inside, and wonder: *What am I even doing on this op?*

I'd been wrong when I thought that killing people would be easy; satos didn't die like this. The Korean woman trembled in my hands, crying while she bled from her mouth, and my concentration broke when thoughts of Bea forced their way in. It pissed me off; nobody would sign up for torturing a human woman. My old assignments in war, training insurgents and fighting on the line, were a dream in comparison, and even killing satos wasn't so bad; they didn't whimper and cry, weren't worth any sympathy even if they did, and although the chick was speaking Korean, you knew what she was saying and that she had a million reasons to live. Jihoon had squeezed everything he could out of her, and the local news had just announced that the police made a breakthrough in the La Tumba murders, so it was time to cut our losses and split; he was in the kitchen, finishing the last uploads of the flexi-tabs so we could burst transmit to an orbiting platform and bail.

"Kill her and get it over with," Ji said. "Isn't that your game?"

Another cigarette burned red. I took a few more puffs, holding the smoke in for as long as I could, and thought, *Fléchettes would be too cruel.* She would have seen me draw, and there'd be that brief moment of horror before I fired, which was an image I didn't want burned into my brain—at least not until I had some bourbon.

She started crying more loudly, and I turned to walk back toward the coffee table. My kit rested on it. It took me a second to decide on what I wanted, but even when I lifted the injector, I couldn't turn, didn't want her to see the hesitation.

"Jihoon."

"What?"

"Tell her that we're going to put her to sleep. That when she wakes up, we'll be gone and she can go home."

He said something to her and then cleared his throat. "It's done but why?"

When I turned, she saw the aeroinjector and shut her eyes. "Because it makes a difference." I knew without looking that Ji was watching. The girl's skin was pale, a kind of white that I recalled seeing once in Georgia, on kaolin roads that stretched forever under overhangs of willows and Spanish moss, and when the aeroinjector pressed against her neck, the skin went even whiter. She whispered something, and Jihoon started to translate, but I didn't want to know, telling him to shut up before he could even get started. Three pulses later she was unconscious.

"The paralytic?" Jihoon asked.

"Truth serum overdose. The stuff has an opiate in it, and I gave her enough to kill an elephant."

When it was over, I swept the area to make sure everything was in my kit, and then we both wiped down the apartment with bleach, taking anything that might have our hairs or skin—sheets, pillowcases, everything. It would be awhile before the Spanish could sift through all the DNA since there had to be thousands of other samples in such a public place as La Tumba, but we needed to be careful anyway. It hit me in a wave of dizziness. The sight of her on the floor and the twin images of Margaret and Bea both made me feel sick, the kind of sick that getting drunk would take care of, and Jihoon's voice—his announcement that it was time to book—sounded as if it came from the other side of the world. I had to make sure. I pulled out my fléchette pistol and squeezed three rounds into her forehead before we left, before we walked down the stairs and into a rainy Madrid morning.

"You on a commercial flight?" I asked.

Jihoon nodded. "Out of Madrid. You?"

"Better if you don't know. I'll see you in Asia; if there's a delay, just keep going to the meeting point every day at noon."

We shook hands and nodded to each other before walking in separate directions.

Cameras. Street cameras, like the ones in the States but hidden to preserve the old city's appearance, and high-altitude police drones—those had done it, allowed the cops to finger me more quickly than I'd anticipated. They'd recorded me entering and leaving La Tumba. Now my face hovered over every one of Madrid's holo casters in a grainy portrait, just clear enough to make out my features. It was night now. I'd spent all day in the sewer, hiding with the rest of Spain's garbage and doing my best to call the next move.

The satellite phone was cold, dripping wet as I phoned in the first report to let them know that the data was on its way and that I'd be moving out on an alternate schedule, and rain fell in sheets, in a wind so strong that it blew the drops sideways. When I finished, I smashed the phone on the concrete and then threw the pieces into the gutter. Flashing lights blinked from the direction of our flat. They turned the rain into a light show of glittering crystal, red, blue, and green, and I froze, wondering if they'd already nabbed Ji but then decided that of the two of us, he was safer since the news was describing it as the act of one psychopath. I leaned against a wall as a group of Guardia Civil jogged by, their boots pounding on the street while their officer shouted something over his helmet speakers.

Now what? A flash of panic made my breath short, but soon the fear turned, shifted into an icy feeling that ran through my veins and refrigerated my mind so that the useless thoughts froze and fell out, leaving the logical options, the ones for which I had been trained. So far I had evaded capture. But the Guardia and Madrid's police would be ready at checkpoints, waiting to find the person who matched the holo image, or if they had found any DNA, the sequence that fit. For now, my appearance would be hard to match given the fact that I was soaked and visibility in the rain was bad anyway. And there were things I could do about DNA, but by now they would have matched my description to my entry visa profile. This last possibility wasn't a problem either, in theory, because it

was possible to counteract a visa match, involving a
method that allowed me to adopt any one of ten identity
chits I carried.

But it would hurt like hell.

My shoes slipped on the wet cobblestones when I
ducked into an alley, and in the distance a dim blue light
shone over a door. I took three steps down to it. The tired
Spaniard manning the bar's entrance smelled of tobacco,
and he looked me up and down before waving me into a
low-ceilinged chamber where white smoke obscured the
far side of the room, and I leaned over to ask him in broken
Spanish for the toilet. The guy pointed and I moved. Once
inside a stall with the door locked, my duffel didn't want to
open until I nearly ripped the zipper off, reaching inside a
concealed pocket to find my extra passport chits and a pair
of special pens that hid things I'd hoped to avoid using—
because there wouldn't be any anesthesia. Both pens were
microbot injectors: One would release a set of invisible
automatons, programmed to arrange themselves under the
skin of a finger where, if subjected to a skin prick, they
would release DNA. The bots in the other pen would
rearrange my retinal capillaries and alter their pattern.
Both signatures would match the next passport. The finger
injection wasn't so bad, an instant of pain as the bots
spread and pushed tissues aside, but I hoped that if asked
for a sample, they would let me choose the digit because
the wrong finger would end everything.

My eyes were another issue entirely. I did both, one
after another, and the pain almost made me pass out; my
eye sockets burned from the inside and tears blinded me
so that at first it wasn't apparent that they consisted of
blood instead of water, and although there was no scream-

ing, someone in the next stall would have heard a soft moaning that no amount of effort could have prevented. When it was over, I could barely see.

Then it was a matter of time. Someone came into the stall next to mine, and I waited, making sure that he sat down before I broke in—slamming my fist into his face, again and again, until he fell unconscious—and stripped him of his clothes. They were big but would have to do. Once I'd finished I dumped all of mine into the trash can, flushed my old passport chit down the toilet, and walked out. The new clothes weren't a perfect solution, but if—in addition to a finger prick—they sampled my clothing, at least for a while the DNA would be someone else's. Outside, I jumped into a cab and told the driver to head for the Atocha train station. The clock was ticking now; although my eyes would be altered forever, the microbots in my fingers had a half-life of two days.

"British?" the cabbie asked.

"American."

"Ah, we used to get a lot of Americans when the war was on, but now not so much."

"Yeah. I can understand that."

"Where are you going, the train to Barcelona?"

Before I could answer he cursed in Spanish, and the cab slowed, its electric motor whining. "La Guardia," he explained. "The cops. They have traffic blocked all over the area."

I did my best to look concerned—which wasn't difficult—glancing at my watch in frustration. "Oh? What do they want? I have a train in an hour; do you think I'll miss it?"

"It depends."

"On what?"

He laughed and looked back at me. "On if you're the one they want to catch. It shouldn't take long. A test here, a test there, and then through."

The rain came down heavier than it had before, and even at full power the taxi's wipers couldn't keep up with it, and sheets of the stuff fell outside my window, turning the sidewalks into a distorted fantasy where yellow lights and shopwindows looked like molten steel. These were the moments that meant everything. They proved I was alive. The important thing about adrenaline, I recalled, was that for me it made time slow to the point where I appreciated a view from a taxi and marveled at the beauty of situations and surroundings. Our vehicle crept forward a car length at a time until they were in sight: the Guardia Civil. Ten of them clustered around a checkpoint where traffic had been stopped in each direction, and two APCs stood guard, their turrets open and their commanders holding rain ponchos over their heads while they smoked. The rain had been fortunate. None of the men wanted to be out in this weather, and they performed the scans as quickly as possible.

When it was our turn, the taxi stopped and someone tapped on the windows. I rolled mine down to see a young soldier, eighteen or nineteen, a stubby Maxwell carbine strapped to his chest, its banana clip pressing up into his cheek.

"You speak English?" I asked.

The taxi driver had already finished with his tests and explained what the soldier wanted. "He wants your passport and a finger—for DNA."

I nodded and handed the soldier my chit. He scanned it, then motioned for me to place my finger in the analyzer, which I did until it flashed green.

"Now a retina scan," the driver said, so I leaned forward, staring into the optics of a handheld unit. A moment later, we had been waved on, my passport returned.

"See, that was easy."

"Who are they looking for?" I asked.

The man shook his head. "A bad one, this man. He killed seven people in a club in the old section of the city and one more not too far from here, where they recovered a sample of his DNA. Stan Resnick. The Guardia think he's still nearby."

"He acted alone?"

"*Sí.* I think so. That's the word I hear, but who knows for sure?"

A few minutes later we pulled up to Atocha Station, and I paid the driver, along with a good tip. He handed the extra money back.

"What's wrong?" I asked.

"This is España," the man explained. "I get paid well for my job, do I look poor?"

I was about to say yes when he sped off.

They had isolated my DNA—or Jihoon's. It was worse than I'd realized, and I moved through the station on autopilot, my feet feeling as though they were detached from my body, my brain floating in a cloud of fear. There was one good thing about them having one or both of our DNA sequences: it meant that they would rely on scans more than visual checks, that my picture wouldn't be the main focus, which was fortunate because once my hair dried I'd start looking more like their holo still. So far luck had been with me, but there was no guarantee that I wouldn't have to go through the whole process again; even if the train left the station on time, there was still the border crossing to worry about.

At La Jonquera.

The train slowed, and I woke with a start, glancing at my watch to find that I had slept for four hours, but it shouldn't have surprised me; I'd gotten no sleep for the previous two days. Until I had passed out, the ride had been uneventful, and my car was empty with the exception of an older couple who sat near the front, but I still shouldn't have slept. Anything could've happened at the stops between Madrid and the Pyrenees. Once more the question of my age crept in, made me wonder if it was time to call it quits before I got myself or anyone else killed, and I struggled to recall what Bea looked like so it would calm me down. I knew her eye color, hair color, everything. But that differed from being able to picture her in my mind, which had dumped any recollection of her appearance and which refused, no matter how much I willed it, to reboot. Phillip. *Him* I recalled, and with that came the memory of Bea, bright and in focus, but rather than reassure me, the fact that I needed Phillip to remember her was a jolt and sent a tremor through my spine. My mind had begun to slip, and sooner or later it could get me killed.

A voice came over the loudspeaker and said something in Spanish, then followed in accented English.

"La Jonquera; last stop before France. Prepare for passport and visa inspection."

I got mine ready and waited, expecting armed Guardia Civil to burst in through one of the compartment doors, but nothing happened. The minutes slid into half an hour. I risked opening the shades to peek out and what I saw made me grab my duffel to lift it from the floor and slam it onto the empty seat beside me; the Guardia was there. Six APCs and about a company of soldiers had arranged themselves on my side of the train, and I knew without looking that it would be the same on the other side, that something had brought them in force, and as far as I knew, I was the one thing that could attract so much attention. My fléchette pistol, when disassembled, looked just like things one would take on travel—a flexi-tablet that wrapped to form the barrel's electromagnetic coil, a pen that was the barrel, batteries, and several other things. I had started to gather them when it hit me: What was I doing? A *pistol*? I dropped the gear back into the bag, fished out the bourbon I had bought at Atocha, and decided to hell with it; now was as good a time as any to get drunk. The first swallow stung on the way down, and my already tender eyes watered more than they should have, but that wasn't any reason to stop drinking. It would be my last one. When the Guardia came for me, I'd make sure that they took me smiling, and the second hit was a prolonged chug, where I swallowed a quarter of the bottle, coughing uncontrollably. Once the fit passed, the third pull went in smoothly.

Phillip isn't really my son. I saw him now, just as clearly as before, and still there was nothing except the warmth that had begun to spread throughout my chest from the alcohol. *He will be fine,* I decided. I couldn't invent love any more than I could assemble my pistol and hold off a company of armed men with APCs, no matter how much training I had, no matter how long I tried. Phillip was left with the lot he'd drawn, same as I'd been, because it was a Resnick family tradition, and maybe someday we'd get together at a reunion and compare notes on how difficult we'd all had it and get drunk together so that once the fists flew none of it would hurt too much, but—

The door in front of me flew open, interrupting my thoughts, and two men in combat suits entered, heading past the older couple and moving in my direction. I stood. I raised both hands in the air and saw that behind the two soldiers, an officer in normal uniform followed, staring at me with a confused look.

The armored men passed, pushing through the car's rear door, and the officer drew even with my seat. I still had my hands up.

"I'll go quietly," I said.

The man looked even more confused. "Sit down. You're American?"

I nodded.

"And you thought we had come for you?"

I nodded again. The man broke into laughter then, which he tried to control and keep quiet but couldn't.

"Why?" he asked, smiling broadly.

I realized that the officer was doing his best to keep his eye on the door through which his men had gone, and it came to me: they hadn't been looking for me at all. *What the fuck answer could I give now?*

I held up my half-empty bottle and tried to smile back at him. "I've had a little to drink."

"Well, we're not here for that. There's a drug gang on board, two cars down, so have another for me," he said.

Once he had disappeared, I collapsed back into my seat, shaking, and finished the bottle.

An hour later, and after an abbreviated firefight, it was over. Compared to that, the standard passport and ID scan was anticlimactic, and although we were so far behind schedule it could have presented a problem for me in catching my flight from Paris, it didn't matter. The train sped through the tunnel and across the French border, leaving Spain behind. I didn't care if I never saw Madrid again. Madrid was where something terrible had happened, an awakening in my soul that I'd always suspected would come but which I'd always prayed would somehow be delayed until later: a self-doubt born from aging. Young men knew everything and never questioned an order, but not me, not anymore. Even the aches in my muscles stayed with me a little longer than normal, and in more lucid moments I noticed the face in the mirror had picked up thousands of lines that hadn't been there the day before. Madrid had been the birthplace of questions and a fear of death, and now that it was receding behind me, now that I was well on my way to getting drunk, I swore that I'd never go back. From here it was Paris, then on to the States, where I'd detour to fulfill an obligation— one that I dreaded—and then Bangkok.

Sunshine, I had already decided, would be my last operation. I'd never take another.

THREE

Binge

Athens, Georgia, was one of those miracle towns that had avoided change during the war years and had even escaped the gristmill of progress for most of its existence so that the summer heat gave its million trees a buzz, the sounds of countless cicadas, their whine and hum ebbing and flowing. There used to be a civilian university there. In its place the walls of a state academy had been erected, and at each entry Marines stood in dress blues with loaded Maxwells, Athens's streets now drained of cadets who would be away for vacation. A few lingered, though. Their heads had been shaved, and white plastic interfaces jutted from just above their left ear, a port where the kids could plug in, tune up, and dial through to the latest military tactics or von Clausewitz in simulation. They looked like the walking dead. The technique had been perfected on the satos, and it made me shiver with gratitude that I had learned the old-fashioned way, in a classroom and on obstacle courses. Our military had used these boys' minds as a dumping ground, and the subjects shuffled down the sidewalk drained of energy, oblivious to anything except the need to salute any officer they passed. Things were gearing up. It was in the air. No news holo needed to report it to me, and none of the press would have noticed anyway because the smell of prewar was something I had learned to identify through decades of having wrapped myself in its sticky blanket. We'd just gotten *out* of the Subterrene War; would the military try it again this soon?

Wheezer's wife, Michelle, lived in a centuries-old house on Boulevard and a sign marked it as historic, having belonged to someone named Cobb. Now it was for bereaved families—a halfway house, in which wives of the dead were given three years to adjust and remarry, find a job, or take the ultimate path of the state: breeding. I'd walked up and down outside the place all morning, smoking, drinking from a flask, just trying to find enough courage to approach the door and ignore the cameras attached to every lightpost in the area. But I didn't have to go in; Michelle saw me and came out to the sidewalk, smiling.

"I was wondering if you'd ever show."

"Nice place," I said.

She took a cigarette and waited for me to light it, drawing in a deep breath. "They told me you got discharged. Medical. I figured they booted you because you finally did something wrong."

"Yeah. I'm out. I have a plane to catch tomorrow from Atlanta, so I thought I'd stop by."

"Were you discharged because of Wheezer?" she asked. "Or did you fuck up and get him killed?"

She was cold now, and her stare felt like twin ice picks jabbed into my throat, rendering me voiceless. What had the military claimed? I didn't know how to convince her that it had nothing to do with me and decided it would have required me to tell her *how* he bought it—through his own stupidity by not listening.

"I didn't get him killed, Michelle."

"So it was just another training accident and you stick to the bullshit, just like he used to. You're still in the Army, Bug; it's all over your face and you and Wheezer were the worst liars ever."

She was crying but with no noise. Tears streamed, and I wanted to rip the cameras from their brackets, stomp on them for preventing me from telling the truth.

"Yeah. Training accident."

"Fuck you, Bug. And him too. Both of you, with your code of silence and dreams of being supersoldiers while we stay behind and make babies. They used to have women in the service, you know. Soldiers. But I've spent the last months trying to figure out what kind of woman would want that duty, and I can't come up with anything because none of this makes sense; we go to war, win or get our asses kicked, grab as much metal from the ground as possible, regroup and repopulate, then do it again. We were going to have a kid, you know?"

I nodded. "Yeah, he told me."

Michelle sighed and took another drag, then kicked a pebble from the sidewalk. "It's too hot here. Ninety-seven in the shade, no breeze, and a hundred percent humidity. It's like Thailand."

"You ever been to Thailand?" I asked. Her observation stuck the jitters to me, like it had been some kind of portent; what reason did she even have to mention the place?

"No. Why would I go *there* when I've been *here*?"

"No reason. But this place isn't so bad, Michelle, compared to some I've seen."

She looked at me and smiled. "Wheezer said the same kind of thing—when we lived in Buffalo. The snow used to bury us, and we lived in one of those underground apartment complexes, ten feet under rock, under forty feet of snow. Winters were so long that I don't know how we never had a kid."

"You're better off that way, without kids. Trust me."

"Yeah." Michelle nodded and blew smoke so it hovered, then sank, cooled to the point where it was heavier than the humid air, giving me the chance to change the subject.

"You know Bea accepted a housing post in one of the reclamation districts out west?" I asked. "She's about forty klicks from the Phoenix hot zone. On days when wind blows from the west, they have to stay indoors from fear of radiation, and they didn't even bother with new housing. She lives in one of those ancient, tiny units from when population was a problem."

Michelle went silent for a second, staring at the sidewalk before looking at me. "Bea called last week. She left you, Bug."

The words stunned me. It wasn't that they hurt as much as it wasn't a possibility that I'd considered. "What'd she say?"

"Phillip got tapped for an academy; Bea didn't want to live down there in the desert, alone, so she asked for a state-sanctioned divorce and went into the breeding program."

"The kid?" I asked, disinterested in Bea completely. "Which academy took Phillip?" But it wasn't me asking, at least it didn't feel like it, because the news had shattered everything. This is what it took to make me feel something—learning that Phillip would be one of them, the walking dead—but I tried to console myself with the knowledge that those who made it through recovered quickly, maybe in a matter of a few months because I'd seen the first ones here and there in the field, and the scientists figured nobody could hold that much information in their brains anyway. It left an imprint more than actual memories. The military data pushed into neurons until they made new connections and networks, which, when it was over, relaxed and dumped as much as they could—kind of like taking a final exam after cramming for three days; you forgot everything the next week. The difference was that with this system, the neural networks had been reformed and shaped to an optimal pattern for strategic and tactical thinking in combat, and those new networks lasted a lifetime. They liked them young because it was easier to shape the brain as it grew, and anyone who showed promise in early testing was snatched up and sent to an academy based on their scores; Annapolis was at the top, with West Point next, then Colorado, and downward from there.

"Annapolis," she said.

Some parents would have been proud. *Phillip isn't my son.* But I heard the whir of a camera as it panned above us and everything snapped, my mind flying into a place uncharted.

"What are you doing?" asked Michelle, and the camera's voice came to life as soon as I started to scale the lightpost.

"You have been identified as Lieutenant Stanley Resnick. Attempts to tamper with the Assurance surveillance systems is a federal offense. Please get down; I've notified the proper authorities."

But I didn't listen. The speaker was the first to go, cutting off the thing's voice in midsentence, and I grinned because I thought that it would at least be silent for a few minutes. But its voice came from a speaker down the street, booming until people started coming from their homes to see what was going on.

"Stanley Resnick. You are in violation of federal statute thirteen-U.S.C.-thirteen-sixty-one, destruction of government property. Desist now and wait for the authorities."

"Fuck you!"

The camera had been fastened to the post more securely than its speaker, and I hung my entire body from the thing before its mounting cracked and the wires snapped, sending me to the sidewalk for a hard landing. It knocked the wind out of me. In the distance the sirens came, making me laugh, and I smashed what was left of the camera against the concrete, then jumped on pieces with my boots, grinding the plastic into tinier chunks.

I laughed again and saw people staring. "This is what we should all be doing," I said, "getting them out of our brains. What right do they have to our neurons? I'm the only sane person on this street, and when I'm done here, *I'm coming for the rest of you!"*

Michelle grabbed my arm. "Stop it, Bug. Please stop. *Now."*

"They're all nutjobs, Michelle. Everyone except Wheezer, and they never gave Phillip the *chance* to be sane because now they'll just force everything on him. He'll wind up like Wheezer or worse. Nobody needs to know how to murder using a tab stylus; do you know what that does to your head after twenty years, especially if you've killed someone with one?"

"Well, then quit!"

Michelle's words silenced everything, sending me into a spin. Now I saw the cop cars, screaming down Boulevard from both directions, but didn't hear them because she had gotten me thinking, sent me into a trance where I had to examine an idea that had never occurred to me before.

A few seconds later the first cop tackled me, pushing me facedown into the Cobb house's dirt yard. "You're under arrest," he said.

"I quit."

"What the hell are you talking about?" He forced my hands back, snapping on plastic ties, and another officer ran up to stand over me.

"This guy's crazy," the first one said.

The second one squatted next to my head. "Son, are you on drugs? Have you been drinking? Have any needles or weapons in your pockets, anything we should know about?"

"I quit," I repeated, wondering why they didn't understand. "I quit because I don't want to do it anymore. I'm finished."

The second one stood and pulled off his cap, scratching his head and looking at the damaged camera. "Lock him up. We'll wait for the Feds and see what *they* want to do."

Michelle yelled good-bye as they dragged me to the closest car, but I was too amped up to respond, too busy grinning and feeling happy—so happy that I screamed it at her.

"I QUIT!"

Once they saw my war record, the Feds went easy and didn't press charges but made me promise never to do it again. I didn't know if that was good or bad. Part of me thought that jail was the right place for someone in my state, someone who was thinking of hopping a ride to Annapolis and greasing every son of a bitch who tried standing between me and Phillip, but who didn't understand why he cared so much about a stupid kid. A chasm had opened. On either side were two versions of Stan Resnick: one the operator, the man whose marketable skill had been an ability to kill and sleep soundly; the other was a version within whom a dormant consciousness had awakened, someone who I despised because he had failed to materialize in time to save his family and whose regret for having failed was a liability. Had the Feds grasped this, they would have kept me in lockup. But now, on the streets, nobody could have predicted what I'd do, not even me, and once I remembered where I'd parked my rental the next decision would be difficult. There was still time for my flight, and the old me screamed to just push on and complete the op, get to Bangkok and start killing again. The new me had other plans.

My car was still where I left it, near the Cobb house, and my gear was still in the trunk. *But where to?* I needed time to think, and Atlanta was the best place for it because from there I could hop a plane anywhere, and so I turned onto the bypass toward the highway, knowing that within three hours I'd be drunk. I started out west but after a few pulls on a bottle decided to hell with it and turned around for the backroads north, toward Annapolis, because whether he was my son or not, leaving Phillip to those bastards wasn't going to work, and I didn't want to deal with an airport or its security.

Small towns flew by in a haze of abandoned gas stations or restaurants run out of people's homes, and my car was

the most modern one that some of these places had seen
in years. The rental had air-conditioning, but the hum
sounded odd over the engine, a strange rattle that hadn't
been there the day before, and soon I began wondering if
the vehicle itself was being monitored, transmitting my
location and anything I said to one of the semis whose
quantum core would parse the data and decide whether it
was worth forwarding to one of Ji's friends. It took a second to pull over. A few minutes later I had ripped apart a
portion of the dashboard, not satisfied that the system was
clean until the sharp plastic cut into both hands, sending
my blood to puddle in the air-conditioning ductwork.
From there it wasn't hard to imagine a listening device
was hidden in the radio or navigation systems. By the
time I had finished convincing myself that those were also
clean, along with the rest of the car, the entire dashboard
had been removed, I'd ripped the seat cushions out, and
covered myself in clay from slithering underneath to
check the frame and undercarriage. When I crawled out, a
group of three boys sat on bicycles about thirty feet away,
each of them with one foot on the ground.

"Hey, mister," one of them called. "What's wrong with
your car?"

The embarrassment nearly left me speechless, and it
took a moment to think. "A snake. Damn rattlesnake got
in, and I had trouble finding it."

They didn't respond but watched as I climbed in to sit
on a metal seat frame and pull onto the road. All of them
stared as I drove past, and their looks said the same thing
I'd begun to think: I'd lost it. Then again, Phillip didn't
have anyone else looking out for him, and it was still more
than nine hours to Annapolis, so between now and then

my nerves would have to settle out or I'd blow the whole thing. I rolled down the window and stopped in front of the kids.

"You boys know where the nearest liquor store is?"

Everyone those days was insane. To me, looking around the bar I'd found off of 95 North, I was the only normal person alive, and while two Marines on leave attacked an Air Force officer, slamming a broken bottle deep into his stomach, I grinned at their technique and laughed until the police showed up and dragged them out. Who knew how much I'd drunk? The bottles kept coming, and there was a breeding facility attached to the place so that one minute I'd have a blonde girl bouncing on my lap and then would black out to find a redhead; some were pretty, others a horror of bad genetics, but it didn't matter to me. This was a place where everything converged, where death and sex and liquor flowed into one whirlpool, with me at its center, mouth wide open and guzzling until I wound up passed out in one of the facility's tiny hotel rooms. Maybe sociologists could have worked it out. They would have said that the letdown from the Subterrene War in Kazakhstan had resulted in a kind of societal *snap*, like two kids who pulled a rubber band to its breaking point and then released it without warning, the result being stung fingers and heat. But instead of heat we got breeding facilities. The Deep South and the Midwest, they were the places where sex was easy and encouraged, where government brothels had sprung up on every street corner right between First Presbyterian and the family pharmacy and where all you had to pay was the entry fee and submit to a quick med scan before stepping onto the floor—slick with the day's production of human sweat and everything else. This was the birthplace of soldiers.

At least a percentage of them. In watching and participating I'd studied the process, and it was like a shot between the eyes when I figured it out: the satos were better than us, not just because of their engineering but because of the fumbling nature of human reproduction. Even here, breeding was a random thing with no control over whose genes went where except for a quick genetic manipulation after conception—at which point the mother was whisked away to some garden spot—to ensure the woman gave birth to another government son. I'd asked myself how many satos I'd killed, but then again how many sons had I fathered? How many other Phillips were there in the world who had no chance of being saved by a crazy man driving shitfaced up Interstate 95? That was the thought that killed my mission. It drove a stake through it, then planted a boot in my face and pushed in the humiliating truth: that my strategy was rooted in hypocrisy, in which I had failed to account for the fact that just because Phillip wasn't mine, it didn't mean I didn't have any children. And if I cared about another guy's kid, why wasn't I driving all over the world to track down my own sons born from breeding sites and who, by now, could be close to twenty? Some of them may have even been operators, knee-deep in the sewers of Dzhanga or some other place.

One night I woke up in a girl's room, still drunk. She grabbed me and begged for me to stay, but it was the grip that got me, that pried loose some petrified crap in my brain and unclogged a torrent of insanity, because I screamed and dropped to the floor. By the time an employee came and got me, the girl was screaming too, and the pair of us had to be sedated by facility nurses, one of whom cooed in my ear as she walked me back to my hotel room.

"She grabbed me by the wrist," I said.

"There, there, it's all right; it's all over."

"The wrist. She had claws, nails that dug all the way in like she was trying to open a vein."

The nurse nodded and caught me when I almost fell over. "I bet it was scary, but soon you'll be in your own rack, and then you can sleep it all off. You know what I'd do if I were you?"

"No, what?"

She grabbed the hotel chit from my hand and waved it over my door lock, pushing me through when it opened. I collapsed in a heap on the rack.

"Tomorrow when you wake up, go into town. On the corner of Main and Battle Streets, there's an empty building next to Gargin's Groceries; every morning at eleven they have a meeting there. I don't know what it's all about, but I see them go in and come out every day 'cause I live nearby, and you might be able to talk to someone and get rid of whatever's on your chest. All of them look like you."

"What?" I asked. "What do I look like?"

"Like one of them that's seen a whole lot. Like an old soldier."

The thought terrified me, reminded me that I was supposed to blend in. "That's not possible. I'm supposed to look like everyone else. I don't even wear a uniform or have a haircut, don't even shave."

"It's the eyes, baby doll. It's always in the eyes."

She shut the door, and I reached out to find the air-conditioning controls, giving up when I couldn't focus and instead calling out the temperature I wanted. The unit kicked in with a rattle. At first it sounded like the snaps of fléchettes, an autocannon spitting red tracers down range or over my head, and I crawled deep under the covers, bringing them around tightly so I could pray for morning to arrive.

The next morning I searched for my car, only to have the hotel clerk remind me that I'd smashed it into a lightpost the week before, but I couldn't recall the wreck even though they showed me pictures and handed me my copy of the police report. The clerk was more than helpful. He got me a ride into town with his brother James, who was all of a hundred years old and drove an ancient alcohol burner with a mammoth engine from the prefusion reactor days, when the aftertaste of oil and gas was still on everyone's tongues, but instead of flooring the thing and letting it loose, the old man peered over the wheel and kept it ten miles under the speed limit.

"Can't see the damn kids," he explained.

I opened the window to let the hot air in and closed my eyes, imagining I was somewhere other than North Carolina in a town with a population of two. "What kids?"

"Them *kids*. Any kids. You gotta watch 'em, sure as hell, or they'll run out in the road, dent the fender all to hell after you splatter them into a ditch."

"Yeah," I said. "There ought to be a law."

"You said it. Look," James continued, "I know it's none of my business, but my brother and I, we served too. Jenny, the nurse at the facility, she said you was a soldier. That true?"

I nodded. "Yeah."

"Well, you ain't have to worry, there aren't any cameras or microphones in our place. We run it clean. Senator Michaelson looks to frequent the place now and again, and he can't have the Federals listening while he's having his fun. The senator hisself made sure that we got a waiver from the BAI: no monitoring."

The thought hadn't occurred to me. I'd been so drunk most the time that I'd forgotten about Assurance and the semis, and the news brought both a chilled reawakening and a wash of relief. "That's good to know. Thanks for telling me."

"Hell. I remember before they wired every street with them cameras, after the first semis was used in weapons systems. Now *that* made sense. Wire a plane up with one, let *it* go and get wiped. But to watch *us*? *Americans?* Something's wrong with that, I'd say."

"I'd say so too." James was all right, I decided. "What else is there to do around here, James? Is it just the breeder?"

"Pretty much. Unless you're from here, ain't no reason to come. You know there's someone lookin' for you, right?"

"No, I didn't know that."

James made the turn into town, a tiny village off the map and miles from the interstate, with oak and maple trees that made it look like some kind of idyllic scene from a storybook. Jebson, North Carolina. He pulled over in front of the supermarket, and I got out, walking around to his window.

"An Chinese fella. Said he was lookin' for a white guy fittin' your description, name of Stan Resnick. That you?"

"That's me." I nodded and looked around. "What did you tell him?"

"Hell. I was in them Asian Wars. I ain't tellin' nothin' to no damn Chinaman." James grinned around the toothpick in his mouth and turned his blinker on, getting ready to pull out. "I have about an hour's worth of things to do at my daughter's house since that worthless son-in-law of mine died in your war. Hour enough for ya?"

I nodded again. "An hour should be fine. I'll just wait here, and if I'm not on this sidewalk," I added, watching the car pull away, "leave without me."

The Chinaman had to be Jihoon, *which meant he'd made it.* In less than a second, the adrenaline rushed in, Ji a reminder of the mission and making me wonder what in hell I was doing there, but the booze had been gone long enough that the thought diluted itself with others—how I'd explain the car to the rental agency, what to do about Phillip, or what I'd do if they found me because, technically, resigning to the Athens Police Department wasn't enough to escape the assignment.

But my mind had been made up the moment I saw those trees. I could live in Jebson. *Why not?* This was what America was supposed to be—small towns that had all but disappeared, swallowed whole by sprawling cities—and what we had inherited from over a century of warfare was a caricature of a human habitat. Jebson had my name written all over it, and it wasn't difficult to imagine finding a job at the breeding facility where I could work, drink, and get laid to my heart's content because goddamn it all if I hadn't earned it. The thought made me smile. It didn't matter what the Army threatened, because now the dream surrounded and protected me with its quiet heat and with men like James, who I'd once looked at as idiots, but who were the few geniuses left. I bet James could figure a way out *for* me. Jebson would be the new base for Stanley Resnick, and I was about to take a walk to admire my new hometown when the reason for my trip hit me again, and I decided it couldn't hurt to see this meeting the nurse had talked about.

There were two empty-looking buildings on either side of the grocer's, and I chose the one on the left, opening the front door before a faint sound of music ran through my mind and registered as to where it was that I had heard the melody before: church. The service had already started. In my haste, I'd been too rough with the door, which banged against its stopper, and about a hundred people, all of them dressed in suits or dresses, turned to stare. They looked happy enough, but under their stares, it was clear that some of them were looking me up and down with mistrust and maybe not just because I was a stranger. I glanced at my clothes. They were the same ones I had worn that day I tried to tear my car apart and were torn in spots, grease stained in others, and when I concentrated, I could still smell last night's women. My face would've been just as bad—unshaven, bruised from my scuffle with the police—and before the door had started to swing back, I turned and ran, burning with shame and the realization that it had been decades since immersing myself in civilization, that for someone like me it would be impossible. *Screw waiting for James,* I figured. It wasn't too far to the breeder, and there wasn't any way in hell I'd be waiting on that sidewalk so everyone in the service could look at me when they left. The nurse must have meant for me to pick door number two.

It wasn't long before the heat and the previous week's drinking caught up with me, forcing me to stop and rest, where my mind raced under the shade of an oak tree. *Jihoon was in America.* This, of course, meant that somebody had figured out that I'd screwed up because Ji was supposed to be in Bangkok waiting for me, and I'd gotten arrested in Athens, and my rental car had been reported totaled in the garden spot of garden spots, Jebson. So my name was all over the system. Someone had probably given Jihoon permission to go and get me, to do me a favor and let me realign myself to the mission before they sent the MPs to lock me up forever, forgotten. *Screw it all,* I decided and got up to resume my walk back to the facility; the MPs might already be there, and if I was going to be arrested, there was no reason to put it off.

The MPs weren't there, but Ji was, sitting at a table in the bar. He stared at me, expressionless, when I sat down.

"You made it out," I said.

"Yeah. No problem, they never got my DNA or picture."

"Glad to hear it."

He sipped his beer and then put down the glass. "You want to tell me why you went AWOL?"

"I didn't. We were discharged, remember?"

"Yeah. I remember. Only you've been spending the government's money for the past couple of weeks on booze and women. You're up shit creek."

"What do you care?" I asked. "After the beating I gave you, I'm guessing you're enjoying this, that you can't wait for them to arrest me."

Jihoon nodded and ran a finger across the table, like he was thinking. I thought I saw a flicker of a smile, but it wasn't clear, and still there was no reading his expression.

"I *told* them to have you arrested," he said. "But someone at Strategic Operations thinks you're the only one who can pull this off, and so they sent me here to find you and reel you back in. They told me about your wife and kid."

"Shut the fuck up." My hands clenched into fists as if they had a will of their own. Who the hell was Ji to talk about my family? As far as I was concerned he was the government, and the fact that he had been with the bureau didn't help matters, made me want to beat the crap out of him again.

Jihoon shook his head. "I went to Annapolis, Stan. Graduated not too long ago. You should be honored; we don't want to go back to those days."

"What do you know about those days? What do any of us know except what they plaster onto billboards and feed through those shitboxes they call holo stations? By now that kid has a million nanotubes coupled to his brain, linked to some semi that can monitor every electrical impulse and feed images, sounds, smells into his cortex. They have a semi-aware raping a six-year-old's mind. Every day. How is that an honor, and *what do you know?*"

Jihoon nodded, taking another sip. "I know because I had it done too." He turned his head to the side and pulled his ear down. It was there. You barely noticed it, but a thin scar, about an inch long, ran across the skin and under his stubby hair where the implant would have been located. It stunned me. I knew he was young but hadn't thought that maybe he'd been young enough to participate in the program.

"I was one of the first," he continued. "My parents volunteered me. It hurt like hell. They sedate you for the operation and once it's over give you painkillers for the first week, but it feels like something has invaded your skull and is ripping at the nerves themselves, tearing apart your brain."

"Do you think telling me that *helps*?"

Jihoon shook his head. "My point is that eventually it stops hurting and just becomes part of the routine. Normal. I was fourteen when they did it, but I hear it's even easier if they do it when you're six, like Phillip. At sixteen, they pull the plug. You want to know the truth, Stan? You want to know what it feels like once the wires are gone and you can't connect anymore?"

"Don't call me Stan."

Jihoon's eyes widened in surprise, and it was a victory to induce some kind of expression in him. "What do I call you?" he asked.

"Bug. It's my call sign, my code name."

"Fine. You want to know what it feels like, *Bug*?"

"What?"

"It feels fine. You don't even miss it, except the way you might miss having access to a really fast computer that once made it possible to do the work of a thousand people. It doesn't change the fact that you're a human being, but it does make you a hell of a lot smarter than the rest of the shits in this world."

"Great. Just what we need, more smart people who act like computers." I said it in a sarcastic tone, but Jihoon's words *had* made me feel better. He was still an asshole; but better for Phillip to be an asshole than a burnout like his stand-in father. "I'm getting too old."

"I agree. If you want to call Momson and bow out of the mission, I think it would be a great idea; maybe then they'll find a new partner for me, and I can get on with this. I mean what was your plan anyway? To go up to Annapolis and break him out, rip your kid from the computer, and kill every Marine guard in the process? You might be a good operator, an assassin, but I doubt you're *that* good. Or were you hoping to screw as many women as possible until you somehow fucked him into freedom? I mean explain that one to me 'cause I'm having a lot of trouble grasping the logic in that part of your plan."

I stared at him, remembering why it was that I'd hated the guy from the start. Jihoon was arrogant. Only that would have been fine because arrogance was a quality that a lot of operators had or they never would have chosen the life. But he was arrogant with nothing to show for it, and *that* made him part idiot.

"What would you have done?" I asked.

"Me?"

I glanced up at the waiter and motioned for a beer, then nodded. "Yeah. You. The almighty Jihoon, son of the semis but still a cherry, a rube."

He leaned across the table until his face was a few inches from mine. "I would have killed every Marine guard in the whole freaking academy until I got my son or died trying."

At first it stunned me. Then he sat back and raised his glass before cracking a grin, and it made me laugh, until we were both laughing, and the waiter left my beer on the table, looking at us as though we were already drunk.

"You know I *am* that good," I said.

"What are you talking about?"

I gulped down half the beer and wiped my mouth on my sleeve. "I could kill every one of those bastards and they'd never know I was there."

"Not anymore," he said, shaking his head. "As soon as you got arrested, you showed up on Momson's reporting, and his people interviewed your ex-partner's wife, Michelle; she told them you found out about your son, and after that they beefed up security around Annapolis. So it was a good idea to stop and get laid or you would have been wiped; probably the only smart thing I've seen you do." Jihoon looked around, as if noticing the girls for the first time; it was early, and just a few sat at the table across the room. He shook his head. "Who would take this as a job, anyway?"

"You think they have a choice?" I asked.

"Sure. Everyone has a choice, so don't give me that crap about how they were forced into it."

"No, they weren't. And neither of us knows what it was like before the semi-awares, but I do know one thing: this country is diseased. What's a woman to do if she can't find a job, or if she marries a grunt and her husband buys it in a war? On the one hand she could keep working at whatever job she has, get pregnant, and have a kid or two on her own. Or she could marry or remarry. But for some, probably a lot, those options don't exist. So here comes the government, saying, 'Go into the breeding program. Take one for Uncle Sam. We'll give you a nice salary, the best health care on the planet, and you get to live on some tropical island until the baby is born, at which point we hand you a fat check, a pat on the back, and visitation rights. Do it again if you want, we don't mind. In fact, we encourage it!' Do you think it's not an attractive option for a lot of women? How much worse is it than what we do—murdering for a paycheck? I read once that they tried a breeding program that didn't involve sex, did it through artificial insemination, but I guess asking guys to jerk off into a test tube didn't attract the kind of numbers they needed. Shit. These girls? They're doing better than we are."

Jihoon thought for a moment and then shrugged, tipping his glass toward me. "OK."

"So what's Momson say? I have to repay the money, promise to never do it again?"

"Nope. Just get on a plane to Thailand and Charlie Mike. No harm, no foul."

"You have an encrypted phone?" I asked.

Jihoon nodded and handed it to me. I had memorized the number on the chit they gave me in Florida and punched it in, waiting for the ringing to stop and the voice mail to activate. "You know who this is. I'm hopping the next plane to the assignment area and will complete my operation on one condition: you get Phillip out of your system. I don't care what strings have to be pulled; I want that kid out of the academy, and I'll come get him when it's all over. Within one week I'll expect proof that you've done this for me, and you'll have to figure out how to get it to me. If you don't, I disappear, and you know what happens when I disappear."

"Disappear?" Ji asked after I hung up. "Why is disappearing a threat?"

"It's not, but they don't know that. Force someone to imagine an outcome in a scenario that's bad to begin with, and usually they imagine the worst one. That's your first lesson in psyops, Chong: let your enemy's mind do the work. Let's go to Bangkok."

He looked pissed all of a sudden and stayed in his seat. "Chong is a Chinese name, Bug."

"So?"

"So I'm an American. My great-grandparents were Koreans."

"Sometimes, *Chong*," I said, getting up, "we don't like the call sign we get. The problem is that you don't get to pick it, your first partner does, and when Wheezer picked Bug for me, I kicked his ass. Twice. Guess what happened after that?"

"What?" he asked.

"Bug."

It had been almost a decade since I'd operated in southeast Asia, and when the plane touched down in Bangkok, I was drunk but not so drunk that the greens upon green didn't strike me as nature's tawdry display of what it could do given the right conditions. Georgia had nothing on it. We deplaned into a hot wind, the air thick with a kind of humidity that only Asia could muster, a thickness that soaked clothes to the point where I wondered if one could drown here by breathing water mixed with biogenerated kerosene vapor from the jets. It was another argument for combat suits. Their climate controls would have struggled, but just the thought of coolant flowing through an undersuit's network of hoses made me salivate for one, a Pavlovian reaction of the aging warrior, one who had forgotten the millions of discomforts the suits carried with them. Anyone who had survived for long on combat rations, with their dosage of stool softeners to keep an undersuit's waste tubes from clogging, developed ulcerative colitis to one degree or another, and mine had been worse than most, a lifelong reminder of service to country, some of which had happened here, days in the bush that I'd hoped to never recall. Even though I couldn't see it, its smell was on the breeze: the jungle. Somewhere out there were the bones of adversaries I'd knifed or garroted, waiting for me to find them again and either pay homage or join them for that last trip downward into dust.

Jihoon didn't think about Thailand the way I did. He looked impatient. *What is it that runs through a guy's head at that age,* I wondered, *and what had I thought on my first operations?* Probably the same thing that I was thinking now, that somewhere in the city or in the jungle would be Margaret, our first target, and that the city streets and jungle creeks would be like arteries, all of them circulating jazz, a kind of nervous energy that would make Jihoon antsy and eager while it made me want to hide.

He leaned over and whispered, "Did you inject another set of bots?"

"Yeah."

"Were they clicked and set for the second ID on your list?"

I nodded. "Yeah. They were. It's all cool, Chong."

"You've got an idea how to find her?" he asked.

"First, we'll hit the hotel. Then we'll start talking to people at the bar. Then we'll do it every day until somebody tells us something useful. Sometimes we'll take walks to try and find our way around, get used to the place, hold hands. Maybe we'll hit a strip club or two, and who knows? If you're nice to me, maybe you'll get laid."

The line for customs lurched forward, one person at a time, and I was next. Jihoon looked pissed, and I understood why because someone with his background would want a set schedule, performance metrics, and guarantees, but how was I supposed to know what to do on an op like this? This was a shitty, high-risk, high-reward op, and I was goddamned if I wasn't going slowly. Jihoon had never faced a sato before, and these chicks in Thailand wouldn't be rotting; they'd be full-blown machines.

I handed the Thai customs guy my passport chit, stuck my finger in the DNA sampler, stared into the retina scanner, and then told him there was nothing to declare.

"Next," he said, and Jihoon made it through just as easily. An hour later we had cleared baggage inspection, moved through the exits to the taxi stand, and stepped into a nightmare.

"Jesus," said Ji.

"They told me that things were falling apart in Bangkok during the mission briefing, but I didn't expect this; it wasn't like this the last time I was here."

"When was that?"

I shrugged. "Seven years ago. Adviser to the Thai military during their bush wars with the Burmese. They've been fighting over metals and resources for a lot longer than we have. But this is new."

The Thai military had positioned itself along the road servicing the airport terminals, with tanks canted half on, half off the sidewalk, and soldiers roamed through a solid mass of people who shouted as they pushed one another, everyone trying to get into the main terminal. To get out. Whatever was happening in Thailand, it had ramped up since the day they'd offered me the mission, and when the closest people saw that I was white, they began shouting and trying to climb the barrier that separated incoming and outgoing passengers. A nearby soldier raised his Maxwell and fired a tracer burst into the air until they stopped.

"What were they saying?" I asked.

"They wanted your passport, whatever good that would do. Some were offering you money for your plane ticket. Hold on." Jihoon approached the soldier who had fired and spoke to him in Thai, but the man didn't respond. He stared while chewing on something until Jihoon came back. "That didn't work."

"Some of them were shouting at you too. What were they saying?"

" 'Parasite,' " said Jihoon. " 'Japanese' devil and a couple of other things, but I wasn't about to correct them that I'm not Japanese. Let's just get out of here."

The taxi stand was about fifty meters away, and we dragged our bags behind us, walking as quickly as we could and trying to stay close to the tanks. The first taxi driver opened his door and smiled. Jihoon gave him the name of our hotel, and we got in, grateful once he pulled onto the road and began motoring away from the near riot we had just experienced.

"Hey," I said to the driver, "you speak English?"

The guy nodded and looked at me in the mirror. "I speak little."

"Why are all those people at the airport? What's happening?"

The man shook his head and lit a cigarette. "Very bad. Bad news. Last month Chinese troops enter Burma, and now they move south toward Thailand border. Everyone want out now."

Jihoon and I looked at each other, and I shrugged. "What's the Thai military doing about it?" I asked.

But the driver shook his head and repeated himself, even after Jihoon tried speaking Thai. "Very bad. Very bad news."

The Mandarin Oriental was almost empty when we got there. Its staff welcomed us, but where I'd expected to see throngs of Asian and American businessmen and- women, the lobby was devoid of anything except a group of hotel workers who had gathered near the front to watch the street, where hundreds of people wearing bandannas ran wild in the traffic, many of them carrying signs. Thai troops had to open a barrier to let our taxi through. Just after we got out and ducked into the building's entrance, someone threw a Molotov, which detonated nearby and was followed by the sounds of cracking fléchettes, so Jihoon and I dove to the floor, covering our heads to protect them from the shattering plate glass at the same time somebody screamed.

One of the hotel workers was hit; a girl writhed on the floor, one hand clutched to her shoulder where a grouping of fléchettes had shredded her uniform to the point where I couldn't tell cloth from torn flesh. She stared at me and screamed again.

"Stay with me," I told Ji and crawled over.

I ripped my dress shirt off, then my undershirt, and used one as a compress, the other wrapped around her shoulders to keep it in place, and then grabbed her good hand, placing it against the bandage; it had already begun to turn red.

"Tell her to keep the pressure on. And that she'll be fine once we get her to a hospital."

Jihoon did it, and the girl nodded. "What now?" he asked.

I waved at the concierge, who had taken cover behind his desk. "Can someone get an ambulance for her? She's bleeding and needs a doctor."

"No ambulances right now," he said. "The entire city has been shut down, and it would take hours for anything to get through."

"How far is the closest doctor?" I asked.

"A kilometer. The clinic on Surasak."

Jihoon and I looked at each other, helpless. I was about to throw her on my shoulder and risk taking her there myself when someone tugged at my leg.

"I take her. I know the clinic."

It was the taxi driver. Somehow he had ditched his cab and followed us to cover, and I lifted the girl to chase him in a sprint, back into the street where the carbine fire continued and bright tracers bounced from the buildings. It looked like the Thai Army was firing randomly. Most people had found cover and were staying in place, having abandoned their cars or pulled them onto side streets to go around. The cabbie dove across the passenger seat and started the car, waiting for me to put the girl in the back.

"You know the way?" I asked, wanting to make sure.

"I know the way, I know the way."

But it wasn't like I could do anything if he *didn't,* and when a burst pinged the taxi's roof, it occurred to me that the guy might gun the engine with me halfway in, and I backed out, slamming the door shut at the same time he pulled away. I waited in the gutter for a break in firing and then sprinted back to cover at the hotel.

Jihoon had already made his way behind the check-in counter, where the desk clerks took our passports and put the rooms on one of Ji's credit chits.

"This is a hell of an introduction to Bangkok," he said.

Already, my idea of going slow started looking bad. I grabbed one of the clerks and pointed at Jihoon. "He's an American soldier. Are there other American soldiers anywhere? Advisers to the Thai military?"

Ji glared at me for giving him up, but the clerk nodded, her attention shifting between us and the windows as if she expected someone to attack at any minute. "Yes. There are American military in Bangkok."

"Where?" I asked. "The Royal Army Headquarters?"

She nodded. "Yes. Your passport chits will open your rooms. Fourth floor, rooms four-seven-five and seven-seven. Do you need help with your bags?"

I shook my head, and we sprinted for the elevators, pressing our backs behind a column until the doors opened. Once we entered, Jihoon sighed with relief.

"Why the hell did you blow *my* cover?" he asked.

"I had to do something. We won't survive long here if we don't make some friends, and she wouldn't have believed *I* was military. You, though? You *scream* Army."

Jihoon noticed something, and I had forgotten that my shirts were on the girl in the taxi. There was no hiding it now. A network of scars covered my shoulders as if both had melted and been reshaped in the form of wax, and I was glad that my back was to the wall so he couldn't see the damage there, which was worse.

"Torture," I explained. "Captured by the Burmese when I was about your age. The Burmese are a special bunch. They like to take apart thermal gel grenades and then dab the stuff all over your skin, one droplet at a time."

"To get you to talk," Jihoon said.

"To get you to scream. If talking would have kept them from doing *this,* I would have told them anything they wanted to know."

We slept in the same room, and Jihoon snored on the rack while I stood watch and smoked. You weren't supposed to, but I doubted with all the riots and an empty hotel that the staff was going to come after me for having a cigarette. My fléchette pistol lay on my lap. It wouldn't do much good against better-armed assailants, but it comforted me anyway, and despite the noise of glass shattering every once in a while, things had quieted some since our arrival.

Already, fate had crapped on our mission. The realization made me feel everything, so the scars on my back gave more trouble than normal, and my knees ached from the almost two decades of jumping out of planes, and running up and down however many mountains had added up over the course of countless ops. It was good to have help. I'd see if Jihoon could prove himself over the next couple of days, but the real test would be when we saw our first action, and with the way I felt, all that mattered was that he proved as good at killing as he was at thinking. Killing wouldn't be a problem for him; you could smell it. I guessed that years connected to a semi, murdering simulated but realistic opponents would have desensitized him by now, made him as clinical about taking life as he was about the calculus of politics. It would all start in the morning. The next day, when the sun rose, we'd have to risk the streets and make our way to the Royal Thai Army Headquarters and then talk our way inside to meet with

American advisers, and the thought made my muscles ache. When I finished my cigarette, I risked peeking out from behind the thick drapes.

A tank sat outside the hotel. The sight didn't make me feel any better, though, because my mind clicked over the reasons for having one at that particular location and told me that it was the wrong place—no intersection, no important strategic or tactical assets, no important political infrastructure I knew of, and the banks were farther down the street. One of its crew lounged outside the hatch, leaning against the vehicle's massive turret, and I saw the red glow of a cigarette until he flicked it away, where it spun in the dim light to hit the ground in a shower of sparks. He looked up. Although I couldn't see well in the dim streetlights, it seemed like he stared at our window and saw through the crack to fix my position, then climbed the turret, lowering himself inside to seal the hatch.

I'm inventing trouble, I decided and shut the drapes. He hadn't been wearing a helmet or vision hood, and in the darkness of my room, there would have been no way for the guy to see me, but still it was odd that they were there in the first place.

With nothing to do and not wanting to turn on the holo for fear that its glow would let everyone outside know which window to take potshots at, my thoughts turned to Phillip. For now I had no way of knowing if the higher-ups had gotten my voice mail or, if they had, that they had taken it seriously and would release him from Annapolis. Even if they did, what then? He'd still be in their care, and there was no guarantee that they'd let him go once we'd finished the op because now, technically, the state owned him. All it took was one parent. By signing him off, Bea had given up all our rights and then booked it herself to some dump like the one in Jebson, hoping for a bigger paycheck and nine months of the high life until she had to hand over her next kid. Bea was younger than me and could handle the breeders for a few years, but the anger toward her grew until I found myself hoping that one day I'd run across her—drugged up on happy pills. Oblivious. *She'd given over Phillip, and why do I even care?* was all I thought about until, without warning, a loud *wumph* blasted through the street, shattering our window and triggering alarms throughout the hotel.

I hit the deck. Jihoon jumped from the rack and crawled over to me, his voice hoarse.

"What the fuck was that?"

A second later we heard a distant explosion, and I shook my head. "A tank. It just fired a plasma round."

"Here?" he asked. "In the city? At their own people?"

I nodded, lighting another cigarette. "Get some sleep, Chong. Because tomorrow is going to be a wonderful day. Welcome to southeast Asia."

FOUR

Occupation

We'd have to cover more than five klicks to Army head-quarters, all of it urban through neighborhoods I barely remembered and Jihoon had never seen. The hotel staff tried to show us on the map. After a mixture of conversations in Thai, English, and hand gestures, I gave up and grabbed Ji's encrypted phone, punching in the numbers so hard that it almost flew from my hands. It took a few seconds to connect to the voice mail.

"Your coms plan sucks. We're at the Mandarin Oriental in Bangkok and need transport to the Royal Army HQ, in addition to combat suits. Ship them to our advisers here. Make sure to send my custom one and Jihoon's size is…hold on…" I paused to hand the phone to Jihoon, who read out his specifications and then handed the phone back. "We need them yesterday. Also, we need priority use of any of our American assets here, so make sure you let our guys know that whatever we need, we get."

I finished by giving the code for my new identity so they wouldn't send it to Stan Resnick, hung up, and Jihoon raised his eyebrows. "What's the plan?"

"We wait. If nobody comes for us by noon, we might risk it."

The concierge shook his head. "Do not try on your own. If the protesters catch foreigners, anything could happen."

"What are they protesting?" Ji asked.

"Some protest against the King and Prime Minister Anupong, who they call dictators, and some of the immigrants would welcome the Chinese as liberators; they want the government to surrender to Burmese forces before an invasion so the city isn't destroyed by war. Last night, the tank you heard fired on a group of them and killed many innocent people. You stay in the hotel. The Army will protect the hotel because we pay them to, but out there? Anything."

I glanced at my watch. It was 8:00 a.m., and already the heat had become unbearable, but we'd asked and were told that the hotel now ran on generators and couldn't spare power for climate control—not when most windows facing the street had been blown out. I crept up to the lobby front, and my shoes crunched on broken glass, a sound almost lost amid the shouts and distant rattle of fléchettes, but it reminded me of bones, and I imagined myself crawling over the skeletons of satos, the hundreds that begged for a longer life but for whom I'd shown nothing except a smile. A smile that was genuine. I was beginning to hate Margaret now; she had brought me here, and the insanity of it all made me want to find her more quickly, and it didn't matter if she was different from the others because her punishment for taking me to my old killing grounds would be the same as it was for her sisters. The heat made it even more unbearable; without normal skin my back wouldn't sweat, and without sweat I couldn't cool. They'd offered me new skin a long time ago and I'd rejected it, but now had second thoughts and couldn't remember why I'd turned it down. But Margaret would pay for that one too.

From the front windows it became clear that since last night, the Thai Army position outside the hotel had been strengthened, and regular troops in combat suits faced south from behind a wall of sandbags and cars, the tank looming over them. Its turret scanned the street. Every once in a while one of the troops would fire his Maxwell carbine at something, sometimes joined by the rest of them, but I never saw any shots returned. I was about to head back to the concierge when it happened again; the tank fired its plasma cannon, and the drapes billowed around me so that at first I lost track of where I was, my hearing shot almost completely.

I'd been close to tanks before when they fired, but there had always been a helmet, its audio pickups cutting off when outside noise reached a certain level, and without protection the experience frightened me. The suits confined, but they also insulated and cradled their occupants in a measure of safety. *Who could know war from inside a cocoon?* I thought and then realized that someone was dragging me by the foot away from the window, and I reached for the tattered drapes, wanting to stay, needing to experience war unfiltered.

Jihoon slapped me lightly, and my hearing returned. "You." I pointed at the concierge. "You bribed the military to protect this place?"

"Not me. Owner. He take care of it."

"How much you think it would take to get the soldiers

outside to take us to Army HQ?" The man cocked his head and looked at me like I was crazy.

"Money," I said, holding up my credit chit. "How many bhat to have them take us to their headquarters?"

"I don't know. Ten thousand, maybe fifteen."

"Would you negotiate it for us?" I asked.

The man's eyes went wide, and he shook his head. "No."

"I'll give you five thousand. Five thousand bhat if you do this for us."

Jihoon grabbed my arm. "Bug, I don't think—"

"That will buy a lot of food," I said, cutting Ji off. "A lot."

The concierge thought about it for a few seconds and then nodded. "OK. Deal." He moved toward the front lobby, grabbing a white napkin from under his desk, and then thrust it through the empty door frames, which the day before had been a glittering crystal. He stepped out. We lost sight until Jihoon and I slithered back to the window and raised ourselves slowly, peering over the sill and into the street.

The concierge was already talking to someone, a sergeant who had removed his helmet as the two sat with their backs against sandbags. The sergeant pulled something from his belt. At first I couldn't tell what it was but then saw our guy stick his finger in for a DNA test, and the next thing we knew, the sergeant had punched him across the jaw, his gauntlet making a cracking noise and sending a spray of blood into the air. The sergeant scrambled for his carbine then and killed the concierge with a quick burst before shouting to his men.

"What's he saying?" I asked.

"Shit. They're coming in. To search the hotel."

"Time to go."

We scrambled back toward the elevators behind us and were about to stand and run for it when the Thais crashed through the front doors, screaming over their helmet speakers. Jihoon and I stopped.

"Raise your hands," said Ji.

I did it and turned to face them. The rest of the hotel staff who had been in the lobby stood still, like us, all of them looking terrified in the face of what had just turned into deadly uncertainty. We waited. Finally the sergeant came in and surveyed the interior until his vision slot pointed in our direction.

"Can you hear if he's saying anything?" I asked.

"Yeah, but I can't make it out. It's too muffled by the helmet and isn't coming over his speakers."

But we didn't have to wait long. The man walked toward us, his soldiers keeping us covered, and he stuck out the analyzer toward Jihoon, who inserted his finger. Then it was my turn. When he was finished, he took off his helmet, and I thought we'd had it, that the next thing we'd feel would be the hard impact of fléchettes and then nothing, but instead, the sergeant grinned and began jabbering in Thai.

"What's he saying?"

Ji started to smile. "He's saying something like 'these are the ones we were supposed to look out for, the two Americans,' and he's telling the others to complete a sweep of the hotel."

The sergeant, still talking a mile a minute, gestured toward the street with his carbine.

"He's saying we should follow him and that he'll get us to Army headquarters within half an hour."

"Jesus." I shook my head. "That phone message moved faster than I thought."

Once we got outside, Jihoon interrupted the man and pointed at the dead concierge; after a back and forth, Ji turned.

"I asked him why he wasted our guy, and the sergeant claims he was antigovernment. One of a hundred half-Burmese Thais who've caused trouble for them over the last year, and they'd been looking for him for a long time. Apparently they keep a list of potential infiltrators."

"Oh?" I spat on the corpse and grinned at the sergeant while we climbed onto the back of his tank. "That's just fine by me."

Tanks and APCs filled the Royal Army's parade ground, and men assembled in any empty space, getting ready for what I assumed would be a push through the city to wipe out remaining signs of protest. How many towns and villages in the bush were being leveled? And how had I returned to this place? Now that we were in the open again, my nose picked out the scent of clay over alcohol fuel, and my skin tingled with a suspicion that the jungle was arranging things behind the scenes, the ancestors of Thailand and Burma moving pieces on a chessboard because they'd allied to lure me back under the canopy and into the banyan roots where the air was still and damp. I hated the jungle. In comparison, Kazakhstan and all the 'Stans had been a pleasure, where any number of systems could be brought to bear and line of sight stretched to the horizon in places, but here the jungle swallowed you whole and cut you off; there would be no autodrones if you wrapped yourself with the bad bush, no microbots, and movement and heat from any number of animals would ping suit sensors to the point where it was best to ignore them. The jungle promised two things to those who stayed too long: solitude and decay.

We jumped off the tank, and the sergeant waved for us to follow him through massing troops, where some soldiers stopped and stared at the unusual parade of two Westerners in casual clothes. Some chuckled. They probably assumed that we'd been brought there for questioning, but Jihoon must have caught wind of whatever they were saying because he dropped back and whispered.

"They're making jokes," he said.

"About what?"

"Something about how you look like a crazy man."

I looked straight ahead and kept pace with the sergeant until one of the soldiers nearby smiled at me, nodding as he laughed.

"Shove your head up your slimy Thai ass," I said, hoping he'd understand. But the guy just kept nodding and gave me the thumbs-up.

"Number one!"

"Yeah," I said. "Number one, asshole. Burma number ten."

We climbed the steps to the main entrance, two at a time, and the heat made my shirt a sopping mass so that when we entered the HQ's air-conditioned space it was as though we'd stepped into a refrigerator, and I breathed the cool air deeply. Dry air. The contrast almost made me giggle since we'd spent most of the previous night and this morning in Bangkok's humidity, which never moved and felt like a warm bath. Jihoon looked at me and grinned, and I almost grinned back until the sergeant showed us where we were heading.

He stopped at a staircase and spoke with two guards, who then performed another ID scan on both of us.

"They show you the way to your advisers," the sergeant said and pointed down the narrow stairs.

"Down there?" I asked, and he nodded.

"You're kidding, right?"

"What's wrong with downstairs?" Jihoon asked.

I shrugged. "Nothing. It's just great."

"You no worry," said the sergeant. "We have no floods down there in a long time."

The thought made my skin crawl. "Floods?"

He thought for a second and then spat something in Thai so Ji could translate.

"He said that sometimes their pumps go out, and because the water table is so high, the tunnels flood, but that there's been no problem like that for a while."

"What happens if you're down there when the pumps go out?" I asked.

Jihoon spoke with the sergeant again, who shook his head. "He said that it's better if that doesn't happen."

The sergeant waved good-bye then and walked off. One of the guards ushered us toward the steps, pointing that we should go down as he spoke.

"What'd he say?" I asked.

Jihoon shrugged. "We take the stairs down for a bit, then transfer to an elevator. There's a subway that will connect us to the Supreme Armed Forces HQ a few klicks north."

"After you."

Ji started downward and I followed, my stomach feeling sick. The staircase was narrow, and we twisted around at multiple landings until the effect—combined with the

sensation that the walls were pressing in on my shoulders—
made me dizzy with the effort of forcing myself onward.
Finally the stairs opened into a medium-sized room, where
pipes and electrical conduits covered every side except for
one, in which an open elevator door waited. We stepped in.
A moment later the floor dropped from under us and the
box sped downward, shaking as it plummeted so that I
grabbed a railing to hold on.

"Are you OK, Bug?" asked Ji.

"Screw you."

"There's medication if closed spaces get to you, you
know. I don't know how you manage a combat suit if an
elevator gets to you this badly."

"I said, *shut up.*"

The elevator opened onto a small platform where a
series of three subway cars sat, their sliding doors ajar,
and we stepped into the first one, waiting for the thing to
move. It took about a minute. The cars sped down a cylindrical tube, which was lit by the single light at the car's
front, and the sight reminded me of the short time I'd
spent at the front in Kazakhstan after the Russian retreat,
to search alone through empty positions in tunnels filled
with abandoned bodies. Man wasn't designed for those
places. But we *had* been designed for war, becoming so
proficient that our weapons drove us into living graves,
places that even moles and snakes avoided, because to
stay in the sun meant certain death. But the memory faded
when the subway cars stopped. A young Thai soldier in
cotton fatigues greeted us and escorted us up the elevator
and stairs into a command bunker filled with the chatter
of tactics and strategy. *Somewhere,* I thought, *in this bunker is one of death's friends, sending the youth of Thai-*

land into a nightmare. Or maybe death had more than one friend. We saw a group of Western men in Thai combat suits; their helmets were off, and ironically, the lack of any emblems or rank insignia made it clear that they were experts in the art of modern killing, American advisers instructing their Thai counterparts on how to fight like the mole men we had all become. Maybe, I thought, the jungle had lost its grip on man, and maybe now we fought below the tree roots, under the countless bodies we had killed in the century before, and I didn't know which method was more horrifying.

Our escort whispered to one of the advisers, and he approached us, shaking our hands to introduce himself as Colonel O'Steen. "We only got word this morning that you two were in country. Want to tell me what's going on?"

"Sir," said Ji, "we're sorry, but it's classified."

"We're here for a girl," I said, and Jihoon frowned, probably pissed that I was about to give up something classified again. "A sato. It's a cleanup mission, sir, and I apologize. It *is* classified, but you should know what's going on in your area of responsibility. And we'll need your help. We're to find this girl, interrogate, and then discharge her."

The colonel shook his head and grinned. "Christ. It's not enough that I have to somehow make sure our interests in Thailand don't fall apart, but now I have to worry about two assassins running around Bangkok? SOCOM wants me to give you whatever resources I have available so you can go after one *sato*?"

"Sir, I'm sorry."

The colonel crossed his arms, their ceramic plates squeaking as they rubbed against each other. "Who is it?"

"She's named Margaret. We can give you the serial number if it would help."

O'Steen looked like I had just slapped him. His face went red, and he glanced around to see if anyone else had overheard. "Jesus. You two do understand that genetics have been given asylum here, right?"

I nodded. "I've never understood why, sir, but yes."

"Then I'll give you an education. The first satos wound up here halfway through the Subterrene War, and Thai officials took a couple of weeks studying them, watching as the chicks putrified. Thailand's laws about genetic manipulation are some of the strictest in the world; natural births, and only those over a certain age are allowed genetic therapy; deformed and disabled kids are allowed to live. So once they saw what we had done in creating satos and the effects of our two-year safeguards, the prime minister took pity on the girls and—with the approval of the King himself—put his best scientists on the job of saving any who floated into their ports. And they came. *Jesus,* did they come. The Thais lost the first hundred or so on operating tables, but they figured it out and were able to deactivate the immuno safeguards— repair much of the damage that had been done to the girls' organs. They even restored their reproduction to normal."

"How?" I asked, keeping my fingers crossed that this guy already knew; maybe we wouldn't have to interrogate Margaret at all.

"Hell if I know. They have some genius Japanese geneticists, and whatever they did, it's now a state secret. But the girls in return pledged their loyalty to the King. Do you know what that means, Lieutenant?" I shook my head, and he continued, "It means that the girls began training his forces. They became trusted advisers—so trusted that a group of satos is now the King's personal bodyguard. Hell. Do you think the Thais even need *me* when they have their own contingent of genetic troops ready to die for the guy if he orders it? These girls know more about tactics and strategy than I could hope to learn if I studied my entire life. They don't need me here."

"Then why *are* you here?" Ji asked.

"Window dressing. The Thais know they can't get rid of the US completely because they need our equipment, and the Royal Army despises the girls since they compete with the generals' access to the King, so the Thai generals want us to stick around too. But any time we try to discuss satos, they make it crystal clear: we wanna run an occasional cleanup operation, fine, but only once in a while. And nobody goes after the head sato."

I had already started getting a bad feeling but had to ask. "Who is that?"

The colonel laughed. "Margaret. Only she's not just a leader, she's some kind of religious icon, a prophet and disciple of the holiest girl they know, some chick called Catherine, who died so Margaret could survive. I don't know all the details. All I know is that you can't touch her and that even some of the local civilian population and all the Japanese immigrants follow the chick; they converted from Buddhism or Shinto to some kind of freakish version of Christianity, and you can't miss them if you see them. They call themselves the *Gra Jaai*. The 'dispersed.'"

A great mission, I thought, *one that keeps getting better the more we learn.* "Can we at least talk to her if we promise not to wipe her?"

The colonel thought for a moment and then turned.

"Wait here." He went to a Thai general and saluted before the two began talking, at which point the general looked shocked and glanced at us; his face twisted in an expression of anger, glaring at me as though we'd been enemies from birth. The conversation got intense then, with O'Steen bowing every ten seconds, until he returned and sighed.

"It's your ass if you do this, you know."

Ji nodded. "He'll let us see Margaret?"

O'Steen nodded. "Oh yeah. But he's not doing you a favor. She's on the front lines at Nu Poe with a mixed force of satos, *Gra Jaai*, and Karen rebels—Burmese mountain people who hate their government even more than we do. Even more than the Thais. And they like the Chinese even less."

"Perfect," I said. "Where's Nu Poe and when do we go?"

"To the northwest of Bangkok on Thailand's western border with Burma. You leave tomorrow. I got word from the States that your gear arrives tonight, and we'll equip you with anything else you need from local supplies so you blend in. They won't spare any air assets to get you there, though. You'll have to go in by road, and it's a long, weird trip. Once you arrive, ask for Major Remorro, the senior SOG adviser for line operations, and between now and then I'll get word to him that you're expected. In the meantime, I'd go down to Khlong Toei if I were you; it's one of the slums."

"Why?"

The colonel waved to someone, who brought us boots and light cotton Thai uniforms with no insignia. When we had finished changing, he handed us pistol belts, and I checked to make sure mine was loaded.

"Because you need a quick education. Khlong Toei is

the black market for people who want genetic alterations or therapy. There's no better place to get a close-up view of what those girls mean to the Thais."

"What about the riots and protests?" Jihoon asked. "We saw APCs and tanks getting ready to move out at the Army HQ."

"Hell," the colonel said. "The protesters are already dead or on the run, and those forces weren't mustering to operate in Bangkok. They're headed to man the second defensive line, behind the sato frontline defenses to the northwest. In case you hadn't heard, the Chinese are coming."

I nodded and grabbed O'Steen's arm before he could leave. "Colonel, have you ever heard of a Samuel Ling, Dr. Chen, or a Project Sunshine?"

He shook his head. "Nope. You want me to ask around?"

"No," I said, letting go of him. "Probably a good idea if you didn't. And thanks for the help, sir."

"Don't thank me, Lieutenant. You're on your own starting tomorrow, and by the time you reach the front, you'll wish we'd never met."

With that, the colonel left. The Thai who had brought us the clothes escorted us from the bunker and up another long flight of twisting stairs until we emerged in the bright sunshine of Bangkok, our light uniforms becoming heavy with sweat. We started down a wide ramp and headed south, back toward the hotel.

"What do you think?" Jihoon asked.

"About what?"

"About the trip to the lines," he said. "Do you think it's a good idea?"

I shook my head. "It doesn't matter, Chong. Who cares

what I think? It's the only mission we have, and Margaret is in the bad bush, so that's where we go. You ever seen combat before?"

"Simulations, but they were realistic enough."

"Yeah," I said, laughing. *"Realistic."*

We made it through several roving checkpoints on our way south through the city. Jihoon had wanted to walk—to see if the protests were under control, but I didn't know if they were "under control" as much as the military had started patrolling instead of holding fixed positions—and every once in a while we encountered a building like the one blown near the Mandarin, its roof collapsed and walls now piles of brick or concrete rubble. The aftermath of plasma strikes were everywhere, and charred bodies lay on the sidewalks since nobody had been there yet to clean up. Maybe nobody cared.

From doorways and alleys, children stared at us with huge eyes, and I could tell it was having an effect on Ji. But what effect and what did he even *know* about kids? I had Phillip, and even having experienced what it meant to be a parent, I'd seen enough eyes like those in Bangkok that it had given me an immunity to the virus they tried to throw around, a sickness that, in the weak-minded, could rot from the inside. You had to be careful about it. If you stopped to help, the overwhelming reality of it all—that there was no amount of help that could save them—would wrap you in an invisible garrote that got tighter the more you tried to give. Only the weak had an instinct to help. So I watched Jihoon, waiting for an indication that he was going under, maybe thinking of throwing them some money or food, and when I saw it on his face, another expression, I studied it, doing my best to figure out what he was thinking. But *this* one I couldn't identify.

"Why are you here, Jihoon?"

"What do you mean?" he asked.

"I mean I don't buy the bullshit about wanting to get in the field. They didn't teach you to be a combat dog; they put you in the BAI, for shit's sake."

He shook his head, and we jumped over a stream of raw sewage. It was past noon. We'd have to shake it to get to our destination and return before sunset, after which martial law would be enforced, and in the darkness—even with the uniform—I didn't trust the Thai Army's identification skills.

"Yeah, they trained me for the BAI. But I also scored well in combat-suitability screens, so they gave me a double major in criminal investigation and military tactics."

"What do you think of the job so far?"

Jihoon glanced at me. He stared for a few seconds and then looked away. "I don't know how you do it."

"Do what?" But I knew what he meant. We were going into the bush the next day and I needed to be sure that this guy wouldn't fold, that he wouldn't turn into a ball of quivering waste under fire. I knew what he was saying, but he needed to explain it out loud, so I could peek behind the words.

"Kill for a living. And how you live this life for twenty years without letting it get to you. When I worked for the Feds, we used to go to the rattiest places on earth and see people that you wouldn't believe. It makes you wonder, you know?"

I shrugged. "You tell me."

"Wonder if we just shouldn't wipe a whole segment of

the population—the ones who don't have any souls. The perpetually useless and wasted."

"Sure. I get it. But I also see the way you look at these Thai kids. You wanna wipe them too?"

Jihoon laughed and held out his hand. "You got a cigarette?"

"I didn't know you smoked." I handed him one, and we stopped so I could light it. He took a deep breath and coughed before trying again.

"I don't. But I figured if you did there must be a reason." Ji took another puff and did better this time, blowing a cloud while talking through the coughs. "I don't want to wipe these kids. I was just thinking that if they're tough enough to survive this, we oughta waste all of ours and replace the academy kids with ones from Bangkok."

And when I heard that, I figured Ji would be fine. "Yeah. Maybe."

We walked until two in the afternoon, waving at passing Thai patrols and occasionally having to submit to identity scans, but for the most part the trip was uneventful. Forget what we'd learn in Khlong Toei. I'd just learned the most important thing so far, that Jihoon was one clinical bastard and that the look of discomfort—if it had been that—shown on his face wasn't related to pity for the Thais, but was one of strategic recognition. Maybe he was thinking the same thing I was—that if any of these countries had developed the same technologies and capabilities as us, they'd have a much better gene pool from which to populate their forces. That we'd be screwed.

We had just reached the outskirts of Khlong Toei when Ji stopped me. "What about you, Bug? Why are you this way?"

"What way?"

Jihoon shrugged. "I've heard the stories about you, read the files. You're one of the best."

"Maybe."

"Not *maybe*, it's a fact. But then you go off whoring and drinking, almost jeopardizing the entire operation and acting like you're insane. Why?"

I had to think about that one. The answer was clear; it just wasn't easy to phrase in a way that he'd understand because he wasn't like Wheezer, didn't have the frame of reference yet.

"It's like this," I said. "I don't fit in the peace world. I don't think you can have someone that operates like me in the field and then instantly turn him off so he can function in civilized society—at least not anymore. At home I look crazy, maybe lose it every once in a while and go off. Out here, though?" I lit another cigarette and grinned around it. "Out here I'm at home, even though I hate the place."

We pushed on across a wide street littered with burned-out cars, and four Thai soldiers stared from their sand-bagged position, their helmets off and lined up in front of them. Jihoon waved to them and laughed.

"So you're crazy, but on an operation, crazy is *normal*?"

"That's it," I said. "You'll get it too, someday."

We saw a gate in the middle of a high concrete wall, with an APC parked outside it and a worn plastic sign that said Khlong Toei in Thai and English. Jihoon threw his cigarette down and ground it into the asphalt.

"I hope not," he said. "I hope I'm never as psycho as you are."

I almost voiced out loud what the conversation made

me realize but figured it was better left unsaid: I had lied; the fact was that Bea had broken me seven years ago, and now I cared about a kid that wasn't even mine and couldn't explain it. The way Jihoon described me was no longer accurate—once but not anymore, not now that caring had wormed its way inside and started laying eggs, because caring was a killer, worse even than fear, and the mantra of "He's not really my kid" wasn't a fix anymore. So I kept quiet, and we ducked through the entrance, letting Khlong Toei swallow us.

Twin smells assaulted my nostrils. An odor of cooking, spices, and fish came first as vendors prepared for the dinner rush, and as soon as we entered, people pressed from every side in a hurry to get from one place to another. That was the second smell's source: unwashed humanity. But it wasn't like in the States when someone failed to put on deodorant, and I'd forgotten that during operations the last time, I'd eaten local food so I would blend in. The locals smelled woody, like a dresser drawer that hadn't been opened in a century. What surprised me the most, though, were the signs written in Japanese; the ghetto wasn't Thai at all. You saw the difference in their faces and the way these people carried themselves, refugees of a war in which Japan and her allies had opted to take out North Korea before it had a chance to attack, while China loomed in the background and drooled for Japanese resources. The people of Khlong Toei were survivors—maybe the last Japanese on earth beside the ones in Australia, the only ones who had bailed before the Chinese nukes fell. A knot of children grew around us, and Ji let me know that they were asking for money in a mixture of Thai and English, so I told him to make it clear that if they didn't leave we'd kill them, and they scattered, disappearing into the crowds.

Nobody had protested here. The buildings showed no sign of damage from tanks or other weaponry, and they had been built out of cargo containers and any other material at hand, barely ten feet from one another so we had to squeeze through the narrow alleyways, fighting to breathe as we made our way deeper into the ghetto. The farther we got from the entrance, the darker it became. We couldn't see the river, but above the walls and buildings the towering outlines of cargo cranes loomed, getting closer, and the smell of dirty water grew. Somehow, we wound our way through the maze and stepped into a courtyard of sorts, empty of people except for an ancient man sitting on a bench. His hair was white, and he grinned at us, nodding as he said something.

"What language is that?" I asked.

"Japanese. He's saying that we've come to the right place."

I shrugged, feeling uneasy. Why did the crowd avoid the courtyard? We hadn't seen any signs labeling it— nothing that would suggest the area was special.

"What place?" I asked.

Jihoon was about to speak when they came from behind. Five men in their twenties pushed past and stood by the old man, bowing before turning to face us, and what struck me first was the fact that they had all been maimed in some way, including scars resembling mine, skin melted by thermal gel. They wore primitive jungle camouflage. Stuff from the history books. But it intimidated anyway, maybe because the men had a look on their faces like they didn't need combat suits—empty stares that I recognized for having seen it in the mirror every day. *Killers.*

Jihoon asked and waited for the man's answer. "He says there's no name for this part of the neighborhood but asked if we're American. When Americans come to Khlong Toei, it's for one reason: to look for Sister Margaret. This is her city, so we're in the right place."

"Ask him if anyone else has been here. Looking for her."

The man grinned and told us that on two previous occasions, men like Jihoon and me had been there to try and find her, to kill her, but that in every case Margaret had taken them first. He was just sorry that Margaret was gone or he would have enjoyed the show. She would be gone for a long time, he assured us.

"Ask him if there are others here," I said. "Like Margaret. Other genetics."

"There are," a girl said. We hadn't noticed her approach either, and before I could go for my pistol, she had leveled a Maxwell carbine at my chest, so fast that her movement had been invisible.

I stared in disbelief. This one also had blonde hair, but her face was empty of tattoos, and since Margaret was in the field, it couldn't have been her anyway, and she didn't confuse me the same way Margaret had; this one was pure machine. The girl's combat armor was muddy, cracked in places, and the helmet hanging from her webbing looked so scarred and pitted that I wondered why she hadn't replaced it.

"We're not here to kill anyone," I said. But my hand almost had a mind of its own, wanting to draw and cut her down. It angered me to see one close-up and with no sign of spoil.

"Not anymore anyway," she said, and the others laughed at her joke.

"You all speak English?" I asked.

The girl nodded. "All of Margaret's human followers volunteer for the tanks. To submit to a procedure meant for the young is their initiation, a test of courage. Some die, others go crazy, but the ones that make it and live are admitted to the *Gra Jaai*."

"What the hell did she just say?" I asked.

Jihoon stared at her as he spoke. "The tanks are what we call the simulators. You're suspended in a fluid-filled tank or vat so you can move while practicing the scenarios they pipe into your head. They also teach languages that way because it's infinitely faster than trying to learn in a standard classroom." He addressed the girl then. "How old are the men you put in the tanks?"

"The youngest was sixteen, the oldest forty."

Jihoon whistled. "That's crazy. You're talking about a mortality rate of more than ten percent once you pass twenty-two, just by having the procedure to get your brain wired. Neuron structure is pretty well-defined by that point. The risk of insanity is about three times that."

"The insane we dispatch out of mercy." The girl looked at Jihoon then and cocked her head. "You have been in the tank?"

He nodded. "Humans train this way. We have since the first of you began using the method in the production facilities and proved it could work."

"If you didn't come here to kill us, why?" She had turned her attention back to me, and the girl's eyes stared through everything, with the same deep blue that had warned me of the attack in Sydney, an ocean of color that didn't care if anyone lived or died.

"We need some information."

One of the men spoke to her in English, his accent almost perfect. "We're wasting time, mother."

She nodded and then gestured to me with her carbine. "Go back the way you came. There is no information here, but you can leave alive."

"Wait; I need to know if the same C. L. Chen means anything to you. Or Samuel Ling or Project Sunshine."

The girl cocked her head again and made me angrier; this was an abomination. The gesture looked too human, and it felt as though someone had stolen something not just from me, but from the entire human race, and that she didn't *deserve* life.

"C. L. Chen, no; nor have I heard of Sunshine. But Samuel Ling is a genetic engineer. He had a small shop in the gene-therapy section of Khlong Toei."

I nodded. "Did Ling ever work with the Thais—to reverse your spoiling?"

"Ling is a very smart man but not that smart. Six months ago we lost a couple of our sisters; they disappeared from their living quarters, and someone suggested that we look into Ling. When we entered his offices, they had been cleaned out—except for the remains of my two sisters, vivisected, analyzed, and dead long before we got there. Otherwise, the offices were empty and pristine, and we do not expect Ling's return."

"Did you run here with Margaret? Did you travel with her when she originally came to Thailand?"

The girl shook her head. "No. Margaret was blessed.

She is the only one to have met Catherine, the most perfect of all."

At the name, all of them bowed their heads, and Jihoon and I glanced at each other. The spoiling affected all the major organs, including the brain, and their manner would have made me think they were all crazy except that the men were human—would never have experienced the spoiling, whereas the satos' own immune systems turned traitor. This was weird, but it *wasn't* a sign of insanity.

"What was so special about Catherine?" Jihoon asked.

Apparently it was another joke, and they all chuckled. She shouldered her carbine and lit a cigarette, handing them out to the others. "They send you to hunt us but don't teach you about Catherine? You are nothing for us to fear then."

And all of them left. They filtered out through the other side of the courtyard, and although my initial thought was to follow, narrow windows dotted the walls around us and there was no telling if someone watched. It felt like there were crosshairs on my forehead. The sun inched lower, and the day had gotten late anyway, so we both turned and headed back for the ghetto entrance.

"What do you think, Chong?" I asked.

"That was the craziest stuff I've ever seen. You hunted them?"

"Yeah. But they weren't like that. The ones I chased rotted alive, incapable in some cases of even seeing. We just saw a sato in perfect form. A killing tool. She could have wiped us both before we even started to draw, and they can all rot in hell."

He grunted and then looked at me. "Why do you hate them so much?"

"Who?"

"Them. Satos."

I started walking faster, thinking about Phillip's father and the jungles. "We have a long way to go, Chong, and frankly, you don't know me well enough to start asking that kind of crap."

We were lost. The maze of rusting and crumbling structures wasn't at all familiar on our return trip, and the best I could manage was to make sure the wharf cranes were at our backs as we tried to find the gate. After a half hour of searching, we turned a corner and stepped into an area that looked like an amusement park for all its neon and terracotta. A narrow route went straight through sets of buildings that were newer than the rest and that resembled what I imagined to be Japanese architecture—more so than either Thai buildings or the makeshift housing typical of what we'd seen so far. These were built by people who had money. Outside each shop hung signs, along with flashing images that showed pictures of animals or body parts.

"What the hell is this?" I asked Jihoon.

"Genetic engineering. That sign says organ repair, and there's a shop farther down selling small dragons, safe for children. I'm surprised the Thais haven't cracked down."

"Well, as long as they restrict themselves to animals and gene therapy, it shouldn't be a problem—especially if they pay off the officials."

A man in a long rubber apron stood in front of one shop, smoking while he gestured to us with rubber-gloved hands. "Come in, come in."

"Why?" I asked.

"You need new liver, yes? I can tell." He chuckled and

looked at Jihoon. "Your friend heavy drinker. The skin says it all. And the nose."

"You know," said Jihoon, "he might be right. You do look a little yellow."

"Screw you." But it struck me that this must have been where Chen had camped out, somewhere in the area. I nodded to the man and followed him in with Jihoon.

The shop's waiting room was gleaming white, its tile extending from the floor almost to the ceiling, and a tiny robot crawled across it, cleaning every centimeter with pulses of disinfectant. One wall had a menu. The writing was in Japanese and Thai, but next to each item was a picture of an organ—everything you could ever want replaced.

"Those prices old," the man said. "No good now. Liver therapy, five thousand."

"Bhat?" I asked.

"Dollar."

"Too steep, friend," I said, shaking my head. "But I'll tell you what. I'll give you a hundred dollars if you tell me what you know about Samuel Ling."

The man's face paled, and he ducked behind his counter, pulling off both gloves. "Don't know Samuel Ling. Shop is closing now, you go."

"Watch the door," I said to Ji and waited until he had taken a position outside before turning back to the shop-keeper. "You're a genetic engineer?"

"Yes. But you go."

I shook my head and put one hand on my pistol. "No, I stay. Samuel Ling. Where is he?"

"You don't understand." The man looked panicked now, his gaze shifting back and forth between the front door and me. "Ling has many friends in Bangkok. Colleagues."

"All you have to do is tell me where he went. Then I'll leave. If you don't, not only could I put a few holes in you, but look at my uniform, pal. I could have every Thai official in here until you'd make more money by burning the place to the ground and selling charcoal."

"He's gone," the man said.

"I know that. Where?"

He ran a hand through his hair and then shrugged. "I don't know Ling. But friend say he bragged about having institute. In Burma. That all I know."

I stared at the man and pulled my fléchette pistol out, but when he started to cry and begged me to believe him, I guessed he'd told the truth. I handed him my credit chit.

"Take a hundred dollars."

With the transaction completed, I left, grabbing Jihoon's arm and pulling him through the alley.

"What's the rush?" he asked.

"Ling. If the shop guy was that scared of someone who's not even here, Ling must have a lot of contacts who still owe him, and I'd bet you anything that the first thing that guy will do is tell them about our visit."

To his credit, Jihoon didn't ask any more questions and moved with me, keeping pace. The sun was about to set. With any luck, I figured, we'd find the gate and high-tail it back to the hotel before the curfew started, but I had that feeling now, like something was about to go wrong, because Khlong Toei had changed. The crowds had vanished as if they knew something we didn't, and I imagined a current running through the place because it was a living thing, a single entity with a unified consciousness taking in everything at once instead of a collection of individuals. We started jogging once we hit a restaurant area, and Jihoon looked over his shoulder for the fifth time.

"We're being followed," he said.

"How many?"

He shrugged, and we quickened our pace when the ghetto's wall came into view. Now all we had to do was trace it north to our gate—any gate—and get the hell out.

"Four. Armed with clubs or something. Not Thai, maybe Japanese."

"Follow my lead and don't hesitate; just waste the bastards."

I pulled my pistol and ducked behind a stall, the vendor shouting at me in English to go away and that he didn't want trouble. Then he screamed something else in Japanese. The guy pulled out a broom and started whacking me with it until I pointed my pistol at him, at which point he dropped the broom and ran. But it had distracted me. Jihoon shouted a warning, too late, so I didn't see it when a guy came from the other side, shouting and swinging a club in a downward arc at my head. I blocked it with my pistol, but the impact knocked the weapon from my hand. It skittered over the concrete. The guy, who looked Asian and wore a T-shirt so tight that every muscle showed, raised his club again and grinned. But before he could strike, three fléchettes buzzed and cracked by my head, hitting the man in his throat; he grabbed his neck with both hands, dropping the club and gurgling as he died.

Jihoon had already wiped two more. The last one ran back the way he had come, and we stood, sprinting for the wall and then heading north once we reached it. I stopped to grab my fléchette pistol, ramming it back into the holster.

"We need to get out of here before any cops show," I said, panting.

"It was self-defense."

"Yeah, but do we really need to get tied up in Bangkok's legal system? It's bad enough I've gone around asking point-blank about Chen, so having to explain everything to the cops just isn't on my to-do list. Besides, if those guys were connected, self-defense might not be on the menu."

Jihoon nodded. A gate was in sight with two Thai Army guards chatting and leaning against the barrier as the sun set. We slowed to a walk, not wanting to look like anything was wrong.

"How'd those guys find out about us so fast?" Jihoon asked.

"Either the shopkeeper was more plugged in than I thought, or our friends with the *Gra Jaai* let someone know about us. Out of courtesy." I thought for a second and then added one more possibility. "Or someone was following us the whole way and questioned our friend, the genetic engineer, as soon as we left."

We showed the Thai guards our passport chits and let them scan our retinas, after which we were back in Bangkok proper and broke once more into a jog, heading north on the sidewalk. I was breathing easier now. Still, my age showed, and both legs screamed with the effort of running so I had to fight to hide my discomfort, not wanting Jihoon to realize that it was a struggle.

"Did you learn anything from the Japanese guy?" he asked.

I waited to answer, trying to catch my breath. "Yeah. Chen is in Burma."

"Christ."

"Well, if we go to the front, we'll be heading in that direction anyway."

I don't know if my voice had betrayed the fact that I was about to give out, but Jihoon slowed down. "You wanna walk for a little while?"

"If you want to, Chong." But secretly, I was relieved at the suggestion, maybe liking Jihoon a bit more. "And you were good."

"At what?" he asked.

"At wiping that guy before he clocked me."

In the morning we'd head into the bush. The colonel had left a message at the hotel, letting us know that our gear had arrived and that a vehicle would be waiting for us outside the hotel at 4:00 a.m.; knowing that it wouldn't be long—a matter of hours before making my return to the jungle—made it hard to sleep. I risked opening the drapes in the darkness and lit a cigarette, sitting in one of the room's chairs to look out over Bangkok. The stillness broke with an occasional pop, far-off gunfire that the heavy air muffled so it sounded like a cracking branch. Bangkok was a tinderbox, a mixture of immigrants who even after at least two generations hadn't assimilated and who panicked at the threat of yet another war; just the word *Chinese* was enough to send them into riotous panic, maybe with a little help from foreign operatives sprinkled throughout the city. Even this late, tiny red lights flared up and then dimmed from windows in buildings across the street, the glow of cigarettes from others who couldn't sleep. We were a brotherhood of strangers bound by anxiety.

And bumping into the sato had unnerved me. Jihoon still didn't understand, or he'd be awake like me, worried that once we reached the line they would surround us, an army of satos who would see me as a murderer. There had been more to Margaret than the holo image. I'd studied what was on the chit, an account of what the girl had seen in Russia, having escaped one of their gulags and made it south through the Chinese invasion of eastern Siberia and into North Korea, where she had braved a nuclear waste-land, finally making it into Unified Korea. Everything had moved so quickly that I hadn't thought of it before: Who had taken Margaret's account of events? She was here in Thailand, so it was possible that someone had gotten the chance to interview her, but I doubted it, and the thing that the sato had said echoed in my thoughts: *They send you to hunt us but don't teach you about Catherine.* Who was Catherine? They'd mentioned her in my briefing, but there hadn't been any data in the files they'd shown me, so some-thing crucial had been omitted and it drove me crazy to think that the answer was just beyond my reach, eluding me no matter how hard I tried to grasp it.

I took another pull on my cigarette and watched as an APC lumbered down the street, its wheels crunching over broken glass and concrete; the vehicle's turret motor whined. By reflex, I hid my cigarette behind my hand and waited for the crushing boom of the thing's cannon, expecting to have to dive to the floor again, but so far everything stayed quiet. Once it had passed, my concen-tration returned. Margaret. She had seen something, had information that the brass wanted—or information they *suspected* she had—and according to Jihoon, the opera-tion in Spain may have been related, but something didn't make sense. The Koreans were spooked and had jump-started a genetic warfare program. But after the war in Kazakhstan, with its associated casualty figures and the holo clips of satos wasting on camera, almost the entire world, including Unified Korea, had jumped on the Genetic Weapons Convention, signing and ratifying it overnight—maybe not so much out of sympathy for satos as for a fear that nobody could compete with our, China's, or Russia's production programs. So it would be better if *nobody* had satos. And the Koreans, also overnight, turned their back on the agreement, despite the fact that if anyone found out, it would be their ass. All of Asia would cry for their heads. A pack of cigarettes later and the answers still wouldn't come, so I stubbed the last one out and glanced at the clock, sighing with fatigue as I stood and turned on the light.

"Half an hour," I said, shaking Jihoon's foot to wake him.

He rubbed his eyes. "Got it. You look like you didn't sleep."

"I didn't. Something tells me we're going to run into a lot of satos out there, and if there's one thing I hate more than them, it's the bush. You take the first shower."

Jihoon went into the bathroom, and I turned the light off again before walking back to the window and peering out. The moon was setting in the distance, and shadows hid most of the area except for a spot under a single street-light that had somehow avoided destruction over the last two days. I was about to close the drapes when something moved. A figure hid in a doorway across the street and I froze, watching as whoever it was worked his way closer to the hotel, until he found a position in an alley. If we'd had our gear, I could have used the vision hood to get a better view, but for now all I could do was stare, hoping that something would happen to give me a look. Eventually there was a glint. The flickering streetlight hit something metallic, and my skin crawled before it occurred to me that I was standing by the window, and I dropped to the floor at the same time a stream of tracer fléchettes cracked through the opening to slam into the far wall. My gun belt was still on. I crawled to the door, opened it, and then stood to sprint for the staircase, jumping down the steps in an effort to make the street before the sniper had time to escape. By the time I made it to the lobby doors, where I hid behind a column with my pistol drawn, the night staff yelled to me that they had already called authorities and asked if everyone was all right.

Keep moving, I told myself. Getting out through the door would be too obvious, so I charted a course to the next column and then sprinted for it, waiting for the fléchettes to crack again, and then jumped through one of the broken windows, firing into the alley where the man had hidden. But by the time I reached it, it was empty; whoever it was had bailed. I spat and kicked a piece of rubble, angry because I was already sweaty from the day before and now there would only be time for a quick shower since my watch said it was already quarter to four. A growl of vehicles sounded in the distance. Soon the Thais would be there, and I ran back up to the hotel room, realizing that I'd forgotten to check if Jihoon had been hit.

He was half-dressed by the time I got back.

"Where'd you go?" he asked.

"You didn't hear that?"

Ji shook his head. "What?"

"Someone opened up on me from across the street. Sniper." I pointed to the holes in the wall, and he whistled.

"That's good."

I stared at him in shock. "Are you a nutcase? What's good?"

"Well," he said, pulling on his boots, "now we know that whoever is after us is a really bad shot."

I pulled my uniform shirt off and headed for the bathroom, shaking my head. Nothing made any sense anymore. It was the worst mission possible for someone at my point, a guy on his last legs and in need of retirement, and it got worse with every passing second.

"Hey, Chong," I called from the bathroom.

"What?"

"Even if we have no clue what's going on, someone is getting ticked off. Maybe *that's* good."

FIVE

Outbound

Nothing had changed since my earlier experiences in Bangkok, which felt like they'd happened yesterday: the Royal Army never hurried unless it was to panic. We waited. Then waited some more. The Thais took their time in preparing for the trip to the front, and we'd be heading northwest toward the Thai-Burma border with a supply column that consisted of six-wheeled trucks in a thousand different forms—cargo, troop carriers, but more than anything, alcohol tankers and armored personnel carriers. Every fourth vehicle was an APC. The Thai version was smaller than the American one, suited to the vile roads we'd have to travel, and if they hadn't improved any since I had last visited (the mountain passages were more like goat trails and were wide enough for only one vehicle) then God help us if someone came in the opposite direction. I wouldn't go inside any of the vehicles, not even the APCs, and Jihoon looked up at me from the assembly field.

"You're riding on top?" he asked. "Why not inside? Are you *that* claustrophobic?"

I lit another cigarette and grinned from the deck of an

APC. "It's not claustrophobia. You didn't learn this one in the tanks?"

He shrugged. "Learn what?"

"These types of APCs have one large compartment, so when they get hit by a rocket, the overpressure liquefies everyone inside at the same time it cooks them. Ride on top, and you'll get blown into the air but maybe survive. I've seen about five guys live because they made that decision, to sit on the top instead of inside. I was one of 'em."

Ji glanced at the loading ramp and then looked back at me again before he sighed and grabbed hold of a tie-down, lifting himself using the nearest tire as a ladder. He had just settled when Colonel O'Steen jogged up. The colonel handed me a computer chit and shook his head.

"Priority transmission from your CO at SOCOM, Momson. For your eyes only."

"Thanks, Colonel," I said.

He nodded and crossed his arms. "You boys see any trouble down in Khlong Toei yesterday? Maybe a group of Koreans with clubs?"

Ji and I looked at each other, and I smiled.

"No. Why?"

"Witnesses said that a Japanese guy and an American shot three Koreans and then ran yesterday. The Koreans had passports and visas, but there's nothing on them in foreign ministry databases."

"Wasn't us," I said. "And besides, Chong here is Korean, not Japanese."

"Well, it's funny because they also caught the guy who took a shot at you in the hotel, and he was Korean too. Found him near one of the Khlong Toei gates, and he still had his Maxwell. They're interrogating him now."

I shook my head, worried, but then again not; once we hit the bush, it wasn't like they'd be able to send anyone to arrest us. "It's a hell of a world. Strange things happening every day."

O'Steen stared at me and frowned, the seconds ticking off. He nodded. "Well, whatever's on that chit, the Thai Army is treating you like special cargo to be delivered at any cost, the highest priority. Good luck up there," he said and left.

I made a mental note of the fact that our pursuers had been Korean, not sure of what to make of it, then settled back into the wait. Then we waited some more. The Thai soldiers laughed and smoked, half of them wearing ancient surplus armor—the only stuff we sold them and which didn't have chameleon skins—and the other half dressed in even more ancient tiger-striped battle suits. Battle suits were basic rubberlike undersuits that had been equipped with cooling units and that were one-piece garments that zipped up the front and had a hood with a clear plastic face; the hoods sealed over the suits' shoulders and would protect their wearers from chemical or biological attacks. Each had backpack power and air filtration. I took a drag and exhaled, thinking how much they'd need the gear where we were going, my cigarette smoke sinking the same way I'd once seen clouds of gas blown over my trench in the bush so that the image made me break out in a cold sweat; gas was the worst. You had to stay buttoned in your suit after they hit because armor was the one thing keeping you alive. Decontamination could take days or weeks—if they got around to it at all— and by then you'd be so crazy from smelling your own sweat that it was almost better to let the stuff take you down in the first place. The mission was getting to me, I decided. The computer chit glinted in my hand, and I turned it over, wondering if I wanted to see it until finally Ji grabbed the thing and slid it into my forearm slot. It took a moment to slip on my vision hood.

It was Colonel Momson. His face flickered onto my heads-up display, and I barely heard him when the camera zoomed out to show Phillip, smiling as he held a Popsicle. The kid's hair hadn't been cut. I grinned at that and almost started crying because it meant the bastards hadn't gotten into his head yet, hadn't corrupted it with the same filth I'd had to endure by choice. He was out, and it was all that mattered for now; I'd worry about getting him later.

The image faded then, and it switched to an audio track with Momson's voice. "There have been new developments since that last time we met. A week ago we sent a team into Wonsan, Unified Korea, to recon the area and see if they could get any information based on the names and addresses you provided us with from the Madrid operation. Unified Korean operatives picked them up within a few days. They held the men in isolation and tortured them until finally one of our guys escaped, barely making it to the US embassy in Pusan, where he told our liaison that the Koreans had been asking about the American in Spain, Stan Resnick—who he was and what the operation was all about. It's no surprise. By now the Koreans have a holo image of you and will be on the lookout for your biometrics, so our analysts advise that if you're still in Bangkok, you should change your appearance as soon as possible. Already Unified Korea has lodged a formal complaint with the State Department, and we're getting a lot of heat from POTUS, who hasn't been briefed yet on the Spain op. Pusan is pissed that you killed all their people, Bug; be careful.

"There's something else. We didn't tell you about a crucial component of your mission because at the time there wasn't a need for you to know, but all the moth-balled Germline ateliers are being reactivated, and construction of new ones began just before you left for Madrid. In two weeks, State will announce that we're formally withdrawing from the Genetic Weapons Convention. China just finished taking the western districts in Russia, and reports are coming in from all over that they're repositioning forces, moving troops toward India and Burma. The Indians, Thai, Vietnamese, Laotians, and Cambodians are screaming for help, and three carrier groups are already prepping to move out.

"As part of the new training regime for genetics, we're going to include a manual called the *Book of Catherine*—the same sato who was with Margaret when the two escaped from Russia and traveled through North Korea. She's someone that the Joint Chiefs spent a lot of money to capture, a perfect killer. We debriefed her as best we could, but once in our custody Catherine just gave us basic information and then demanded discharge. But one thing came through during the sessions: she considered herself to be in direct communication with God. We don't consider this insanity because it's what they're trained to believe, and it made her totally fearless. Deadly. What *was* odd was that at over three years past expiration, she was in better mental form than when she was first fielded; totally fearless instead of being a mental basket case. Margaret likely absorbed some of Catherine's ideas, and from the little information we have, she's more than just a sato to the other escaped genetics in Thailand, and considering the shit that's about to rain down over southeast Asia, we're canceling your kill order; the higher-ups want Margaret alive. In the coming months we may need those satos to slow down a Chinese advance if they decide to invade Thailand because we're not ready yet and production will take time. Get the word to Margaret; convince her any way you can that we're on the same team and that she needs to slow down a Chinese invasion force if one should cross the Thai border; only then proceed with the plan to find Chen, whose voice and physical biometrics are now uploaded to your system. Your mission just got bumped up to priority one. End of message."

"*Real* special," I muttered and then worked my forearm controls to delete the video portion of the chit; there was no reason for Ji to see Phillip, but whether the message was for me alone or not, he needed to hear Momson. I yanked the chit out and handed it to him. "You gotta freakin' hear this."

"It said for your eyes only."

I pulled my vision hood off and picked up the cigarette I'd placed on the APC deck, taking one last drag before tossing the butt away. "Yeah, but you're not going to freaking believe this one."

"I was looking at your backpack computer unit," Ji said. He inserted the chit into his slot. "It's bigger than any I've seen. You have a semi-aware in that thing?"

"Yep."

"How do you keep it juiced? Those things suck power."

I pointed to my helmet and shoulders. "The chameleon skin polymer is also doped with a photovoltaic material, and the suit's inside is coated with a piezoelectric nanocoating. So anytime I'm in sunlight or moving, my batteries and fuel cells get a little extra charge."

He laughed. "I never would have guessed it—that you, of all people, would have a semi-aware."

"This one's different," I said. "This one is female and has a really sexy voice and promised not to tell anyone my secrets. She's the only girl for me."

Jihoon slid his vision hood on. A few minutes later he yanked it off and slid the chit out, snapping the paper-thin plastic between his fingers. "Looks like a mission."

"Yep." Thai officers blew whistles, and everyone loaded up at the same time the APC engine ground to life beneath me. "But it's some mission."

There was no forgetting that road. The highway took us over a bridge to the far side of the Chao Phraya River, in an endless line of vehicles that downshifted and ground their gears as the gaps between them shrank and expanded so that from above the convoy must have resembled a spring. Seven years hadn't changed anything. My mind had altered the memories and played tricks, the kind where I swore that a particular fuel-alcohol station had been on one side of the road but was actually on the other, and some places had been torn down to be replaced by new buildings, but it didn't take long to repair the image in my mind. It wouldn't be long, I thought. Not much farther until we hit the endless rice paddies and fish farms, beyond which the jungle would form a dark green scar on the horizon.

Jihoon had laid out his equipment on the bouncing APC deck. He checked and double-checked the Maxwell carbine, its long barrel a dull black and formed by bands of ceramic under which coils of superconducting wire would juice themselves into magnets at the squeeze of a button. Unlike the smaller police models I'd seen in Spain or used in Sydney, these ones were for combat. A long flexi-belt fed thousands of fléchettes from the carbine's breach to a hopper that would perch on the left shoulder, the weight a comforting reminder of the power in one's hands.

"Seven years," I said.

Jihoon yelled over the noise. "What?"

"Seven years. Seven years since I've been back in this awful country."

"What's wrong with Thailand?"

Jihoon could have his equipment. I searched my pack for one of the bottles I'd brought and uncapped it, offering him some but he declined. "There's a different way of doing things out here, Chong. Not like in the simulators. We'll see if it makes *you* sick."

"You think I can't hack it?" he asked.

"I think after the BAI you did your time in the regular Army, just enough to find your way into Special Forces. I also think you're a good Korean American who salutes the flag every day and jerks off while reciting the pledge of allegiance."

Ji started packing his kit, making sure that everything went in the proper place. "You really can't stand Asians, can you? Not just me, I mean anyone who even resembles one."

"That's not true. I love Asians. Bangkok has some of the best hookers around; it's a real shame there wasn't time to try one or two while we were there." The bourbon went in smoothly and took the edge off, but you couldn't mess around in this heat, even with the suit's climate control; I reminded myself to drink plenty of water once I'd finished.

"All right. If you won't tell me why you're such a bigoted prick, how about you tell me why you hate satos so much?"

I thought about that one. It was a good question, one that warranted another drink because it was the second time he'd asked it and the guy wouldn't give up. But even then the answer wouldn't come, and several responses swirled in the cesspool of my brain, each of them almost right but none of them close to the whole truth.

"You were there, in Khlong Toei," I said. "Didn't you *see* that betty?"

Ji nodded. "Yeah. I saw her. She looked exactly like the pictures I've seen, but nothing there to hate so much."

"Give it time. Maybe one of them will shove her hand through your best friend's stomach and snap his spine while quoting their bible. You ever read their combat manual, Chong?" I didn't bother to look if he nodded since it was likely he *hadn't* read it. "It's not about small unit tactics; it's about how to get closer to God through killing. None of them should be breathing the same air as you or me. And some asshole like you and me made them." *Assholes like Phillip's father.*

The convoy slowed, and ahead of us the lead vehicles took an exit ramp off the highway so they could turn onto a two-lane road, heading northwest into haze. It was late morning. We had our hoods and helmets off so the hot wind blew across my face, and the trucks' exhaust made the air wetter, their alcohol-burning engines screaming as they shifted into low gear to slow down. When it was our turn, we took the ramp slowly, spiraling around until facing the right direction again and in front of us saw nothing but green. Rice paddies lined each side of a small country road, and I wondered how many armies had taken this route north. You almost smelled the leftovers of war in this place, and thinking about it didn't help because the more you thought about it, the more you wanted to pick up your Maxwell and hold it close, keep it ready. Paddy dikes could conceal anything. The trees topping them would make good cover, and before I could catch myself, I'd started to reach for my vision hood to take a closer look, scan the road ahead for signs of ambush, but the rough canvas was like sandpaper and made me laugh at the thought, so instead I took another drink.

Thailand made me feel old, I decided, but then it didn't take much to make me feel old these days and Wheezer should have been there, not Jihoon. Wheezer would have gotten everything, could have said something to pull me out of the gloom. It was funny how dark everything had become despite the fact that the sun couldn't have been more brilliant on its climb upward from the horizon, and the thought occurred to me that it had been years since I'd seen the ocean—*really* saw it, not just flew over or drove by. The last time had been with Phillip when he was two. In Beaufort. It had been a strange place where the forest went almost all the way to the ocean and where the surf pounded in booms so loud they drowned out the noise from the naval air station and its constant, roaring fighters. And there it was, the entry of another memory, one that I wanted least of all because it threatened to ruin the focus I'd need to complete the task at hand. Old age rode the APC next to me, laughing not at my jokes but at

me, poking its finger in my eye because it knew that
there wasn't anything a guy like me could do and that the
cracks had started to show, cracks into which it could
push its fingers and work to wedge them even wider.
Old age and a rube named Jihoon were the APC's only
other riders.

"They took Phillip out of the academy." The words left
my mouth before I'd thought about it, and after they did I
wanted them back, but it was too late.

Ji glanced at me. "Oh."

"Yeah," I whispered before chugging the rest of the
bottle. "And here *I* am." *Wondering why it is that I care
about another guy's kid.*

We spent the rest of the morning cruising northwest along
narrow paved roads, forcing oncoming traffic to pull off
to the side or risk getting crushed under the ceramic-
armored APCs, and people stopped to stare with quiet
curiosity. We had jumped back in time. Despite the progress of the last two centuries, *here* were old men walking
behind water buffalo, their feet protected by nothing
except sandals as they guided plows through the clay.
There were women in conical hats; they stooped over in a
dry field, yanking rice from the ground with hands that
were darker than the clay itself, the sun having baked
everything to well-done. Some wore white turbanlike
things on their heads. But they all stood when the convoy
roared up, holding both hands to their eyes, shielding
them from the sun. Jihoon pulled an item from his kit, a
tiny rectangle, and placed it against his face. It took me a
second to realize that the guy was taking pictures.

I was about to laugh and give him hell for it when something else caught my eye. We were moving out of one farming area into another, and there were no fences to delineate separate areas, but I sensed it from the tree line and the fact that the new area hadn't been tended as nicely; huge weeds and brush had overgrown much of its fields. To our front, a narrow concrete bridge spanned a canal. From where I sat, it looked like something was on the bridge so I yanked my vision hood on and stood, grabbing hold of the APC's turret rear so I could see over the forward vehicles while zooming in. A truck had broken down. It looked like an ancient vehicle, rusted out in spots, and the engine hood had been propped up as if the truck had stopped and been abandoned when its owner couldn't fix the thing. I looked back. Jihoon was still taking pictures, but the farmers had stopped staring and were moving in the opposite direction, some of them sprinting away once they climbed the dike and made it to the road.

"Chong!" I yelled, dropping back to the deck to grab my helmet. "Ambush. Get your hood and lid on, and let the Thais know that the vehicle ahead is part of a trap."

He didn't even pause, and I had to give the guy credit. Jihoon slipped the camera into a pouch and geared up in under ten seconds, calling over our radio in twangy Thai that crackled in my ears. But it was already too late. Our road ran along the top of a dike, with steep dirt and gravel sides that dropped about ten feet into the fields on either flank; although the APCs could make it down such a slope, the trucks would have to stay put.

I had just grabbed my carbine, which had been slung over a shoulder, when the first rocket streaked out of the tree line ahead of us, clanging into the lead APC after a loud *whoosh*. Time stopped. I don't remember deciding what to do or telling Jihoon to follow, but we leaped from our APC as it screeched to a stop, and both of us rolled down the sides of the dike after an impact that snapped my jaws together; I tasted blood from having bit the inside of my cheek. Jihoon rolled to a stop beside me. We stood in a crouch and jogged toward the trees where the rocket had come from but kept to the area where the fields met the dike, our feet sucking in and out of thick mud in a shallow ditch. We had made it about ten meters when daisy-chained geysers of asphalt and clay leaped up to our left. At first it didn't register. Then I noticed that my speakers had cut off to shield my ears, and shadows appeared where none had been before, so there was just enough time to look left and see the line of explosions work their way down the road, hitting the APC on which we had just ridden. The vehicle leaped up. A fraction of a second later the fusion reactor went and small jets of plasma shot out from cracks in the hull. The vehicle broke in two, already burning before the separate pieces landed. A few seconds later my hearing came back as bits of uniforms, armor, and ceramic chunks from the vehicles either floated down around me or thudded into the brush, along with, miraculously, our packs; they hadn't even been singed.

"Mines," I said over the radio.

Jihoon sounded shocked. "What?"

"Mines. They mined the road. Look sharp, and move up quickly. Whatever you do, don't stop until we hit the tree line."

Things were clicking again, making me smile with the feeling of being in my element. The APCs that survived whined as they turned off the road, crashing down the dike face in front of us at the same time their autocannons and plasma guns opened up. Jihoon and I sprinted behind them, trying our best to use their hulls as cover. The vehicles blocked our view of much of the way ahead, but between them we saw the flashes of expanding plasma, which ignited dangling tree branches into long torches and crisped anything on the ground. Tracers from the APCs also rocketed downrange, chewing up the dirt in small puffs. It was hard to keep track of time during that advance, but when the APCs reached the far dike, they stopped, and by then I noticed that sweat had soaked through my undersuit, suggesting we'd been running for at least a few minutes.

The embankment, on top of which the trees burned, was steeper than the one supporting the road, and the APCs couldn't climb it. They idled there—a pack of frustrated tigers.

"Tell them we're moving up," I said to Jihoon; there was no way I'd sit in the open for another second. "And make sure those asshats don't shoot at us." And I started up the slope, not waiting for Jihoon to let me know it was OK.

The trees crackled overhead, and one of them fell next to me, crashing to the ground and sending up a cloud of sparks. Two bodies had been charred. At first it was difficult to tell the difference between them and the scorched grass, but the remains of a rocket launcher rested between them, suggesting the Thai APC gunners had targeted the right location. I stayed down. Jihoon crawled up next to me, pointed right, and I nodded; we split up, moving in separate directions through the smoldering underbrush.

A figure jumped up in front of me but then vanished into

the brush. I'd chosen to head back in the direction of the road and had passed out of the burning zone into an area of dense grass, so by the time I lurched to my knees, he was gone and only the sound of crashing brush came from the far slope. I stood and ran. The adrenaline was kicking in now, and I heard the sound of my breathing as my feet slipped over the edge, sending me into a downslope slide to land in the far field. From there I saw the bridge to my left about ten meters away. It was quiet again. I moved toward the road, and stands of sawgrass swayed in a stiff breeze as my carbine rose so I could tuck it into my shoulder, the sighting reticle flashing onto my goggles, and a sense of satisfaction crept through my gut; the guy couldn't be far. At the same instant, a group of men broke cover to my right; I reported the contact and fired as they fled, not stopping until the last one dropped in a spray of blood, my fléchettes kicking sparks when they passed through ceramic armor. The whole thing took a few seconds from start to finish.

After an action ended, you sensed it—a letting out of pressure as if you were an overinflated balloon that had been on the verge of popping but now could relax, and you didn't know the pressure had been there until it was gone. My legs burned from all the running, and when Jihoon showed up, sliding down the bank to my right, they felt on the verge of giving out. Killing had filled my head with fog, and I sensed rather than heard him say something until I had to shake my head clear, waiting for the buzzing to leave.

"I said," Ji was yelling, "*are you OK?*"

"Yeah, I'm fine. Six KIA. Come on."

We followed the beaten grass until we had found and counted all the bodies. Jihoon radioed it in. We couldn't see them, but behind us we heard the APCs resume their drive, turning around and climbing back up the dike and onto the road.

Ji stood over one of the dead. "You shot him through the head. Clean."

I nodded. "Burmese."

"How can you tell?"

"Chinese armor. This is the stuff they used in the Asian Wars, way obsolete, and no chameleon skin. Burmese infiltrators."

Ji stooped and removed the guy's helmet but dropped it when brains and blood slid out, spilling over the ground and making the grass bright red. He turned, fumbling for his locking ring. By the time he got his own helmet off, Ji was heaving and threw up into the bush to leave a little of himself in Thailand, and I understood because it was a normal reaction that everyone had when faced with the reality of what lived inside their skulls. When he finished, I picked up his helmet for him.

"Different from the simulators, I guess, and let me warn you; that won't be the last time you puke. Come on. We have to see how many vehicles are left on the road and get our packs."

Jihoon caught up with me and pushed his hood off, so it hung from the back by its wires. "Where'd you get your armor, Bug?"

"I had it custom made. Once you get the rhythm of all this, you should do the same. Think about what features might help you do your job, and get the armorers to put it all together."

"Why does your helmet look that way, all elongated?"

I reached up, running my gauntlet along the extended

snout, wondering why I hadn't just asked to have a standard suit sent since there wouldn't be any reason to use my add-ons, and told him what it was for.

"Jesus," he said. "Now I know why they call you Bug."

"Now you know it all, Chong."

We got back to the road to find a crowd of pissed-off Thais. Jihoon spoke for about five minutes with the convoy commander while I walked through the wreckage, staring at the two-meter craters that had appeared where once there was blacktop. It could have been worse. When I'd seen the mines go off, it looked as though the entire line of vehicles had blown, but in reality the Burmese got about ten trucks and three APCs, which the Thais were now pushing off the road and down into the fields. A couple of the men cried; soot covered their faces, and the tears cleaned off narrow lines from their cheeks so that it looked as if the Thais, in reality, had black faces and had smeared on thin, ruddy lines of makeup. Their presence made everything surreal—a troop of crazy clowns that had popped into the war for a pantomime.

Jihoon tapped me on the shoulder, yanking me from my thoughts while handing me my pack. "The Thais are going after the locals."

"Good."

"Good? What if they kill them all?"

I shook my head and ran a gauntlet through my hair, which had matted with sweat, and when I pulled my hand off saw that water had mixed with soot from the burning vehicles to turn the gauntlet gray.

"How do you think the Burmese operated here, Chong, this far inside Thailand? We're barely outside the Bangkok urban zone. I don't know, maybe the whole area is sympathetic to the Burmese. Maybe they're all Chinese immigrants from the war or Japanese. Maybe they're Korean."

"That's a load of crap," Jihoon said. "We have to do something. These guys are ready to go round up every person in town and execute them."

This was getting out of hand, and if Ji had taken the time to look around, he'd have seen that we were the only two Americans for miles. "Shut up and listen. You will do *nothing*. Just stand there, and let the Thais do whatever it is angry soldiers do in this crappy little country because you don't know shit. I do. I've been here. If you get in the way and try to be some kind of hero, these guys will take your head off and piss into your neck before you're half-dead. They don't fight like we do, Chong."

Ji clenched his carbine in both fists and turned around to watch as the soldiers in the convoy, escorted by one of the APCs, jogged toward the town. The APC pushed the broken-down truck off the bridge. When they reached the other side, the road sloped downward and we lost sight of them, the last thing visible a radio antenna that swayed with the motion of its vehicle.

"This is shit," Ji said.

"Yeah. But you signed up for it. Sometimes, in this job all you can do is stand back and watch, stand back and take it because the mission is what matters and you never do anything to jeopardize it. We're all alone here, Chong, and nobody will help you if these guys decide you're a liability. Think about *that*."

I was sorry for him. He didn't realize that from here on out it would get worse and that the closer we got to the mountains and their jungle it would get crazier, the insanity ramping upward until he'd have to accept the fact that there wasn't any limit to what could happen in the bush. The jungle's canopy was impenetrable. Dark. It gave men the feeling that no matter what they did, nobody would ever see a thing, but I knew that idea was wrong; the jungle saw it. The bush had its own mind and marked the players, put an indelible stamp on their souls so they'd wake up in the night and swear that the shadows were out to get them. Now that we had moved out of the city, it was on the wind, and I broke into a sweat, hating the fact that we were headed to another place I swore never to see again and that soon, whether he wanted it or not, Ji would change forever. The funny thing was that he wanted this life and had volunteered for it; we all had. There were no saints on the road that day, no saints in all of Thailand maybe, and if he wanted to make it out alive, Jihoon would have to armor his brain with an excess dose of the *fuck its* so that none of it would make any difference. And he'd have to do it soon.

Maybe that's why I cared so much about Phillip; they'd tried to steal his right to choose: saint or anti-saint.

The sun nailed itself overhead when we passed through the town. I refused to look at the signs on buildings because I didn't want to remember the place's name, and that was because the Thais had snatched the mayor and his wife and strung them up by their necks. We passed them along the main road, a pair of corpses that swung in the breeze, their empty eyes looking through me, and already the heat had started the swelling so their faces were bloated and gray. Although they couldn't have stunk yet, I held my nose shut until the APC turned a corner. Finally they were out of sight. But you knew that they saw through the walls of the town's buildings and followed you with the X-ray vision of the dead, a stare that ripped your skin off until they saw your heart and laughed without twitching a muscle.

Jihoon wasn't talking. That was fine with me because there was a lot to think about, and after we cruised through the town, the convoy made good speed, driving for at least two hours until we hit a city, the first one outside Bangkok that we'd seen. The convoy slowed and pulled over into a huge bus station. One by one the remaining tankers lined up, and the other trucks and APCs refueled while a platoon of Thai soldiers formed a perimeter to stand guard.

"I'm hungry," said Jihoon. We had jumped off the vehicle to stretch our legs, and I rested the carbine behind my neck, hanging both hands over either end like a yoke.

"Don't eat the local food. Stick to your ration packs, or you'll have problems pushing solid waste out your port."

"Don't remind me."

Ji looked uncomfortable and pale, and I started laughing. "When was the last time you wore a suit?"

"This is the first time in a few months. Does your ass always itch like this?"

"Always." I nodded. "It takes awhile to get used to the waste tubes. Drink plenty of water, and do yourself a favor and give yourself the trots."

"How?"

I unsnapped a pouch and pulled out a plastic bottle, tossing it to him. "Take a swig of this. In an hour, take another swig."

"What is it?" he asked.

"Trooper's best friend: castor oil. I got a bunch from the motor pool back in Florida a while ago and never travel without it. The problem is that I can't take a solid dump anymore."

"You didn't need to explain all of that."

His expression made it look as though Jihoon would vomit again, but he swallowed a dose and then sat beneath the shade of a palm tree, laying his carbine down and pulling both knees up to his chest. It didn't matter how tough you were. The suits reduced even the hardest to crying babies during their first couple of days—from feeling confined and not being able to itch the hundreds of spots that you'd forgotten existed. Claustrophobia came later. The helmet wrapped you in its ceramic, and once you couldn't run a hand through your hair, it started to make you wonder if the world existed, and the fact that you couldn't see in your periphery or turn to look behind you stuck a pin in some guys. Most people would look at me in the States and wonder how I could stand the fighting—the chance of dying. But those weren't the toughest things for me. Things like having to deal with the suit made them pale in comparison because you saw combat every once in a while, but the suit was with you every day, even when you slept.

"What's the longest you've gone in a suit?" Jihoon asked.

"Without a break?"

"Yeah."

"Four months." I'd pulled out my bourbon and drank some, wishing that I could get drunk, but I wasn't *that* stupid. Out there, I might need to be wired at any minute. "It was early in the Subterrene War in Kazakhstan, when they weren't sure how to use us, so I got attached as a forward artillery observer to some line outfit."

Ji nodded. "How many fire missions did you call in?"

"None."

"None?"

"None. For Christ's sake, we were over a kilometer underground in a freaking tunnel near the main mining area, so what was there to observe? That's logic for you. Put me in as a forward observer to call in artillery for an underground unit."

The whistles blew, and Jihoon picked himself up. He walked bent over, like an old man, and I grabbed his weapon for him, removing the fléchette hopper from his shoulder when something started bothering me; my antennae were up. Over the noise of the vehicles, I heard Thai soldiers speaking loudly, hurriedly, and then noticed that some pointed down the road to the north where a line of vehicles approached from the opposite direction.

"Put your hood and helmet on," I said.

Jihoon moved slowly, and I tossed our weapons onto the APC so I could free my hands to put my helmet on too. We had just finished when the first vehicle crept by.

Four satos sat in an open scout car. All wore Thai combat armor, which they had painted in different patterns with bright colors, and one of them had put black-and-yellow stripes on her gear to channel some kind of construction warning sign, but it got your attention. These ones didn't want to blend in with the jungle. All of them had short hair dyed in crazy colors as if someone had replaced the hair fibers with tiny neon tubes that glowed even in the daytime, and it was all so distracting, I almost failed to notice that the girls didn't even bother to glance our way, leaving me with the sense they had already judged our column as insignificant. It made me angry; they didn't know who I was or what I'd been doing for the last several years. I put my hand on my carbine as I climbed back onto the APC deck, wishing I could lift it and open fire, get a clean shot at them from the back as they lumbered away.

Behind the scout car was a string of four trucks, each one filled with soldiers who had made themselves up in ways similar to the girls, but these were men. Some of them looked Thai. Others had the paler features of Japanese and stared at me blankly, and one had a white bandage wrapped around his head with red blood that had seeped down his face while he smoked. The man smiled. A few of them shouted things at our convoy, and I nudged Jihoon.

"They're insulting us," he explained. "Loosely translated, they're calling the regular Thai Army a bunch of lost little girls."

"I've heard worse," I said.

"They're speaking Japanese. I'd say most of those guys were Japanese."

"*Gra Jaai*. Looks like we're heading in the right direction."

"Yeah," said Jihoon. "Right."

The trucks wound their way through the town and disappeared in a cloud of exhaust that blended into the day's haze at the same time our APC lurched forward. Jihoon lay down on his back, not bothering to take his helmet off.

"How much farther to the mountains?" he asked.

I pulled my helmet and hood off, sticking a cigarette in my mouth but was too tired to light it. "Tomorrow. We should get there by tomorrow."

The convoy crawled northward at about thirty kilometers an hour, just fast enough to get a nice breeze but slow enough that we knew we'd be spending the night on the road. We passed towns that were so poor that at some point I stopped looking; there were only so many crumbling structures and water buffalo that you could notice without yawning. Then the towns disappeared for a while, to be replaced by tiny villages dwarfed by huge fields that stretched from horizon to horizon, the green of their crops making me grin with the realization that I was free. Out here there was no Assurance, no microphones hidden in the rice paddies, and it had been some time since I'd seen any surveillance cameras. Progress, I decided, was overrated. Although the average Thai farmer would trade places with me for a chance to live in the States, how long would it be before he got sick of having the government watch his every move and how long would it take him to go crazy wondering if tomorrow he'd do something wrong and bring the full focus of the BAI on his life, their sole mission to build a case against him—whether one existed or not? It hadn't been reasonable to blame Ji for the Assurance program or the semi-awares; but the hatred returned nonetheless, and I shook my head, trying to clear it.

A gray hair clung to the inside of my vision hood. I pinched it between two fingers and stared at the thing, wondering how it had gotten there and where it had come from, the recognition of what it was making me feel older and giving me phantom pains in my back until I sucked at the bottle, draining it of bourbon and throwing it from the APC into an empty field. *To be in my thirties shouldn't be this horrific,* I figured; how many people my age could point at all the things I'd done and come close to measuring up with their life? Then again, how many people could I tell about what I'd done? None. The depression of having now seen my life from the perspective of near middle age slammed into my brain with the force of a pickup truck, machine-gunning me with questions and doubt, and at the top of my list was the fact that I had no idea what I was doing there. This was a young man's job for guys like Jihoon. The Asian Wars had lit up when North Korea and China teamed against South Korea, at which point mutual defense treaties kicked in to force Japan, Russia, America, and about half of Taiwan to Seoul's defense, just to have more nukes than we could stomach tossed our way. Japan was gone. Taiwan was half-radioactive, the other half cratered beyond recognition when China used its space-based kinetics. So what did we do? We repopulated and went straight to war again in Kazakhstan, this time for rhenium and every other trace metal we could find, this time against our former allies, the Russians, who also had a thirst for resources. And now China was back. We were down in population, not reconstituted for war, and yet war had reconstituted for *us* whether we wanted it or not.

Old age was a hell of a thing, I thought, because it made you see—not what you hoped or what you wanted, but how it *was*. The US wouldn't be coming to Thailand's aid any time soon. Moscow now belonged to the Chinese, who had attacked Russia en masse after we weakened them in Kaz, and what Japanese were left had decided to follow a bunch of psychopathic genetic soldiers trying to make their own death wish come true via the *Gra Jaai*. And the Koreans? *Well*, I figured, *that's what we are here for—to find out what the hell they are doing.* It was funny, though, that we had to go to *Thailand* to find out what Unified *Korea* had up its sleeve. It all stunk to hell, and I was too old for any of it.

Jihoon raised himself on his elbows at the same instant I smelled something foul, the sign that his waste port had opened and sent its filth to spill on the APC deck. I moved away and waved the air in front of my nose.

"Jesus, Chong. Next time ask for a bathroom break."

He pulled his helmet off, grinning. "I feel a hell of a lot better; the castor oil worked. What time is it?"

"I have no idea." The sun had started to approach the mountains in the west, and the eastern horizon had turned a deep purplish color that I had forgotten about; it had been so long that the sight left me speechless for a second, hypnotized by the colors. "I'd say almost five, but I'm too tired to put my hood on and check the chronometer."

Jihoon nodded and gestured for a cigarette. I lit it for him.

"What's it going to be like?"

"What's what like?"

"Out there." He gestured toward the northwest, and my gut churned when I realized that I hadn't factored in their significance when I'd looked at the sun: mountains. We were getting closer now, and tomorrow I'd be back inside. Hidden from the scrutiny of civilization under a green blanket, where death and I had become first cousins.

"It's going to be rough. You know as much as I do, though, and I have no idea if the Thais have borers. Don't know if we'll be above- or belowground."

We ducked at the sound of an explosion and had to look around since it wasn't clear where the blast had come from. A small black cloud rose from far in front of us. Then a second detonation made the APC vibrate, and those damned whistles sounded until the convoy ground to a halt so all the Thai soldiers could jump down and spread out, and we got clear of our vehicle before it veered off the road, repeating the maneuver it had made at the ambush. It crashed down an embankment and disappeared.

Jihoon was about to sprint after them, but I grabbed his arm. "Stay put for this one. Have a cigarette."

"There's a lot of chatter over the radio. Another group of infiltrators; Thai troops from the town ahead of us have encircled Burmese saboteurs and are asking us for the convoy's help."

"So?" I asked. "Then the Thai boys can handle it, and we'll stay here with the trucks. We're close to the mountains here, Chong." I pointed west. "Out there is the bush. You'll get plenty of action once we're in, and I bet you can't even feel it yet."

"Feel what?"

"Eyes. The jungle has 'em, sure as shit. And right now they're watching us, waiting for a taste of our spines, so you don't want to go and get killed or wounded now because it wouldn't do to leave the bush hungry. That wouldn't do at all."

Jihoon just stared at me, probably thinking I was crazy. And maybe I was. But as the sun winked out of sight, you saw the mountains outlined, a long jagged line of black with a tinge of green at the edges that fooled you into thinking they were the only mountains around, but they weren't. These were part of a network—a wide and branching web of the earth's veins, with its heart in the Himalayas—a silent organism with the patience of an entire planet and that hated us, hated me. And we'd be in its grip soon enough.

To our north the explosions continued, punctuated by

plasma flashes and crackling fléchettes, until they died out so we could hear the bugs. They filled the air with a humming kind of music. Mosquitoes buzzed my ears, and I pulled on my vision hood, then buckled my helmet around my skull, finishing by sliding the locking ring in place to get a seal before I powered up my girl's systems one at a time.

"Kristen."

The computer hummed to life. "It's been several months since last we spoke, Lieutenant. Congratulations on your promotion. Systems are all nominal, and records indicate that I had routine maintenance less than one week ago. New hardware detected."

"What?" I asked. *Nothing should have changed.* "What new hardware?"

"Standard tracking device, burst transmitting on random frequencies."

"Can you deactivate it?"

She sounded amused. "Of course, Lieutenant."

"Call me Bug, Kristen. Do it. Deactivate the hardware."

A second later she chimed, "Hardware deactivated. Was there anything else, Bug?"

"Yeah." Jihoon had started talking, and I held up my hand to shut him up for a second. "Geography. Given our current location, I'll need to know how long it will take to get to a place called Nu Poe, near the Burmese border to our west."

"One moment." Kristen went silent and then came back immediately, a light green map opening on my heads-up with a red line tracing a path. "Your current location is the town of Mae Poen, and straight line distance to Nu Poe is approximately fifty-three miles. Road distance is 133 miles, which factors in elevation changes in the Thai Highlands."

"Thanks, Kristen. And can you do real-time translation of Thai and Burmese into English?"

"Of course, Bug. And as we did in Kazakhstan with Russian, I can route my voice to output speakers and relay your English answers into those languages."

I sighed, grateful that on the line I wouldn't have to rely on Jihoon to understand what people were saying. "One last thing: scan the guy wearing type-ninety-seven armor next to me, look for tracking devices or any anomalous transmissions."

"Of course." She did it and chimed back in, "An identical tracking device located at the base of his backpack unit in the fuel cell compartment."

"Thanks. Go ahead and power down. And Kristen?"

"Yes, Bug?"

"You are so damn sexy."

"Thank you."

I nearly lost it while ripping my helmet off and then yanked the hood from my head, spitting once my mouth had cleared. *"Assholes."*

"What's wrong?" Ji asked.

"Data. Information. It's all those pencil-necked bean counters care about, Chong, all they freakin' know, and so it's not enough that they bug our houses. Now they have to bug our suits." He said he still didn't get it, and I explained what Kristen had told me, making him turn so I could dig the thing from his backpack and toss it into the field.

"It doesn't matter," said Jihoon. "I don't care if they know where we are or not, and besides"—he pointed northward—"it sounds like the APCs are on their way back, and it's getting dark."

He was right. I'd forgotten so many things about Thailand that it made me wonder if my mind really was starting to slip because once the sun dipped under the mountains that was it. Night came almost immediately afterward. Ahead we saw the flickering lights of a town, which lit the valley in a yellow glow and glittered with the colors of neon signs. It was almost surreal. A moment ago, a firefight had raged to the town's south, and even now the fires still burned in fields, with flames that leaped upward in orange flashes. But the neon made everything happy.

Tomorrow, I thought. Tomorrow I'd see whether I was too old for this kind of op or not.

We drove toward the jungle just before sunrise. A dirt road wound its way through the hills outside town, where we saw a long line of Thai observation bunkers spaced a few hundred meters apart and strung together with multiple rows of bots whose autocannons pointed northwest toward the Highlands. The bots were ruthless. Concrete mushroom caps equipped with infrared cameras, motion sensors, and shape detectors, they would pop up at the first sign of a living organism and check for a friendly response from anyone or anything approaching. If you were supposed to be there, your suit computer would ping the appropriate encrypted response. If you weren't supposed to be there, they'd open fire. Their presence meant that somewhere below us were underground tunnels where the bots' ammunition was stored and where Thai soldiers would live, in tunnel fortifications that had been prepared as a second line of defense against invasion from Burma, and I was glad to not be going down into the deep.

When we reached the checkpoints through the bunker line, a group of Thai boys scurried around the vehicles and yelled at the troops or drivers, until they caught sight of me and Jihoon; then the entire lot converged around the slow-moving APC, so reckless that I thought one or two might get sucked under one of the huge wheels. They laughed and pointed.

"Hey, American, got money?" one cried. This set off a chorus of different efforts.

"Candy? You got candy?"

One of them slapped two fingers against his lips. "Smoke?"

"Sure," I said. I dug a pack from my pouches and ripped it open so the cigarettes spilled into my hand, then threw them as hard as I could, watching the kids run up to the edge of the safe zone, which had been marked by a series of yellow stakes. Some of the cigarettes landed beyond. You saw their little minds working at the problem, thinking that if they moved fast enough or slow enough or stayed low or jumped high, maybe they could get the cigarettes and dash back to safety before any bots opened fire.

"Number one," I yelled. "American cigarette, number one. Burmese, number ten, right?"

And we were through the checkpoint without even having to stop, without having even seen anyone manning the guard stations. Only those kids existed. And to them, a few cigarettes were just as good as bhat and could make anything happen, would give them something to trade back in town and render everything greasy and paved, so that within ten minutes, after the bunkers spat us onto the other side, I smiled. In that moment I was happy; the kids had reminded me of Phillip, and Ji scowled at me—either for giving cigarettes to the kids or for sending them so close to the bot field—but I figured to hell with him, because those kids didn't care that they weren't old enough to smoke, and if they decided not to trade them, but to light up for themselves, so what? Smoking was the least harmful thing to them in this place, and maybe they needed cigarettes more than I did.

But the happiness didn't last long. Our line of vehicles crept upward along the road, weaving its way through boulders and elephant grass, and then we climbed a steep hill. Once we crested it, the jungle spread out before us, an endless rampart of dark and light greens so that it made me wonder if my goggles had somehow been filtered, letting nothing in *except* green, a color that made my stomach churn and wish we were back in Bangkok. Each moment brought me closer, the jungle looming larger. I looked for signs of life, like birds or monkeys, and then listened for any sounds that might suggest the jungle wasn't a crypt and that at least some animals could exist in such a place, but the one sound I heard was of engines growling, struggling to make it up the road, which had gotten steeper.

Jihoon pulled his camera out again and started snapping pictures.

"Amazing," he said. "I've never seen anything like this."

I opened another bottle. "I have."

"How do you even fight in that stuff, Bug? I mean we simulated jungle warfare, but this is insane. It's so thick you can't see ten feet."

"It's so thick," I started, but the first bourbon of the morning burned my throat and mouth, making me pause before finishing my thought. "That you can't see the guy walking in front of you, even if you're marching crotch to ass."

"What are those?" Jihoon asked.

I looked where he pointed and saw a series of poles arranged in random fashion on either side of the road but couldn't bring them into focus until I'd pulled my vision hood on. The goggles zoomed in. Each pole held a corpse in varying stages of decomposition, some new and some already bare skeletons that had started to fall apart at their joints, and at the top of each, a sign in Thai had been painted on a wooden plank.

Jihoon had also pulled his hood on. "The signs say that 'no man or woman can come further unless their souls are prepared.'"

I shook my head and took another drink. "Satos."

"What's it supposed to mean?"

"That we're getting close. But not close enough to button up. I'm not sure if we'll get there by tonight or not, but I'd hate to have to spend a night in the open, in the jungle, and I'd bet these guys feel the same way. I just hope they don't drive off the road in a hurry to get us to Nu Poe before sunset."

Jihoon lifted his carbine and checked its power level. "I'm beginning to see what you meant, Bug. About the jungle."

"What about it?"

"It's spooky."

"That it is, Chong," I said, taking another swig. "That it *is*."

The road snaked toward the bush through the rows of bodies until at last it hit the first trees and took us inside, and I glanced once over my shoulder, back into Thailand, to see the hole we had entered disappear around a bend at the same time the light dimmed, huge trees blocking every part of the sky. The bush made you feel abandoned, cut off, like someone had just slammed and locked the door behind you. It was dead quiet. Leaves absorbed the engine sounds and made it feel as though everything was muffled, and the air became heavier now that the trees blocked any breeze, so that climate control could barely keep the heat out, and I began to feel as though there wasn't any air, that we had just entered an underwater nightmare. I lifted my carbine and shook it, making sure the fléchettes ran free in their flexi. Then I adjusted my hood to make sure it was snug and buckled my helmet on. Jihoon noticed and did the same. The troop truck in front of us had been packed with Thai soldiers, and without having seen us, the Thais also helmeted up or sealed their battle suits' hoods tight around their shoulders before they all rested their weapons on the truck sides, pointing them outward.

"Is anything wrong?" Jihoon asked, his voice sounding loud in my helmet speakers.

"Yeah."

"What?"

"We're in the jungle."

"So what?" he asked.

"So now everything's wrong. Shut up. We're not that far from the Burmese border, and I need to concentrate."

SIX

Secret War

The convoy had stopped, and now people were shouting. Thai soldiers jumped from their vehicles and scattered as far into the jungle as they dared, which wasn't far at all, and most of them kept checking to make sure they could see the road after dropping into the foliage. It was noon, but you wouldn't have been able to tell. Banyan trees crowded us on either side, their roots snaking far enough onto the road that for the last four hours the APC had bounced so hard that I'd had to hold on for fear of being thrown off. Branches crowded overhead. The limbs scraped the highest of the convoy's vehicles and sent clusters of roots into the clay so that they looked like tentacles reaching for something that rested far belowground and lent an alien feeling to an already growing sensation that we had landed on another planet. I jumped from the vehicle and motioned for Jihoon to follow.

By the time we reached the front of the column, the convoy commander, a lieutenant, had already asked for the two of us, and as soon as Ji rounded the front APC, the guy started jabbering—so quickly that I couldn't activate

Kristen in time for a translation. He sounded terrified. Kristen translated Jihoon's response in my ear, her voice a perfect imitation of his.

"We can't stay *here*," he said.

"My men will not move forward. Not under these conditions."

"What do you mean? I can't understand half of what you're saying, and the other half doesn't make any sense."

"*These are madmen*," the lieutenant shouted. "The *Gra Jaai* will kill us just as soon as they would kill a Burmese. I'm radioing this in."

"How will you even turn around? *And what the hell got you so spooked? Radio what in?*"

"*That!*" The lieutenant pointed farther up the road. "Those men went missing from the convoy when we were ambushed on the first day."

Three Thai soldiers had been tied to a banyan tree with wire. Even from this distance you saw that their throats had been slit and signs—like the ones we had seen before entering the jungle—dangled from their waists; I zoomed in so Kristen could see the writing.

"The signs all say the same thing," Kristen told me. "*Spies*. And Lieutenant?"

"Call me Bug, Kristen."

"Yes, Bug. The Thai officer is radioing to the rest of his men to reverse down the road. He is taking the convoy back to Bangkok."

I pushed Jihoon out of the way and swung my arm, slapping the side of the Thai lieutenant's helmet so he fell, sprawling facedown across the road and dropping his carbine. I knelt on his back. The man's backpack unit was simple, and his radio light blinked as it sent bursts upward through the canopy, invisible pigeons that by now could have given away our position to either Burmese infiltrators or the *Gra Jaai* themselves, but then the satos already knew where we were, and the bodies had been a message: the mayor and his wife had been innocent. It took less than a second to deactivate his radio while the lieutenant struggled.

I yanked him to his feet and slapped him again. "You don't turn this convoy around *unless we tell you to.*" Kristen sounded like she had put just the right amount of anger in the words, but it was hard to tell.

"The *Gra Jaai* are crazy," he said. I heard him sobbing now and wondered how old the guy was. "They'll kill us all. This isn't my first time on a supply run; I know what I'm talking about."

"Well, *I* don't know what you're talking about. Explain it to me."

The lieutenant removed his helmet and vision hood, then wiped sweat and tears from his face. "Up there, the *Gra Jaai* are in charge, not the Army. We supply them— on orders from the King himself—but once we enter the mountains, it's like entering another country, a nightmare. They fear nothing. Can do anything they want."

"Were those men," I asked, pointing at the bodies, "spies? Could they have given away the convoy information?"

He looked down. "They were new to my unit. I didn't know them well. None of us did; they didn't really try to make friends with the other men and disappeared last night."

"Then they got *exactly* what they deserved. Gear up, Lieutenant. Get this convoy moving forward; we can't waste any time unless you like the thought of sleeping out here tonight."

"I am not moving another centimeter forward."

I sympathized with the guy. He hated satos more than I did, and now that I saw his face, I knew he was younger than Jihoon—maybe hadn't been exposed to the horrors of a bush war until recently—and from behind me I sensed that the bodies had an effect on Ji too because he shifted nervously, the sound of his carbine clicking every time it changed hands. But there wasn't time for any of this.

I pointed my carbine at the lieutenant's forehead and clicked onto the general frequency so everyone could hear Kristen's translation. "We're on a priority mission and have to make it to the line today; you know it and I know it and nobody in Bangkok will mind if I shoot you here. So get this thing going, Lieutenant. Forward. *Now*."

By now, all the vehicle engines were off, and I realized just how weird it had gotten. Silent. When it got that quiet, bad things happened, and the jungle secreted anticipation, holding its breath until the shit started flying, the infinite shades of green surrounding us with a sickening sensation of being in a place that was part fun house, part nightmare. You just knew that the *Gra Jaai* loved the jungle and bathed in its heat, wiped their asses with the morning fog that settled in low spots. They breathed the bush. Out here there were worse things than the Burmese Army, things that nobody wanted to see, and while I waited for the lieutenant to tell his men to load up and push on, it occurred to me that the *Gra Jaai* had taken root in the deep green the same way the banyans had; if I were a Burmese infiltrator, I would never go here alone, never with anything less than a platoon or maybe a battalion. Finally the lieutenant nodded and pulled his helmet on.

"Let's get our gear," I said to Ji. "From here on out, we

ride on the lieutenant's APC so we can keep an eye on things."

"Even the Thai troops are scared of them," he said. "Of the satos."

I nodded, and we jogged back to grab our gear and then made our way to the column's front. Jihoon helped me onto the lead vehicle.

"Are you scared of them?" I asked. "The *Gra Jaai*?"

"I don't know what I am. It makes sense that three men from the convoy would have been responsible for the ambush, though. On the other hand, who's going to pay for the fact that the Thais screwed up and killed the mayor?"

The lieutenant's APC jerked forward, and I risked taking my helmet off for a cigarette, breathing the smoke as deeply as I could and then holding it there, willing it to calm my nerves. "Why should anyone pay, Chong? It's just war."

The trucks behind us kicked up red dust and slid from side to side until their wheels found traction, taking all of us farther into the bush. Closer to *Margaret*. The convoy slowed to a crawl a few miles later, and one by one the vehicles turned onto a rocky track, even more narrow and rutted than the road we left, and we headed up the side of a steep mountain so that at times my legs—which hung off the APC's side—dangled over near-vertical drop-offs. Other times you couldn't see the cliffs because the jungle was too thick, but they were there, and I knew it the same way I knew that we were being watched; the girls were in the bush, and I didn't need sniffers to tell me because it made sense that they'd want to observe, to gauge our reaction to finding the Thai soldiers. Satos and the bush were synonymous.

The deeper we went, the hotter it got.

*   *   *

It didn't matter that we were aboveground; out there, the canopy formed a different kind of subterrene. At one point the road narrowed and vegetation formed a tunnel through which we pushed at five kilometers an hour, branches cracking as the APCs squeezed through the shadows and into a dim kind of green light that made everything look sickly. We heard firing in the distance. Not plasma weapons, but a deep rumbling that I hadn't forgotten since the last time I was there, when ancient artillery—of a caliber that sounded immense—drove everyone into holes. As we neared the line, vibrations shook the branches around us and every once in a while a limb would crash and the convoy would stop to clear the road, making the last part of the journey a crawl. It was just before sundown. But even though the sun must have still been visible from other parts of the country, where we were the road had gone dark so that my thermal imaging kicked in, changing the scene from green to varying shades of gray and white; I felt better when the green faded into memory.

On thermal, the banyans looked even more alien, things that had landed from above to spread gray limbs over rocks, cracking boulders at the roadside to send fragments into the path of our wheels. Nothing resisted their roots. Even if it took a lifetime, the trees had the patience to wait infinitely, however long they needed to destroy rock and earth. Our motors whined and spat, echoing against the distant mountains while we tried our best to stay on the trail, bouncing over the rocks until the path emptied into a clearing and dumped us in front of a structure where everyone dismounted. The sight of it made me shiver—an ancient Buddhist temple that had been partially destroyed by engineers who'd mined a circular, ten-meter hole through its side.

A sign over a main tunnel entrance said *Supply* in English, but Kristen translated the Thai anyway, and I watched as the soldiers began stringing hoses into the tunnel's mouth, disappearing as they went to hook up with underground storage tanks. It would be some time before the tankers drained their loads. Other Thais began ferrying cases and crates from the trucks, and at first there was no sign of anyone manning the place, but as the men moved their materiel, a single sato emerged to lounge against the temple wall so she could watch and light a cigarette.

"She's staring at you," said Jihoon, and his voice crackled on helmet speakers.

It was true. The girl looked at me as she inhaled, a white spark from her cigarette obscuring everything except the eyes and a bizarre insouciance, out of place in our current surroundings and with artillery still impacting a klick up the mountainside. "Maybe she likes my helmet."

"You ever think that maybe those chicks are psychic?"

"Are you nuts?"

Ji chuckled, and in the distance we heard the impacts stop, a sudden silence that made things even creepier.

"I'm serious. Like she knows who you are and what you do for a living."

"She knows what we are because we're wearing modern US armor and stick out like a sore thumb. So sure. If that's your definition of psychic."

He motioned with his carbine at the entrance. "We'll have to go in there, Bug. Once they've finished shifting supplies."

"I know."

"I'm just sayin'. Don't freak out or anything."

The tunnel was like none I'd ever seen, and it struck me as blasphemous that they'd bored through such an ancient structure, a tremendous monument consisting of eight-foot rock slabs that interlocked seamlessly; much of the temple had become so overgrown with vines that it seemed to have sprung from the earth as half tree and half stone, belonging there, and even the patches that weren't shrouded in stranglers had gone black with mold. Then again, tunneling through it made perfect sense. To the satos, the *temple* would have been blasphemous, a monument to their God's competitor, and so taking a fusion borer and watching it melt its way through the stone would have brought smiles to their faces, and for all I knew it was why the one watching me was so happy right now.

When the trucks finished unloading, the troops loaded back into their vehicles, which managed to turn around and head back onto the road that had brought us.

"I thought they'd stay here for the night," said Jihoon.

"Guess the lieutenant would rather risk going over a cliff or getting ambushed than spend a night with these chicks."

"Or in this *place*."

"And I can't say I blame them." I slung my carbine and headed toward the tunnel entrance, just as the barrage started again, bringing shells closer this time. The girl stopped us before we could enter.

"Who are you?" she asked.

"American advisers. We're supposed to report to Major Remorro."

She didn't say anything at first and just stared some more. Then the chick ground her cigarette on her armored forearm and motioned with her carbine that we should walk ahead. "We'll see."

Jihoon cleared his throat, and I tried sending him a psychic message to just shut up but knew it wouldn't do any good.

"What's your name?" he asked. When she didn't answer, he tried again, but the chick wasn't about to talk with us, and it pissed me off.

"I think I recognize her, Chong."

"Yeah?"

"Yeah. She looks just like a hundred other engineered betties I've wasted."

But she was cool. The girl never even breathed faster as far as I could tell and just kept walking behind us, staring beyond and in front, her eyes not needing infrared or light amplification to see in what must have been near total darkness. Our feet splashed in a shallow stream of water that grew deeper as we advanced, the tunnel floor sloping downward so that with each step it was as though the pressure increased, rock overhead getting thicker and heavier. Finally, the main tunnel opened into a large chamber—a hangar—and overhead lighting forced our vision kits back to normal.

Before I knew what had happened, the sato behind me pushed us to the ground while six others jumped out on either side, stripping us of our weapons and pressing their carbines against the back of my helmet so that I couldn't move my head.

"What is this?" I said, getting even more pissed off. "We're here on orders to meet with a Major Remorro."

I couldn't see the girl who answered. "You're Special Forces. *American*."

"So?"

"So we can't use you here."

I closed my eyes. It was funny, but at that moment when I thought it was over, there wasn't any fear but there wasn't any peace either, just a sense of amazement because it had all happened in a few seconds and left me wondering: Would it hurt? What did dying *feel* like? I sensed that the girls had all tensed in preparation to squeeze off bursts into our heads, but then someone ran up to us shouting.

"They're here to see me," the guy pleaded, but I couldn't see him. "Jesus, do we have to go through this every time one of my guys shows up? They're number one, not here for genetics; number one, I swear to God."

"Don't say *God* ever again," the one behind me said.

"OK, but I swear these guys are number one; they're not here for you or your sisters."

Silence. I lifted my head, pushing against their carbines so I could get a better look, but one of them kicked me, jamming my faceplate into wet rock, after which they let us up. I watched as the group sauntered away in silence with carbines perched on their shoulders. The man who'd saved us helped me to my feet, then waited for Jihoon and me to collect our gear before shaking hands.

"Major Remorro, Special Forces adviser to the Thai Army."

I pulled my headgear off and grinned. "We always get such a warm reception up here?"

"This?" The major glanced at the girls and whistled. "That was nothing. You should see them when they capture a Mimi."

"Mimi?" Jihoon asked.

"Myanmar troops," Remorro explained. "The Burmese Army, the Tatmadaw."

Major Remorro was tall and so thin that with his helmet off it looked as though he could wriggle out of his armor through the neck ring, and you almost heard his arms and legs thumping against the insides of his carapace. He looked like he was in pain. A thin beard grew from his face, and his head was bald, shaved, so that my focus shifted to the eyes, a pair of glassy ones that saw everything and around which dark circles had formed to make the guy look half–beaten up. It was a vacant look I recognized at once—either he was sick, exhausted, or mentally gone, and maybe all three.

"Follow me," the major said. "And hurry up before they change their mind."

He led us through the hangar, where we wove our way through countless APCs covered with dust from never having been used, and stacks of crates and supplies took up every spare inch so that we had to wriggle our way between them before the major led us to a wide exit tunnel leading deeper under the mountain. Deeper into rock. On our way we passed more of the *Gra Jaai*. The dim blue of combat lights made their faces look pale, but most of them were men with a few Asian women, and all had dark stains on their chins. They spat on the tunnel floors. Their eyes were half-glazed and watched us with a passing interest that showed no understanding of who or what we were.

"What's wrong with them?" I asked.

The major glanced at one. "A lot of the *Gra Jaai* take drugs in addition to chewing betel nut. To get closer."

"Closer to what?" asked Jihoon.

"To her. To perfect. Who the hell knows for sure, but welcome to the world's deepest crap hole because you've stepped into it now."

I glanced at another one, a Japanese-looking woman who smiled up at me as she sprawled along the tunnel floor, half submerged in the stream of water and waste that ran down its center. "Closer to Margaret?"

The major shook his head. "To Catherine the Eternal, the maker of the one path. You assholes have a lot to learn. Now shut the hell up before you get us all killed."

The deeper we went, the tighter I wound, and soon water dripped from above, pattering on our helmets so that it sounded like rain; at the same time it made our footing slippery and the walls glistened in the dim lighting. This was like no tunnel I'd seen. While on the one hand everything looked disorganized and filthy, on the other you could tell that this was the look of war, of a place and people who had lived with it for years, and so while filth accumulated, it was a sign of having decided to spend time on more important things instead of cleaning up. I warned myself not to underestimate the inhabitants. We were rubes here, and my face was hot with shame—of having thought that I had known the bush. I did know it. But since then the bush had married with subterrene, and this was their deformed child, a kind of mutant and decrepit earthworm that had swallowed me whole, and this was its guts.

Eventually the major led us into a bunker, through a one-meter tunnel that forced us to crawl for at least five minutes, and by the time we exited, my knees ached to the point where I had trouble standing. With the exception of us and the major, the bunker held one occupant—just as skinny and pale as Remorro.

He grinned at us from around a long clay pipe, its thick smoke filling the tiny area. "Welcome to our little corner of hell, Lieutenants. I'm Captain Orcola. You two can have the top racks."

The major collapsed on one of four bunks without removing his armor. Other than racks the room held a pair of chairs and a desk, on top of which lay computer after computer, and multiple video screens that showed views of the jungle somewhere far above. Jihoon peeled his helmet and hood off and glanced at me. We stood there for a moment, the artillery above shaking tiny clouds of rock dust from ten feet overhead.

"There's no exit tunnel," I said. "Nothing except the one we came in."

Remorro nodded, his eyes already shut. "Yeah."

"So what if it collapses behind us?"

"Then it collapses. Now if you don't mind, Lieutenant, I'd like to get some shut-eye. There's plenty of time to get acquainted in the morning."

"If there is a morning," Orcola added.

Jihoon and I stowed our gear in a corner, and when he began peeling off his armor, I stopped him.

"Why?" he whispered.

"Because we're on the line now. Jack into the waste port every few hours and you never take it off from here on out, except your helmet."

"That's right," said Orcola. "Last night we had about a hundred Burmese infiltrators make it almost all the way to our command bunker, about half a klick from here. It's not a great war, but—"

"It's the only one we've got," Remorro finished. It sounded as if he had spoken the words in his sleep, and Jihoon rubbed his hand through his hair, wiping off the water that had already dripped onto him from the leaking roof.

"How are we supposed to sleep on the top racks?" I asked. "The mattresses are soaked, and this whole place leaks."

"Ain't this five star?" Orcola asked, laughing. He finished his pipe and knocked it against the metal bunk, dropping the ashes to the floor where they hissed in a puddle. "Wear your helmets or use a poncho. Two ponchos work better, though: one to rest your head on and the other to cover it so you don't get wet or gnawed by rats."

"Rats?" Ji asked.

"Some people call them rats." Orcola rolled over so we couldn't see his face and then pulled a dark green plastic sheet over his head. "Others call them dinner. You get used to the taste eventually."

Jihoon glanced at me once more, and I grinned. "We don't want to go back to those days."

Ji shook me awake the next day. By the time I got my helmet off, the room had filled with so much tobacco smoke that it was difficult to breathe let alone see, but I lit up a cigarette anyway to get rid of my last dream—that I'd lain in bed forever, eaten by fungus and mold as warm water dripped over my chest and legs.

Major Remorro turned on a holo map and pointed at it with a clay pipe, identical to the one the captain held. "We're here," he said, pointing to a green dot in the middle of a long line of green dots; solid or dashed lines connected each one. "And this is the Thai border defense network, which consists of underground strong points and bunker complexes like this one, connected in some places by trench lines."

"So the border is completely defended," said Ji. "How are infiltrators making it through?"

"Don't kid yourself; it's a long border, and I said they were only connected in *some* places. Most of the gaps are filled with cameras, motion sensors, and basically anything electronic we could put in there to detect it when the Mimis try to cross. But there are gaps wide enough for a division to move through."

"What's the main Burmese objective?" I asked.

"Up until recently, they wanted this." He punched at the map controls so another dot appeared to our south and within Thailand, just a few kilometers from the Burmese border. "A minor gold and copper mine with some trace metals. It's one of the few working mines in southeast Asia with decent reserves."

"And now?"

Remorro clicked the map off and pulled at his pipe before answering. "Now they're getting bolder. That ambush you encountered a couple of days ago never would have happened last month, and it looks like they've decided to ignore the Thai mine completely. With the arrival of a Chinese expeditionary force, we're guessing that they're planning on an eventual invasion."

I nodded and thought about what I'd seen, realizing that if the Chinese ever concentrated at a single point, the line would be almost useless. With so few underground complexes and so much unprotected border, the Chinese would almost be able to choose their entry and stroll through without having to worry about resistance until reaching the secondary defense line we'd encountered on our way up. *But,* I thought, *has that even been occupied?*

"Who's manning the line? *Gra Jaai* and Thai Army?"

Both men laughed before the major leaned forward and blew smoke in my face, grinning as he spoke. "Thai Army? Who's that?"

"Listen," Orcola explained, "you have to understand something. Not everybody in Bangkok shares the King's love for satos and the *Gra Jaai,* especially generals in the Thai Army who used to be the royal favorites—if you catch my drift. In fact, the American advisers to the Royal Army HQ have one job as their primary mission: to try and screw the satos over and find a way to make the King hate them."

"But the Royal Army is at least supplying you, right?"

"If you call it that." Major Remorro leaned back in his chair and waved at the space where the holo map used to float. "That map is misleading. The supplies they give us are enough to keep us running, but not enough if we want to push into Burma. It's the one way they can keep some kind of leash on these girls. Outposts not manned by the *Gra Jaai* are manned by Karen mountain people, rebels against the Burmese government, and although they're ruthless as hell, it took us nearly a year to teach them armor and Maxwell carbine fundamentals. They're not cowards. They're just a little overwhelmed at the moment."

Captain Orcola nodded. "We're barely holding on. It's like the Stone Age out here, and something is up because last week a sato patrol came back with combatant prisoners."

"So?" asked Jihoon. "Why's that so odd?"

"Because the *Gra Jaai* don't *take* prisoners," he said, "unless they're civilians. If these satos weren't on the line, Bangkok would have been speaking Burmese years ago, and holding them back has taken a level of violence that you guys haven't even begun to imagine. Hell. These chicks and their human units are so badass that their atrocities have atrocities."

My helmet had been off for a few minutes, and already the hair on my head had soaked through with the damp but it felt good in the bunker's heat, which had been born from radiation and a geothermal gradient that made everything warmer with each meter downward you went. Drops ran the length of my neck. They slid into my under-suit and along my back so that I fought the urge to peel the ceramic off and scratch at them, the sensation of water making me want a shower more than anything. But at least in our bunker, the jungle had lost its hold. The kilometer of overhead rock separated me from the banyans and strangle vines, from the snakes and insects—spies and sappers the bush used to wage constant psyops on my brain, making it crawl with uncertainty. It took all my strength to keep my thoughts on target and on the conversation because they just wanted to turn back to Phillip or to Wheezer. To anything except this place.

"What's the *good* news?" I asked.

The major shook his head. "We thought *you* were bringing some. You want to tell us why you're here?"

"The US is putting the Germline program back online—pulling production ateliers out of mothball and starting construction of new ones. They're going to try and get back onto a war footing so they can stop the Chinese advance into Thailand using new genetic units."

Both men stared at me. The air in the room had become still, and I sucked on my cigarette, hoping it would prevent the onset of a bad headache, then drank a mouthful of water while I waited for them to respond.

"There isn't time," Remorro said. "That'll take years, and there's no way they'd get here in time."

"I know. That's why we're here. We need to talk with Margaret because SOCOM needs her help, and they want her to ally with us—stop the Chinese invasion if she can."

"Jesus Christ." Remorro stood and leaned against the wall, pressing his forehead against it. "They don't understand shit."

"What's the problem?" Jihoon asked.

"The *Gra Jaai* aren't just here for a tour or rotation, and this isn't some military op for them. It's a home. Nu Poe is holy ground, the headquarters for their freakin' religion, and they have everything here—families, children, underground schools for the kids, and training tanks for potential converts. Everything. So of course they're going to try and stop the Chinese. But it doesn't matter how well they fight or how dedicated they are, and the last thing they'll do is negotiate some kind of deal to work with us or US forces. There isn't any way to stop the freakin' Chinese whether you talk to Margaret or not; *don't they get that?*"

Orcola nodded and pointed at me with his pipe. "And you better not tell these chicks about production ateliers. I have no idea how that will sit with them because they're *all* freakin' crazy."

"I still need to talk with her," I said. "Can you arrange it?"

Major Remorro sat back down and relit his pipe. "They think you're here to kill Margaret."

"I'm not here to kill her; I just want to talk. I mean, what the hell are you guys doing up here anyway? The *Gra Jaai* are in charge, and there's no Thai Army, and from what you say it sounds like the satos won't accept

US help anyway. So who the hell are you *advising* in this place?"

"Nobody. And other than radioing in occasional sit-reps and being the eyes and ears of the Royal Thai Army and SOCOM, I have no idea why we're here," the major said. "No fucking clue. So yeah, smart guy. We'll take you to see Margaret, and you can see for yourself how crazy this place is. And then maybe *you* can give these chicks some god-damned *advice*." He and Captain Orcola stood, slipping into their vision hoods and helmets. "Do exactly what we do, and don't say a damn word until I tell you to. Follow us."

Orcola knocked his pipe clean and slipped it into a loop of webbing on his chest. "*This* oughta be fun."

We squirmed through the entrance tunnel and back into the main one, which took us farther into the complex, and it wasn't long before I got lost; the place was like a small city. Remorro led us through underground villages where children of the *Gra Jaai* squealed at seeing four Americans and then ran to hide. Nobody trusted us. The kids, even the girls, were bald and all dressed in white pajamas, and at first something bothered me, but it took a few minutes to figure out what was wrong, and when I did it chilled me to think what the *Gra Jaai* might be doing; the kids all looked under the age of ten. None of them was even close to their teens, and there were even fewer old people—a gap that underscored the sensation something was off. The two or three aging men and women we *did* see sat in front of automated looms and sewing machines, putting together uniforms or repairing ripped undersuits, and none of them paid us any attention. So there was just one conclusion to draw: everyone between ten and fifty was either dead, on the line to fight, or in the training tanks.

The major led us to a bank of mining elevators where three men stood guard, their hair clipped into short Mohawks and faces scarred from more wounds than I could count. One of them pointed his carbine at us.

"Go back."

The major pointed at the elevators and bowed his head while speaking in Japanese. "With respect. We need to see the sisters."

"Access to the command bunker is sealed. *Go back*."

"It's an emergency," Remorro insisted, "and it can't wait. Please contact them and ask; the new ones"—he then pointed to me and Jihoon—"have important information about Chinese and American forces."

The man looked at us and took forever to make a decision, finally slinging his carbine over a shoulder and disappearing into one of the mining elevators—small steel cages that ran on cables into a narrow shaft overhead. I looked at Remorro while we waited. Even through the armor you saw him shiver, the plates of his carapace vibrating against the ceramic carbine, and he stooped over so that at first I thought he was continuing to show respect to the remaining *Gra Jaai,* until Remorro burst into a fit of coughing and almost fell over. Orcola wasn't much better off.

"Are you two OK?" I asked.

Remorro tried to straighten but amazingly wound up more stooped than before. "Dysentery."

"Or," said Orcola, "malaria. Or dengue. Pretty much any cruddy tropical disease you can imagine is on the list."

Even over the helmet speakers, Jihoon sounded scared. "Biological warfare?"

"Yeah," said Remorro, "if you call Mother Nature biological warfare. That's the thing. You don't need the manmade stuff to have a real good disease out here because in reality the bush is already one big stinking petri dish, with all the warmth and nutrients you need to get a good epidemic going. The smoking helps, though. And we have some drugs."

"Christ," said Ji, "all you'd need are the right antibiotics and antivirals, and haven't you been vaccinated anyway?"

Orcola shook his head. "Kid, you don't get it. We've been vaccinated. But there are things up here that nobody's heard of, and all our medical supplies get intercepted anyway for the *Gra Jaai* and their war effort."

The thought of it made me cringe. Both men seemed so weakened with disease that I wondered if it would be a good idea to stay suited for our entire trip to the front, to keep at bay an entire universe of invisible biothreats that hovered all around us. Nobody said anything, and what was there to say? In Bangkok, whatever the two had contracted was probably treatable, but out here you managed on your own, and in our silence the remaining *Gra Jaai* guard watched us, grinning. I hated the guy; I stared back at him, fingering the stock of my carbine, and figured he knew what we were saying and that his grin resulted from hatred returned, a wish that disease would take all four of his non–*Gra Jaai* visitors sooner rather than later. If we'd had to wait much longer it wasn't clear what would have happened, but a moment later the elevator returned.

Remorro bowed his head again to the guard who stepped out. "Will they see us?" When the man didn't answer, he motioned us forward. "OK, this is it. We'll go up first. Leave your carbines here, and after our car goes, you two get in the second one and wait a few seconds before hitting the button. When you get there, bow to the girl speaking to us and don't say a word until I give a signal."

I nodded, and they disappeared. A few seconds later Jihoon and I had dropped our carbines to the floor and stepped into a metal cage that rattled into the darkness overhead, and I closed my eyes, not wanting to see rock a few feet from my face, the streamers of water looking like white strings that would encase us in a spiderweb of heat. The cage screeched. In places it scraped against the rock and promised to become stuck, trapping us there forever, but I consoled myself that even if the *Gra Jaai* wouldn't want to waste time to rescue *us,* they'd have to if they wanted to recover their *elevator.* Finally, it dumped us into another bunker somewhere above, where monitor screens covered every wall, and holo stations blinked and shifted to portray different aspects of the defensive line.

There was one sato; she spoke with Remorro while about thirty *Gra Jaai* women jabbered into radios or worked at their computers in a dance of strategy that neither Jihoon nor I had time to grasp.

"Drugs and therapeutics are reserved for those who have seen the tanks," she said, "and aren't for the nonbred who killed so many of my sisters. Catherine's blood is on your hands. And don't forget that there's another way to get drugs, Major."

Remorro had removed his helmet and shook his head. "I'm in no shape for joining the *Gra Jaai*."

"The Karen don't require medicine for disease," she said, sounding disgusted. "Why should you?"

"Because the Karen are natives. They have their own

remedies and immunity to the local stuff. If you can't spare any medicine, then tell the Thai Army to relieve me, have them send a replacement."

She laughed, and the sound sent a chill up my spine; it was empty of joy, and hearing it reminded me they were pseudohuman things—almost people, but not quite.

"We can't do that either," she said.

"But *why*? You know the agreement, that I can't be relieved without your or Margaret's endorsement. And your people are stealing the medicine that's supposed to be reserved for us."

"Why keep you here? Because we like you and think you can be so much more, if only given the right motivation." The girl looked at me, and I froze, embarrassed for having almost stepped back. "You are the two from Bangkok," she said, "the ones with news from America."

"Take your helmet off," said Remorro. "This is Lucy, Margaret's second-in-command."

I did, then peeled my vision hood away, staring at the girl without blinking and annoyed with the thought of having to show respect. "What's your serial number?" I asked.

The entire room went silent. Other women stopped talking into their radios and looked up, and if anyone had asked me why I'd done it—why I'd said something that was sure to piss her off—there wasn't any answer other than it *felt* right. This was a sato. I was goddamned if I'd treat one with deference after I'd hunted them for so long and seen them rotting in terror, and the way she'd treated Remorro and the way he'd just taken it...I'd never thought a Special Forces operator could sink so far. But what really got me was that I couldn't stop seeing

Wheezer as she spoke, couldn't get the image of him out of my head.

"It's OK," Lucy said, smiling as she waved the *Gra Jaai* women back to work. "I like this one, Remorro. Maybe I'll let *him* replace you."

"Where's Margaret?" I asked.

"Jesus, Lieutenant," Remorro pleaded, "shut your damn mouth."

"I said it was OK!" The girl moved so quickly that her hand disappeared one second, then reappeared the next to hold a knife against Remorro's neck. "And to answer the lieutenant's question, I can't remember my serial number. Before I let you see Margaret, I'll have to know why you want her."

"The last of your sisters I killed were in Australia. Before that, I got one in Turkmenistan. She begged me not to take her life and died just like a scared little girl. A coward."

"You like killing us?" she asked.

"I *really* like killing you."

The girl leaped without another word, diving toward my right leg in a roll, but I'd been ready for it and my adrenaline kicked in, ridding me of the aches that had racked me a minute before. I spun on my left foot, bringing my right around in a kick that landed against her temple. She rose and shook her head from the blow as I drew my own knife.

Neither of us spoke as we circled. It was the first time I got a close look at her and saw that Lucy's face had been pockmarked with thermal gel burns and that her armor was patched in multiple spots with quick paste—a kind of epoxy that sealed suit breaches in seconds. It didn't faze me that this one wasn't wasting away, and although she was fluid in her movements, suggesting a level of comfort in combat that I hadn't seen in rotting satos, a sense of stillness settled in my gut. She'd win. But maybe I'd get in a lucky shot or two, and what mattered now was that the girl understood I wasn't afraid; I was calm because something told me this was the right thing to do.

Lucy attacked, swinging her knife with precise cuts that slammed into my forearm and chest plates before one stroke flicked upward, slicing open my lower lip. The blood was warm. A strange thought crept in then, almost making me laugh—that with blood dripping down I must have looked just like the *Gra Jaai,* with their chins stained red, marking them as betel nut fanatics.

The fight ended a second later. Lucy attacked again, and I rammed my knife into the joint at her shoulder, intending to rip it out and back away, but the tip stuck when she threw her shoulder back; I lurched forward and stumbled, landing facedown. Lucy knelt on me and yanked my head back, placing the edge of her knife on my throat.

"Why are you here?"

"I told you—to see Margaret."

She dropped the knife and used both hands to grab my head, twisting it slowly; the girl's grip was so strong that she could have pushed both thumbs through my temples, and a second later I screamed, my neck muscles close to the point of tearing.

"Why?" she asked again.

"The US is reopening ateliers to produce more Germline units like you. They're afraid that the Chinese will take Thailand and sent me to speak with her, to convince her to fight and hold the border for as long as she can, maybe until US forces land. I've been ordered not to kill her."

"How long before they come?"

I wanted to scream again but held it in, not about to give her the satisfaction of hearing my agony. "I don't think they'll get here in time. Years, maybe."

"You've been ordered not to take Margaret, but do you want to? Will you kill her anyway?"

I considered that one for a while. It must have been a few seconds, but the pain made it feel like an hour and threatened to destroy my thinking process.

"I don't know," I said. "But *all of you should be dead*."

When she let go, I wondered for a moment if she'd cracked my neck and that *this* was what death was like—a complete release from all pain—so I lay on the floor for a moment just to press my face against the warm rock and convince myself that my body was in one piece. Ji helped me up. Lucy had retreated a few steps and leaned back against a workstation, her body half inside a holo projection, and she stared at me while the blue lines moved across her face.

"It's good," she said.

I rubbed my neck, trying to figure out if anything had been torn. "What's good?"

"To reopen our birthplace. We've been fighting for the Thais for years now, and our numbers have gone down into the low thousands despite the fact that we reproduce. Our children and those of the *Gra Jaai* make reliable soldiers, but even my children are half nonbred, like you, and this is a weakness that they sense the same way you know that your neck hurts. Catherine taught us this, that we are more perfect than you and closer to God. And we need more of the pure. Have they changed anything?"

"I don't know what you mean." Jihoon and the other two watched us intently, and I saw a look of amazement on Remorro's face, his jaw half-open as if he couldn't believe the conversation was taking place.

"I mean production plans. Will the ateliers produce women like us or something else? Something *not* in his image."

I shook my head, not sure if I understood what she was asking, but the question reminded me of the armor schematics that we'd stolen. "I have no idea, no way of knowing. Does your question have anything to do with Project Sunshine?"

Lucy smiled. The whole mission had been wrong from the start, one that still refused to add up and that had already made me kill a young girl, a secretary, and took me from Phillip so that the government had been able to stake their claim on a kid. A child that, given all I felt, *may as well have been mine.* But my reason for asking Margaret had as much to do with obsession as it did with my mission, a need to learn the details of Sunshine because for all I'd given up, it *had* to be an important operation, one that justified the sacrifice. Lucy's smile made me feel closer to the end. She knew something, and waiting to find out if she'd tell us was a kind of slow torture.

"It has everything to do with Project Sunshine," said Lucy.

"What do you know about it?" I asked.

"And what does Korea have to do with it?" asked Jihoon, unable to restrain himself. "Why did they break the Genetic Weapons Convention?"

Lucy thought for a moment, then spat something in Thai to the *Gra Jaai* working closest to her; I had switched off Kristen to conserve power so missed the translation.

"Come with me," she said and made her way to the elevators. "I'll show you why the Koreans—why everyone in southeast Asia—is preparing for war."

Down we went, and whenever I guessed that we'd reached our limit and couldn't go deeper, Lucy found another narrow staircase or a shaft with rusting iron rungs set in the stone so that our boots clanged as we hurried to keep up. Remorro and Orcola had a rough time. The heat grew more intense as we descended, and even when we got deep enough to feel air handling kick in, sending a breeze across our faces, the wind hit as though it had just come straight from an oven and did as little to cool our skin as the undersuits, which couldn't keep pace with the temperature. Bare fluorescent bulbs lit the way. Finally, she led us to a vault door made of dull gray steel, its control panel set in the side of the tunnel, and she entered the code on a black pad before stepping back to let the door slide upward with a loud bang.

A cold fog rolled over us as soon as the hot tunnel air met that of the room beyond, and at first we couldn't see anything since the vapor obscured our vision. The door slammed shut behind us. Eventually, chillers whined overhead, and we breathed with relief at feeling an icy breeze leak into our suits through their open necks, the sensation of standing in front of a freezer making me smile. The fog cleared a few seconds later to reveal a long tubular tunnel, each side of which held banks of tiny steel doors.

"This is a morgue," I said. "But why the security? And why put it so far down where it's hard to cool?"

Lucy reached for the nearest door and opened it, pulling out a thin tray. "Because these are too valuable. These are what Margaret foresaw and are proof of God's word, so we can show the King when we get the chance; proof that the beast is here."

The tray held what looked like a baby. But it wasn't human, and my stomach churned at the same time Jihoon threw up, filling the chamber with a smell that made me feel even more like vomiting. The thing was a human torso about the size of a small child and with a head almost twice the diameter of mine. There were no arms or legs. It hadn't been dismembered, though; the thing had never had arms or legs in the first place, and instead of eyes, bundles of fiber optics stuck from its sockets like sheaves of wheat or twin fountains that shifted in eddies of the air-conditioned space. Flexible tubes ran from holes where its nose and mouth should have been and dangled over the tray's edge where they dripped a light blue fluid.

"What is this?" Remorro asked.

"A Chinese scout. We got thirty of them last week behind Burmese lines when they fell into our tiger traps off the main trail. My girls took their time killing them, but still the things put up a fight. They would have done better against us in the open."

The schematics popped into my head again, the ones we'd taken from the Korean secretary. "Powered armor. These things are genetically designed but live out their lives in powered armor."

"That's right," said Lucy. "And it is as Margaret foretold. She saw this in her dreams, and Catherine warned her that we would encounter a beast, something made by man in the image of himself and not God. The judgment will happen soon."

"Judgment my ass," said Jihoon, who knelt nearby and struggled back to his feet. "This is just some Chinese nightmare, the dream of a people who lived underground for decades because the rest of their country had been nuked. This *thing* is a manifestation of Beijing's insanity."

I leaned closer to it, running my gauntlet along the corpse's stomach, and welcomed an admiration that surprised me because it matched my revulsion. A small black nodule protruded from its throat, just above its chest—a voice synthesizer. The thing had no reproductive organs, nothing that didn't serve some absolute necessity, and although the idea of creating monsters like this registered as insane, I knew the execution had been absolute genius.

"They're perfect warriors," I said.

Lucy nodded. "Yes."

"Not a speck of humanity. No knowledge of anything except living within armor, and they must see *us* as the animals—things so foreign that the sight of us makes them sick."

"Fuck perfect," Orcola said. "Have you lost your mind? *Do you even know what this means?*"

It was as if something had taken over my mind, calming it and nudging me into the zone, the same one within which I killed satos, and I looked at Orcola with pity because he never would have made it as a hunter. There was no value in appraising an enemy the way he'd suggested. Data was what mattered the most, and once you stripped the crap away to expose valuable facts then you could begin targeting weaknesses and vulnerabilities—learn the best ways to kill. The thing in front of us was something brand-new to me, and I imagined that the way I felt now was the way Napoleon might have if he'd been shown an old biplane.

I pointed at the fiber optics. "Range of vision?"

"Full infrared and visible," said Lucy, "in addition to a portion of the UV spectrum. Zoom is handled by the vision ports themselves. A weakness. Damage their vision ports and they are blind, unable to replace the lenses in combat."

"Brain. Twice our capacity?"

"Roughly three times the normal human brain by volume. Our Japanese scientists are studying neurological function and have some time left before tests are complete. They only just began late last night."

I nodded, estimating the body size again. "Their nutrition requirements must be lower than ours."

"All intravenous. A small container carried inside the suit can be refilled externally. So far it looks like a glucose protein mixture, and one container might last three weeks. Power is supplied to the armor servos through a new fuel cell design, rechargeable in specialized wall outlets, in addition to having a much slower solar recharging capability."

"How about variants? Have you seen more than one kind?"

Lucy stared at me and smiled. "We've seen two. One in heavy armor, which is slower but harder to bring down, and a second in much lighter kit, barely armored at all, but which travel at high speeds. About forty kilometers an hour. This one here is of the latter variety, one of their scouts."

I nodded and placed both hands against the tray, leaning forward and over the body to give it one last look. Without any arms or legs it didn't match the armor schematics we'd stolen in Spain; this, I decided, was something altogether different. Unlike our satos, these might feel pain. Girls like Lucy could cut their own nerve impulses and control blood coagulation in the event of a catastrophic wound so they'd continue fighting after losing an arm or leg. The Chinese ones *had* no arms or legs—not ones made of human tissue anyway. So I made a mental note: if I ever got the chance, I'd see if I could make one hurt.

"Brilliant."

"You have got to be shitting me," Ji said.

I looked at him and shrugged. "What?"

"You *admire* these things?"

"It doesn't matter if I admire them or not, Chong. Think about it. We've answered one important question: Why are the Koreans so scared? The Chinese have taken bioengineering one step further and created the ultimate semi-aware—except these aren't semi-aware, they're fully aware. At least as aware as what the Chinese teach them and what they can then learn for themselves on the battlefield. Think of the implications. Who needs artificial intelligence and all the production costs? Now you can grow one of these things and train it to be a drone pilot, a tank commander, or an infantry soldier. Hell, you could even grow them for the Assurance program back home if you wanted to. When they're ready, you just hardwire them into the system they've been designed to handle."

Jihoon looked angry enough to hit me, and for the moment it was as if we were from two different species, and why didn't he get it? This was war. War was about weapons. The ones with the biggest armies also better have the best weapons or their size wouldn't matter a bit, and now China would have both; now it was clear how they'd rolled over the Russians.

"The Koreans," I said, "found out about it and kick-started their own program in an attempt to keep up. They probably were going to keep it a secret from us until they made significant progress; that way they could sell the technology and make a killing."

"These are *human beings,*" Remorro said, horrified. "Not weapons systems."

"No!" Lucy and I said it at the same time, and the thought of sharing an opinion with a sato made me feel sick, but I continued and pointed at her. "Lucy isn't a human, she's a sato." Then I pointed at the thing on the table. "And that isn't a human. It's a tool. Both are manufactured by us, to be used by us and to be discarded by us. *By* humans."

I glared at her as I finished. "Any time we want."

"You," she said, "are exactly what we expect of the nonbred."

I cocked my head—the same way I'd seen so many of them do it—and smiled. "Thank you. Jihoon, get pictures and tissue samples, assuming it's OK with our hostess."

SEVEN

Outbound

We need to speak with Margaret." I checked my suit chronometer and saw it was now late morning, and Lucy had taken us back to the bank of elevators where she stopped, indicating we should go no farther.

She shook her head. "Margaret isn't here; she left two days ago, and we don't know when she'll be back."

At first I was disappointed. But the feeling soon faded because we had already accomplished a key part of the mission and now high gear had kicked in, pushing me forward so that meeting Margaret was the most important thing, more important even than Phillip, the mission a black hole that sucked me in and forced all other concerns to melt into the distance behind me. And the answer I'd given Lucy when she asked me if I would kill her had been true: I didn't know what I'd do to Margaret. That would be the jungle's decision. The bush had taken its hold on me again, awakened instincts long forgotten, and the mountains soaked into my skin, maybe along with the water that dripped onto our heads, a kind of aqueous tincture that acted on the brain. We still didn't know what

Sunshine was, but something told me that Chen did. And Margaret might know more.

"Where did she go?" I asked. "Back to Bangkok?"

"Into Burma. She's chasing a man who killed two of our sisters."

"Chen."

Lucy nodded and stepped into an elevator, sliding the gate shut. "Yes."

"We need to find Chen too before she kills him. Can you tell us where she went so we can follow?" From the corner of my eye, I saw Ji look at me; I didn't want to go into Burma any more than he did, but it was impossible now to resist the urge that had been reborn. This is what the bush did; it filled you with a sense of being able to do anything and combined it with an overwhelming feeling of dread, the combination of which, in turn, made the calculus of a mission easy because staying on the move was all that counted—getting things done so you could get out of the jungle as quickly as you'd gotten in. I wanted Chen dead. But I wanted his information first so we wouldn't have to stay here any longer than necessary. "If she kills him, we could lose important data on Project Sunshine, and we can jump off now—get out of your way and catch up to Margaret."

She shook her head. "Nobody is going into Burma; the line is closed, and even if she finds Chen, Margaret will most likely die on the return. It will be difficult for her to make it through Chinese forces. Margaret left us because she wanted to die."

"Staying here isn't an option," I said, beginning to get angry. "If Chen is in Burma, we *have* to go."

Lucy frowned and paused before pushing the elevator button. She glanced at Remorro. "Take them to the line. A patrol is preparing to leave tonight. We have new weapons that we want to test against the Chinese abominations, and if the lieutenant can survive the mission, he can leave when it's over. I'll send Chen's coordinates to your suit computers before you jump off."

The elevator began sliding up, and I called after her, "How did you find out where Chen is?" but she was already out of earshot.

"You're insane," Remorro said.

"It's our mission."

Jihoon lit a cigarette. "Yeah. But nobody said anything about going into *Burma*."

"Nobody said anything about not going there either, Chong, and if that's where she is, then that's where the shit happens. You can stay here, I don't really care." I slipped my vision hood back on, then my helmet, and gestured toward Remorro and Orcola. "You want to show me where the line is?"

Remorro stared at me for a second and then sighed. "Screw it."

The walk gave me time to think, and I lingered in the rear while Jihoon machine-gunned our escorts with questions, wanting to learn as much as he could about the line. It wasn't luck that tossed this mission into my lap. The fact that the satos revered Catherine as some kind of saint and ascribed Margaret's knowledge of the Chinese genetics to precognition made me laugh at them, not pity the girls, and the brass had known it would be my reaction. They counted on my disdain. There were plenty of other cleanup crews available for the job, but none of them had the kind of hatred I did for satos—an instinctive disgust that the girls were nothing more than frauds in human tissue—which kept me insulated from fear. Now that *they* wanted her to live, though, the brass had made my footing slippery. Dangerous. I wasn't the right guy for the kind of negotiation they needed, and the decision was an order that ran counter to everything I believed, leaving me with an empty feeling that the military had betrayed mankind. *What a fucked-up way to fight a war,* I thought. To instill satos with a safeguard that resulted in their destruction only to have it hacked by some Japanese or Thai bioengineer, then to let these chicks roam freely—a series of mishaps that had allowed the girls to exchange the insanity of living rot for the insanity of belief in Margaret. *And in Catherine.* I preferred the ones that I'd seen in that last operation in Turkmenistan when the sato had begged for her life, asking me if I was God. When they were in that state, it was clear that the girls were something to be discarded or stepped on, an insult to the rest of us. And how exactly did one negotiate with a chick who *wanted* to die?

Bright sunlight surprised me in midthought. A new set of elevators had dumped us into a trench, and I looked up to see that the jungle canopy was gone, allowing the sun to burn down on red clay where lines of huge ants scrambled over it as rapidly as they could. I stepped into mud. A rat squeaked in anger and ran, joining a group of three others that bounded away from our group before stopping to look at us one more time and give me a chance to raise my carbine. Before I could fire all hell broke loose. Someone in the distance screamed in Thai, and Kristen said something like "incoming artillery rounds," but I stood there like an idiot when the first shell landed a few yards to my right, outside the trench. The impact shook the ground. A wave of dirt flew over us and struck my helmet, rocks and tree roots slamming it against my head and forcing me to collapse into the red mud. Then a bright light seared my eyes before the goggles frosted over, and the suit's temperature indicator jumped upward at the same time I screamed. *Plasma.* It had to be the Chinese, I thought. They'd brought plasma artillery, mixing it with the ancient guns of the Burmese. Bright tendrils of the stuff played over the trench above me at the same time chemically propelled rounds thudded all around and shook the walls, and the ants and rats knew what to do; the ants and rats had disappeared.

Jihoon shouted over the radio. "This is crazy. Nobody can survive up here like this. We should go back until the barrage lifts."

"Sure they can," I said. "Just stay low and move forward. There has to be a bunker somewhere ahead."

"It's a hundred meters up, take the first left fork." Remorro pointed ahead of us with his carbine, and we moved out.

The crawl lasted forever. I led the way, gritting my teeth with each impact, and artillery overwhelmed my senses so that perception shifted, blurring my eyes and tricking them into seeing things. A huge banyan trunk had fallen over the trench at one point. Three Burmese artillery rounds landed on it at the same time, obliterating the tree's remnants in a cloud of splinters that stuck into the mud around us to create a field of wooden spikes, some of them a meter long, and when I started moving again, I realized that a splinter had gone through one of the rats to nail it into the mud where the animal now tried to run as fast as it could, all four legs scraping bits of clay from the ground. It couldn't have been real. But I stared at the thing, which fell limp while I crawled past, and I hoped that the first shell hadn't given me a concussion because it just *couldn't* have happened.

I turned at the fork and saw the bunker entrance. A squat concrete structure rose from the clay ahead of us, and the trench sloped downward so that the enemy would only see the bunker's narrow horizontal slit under a meter and a half of steel-reinforced concrete. Someone stood outside. His skin was dark, almost a reddish color, and he was naked except for an orange strip of woven cloth that wrapped around his waist like a sarong. The man saw me and grinned. He made no effort to avoid either the plasma or the artillery shells and, as if to show off, lifted both arms and laughed just as the barrage tapered off. The man looked back at us then, and I recognized that we had stopped moving, frozen in the mud by incredulity, and he was about to say something when we heard a series of pops in the distance followed by a screeching sound. More shells detonated. But these ones never touched the ground and instead burst overhead to blossom into a thick fog that settled over the line and draped itself around everything, hiding the bunker and the man so that for the second time I thought I'd gone crazy.

"Did you guys see that man near the bunker?"

"The one in the orange skirt?" Orcola asked.

I breathed deeply, relieved that it hadn't been an illusion. "Yeah."

"Karen recruit to the *Gra Jaai*. If anyone shows the slightest bit of fear, that's one of their punishments; they have to stay in the trench for an hour during a barrage—"

"Chemical agents detected," said Kristen, interrupting.

"Checking seals, Lieutenant." She stopped talking but came back with a gentle chime. "All systems sealed, filters nominal."

"Can you tell what kind of agent it is?" I asked, trying to hide the sound of my fear.

"The presence of carbon phosphorus bonds suggests nerve agent, Lieutenant."

I clicked back onto our group's frequency. "Chemical weapons. Make sure you have a good seal."

"No shit, chemical weapons," said Orcola. "Now would you mind moving forward so we can take cover? *You're blocking the whole freakin' trench!*"

Chemical agents. The thought made me want to get up and run, and as I moved forward, my armor started to glisten because the fog had begun to coalesce, forming tiny droplets that stuck to the ceramic on my forearms. Just the thought of a suit breach almost drove me crazy during those last few meters because I knew that it wouldn't take much to kill, and a microtear in the suit's joint material could let in more than enough. The drops or their vapor would seep through and make contact with your skin so that the next thing you knew you couldn't breathe. Training kicked in then, but not in a good way; my mind ticked off the symptoms one at a time so that by the time I reached the bunker I had traced them all the way from tunnel vision and runny nose to seizures and eventual suffocation.

Jihoon was the first to notice the man—the one who had been standing there a few minutes before. "Look at that shit."

"He's definitely a Karen. And one of the *Gra Jaai*," said Orcola.

"So?" I asked.

"Yeah. Just saying."

"Any chance of giving him an antidote?"

Orcola shook his head. "He's gone, and I'm not wasting it on the *Gra Jaai*."

The man twitched in the mud as every muscle in his body contracted, the agent forcing his nerves to fire out of control and send signals that should never have been dispatched in the first place. He stared at the sky. Both pupils looked like pinpricks and streams of mucus ran from his nostrils until it all ended when Remorro fired a burst of fléchettes across the man's chest.

I stood in a crouch, making sure that my head was below the top of the trench, and reached for the bunker door. "Looks like another one gets to see God before we do."

Gra Jaai, most of them in flexible battle suits like the ones we'd seen Thai soldiers wear on our ride to the front, filled the bunker. Most of them sat on the floor with legs pulled up to their chests, but a few stared out the bunker's slit to stand watch over the field; their battle suits were ill fitting, and some looked like they wore an oversized trash bag so that it took a few seconds for me to realize that these were children and that their Maxwell carbines were as long as they were tall. Instead of the gaudy colors we had seen on some of the *Gra Jaai*, a single Japanese character had been printed in yellow on their chests.

"That character is Japanese for death, Lieutenant," Kristen said.

"Thanks. Get ready to translate and call me Bug."

"Yes, Bug."

I spoke as loudly as I could—without shouting—as Jihoon and the others crowded into the bunker behind me. "Who's in command?"

"Are you here to fight?" The question came from one of the *Gra Jaai* at the view slit, a woman who had been watching the Burmese line.

"We're here to go on patrol. Tonight."

"Lucy sent word that four nonbelievers would be going with us, but the patrol has been canceled. We will have to wait until after the Chinese attack."

"When will that happen?" Jihoon asked.

"When will the sun die? When will the rats come back to feed on corpses, since their more greedy cousins hadn't known that nerve agent is deadly? God commands the Chinese even though they don't realize it, and God will determine these things such that they will come to us in blessing, as a holy test of our belief. Come. It is time to pray."

The entire group went onto their knees then, and one of them held a tiny package—a miniature battle suit—from which a baby began crying so that the woman or man holding it began rocking back and forth, shushing the infant quiet. The bunker made me feel sick. When some of its occupants shifted to begin praying, they revealed piles of rats that still twitched from the chemical attack, and a mixture of mud and human waste covered the floor on which the mother held her baby. Behind me, Ji gagged, and I grabbed him.

"Don't throw up in your suit."

He looked through his faceplate, both eyes magnified by the goggles underneath to show dilated pupils. "This isn't what I expected, Bug."

"Get your shit together. Throw up in that suit, and you won't be able to clean it for days, maybe weeks, because we'd have to decon before removing our helmets. Your suit is coated with nerve agent. Don't freakin' throw up, or so help me, I'll just shoot you now to get it over with."

"I asked for this, huh?" Jihoon's eyes narrowed, and it took a second to realize that he was trying to smile. "We don't want to go back to those days."

"Right. Just shut up. And if you have to, go back into the trenches but keep low, and whatever you do, don't puke."

The *Gra Jaai* ignored us then as they prayed in one voice, and Kristen's translation crackled in my ears. "I have sinned through my own fault. In my lack of conviction and through those I have failed to kill; in my actions and actions I lacked the courage to take. I ask the blessed Catherine and all the fallen before us, and you, my brothers and sisters, to pray for death and faith, for glory and sacrifice, to our God whose blessings bring war."

Now *I* felt like throwing up. This was my first close-up look at human converts to the satos, and it strengthened my belief that we'd be better off without genetics—not just because the ones in Thailand were past their shelf life, but because without them, people like this, who had nothing to lose and just wanted to trust in *something,* never would have been created. The Japanese and Karen must have been desperate if they'd reached out for Margaret. Then again, all it took were the memories of the children in Bangkok, the squalor of Khlong Toei, and the riots at the airport, and I came close to understanding how people in those situations might have chosen a faith based on madness because it promised at least one thing: a home. Maybe a family. But that still didn't make it right, and I stepped over and through the *Gra Jaai,* who now prayed as I worked my way toward the bunker's vision slit. With my back to them, I wouldn't have to watch; I wouldn't have to think about the fact that they'd been fighting in at least six inches of their own waste.

A thin haze hovered over the ground as the nerve agent evaporated in the heat. But it wasn't enough to conceal the secret of the line or hide the fact that beyond the vision slit a wide swath of ridgetop jungle had been erased for as far as I could see, leaving jagged stumps of banyan, palm, and hundreds of other trees, their trunks lying in every direction and splintered from having been struck by artillery. The line's secret was this: it was artwork, a tapestry that described easy ways to die. Fallen trees would slow anyone who tried to work their way up a steep slope out of Burma, where they'd then have to cross five hundred meters of no-man's-land, and every time the enemy tried to push forward they'd have to climb over the fallen trunks, exposing themselves to fire from our trenches. So many bodies had collected that you couldn't see the clay. Men and women in loose battle suits lay between the fallen trees and had been dead long enough that decomposition and heat inflated the fabric like balloons, while artillery had burst through others and scattered parts for some distance. But for the *Gra Jaai*, this wasn't enough death. In front of the bunker, and at regular intervals in either direction along the trench lines, they had impaled enemy soldiers on tall stakes to allow them to rot for everyone to see. *This is nothing like the last time I had been here,* I decided again; the bush had decayed even further in my absence, its constant war cry resulting in the early onset of cancer.

I clicked into Remorro's private frequency. "You were right. Even their atrocities have atrocities."

"You haven't seen anything yet."

"Why? What else have they done?"

Remorro joined me at the bunker's view slit, but he

spoke over the private frequency and kept his helmet speakers off so nobody else would hear. "Before the Chinese arrived, the *Gra Jaai* and Karen troops would raid behind Mimis' lines. All the time. Sometimes they went for enemy assets—ammo dumps, you know. But most of the time they went to capture children from the Burmese villages."

"To make them into *Gra Jaai*?" I asked.

"That would have been better. No. Whenever the Burmese attacked, they'd raise them on the stakes, alive, where they died from stray fire. And the stakes weren't that sharp. So even if they lived through the battle the kids' own weight would make it take hours, sometimes days to impale them; it was so painful that I saw some of the kids jerk around, forcing the stakes through themselves just to get it over with."

"I understand," I said.

Remorro's voice sounded sharp then, angrier than I'd yet heard him. "Oh. You *understand*? Explain it to me then, asshole."

"This isn't my first time in the bush, Remorro. And I hunted these chicks across central Asia. You get exposed to their beliefs, and they've been so indoctrinated in the tanks that even the ones who've gone insane still haven't given up on *God*. They've just given up on the idea that dying for mankind is the only way into heaven. So to the *Gra Jaai* and true believers, when they kill children they probably believe two things: one, that it will make the enemy act irrationally, and two, that kids go straight to heaven when they die. To the satos, killing is an act of kindness. So I may not like it, and it might still make me sick, but yeah, I'm starting to get it."

"I get sicker every day." Remorro leaned both arms on

the view slit, resting the chin of his helmet on his hands. "So now that the Chinese are here, what do we do?"

I glanced at the *Gra Jaai* and saw them sway back and forth, then looked onto the battlefield. "There's nothing we *can* do except pray for them to attack us topside, that they won't bore underneath us or build a road to a section of the line that's undefended. What happened to the mining gear—the stuff that made all these tunnels?"

"Gone. I only got here a year ago, though, so for all I know it's around here somewhere, hidden in one of the side hangars or something."

Only a year. Looking at Remorro, you'd think he'd been in the bush for a lifetime, during which it had bored him from the inside and emptied his body into a thin husk that shivered within his suit. He wouldn't last much longer. We all had our own missions, and his was to stay here because the satos had worked it so that if he left they wouldn't allow a replacement, and the brass would figure it was better to have someone—anyone—on the inside, even if they were dying; SOCOM lived for its reports and had probably ordered him to stay put until he kicked it. On the other hand he'd made his own decision and could have told both sides to go to hell, so at first I hadn't been sorry for him. But now that I'd *seen* the field . . .

"Why don't you just go back to Bangkok?" I asked. "You could get treatment there."

"Thought about it. But Orcola and I decided to stay put until the Chinese break through; then maybe we'll haul ass. To tell you the truth, though, we don't really *want* to leave."

The statement left me speechless, and I almost laughed. "What?"

"I'm serious. Have you been back home recently? To the States?"

"Yeah."

"Out here you get to do whatever you want as long as it doesn't bother the satos, and there's nobody telling you how to take a piss so you don't waste water, and I don't miss being threatened by some semi-aware just for complaining about Congress or the president. And I *like* the people. The *Gra Jaai* aren't so bad once you get used to them. If I weren't so old and so sick, I might give their training tanks a try."

I did laugh then and ducked when a stream of tracer fléchettes leaped from somewhere on the enemy side of no-man's-land to smack into the concrete over my head. We slid to the floor and sat in the bunker's filth.

"You have no idea how screwed up that way of thinking is, but I agree with you."

"Why is it screwed up?" he asked.

"Because these days the one way to get any privacy is to leave the States, go to war. In Thailand. In the bad bush where there are thousands of ways to die, and all of them are ugly."

My eyes didn't want to stay open. The day's action had worn me out quicker than I'd realized, and now that all the firing had stopped the jungle insects started in with a mixed orchestra of buzzes and chirps, their music shifting in some rhythm that the jungle understood. Our bunker mates still prayed in front of me. I wondered how long they'd go at it before I realized that they were mumbling something, but it was too low to pick up on my helmet mics, and Kristen hadn't offered to translate.

"What exactly do the satos teach them?" I asked.

Remorro rested his carbine across his lap and began disassembling it to clean the parts. "I only know what I heard. By the time I got here, the satos were pretty much the same way you see them now, and Margaret herself came close to killing me once when I stood up to her. I've never seen anyone fight them like you did."

"What did you hear?"

"That when the satos first arrived, they had lost it mentally—all of them past the two-year discharge point so their minds were frying. And whatever they'd been taught in the ateliers about dying in combat or reporting for discharge once they reached eighteen, it was all gone. They were terrified. Even once the Thais managed to reverse the genetic safeguards so they'd stop rotting, the girls still couldn't get their shit together. But then comes Margaret. She traveled across Russia and Korea to get here, along with a sato named Catherine, 'Catherine the Eternal,' who taught her how to get back on track, to reach God's side again. Margaret started preaching to them about 'the one path,' and from then on these chicks have been holy hell for anyone who gets in their way. Now they're more deadly than they were when we first fielded them."

"Why?" I asked.

Remorro pulled out his combat knife and used it to skewer a huge cockroach. "Because now they're convinced that we, the nonbred, are inferior. We're not even worth talking to. *Unless* you're a *Gra Jaai* human."

It was late in the afternoon when Jihoon woke me. The bunker had gone quiet. Prayers had ended and just a handful of *Gra Jaai* remained, two of them struggling with an object that at first refused to come into focus as my eyes blinked from exhaustion. Finally, when they came closer, I saw a huge Maxwell autocannon; the pair lifted it to the vision slit, where they slid the weapon into place and then locked it onto a fixed mount. The autocannon was an impressive weapon. It fired thousands of rounds a minute, and each fléchette—about ten times the size of a carbine's— had alternating high-explosive, armor-piercing tips or tungsten penetrators, but the high rate of fire also meant it consumed ammo like mad. Both men shuffled back and forth, ferrying ammunition crates to arrange below it.

Orcola clicked in. "Keep your speakers off, and don't switch to the general frequency unless you need to because the *Gra Jaai* hate it when someone uses it for nonpriority traffic. Remorro will monitor it anyway to let us know if anything comes up. We're all on a private group frequency; I sent you the key."

I flicked on Kristen's power with my tongue. "Kristen."

"Yes, Lieutenant?"

"Key me into the frequency that someone just sent. Check the system in-box."

"Done," she said.

I stood and almost cried out. The morning's trek through the tunnels and then crawling to the bunker under fire made both knees feel as though they'd give at any moment, and my back ached from having fallen asleep at an odd angle, but I did my best to hide the pain. I stretched, then leaned against the concrete wall for balance.

"Where did everyone go?" I whispered. "The *Gra Jaai*?"

Remorro was still at the bunker's vision slit, and he pointed toward the door we'd come in. "Outside. The whole complex is on alert, and everyone took their positions."

"Everyone except the satos," Orcola said. "We just couldn't bring ourselves to wake you."

"Where'd the satos go?"

"Nobody'll tell us," said Remorro, "but something's up. All the *Gra Jaai* are grinning ear to ear, and it's not their usual smile—the one they use when they think they're about to die in battle. This one is more slippery."

"Slippery?" asked Ji.

Orcola coughed for almost a minute before answering. "Like they have a surprise for the Chinese because it's the kind of smiling they do when the Burmese are about to be slaughtered. But I'll be damned if I know why they think *that* will happen."

The sun drifted downward as we waited. To our west was another mountain range and beyond that, I figured, another and another until you hit the ocean or India, and my goggles frosted over as I struggled to look into the sunlight, begging for the thing to set. But darkness in the bush was another matter, and I'd been back for less than a week—hadn't experienced night in the deep jungle for years. It couldn't have changed much, though. From what I remembered, the jungle came alive at night with sounds different from the ones you heard during the day, and on moonless nights the varying shades of green transformed into blacks and grays, shapes that moved on their own and convinced you that something was out there. Ghosts roamed the bush once the sun disappeared. So at the same time I wished for night, I dreaded it.

A shimmer caught my attention. The spot was midway between our position and the Burmese line, and I fixed my eye on it to try to see better, then looked on either side to define the borders of whatever it was. At first it looked like a heat mirage. But then the spot inched to my left before zipping back in the direction of Burma where it disappeared into the jungle below.

"Anyone see that?" I asked.

"Affirmative," said Ji. "Something with chameleon skins activated, moving fast. Really fast."

Orcola cursed under his breath. "Mimis' armor doesn't have skins. One of the Chinese scouts Lucy described?"

But nobody answered him. How would *we* know? We knew simply that somewhere out there the Chinese waited, and nobody had told us the size of their force, which for all I knew could have been a single battalion of genetic horror or more than a division. Why was I pushing on? I glanced over at Ji, who stared downslope and aimed over the top of his carbine, and from inside his helmet came the sound of muted whines as his goggles zoomed in or out. He was searching for the enemy. This would be Jihoon's first real taste of combat, and it could be his last. The thought of calling it quits, right then, occurred to me, and the more we waited the better the idea seemed because this was insane, and I struggled with the temptation to run. A tiny voice kept begging me to quit. Who would blame us if we left? Who was going to survive in this place anyway? There wouldn't be anyone to tell the brass what happened, and Jihoon and I could make up any story we wanted, and besides, maybe Chen was already dead. Margaret had gotten a head start on us, and for all we knew she'd wiped the guy and was on her way back, or the Chinese had gotten *her*. We knew nothing. One thing, though, was certain: Ji wouldn't live to see his thirties. Whatever drive to follow Margaret had been there that morning, it evaporated in the face of Chinese invasion, and I was about to tap Ji on the shoulder—to tell him we were leaving—when Remorro clicked in.

"Getting something on the general frequency." He listened for a moment and then made a swirling motion with his finger. "Make sure your suit comps are synched with mine; we're getting a dumper."

"A data dump?" I asked. "From who?"

"*Graa Jaai*. It's terrain data. Incoming now."

My map blinked onto my heads-up display in light green and now showed the same information we'd seen earlier on Remorro's holo map: the Thai-Burma border with our strong points and trenches shown as dots and lines. But now there was something else. Red blocks representing Chinese troops blinked onto the map on the Burmese side of the border, in a pattern that suggested they would concentrate forces on Nu Poe. It made sense. The mountains were lower to our south, but the Burmese roads to them were either nonexistent or impassable, and the mountains to our north were even more remote, that much farther from Bangkok. Nu Poe was the perfect border crossing, and why make the effort to bore when a topside attack would succeed? I flicked through the troop data and saw that there were no armor or motorized units, which made me feel better because it meant Chinese APCs and tanks were too large for the mountain roads and so had been left behind. My relief evaporated, though, as I read further.

"How'd they get this data, and do we know if it's reliable?"

"No idea," said Remorro, "why?"

"Because it's an entire Chinese division of genetics in powered suits—heavy infantry with supporting scout elements. *An entire goddamn division.*"

"Nobody told us war would be *easy*," Orcola said.

"Fuck this." I grabbed Jihoon by the arm and slung my carbine, pulling him toward the door.

"Where are we going?"

"Anywhere but here. I'm aborting the mission. We don't even work for the Army anymore, remember?"

Remorro turned and called after us, and I looked back to see the *Gra Jaai,* six of them, watching us yell at each other.

"What the hell are you looking at?" I screamed at them.

Remorro sounded shocked. "It's over two hundred klicks back to Thailand by road, and you can't move in a straight line unless you sprout wings. You're freaking crazy. If we get overrun, you won't get halfway to the secondary line before the Chinese catch up with you. At least here you have a chance."

"Here," I said, turning for the exit, "is the only place we have *no* chance."

But before I could get out, the door swung open and a mass of *Gra Jaai* swarmed in, including their children, pushing me and Jihoon against the wall in their effort to find cover. Most of them jabbered. It reminded me of a group of tourists who had come to a zoo because some of them lifted their kids so they could get a view out the vision slit, just before bombs and missiles struck the jungle around us. There had been no warning of aircraft. Later I figured that high-flying drones or strategic bombers out of China must have done the job because there had been no sound or giveaway at all until the explosions rocked the concrete overhead and sent bursts of flame to jet through and engulf us. Our suits—even the baglike battle suits of the *Gra Jaai*—could withstand exposure to the flames, and some of the children laughed or screamed with joy. I let go of Jihoon. The attack lasted an hour, and I marveled at the fact that none of them showed the least sign of fear, and once it ended the *Gra Jaai* acted *disappointed* it was over, shooing their kids back out the door and into the trenches.

"How did they know?" I asked.

Before anyone could answer, Kristen chimed in. "Lieutenant, I've been monitoring local friendly force communications and have managed to decode one of their encrypted command channels."

Remorro started to talk, and I waved him quiet. "I love you, Kristen. What can you tell me?"

"The locals have full access to Chinese communications and have, themselves, developed the means to monitor and decode all Chinese transmissions—even ones using frequency hopping. The Chinese have been preparing to launch an air attack out of Rangoon, and the girls knew about it half an hour before the assault began."

"How are they doing it?"

"It's not clear, Lieutenant."

I told the others and glanced at the *Gra Jaai* nearby. Most of them had left, except for the six who had manned the bunker with us previously, and they sat against the far wall playing cards. It was nighttime now; my infrared had kicked in, and it wouldn't be long before I'd need a new fuel cell.

"Sometimes I really hate these chicks," Remorro said. "They can do stuff I've never dreamed of, and we only learn about it after the fact."

"You didn't know they'd broken the Chinese codes?"

"There's a lot in this place they haven't shown us. The

satos have labs and production facilities for repairing weapons and armor. Today was the first time I ever knew they had a morgue. Look, a lot of the *Gra Jaai* were scientists, engineers, and doctors before they came here from Japan and signed up for this mess, so it's not surprising they can break encryption and make things. But I didn't have any clue about this."

Before I could answer, the *Gra Jaai* tossed their cards aside and got up, running to man the autocannon. Now it was too late to get out. We heard the *whump* of friendly artillery firing from somewhere behind us and the low roar of shells as they passed overhead, and I waited for the impact. *Nothing.* All of us moved to the view slit and peered out. The artillery continued firing, and from no-man's-land to the distant jungle below, we saw tiny flickers of detonations that sounded like muffled firecrackers, after which a cloud of sparkling material settled into the trees and over the ground. From what we could see, it looked as though the barrage covered almost the entire front and penetrated several kilometers into Burmese territory.

"What is that stuff?" asked Jihoon. "Chemical rounds?"

I shook my head. "It reminds me of when we used microbots to hunt satos; the bots would transmit precise location data of any power source like the ones used in armor or small electronics, and looked exactly like that on infrared after you fired them from their launchers. But I've never heard of micros fired from artillery shells."

"Jesus Christ," said Remorro. *"Look."*

At first, when the material settled over the open area below us, nothing happened. Then my heads-up went crazy. Our suits were equipped with short-range shape detection to assist with targeting, and until that point there had been no indication of anything unusual, but soon outlines began flickering in red—a sea of shapes, two hundred meters away and moving too slowly for motion detection to kick in. The Chinese had arrived.

"I see it," I said. "Do the *Gra Jaai* vision hoods have shape detection, Remorro?"

The autocannon opened fire before he could answer. It sounded like a huge zipper, and the gun's thick barrel spat so many rounds that its tracers formed a laserlike beam, piercing the air and cutting into shapes that crept toward us. It was a signal for the other *Gra Jaai*. Everyone in the trenches and the bunker started firing whatever they had, and I watched my carbine's fléchettes burn red as they streaked into the mass of oncoming shapes, only to bounce off, ricocheting into the air or fallen trees. The mass kept coming. When the Chinese reached a point a hundred meters from us, flashes erupted from them and grenades pelted the front of our bunker, some of them flying through the view slit and detonating behind us so that thermal gel hissed on the ground. They were close enough that we could see them now, and I stopped firing, awed by what had taken form.

"Are those Chinese?" asked Jihoon.

It was the first time I'd seen anything like it, and the fear was so intense that the sound of my own voice surprised me, making me wonder if someone else had spoken. "What else would it be? *Just look at those things...*"

Thousands of Chinese troops walked toward us in heavy armor, their arms and legs solid metal or ceramic that carried them over the fallen trees, and grenade launchers attached to their shoulders fired without stopping. They looked like robots. A tiny hemispherical turret rested where the head should have been, and I focused on one as it rotated, bristling with sensors and antennae. The realization that somewhere inside these frames were those things we had seen in the morgue filled me with dread because we weren't fighting *men*; these were semimachines, and for all I knew the Chinese genetics hadn't any humanity in them to speak of—wouldn't discriminate between man or child. Most of them targeted the autocannon. Beside me I heard a scream, and the weapon went silent, the *Gra Jaai* now writhing on the floor as thermal gel smoked through their battle suits and ate them alive.

"Chameleon skins," I said. "And cease-fire."

"What?" Jihoon asked.

"Do it!"

We flicked on our chameleon skins; except for the dead *Gra Jaai* and a slight shimmer where Jihoon and the others stood, the bunker looked empty.

"Now what?" someone whispered.

"Now," I said, "we wait. Get down and don't move. Those artillery shells we fired must have been some sort of microbot, one that deactivated Chinese chameleon skins."

"So?" hissed Jihoon.

"The satos were expecting this. Let's see what happens next."

In the silence we heard Chinese armor servos; the motors buzzed to translate heavy feet, which made an odd squishing and clunking noise that got louder as they approached. At fifty meters out, the Chinese switched from grenades to fléchettes, and it wasn't long before the sound of return fire from the *Gra Jaai* outside died off to nothing so that except for the enemy's noisy advance, the battlefield went silent. We waited. Jihoon's breathing had become shallow and rapid, and the sound made me concentrate on mine, willing it to slow down because panicking wouldn't do any good. For a while it worked. Then the Chinese began systematically working every possible location where *Gra Jaai* could be hidden, which included our bunker, so that tracers pinged off the far wall to ricochet everywhere, some of them glancing off my chest and helmet. I caught a glimpse of what happened next; I popped my head up for a fraction of a second, catching it when the satos sprang their trap.

Several explosions ripped upward through no-man's-land. The blasts threw fallen trees into the air along with multiple Chinese, the rest of whom stopped to survey the damage, and from my vantage point you could almost sense the confusion the detonations had caused. Then meter-wide circular turrets rose from the ground. The turrets had been spaced along the strip of cleared ground, from our trenches to the jungle below, and I realized that the explosions hadn't been mines intended to kill the enemy, but had instead been planted deliberately to remove debris and clear the way for the turrets to pop from deep underground. A long pipelike apparatus jutted from the turrets' tops, which spun slowly, each one fixing on a target.

The Chinese closest to us faced the new threat and began firing, pelting the turrets with grenades. Still nothing happened. Finally, the pipes sprayed fluid to coat the enemy, and although I couldn't see him next to me, Orcola must have also raised his head to look out.

"What are they doing?" he asked.

"Hell if I know. It looks like—"

The roar of flame interrupted me, and its brightness overloaded infrared so my vision kit shifted to visible light, after which I saw the turrets jetting white-hot flames. I wondered what good it would do. The Chinese armor would have been resistant to elevated temperatures— like ours—but when the flames enveloped their targets, they burst into bright spots of light, followed by a second round of sparks that were so bright my goggles frosted over for protection. Even from that distance you felt the heat. It baked my helmet and radiated through the hood onto my face, and the suit's temperature indicator climbed until I realized that I needed to duck again.

"Kristen," I asked, "did you get a temperature on those flames?"

"Temperatures varied from approximately twenty-five hundred to forty-five hundred degrees centigrade before suit sensors overloaded."

"Would those temperatures be able to damage ceramic or systems on standard armor?"

She took a second to respond. "It depends, Lieutenant. Your armor is designed to withstand short exposure to high temperatures but would not survive a direct hit by standard plasma artillery or long-term exposure to a forty-five hundred degree heat source. The ceramic would be fine, but the heat would damage or melt metallic components as well as joint sections."

I clicked onto our group frequency. "This is genius."

"What is?" Ji asked.

Outside I heard popping now over the roar of flames, but it didn't sound like the Chinese grenades; this was more like the sound of a car that had caught fire and was out of control, its metal parts hot enough to burn. With each pop the fear dissipated to the point where I crawled over to the bunker door.

"The satos fielded some kind of flamethrower, and it has something in it that's hot enough to damage Chinese armor, which I'm guessing is impervious to thermal gel. Jihoon, I'm at the door. Let's go take a look."

The trench had filled with dead. I crouched to stay low and moved out in the direction of the elevators, careful not to fall as I walked on *Gra Jaai* corpses and making sure not to look down for fear of seeing a child. Ji tapped me on the shoulder. We paused, and I lifted myself carefully, inching my carbine up and poking it over the top of the trench to get a view from the gun camera. With my free hand I tapped at my forearm controls, piping the feed over our group channel.

The turrets had gone dormant. On the far side of no-man's-land, Burma's jungle burned, and limbs of trees had ignited to form what resembled miles of huge torches, their flames illuminating the entire area. The Chinese were still there. But none of them moved, and although the picture quality was poor, it showed spots on them that still glowed white-hot, and gobs of metal dripped to crackle on the ground.

"They were too bold," a girl to my left said, and I swung my carbine to aim at her. Nothing was there. A second later, whoever it was deactivated her chameleon skin and a human figure formed, wearing a long robe that dragged on the ground, her head hidden by a hood with a wide vision port of dark glass. When she pulled the hood off, I saw Lucy. "Our Japanese engineers developed a nanomaterial that shorts out chameleon skins and makes the enemy visible."

"You knew what needed to be done," I said. "Everything."

"I told you: Margaret foresaw it. We've been preparing for this for years, the arrival of the Chinese, and without access to plasma artillery and in a location where APCs and tanks can't reach, we needed new weapons. Thermal gel and fléchettes are useless, rockets too expensive."

"What were those turrets?" asked Jihoon. He and I had deactivated our chameleon skins, and I pulled my spare fuel cell out, replacing the one that was about to die.

"They are modeled after an ancient weapon, one that most thought obsolete for over a century. Flamethrowers. We modified the historic recipe, however, and added powdered metals and oxides to a synthetic hydrocarbon gel carrier. The fluid sticks to the armor and drips into joints. Then we follow with a burst of flame. Three different kinds of metals ignite in steps, each one hotter than the last, and in addition to the turrets, all my sisters are now in the jungle below with handheld versions, chasing the enemy that still lives."

"They're running," I said. "The entire Chinese assault group, the better part of a division."

Lucy smiled and shook her head. "There is no honor in this. Except"—Lucy paused to gesture toward the dead at our feet—"for them. They faced the Chinese with Maxwells and grenades and would have gone hand to hand had it come to that. I will miss them."

"Lucy. Someday we'll see these weapons used against us. I'm surprised it hasn't been thought of sooner."

"Until now," she said, "plasma has done the job. But as I said: we have no plasma weapons that can be fielded in this terrain."

From far below on the Burmese side, the sounds of combat rose out of the jungle, distant firecrackers and the deeper thumping of artillery that flashed within the canopy and turned the sky green. White flames leaped up here and there. While we watched, silent teams of *Gra Jaai* came and collected their dead, placing them on stretchers with a dedicated gentleness that suggested the corpses were worth more to them than any of their living, and you knew that the bodies would be treated with respect. It was a strange backdrop. The sounds of war juxtaposed with the somberness of undertakers made me feel as though there was no shame in what had happened—on that day or any other. There *were* no atrocities. This was a war of survival, and as far as the *Gra Jaai* and satos were concerned, the Burmese had threatened to invade their home, the only one they had, and so to die in defense of it made perfect sense, their more extreme methods forgivable. While I thought, one last piece clicked into place and made the whole picture clear: the Thai King had been a genius; putting satos on the line would buy him time if nothing else because these girls weren't just fighting out of obligation to him, they were fighting for the right to call this home.

"You and Margaret have done well," I said. "The next time the Chinese attack they won't make any mistakes, and it'll be an underground assault. But tonight you did well." I saw Jihoon and the others turn to stare at me.

Lucy didn't indicate that she'd heard me at first. "So far, we hold," she finally answered, then started scaling the trench wall to head into no-man's-land. "Come with me; there's something you'll want to see." The others started to follow us, and Lucy waved them back. "Not you. I just got a transmission and enemy drones are incoming. They'll be in firing range within ten minutes, followed by a barrage, so return to the underground complex. Decontamination stations are at the bottom of the elevators. Wait for us there."

She led me onto the battlefield. My boots crunched over the Burmese corpses I'd seen earlier in the day, the fabric of their battle suits now so burned that they crumbled underfoot, and flames here and there provided enough illumination that we didn't need infrared. Lucy approached the nearest Chinese soldier. Its armor made pinging noises as the plates cooled and contracted, and metallic portions glowed in dull orange shapes that the flamethrowers had twisted and deformed. Lucy made sure to stay out of the way of its weapons systems, but it didn't look like she needed to; the barrels of its Maxwell carbine and grenade launcher had almost melted off.

She flicked a series of latches on the side, and the armor's main frontal plate swung open, then fell off because its hinges had melted, so Lucy had to jump back. I barely noticed the noise. Instead my concentration focused on the armor's interior, where one of the genetics lay strapped into a harness, its fiber optics glowing and twin tubes running into nose and mouth sockets. If not for the size of its head and fiber optics for eyes, it looked like an infant on life support.

Seeing the Chinese genetic within the armor was more shocking than what I'd seen in the morgue, and it consumed me with sickening curiosity; if I believed satos didn't belong on earth, then where did these? They were so far from the human template that it triggered thoughts of obsolescence, that humanity was on the verge of designing itself out of existence, and it made me want to scream at the same time I wanted to smash the thing into a pulp. Who was responsible for this, and what could they have been *thinking*? I leaned closer and saw where the fiber optics joined with the suit at a small conduit that twisted upward into the turret, its cameras and antennae now shattered or melted. You couldn't have predicted what happened next. The thing must have sensed my proximity and spoke, its synthesized voice similar to that of the Assurance system except that this was in Chinese, and I leaped to the side to aim my carbine at its head.

"It's OK," said Lucy. "There is no danger."

I'd switched Kristen off. "What did it say?"

"It's begging for us to kill it."

"Will you?"

"Why?" asked Lucy. "Why should I put this thing out of its misery? I wanted you to see them in place, in their armor, so you know that we didn't lie and that what I showed you this morning was real."

The thought hadn't occurred to me because I knew satos and had never seen one lie. "They're real. And horrible."

"This is the first time we've met the assault units in action, and everything Margaret said was true, her word perfect. I also wanted you to see them so I could ask you a question."

I waited, but Lucy was having trouble. She stared downslope at the forest of immobilized Chinese, each of them frozen in different poses, and I wondered if they were all alive inside their suits, trapped within a coffin of ceramic and alloy. It made me want to take my own suit off. There would be no quick death for the Chinese, and I got it because nobody would take the time to walk through the rubble of no-man's-land and open all those carapaces—some of which had fused shut—tempting enemy fire with the time it would take. We were safe now that the enemy had retreated, but eventually they'd return.

"What did you want?" I asked.

"Do you think these things will go to heaven when they die?"

There wasn't an answer to the question. The last time I had been in church was in Jebson, and except for the occasional and accidental prayer, the last time I'd thought about God was long before that, but she'd asked with such sincerity that for a moment Lucy sounded less like a sato and more like a young girl. It choked me up, partly from confusion. I still hated them, but the urge to kill her and Margaret had eroded—so quickly that it made me wonder if I'd been right in Spain: that I was cracking up. Part of me wanted to tell her that the Chinese genetic was a thing, an object just like her, and how could she be so stupid to think that it or she had a soul? Another part wanted to laugh and explain that we'd pulled a fast one on her and all the satos because *none* of us were headed to heaven; *God* didn't exist.

I sighed. "No. I don't think it will go to heaven. It isn't even close to being human."

"Then," said Lucy—and I cringed at the inevitable follow-up question, the one I'd been fearing—"what about us? Will *we* go to heaven?"

"Yesterday I didn't think so."

"And now?"

I slung my carbine and spat on the Chinese genetic, seeing it flinch; I figured it was a painful experience because the things lived their lives in a cocoon of metal and weren't used to any human contact whatsoever. So I spat on it again, just for fun. Lucy pulled me away, back toward the trench.

"What do you think tonight?" she asked.

"Now I think maybe God has a plan for you. And yeah, maybe, if you're lucky, you'll all go to heaven."

Lucy pushed past me and almost knocked me over, making me think at first that I'd said something to piss her off, but when she spoke, it sounded like she'd started crying.

"Luck has nothing to do with it; you nonbred are all the same. Hurry up, I don't want you to die if the Chinese send in their recon versions because other than the ones we captured, we haven't seen them today. There are many more of them out here. And they are very, very fast."

After decontamination the four of us headed back to Remorro and Orcola's bunker, where we lay down to get some sleep. I had forgotten about needing a poncho, and it pissed me off, but I decided one night without a helmet would be worth it, and I was too tired to worry about rats anyway. There was no process of falling asleep. As soon as my head hit the rack, I was out cold, exhausted from the night of combat, and the chronometer showed that we had been fighting until 3:00 a.m. Someone shook me awake almost as soon as I passed out, and I grabbed my knife, thinking it was a rat.

"Relax," said Jihoon, "it's me."

The room was pitch-black, and I probed the concrete floor for my vision hood, attaching the wires to my suit by feel. The infared clicked on. Jihoon and Lucy stood by my bed, and she motioned with her hand to follow so I grabbed my gear and ducked into the narrow tunnel.

In the main passageway, ten *Gra Jaai* waited, equipped with modern combat suits and the cloak and hood that

I'd seen Lucy wear during the fighting. She handed me
and Jihoon a set. The others showed us how to wear it and
attached the hood with strips of webbing so that it hung
on my back out of the way.

"What's going on?" I asked.

"There are two hours until sunrise. These men and
women are going on a long-range patrol, and you'll need
thermal protection for your metallic gear if you join them;
these cloaks and hoods can withstand very high temperatures and also function as chameleon skins. Our sisters
pushed Chinese and Burmese forces back over ten kilometers. Two reserve Chinese battalions were so surprised
that they retreated toward Moulmein, thinking that Americans had arrived unnoticed; now is the right time for you
to get through the line."

"What about Margaret and Chen? How will we find
them?"

My incoming message light blinked on, and Lucy
smiled. "The *Gra Jaai* patrol route is mapped so that
much of it heads in the right direction, and you will see
when to break off, near the river. I just sent you Chen's
coordinates. Do you need power?"

I nodded, and Lucy handed us both a bandolier, each
loop of which had been stuffed with a fuel cell.

"The cloaks are wired to your suit and should synch
with the main computer. Activate their chameleon mode
the same way you would your armor."

Lucy spun and walked away then, calling over her
shoulder, "Margaret is expecting you, Lieutenant, both of
you. Take care to mind your manners; she's not as forgiv-
ing as I am."

EIGHT

Snipers

Our path took us far south of Nu Poe and into the mountainous jungle where we stayed clear of paths for fear of Burmese traps or electronic surveillance. The *Gra Jaai* escorting us were all Japanese. One of them walked point tens of meters ahead, impossible to see except for the blinking dot on my map that showed me where he and everyone else were. Even if we'd wanted to move fast, we couldn't have. The jungle was so thick that bushes and leaves slapped into my helmet almost continuously, and in some places they obscured the very ground, so I had to feel my way through, hoping that I wouldn't step off a cliff or onto a mine. We stopped every few minutes to listen in the darkness, but everything was still as if the jungle was satisfied that to our north so many had died that the blood would eventually reach this far and saturate the clay, feeding it.

Before sunrise our patrol stopped. The *Gra Jaai* flicked off their chameleon skins and arranged themselves in the bushes to pull leaves over their bodies and disappear as if they had transformed into foliage themselves, and one of them clicked over the radio that we should do the same to conserve fuel cells. I helped Ji and made sure he was hidden before finishing my own camouflage and then lay there. It was pitch-black in my helmet; my anxiety amplified the sounds so a mouse nearby made me think that a Chinese scout was moving in, and I heard my own breathing in the tight space of my helmet. Those were the most horrible moments for me. Blinded by the darkness and, once morning arrived, the layers of green over my face, the only place to retreat was further into my mind, which turned its focus toward Phillip; before I knew it tears had started to form, fogging my goggles so that I prayed for sleep to come quickly.

"Jihoon," I whispered over the radio.

"What?"

"You asleep?"

"No."

"What do you think?" I asked.

"About what?"

"About this," I said. "About everything so far."

There was silence as Ji thought. It took so long for him to respond that at first I assumed he'd fallen asleep and I was about to say something when he cleared his throat; his voice shook. "This is way insane, Bug. I think I made a mistake."

"No, you didn't. Hang in there. It takes awhile to get used to all this, and it's your first action."

"Bullshit. I trained for half my life in the tanks, and it's not like they didn't make it seem real. There were even smells. But they have kids on the line. The kids laughed in the bunker, even when the missiles hit us. What the hell is that *about*?"

I wanted to leave my hiding place and shake the crud from his head, but all I could do was whisper, "It's the satos. They've changed things here and to hell with them—Chinese *and* satos. But it's samba time now, troop, so get some rest and study your map because we'll be covering a lot of ground tonight. When we find Margaret, I'll decide what to do with her."

"You still haven't really told me why you hate them so much," he said. "The satos."

Maybe it was the exhaustion. At first I didn't want to answer, but as the silence wore on and sleep refused to come, my mental guard slipped, and it wasn't until it was over that I realized what I'd said.

"The Army chose Thailand as my first area of responsibility, and the bush wars went on for years. Last time I was here, SOCOM decided they wanted to test a new weapons system, and I was to hold off offensive operations until it was deployed with my unit—a battalion of the Royal Army. I loved those guys. The Thais were incredible fighters, really pissed that the Burmese had ever stepped foot in their country, and they had one officer named Major Po who saved my ass. The Burmese ran a snatch and grab and pulled me off the line into the bush one night, and as soon as they took me into Burma, they started torturing me. In the open, right in the jungle. Po came after me. By the time the Thais arrived, I was close to dead, with half my back burned off. Po carried me all the way back.

"I had just recovered and returned to the line when SOCOM's weapons arrived. It was close to the end of that particular border war, and the brass wanted to get this system in the field before the Thais ended hostilities because Kazakhstan was on the books but hadn't really kicked off yet. The weapons were satos. Boys. Winchester plant's first batch of prototypes and I didn't know what the fuck to do with them, but they sent another adviser whose job it was to lead those assholes, and you could tell that it wasn't going to be pretty; the Thais hated them from the start because those kids were just…odd."

"Boys?" Jihoon asked. "I never knew they produced male Germlines."

"They didn't want anyone to know then and don't want you to know now. On our first operation we pushed into Burma and took one of their villages, which was great because it had been a strong point for Burmese operations in the area, and at first the satos impressed me. They had no fear. Enemy troops freaked out because the kids were so ruthless, and overnight word of the armored devils got out, so we probably could have taken the whole country. I don't remember the name of that town. But I remember that after we took it, the American adviser told the boys to stand down and they refused, knifed the guy so badly they took his head off, which really sent them into a frenzy where they started killing anyone in sight, including Burmese kids. Including Thais. Major Po and I retreated with what remained of his force, and the satos followed us, attacking all the way so that by the time we got back to the line, it was just me and Po. The satos shot him before he reached the trenches. When I got there I turned around to see a bunch of them dismembering Po with their bare hands."

I stopped talking. The story had brought with it memories forgotten, and they became so real that I swore I could have reached out and touched Po, his screams echoing in the jungle.

"What happened to them?" asked Jihoon. "To the satos?"

"I called in artillery and ordered the Thais in the trenches to open fire. Then sent a report back to command and never heard another fucking thing. So yeah. I hate freakin' satos. Later I heard that they tried to use the boys again, early on in Kaz, and the same thing happened so they went with girls from then on."

Jihoon said something else, but his voice had already started to fade as my eyes fluttered shut with the exhaustion of having trudged through the mountains and now having dredged up the past. It was a mental weight. Pulling out my memories had been like trying to drag myself out of quicksand, so once it was finished all I could *do* was sleep, and that was without telling the whole truth: that Phillip's father had been part of the team that manufactured them—the same things that killed Po, the same things that I had hunted ever since.

We woke in the late afternoon and flicked on our chameleon skins so we could eat in the open. It was a bizarre sensation—no matter how many times I'd done it. My ration pack floated in midair, held in hands that had become invisible, and I squeezed the thermal capsule to wait for the meal to heat. We'd settled in a dense area so that I couldn't see Jihoon; the one other visible person in our group was a Japanese *Gra Jaai* who ate under his cloak and hood, lifting fingerfuls of rice to disappear under the shimmer of his chameleon skin. I stuck the feeding tube through the membrane in my helmet and squeezed, finishing the mush before realizing that it had resembled franks and beans even though the label said steak and eggs. Everything tasted like franks and beans.

Whatever they did to process the food and mash it into a state where it could travel through the narrow tube added a flavor to it so that no matter what you ate, it all tasted the same. Or maybe my taste buds had deteriorated. I washed it down with water and wished that I had brought some bourbon with me, wondering if my bottles were still safe back in the bunker complex.

The sun had gotten lower and would soon set. Around us monkeys screamed, and in the jungle the bugs sometimes got so loud that they triggered my speaker safeties, cutting them off in a kind of stutter that soon threatened to make me crazy. And the sounds mesmerized so that at first I tried to count the number of different insects only to realize that the number was infinite and that I'd spent ten minutes in the effort before losing count and having to start over. I'd just begun to try again when it all stopped. You knew if the jungle got that still, that quickly, it meant that something was out there, and I dropped the pack to reach down for my carbine, flicking off the safety as my heart raced. I was about to scoop up my empty rations, to slip the pack into a pouch where it would be hidden, when the leaves next to me parted.

Time stopped. With breathing on hold, my heart pounded so that anyone nearby would have to hear it, and I willed myself not to shake for fear that the carbine, camouflaged now that I held it, would rattle against my armor.

It had to be Chinese. The thing turned the air next to me wavy and buzzed with electric motors that pushed through the shrubs at a creeping pace, which gave me minutes to pray that it wouldn't collide with me and would keep on going. Instead it stopped. The spent ration pack lifted off the ground for a moment, and I heard a soft chime followed by a mumbling voice as if someone spoke from deep inside a helmet. From there things got confused. The rations fell to the ground, and another shape crashed through the foliage to land on whatever it was next to me, knocking me down the mountainside into an uncontrollable roll where I grabbed at anything to break my fall. When I stopped, it was quiet again. Above me I heard a thump followed by a hissing and then a shriek that went on for at least thirty seconds before something cut it short. I moved back up the mountain, following the path of plants I had crushed until I stood among the red dots on my map, Jihoon and the others still masked.

In our midst lay an armored wreck, its carapace still smoking from whatever the *Gra Jaai* had done to it and its chameleon skin flickering on and off.

"What is that?" I whispered, and Kristen translated this into Japanese.

"Chinese scout," someone answered.

Jihoon clicked into my private frequency. "It looks like a big dog. And look at those things on its front, what are they?"

A dog was a good description. The scout's powered armor was low to the ground and had four widely spaced legs, articulated in two spots with alloy push rods that attached to armored motors. Its head was similar to the ones we'd seen the night before—a hemisphere dotted with glassy ports and short antennae. From its size, the main body looked large enough to hold one of the Chinese genetics along with whatever they needed for battery and food storage, and along the top ran a short Maxwell carbine in a fixed-forward mount. But what Jihoon referred to was something neither of us had seen. Twin blades, short and square, protruded from the thing's front and joined with hydraulic lines that pushed them together so that anything in between the blades would be severed clean.

"It has a carbine," I said, nudging it with a boot to make sure it wouldn't move. "And those things are mandibles, probably powerful enough to cut through our armor. How'd it die?"

"Thermite grenade," another *Gra Jaai* said. "I jammed it under the chest plate. Let's go. There is no time now; we have to move as fast as we can before more arrive."

It was still light. We weren't planning to move until darkness, but now the *Gra Jaai* led us in as fast a pace as we could manage in the steep, overgrown terrain. My legs started burning almost immediately; *age,* I thought, *is worse than death.* There was also a new kind of fear that made me think of being chased by wolves because the Chinese scout suits had evoked a sense that they were more animal than human, even though I'd seen an example of their occupants in the morgue. Thinking became difficult. Instinct said to run, and for the moment my heart threatened to pound out of my chest with the adrenaline that kept me going.

A half hour later we stopped. The map on my heads-up put us two kilometers inside Burma, and for a brief moment the thought made me want to give up because it looked as though we hadn't moved. Ahead of us was a river. The *Gra Jaai* patrol route turned north to follow it, but the coordinates that Lucy had given us planted Margaret's position almost ten kilometers due west, and the realization that we'd have to split up made me wonder if it was worth it; Jihoon and I would be alone then in the deep jungle. *We could give up.* For the second time, doubt crept in and made me question the decision to keep going, but I knew there wouldn't be any going back. I smelled the mission. It was a mating call that the bush relayed from tree to tree and transmitted to the primal parts of my brain, which transformed the operation's completion into an autonomic need, just as important as breathing.

We listened to the jungle sounds, which returned a few minutes after we fell silent, and I had to suppress the fact that my stomach wanted to vomit out breakfast. The bugs had become our early warning system. No matter how good your chameleon skin was or how slowly you moved, the insects knew everything and would give the enemy away long before he reached you but only if you stayed still, stayed quiet.

"We have just over a kilometer to the river," a Japanese woman said.

I nodded, catching my breath and wondering what she looked like. "We'll have to leave you there."

"You will need a way to cross the river. This time of year, the current will be strong. And on the far side was an enemy garrison, but our reports indicate they retreated with our counterattack yesterday."

"Do you know of any boats in the area?"

A dot appeared on my map, a kilometer south of where we'd split up at the river. "There is a village," the woman said. "You'll probably find a boat there."

I waited for the *Gra Jaai* to decide to move, but instead we waited. In a few minutes the sun would be gone. Around me the jungle darkened so that the million shades of green shifted into black as the shadows took over to send me a message: the bush was glad to have me back.

Here I had led Thai actions to murder villagers and soldiers; here were my secrets, the ones I'd learned to keep in my twenties before age had started to erode my mind with doubt and regret, and they laughed at me from the foliage so that when the woman spoke again it made me jump.

"Why do you need Margaret?"

"The US wants her to help. They're sending more soldiers like her to keep the Burmese and Chinese from invading Thailand." She and some of the other *Gra Jaai* chuckled at me, and it made me want to punch someone. "What's so funny about that?"

"Help?" she asked. "What help do we need? This is a blessing, not a problem. War is our way of life now, and we see the path set down by our ancestors the day our homeland was obliterated. Tokyo had become soft. Delinquent and corrupt. War is the way to reach God, and we honor our ancestors by returning to a way long forgotten by Japan, a way to see beauty and light."

"That won't be possible once the Chinese take over your new home," I said. "When they tear your children apart with grenades."

They laughed again, and the woman had trouble talking, trying to form words around what must have been a tremendous smile. "Our new King has friends, Lieutenant. Nobody wants the Chinese to even exist, and *they* have other enemies beside Thailand and America. We have allies who will arrive soon, and when they do, the Chinese will meet another angry people who have never forgotten them, not even after hundreds of years."

"What are you talking about?" Jihoon asked. He sounded as skeptical as I was, and the sensation that these people were crazy—more insane than satos—made me wonder if it wouldn't be better to just let the Chinese have Bangkok.

"If you live," she said. "If you make it to Margaret and return safely, then you will see everything, including that we don't want or need *American* help." The woman clicked off, then came back a minute later. "We move. A patrol three kilometers to our north was just destroyed by Chinese scouts and are now at God's side."

"Are you going back?" I asked. "To Thailand?"

"No. We push forward and finish the route."

"Fuck this," Jihoon whispered to me. "Her and all the King's *friends*."

In infrared the mosquitoes and moths looked more like shooting stars as we eased through the brush, and by now we moved downhill, descending from the mountain until we reached the edge of an immense flat clearing filled with rice paddies and low dikes. The Japanese woman led the patrol. She had indicated for us to hold at the clearing's edge, where we spread out to leave about five meters between us, and it was enough space to make me feel alone, sorry for myself until I saw her marker inch out into the paddies; she'd be exposed, and the woman made no effort to move slowly, jogging as if she wanted to be seen, heading alone into the empty field. I flicked my safety off and got ready.

The woman reached a spot about three hundred meters away before she froze. At first I wondered if she had bought it because her dot stayed put for almost twenty minutes, at which point streaks of tracer fire broke the darkness in front of me so that I stared through the reticle that had appeared on my heads-up, praying for a target—anything to shoot at and break the tension. She shouted on her way back to us, the dot moving so fast it occurred to me that she could have been an Olympic sprinter.

"Five scouts," the woman screamed. *"Get ready!"*

A hand grabbed my shoulder, and I nearly opened fire. "Don't shoot," someone said. "Hold and we'll handle them." The guy moved off in the direction of Jihoon, and I struggled to keep my finger from squeezing the trigger.

The woman was almost to us, and when she got into range, my vision kit's motion and shape detection outlined her and at least three other figures approaching fast, otherwise invisible on infrared except for a faint gray smear and the firing of their Maxwell carbines. The things chasing her were close to the ground. At first it looked like the Chinese scouts would get close enough to pounce before she could reach us, but finally the woman put on a burst of speed that carried her back to the edge of the paddy, while just behind her the splashes in the paddy water stopped when the scouts leaped. *Gra Jaai* flame units opened fire. Beams of white leaped from the line to swallow the Chinese in midair, where they twisted through the leaves before crashing into the jungle behind us so the *Gra Jaai* followed them, pumping several bursts at the scouts as they ran. The Chinese thrashed into the brush, trying to get away before the burning metallic fuel damaged their systems to the point where all of them fell still.

"That's three," someone said.

The Japanese woman was out of breath while she whispered over the open frequency. "Stay still. Two more are out there, and there may be others I didn't see."

"Can they see us?" asked Jihoon.

I clicked into his private frequency. "We don't know all their systems yet. Assume they can detect movement and shapes unless you stay absolutely still or move very, very slowly. And only use burst transmission, but stay off the air unless it's an emergency. They might have direction finding."

Our group stayed put for over half an hour. After that, a chorus of frogs erupted from the paddies, their croaking a source of comfort because like the insects the fact that they made any noise at all meant that the animals hadn't detected either us *or* the Chinese, and with each splash the frogs made, I had to hold my breath in an effort to keep from moving. At first the thought of the scouts terrified me. This wasn't like the satos, who I knew and were a familiar enemy; these were the unknown, and a sensation of being stalked by some kind of monster made me wish I was back on the line where at least there was a measure of safety. Not doing anything was the worst for someone like me, inaction eating at my mind the same way waiting for a mission did until I'd had enough.

"I'm going out there," I said. "Someone give me a flame unit."

The woman clicked in. "Are you sure? You're not one of us." She said the last part as if the woman was sorry for me.

"Just give it to me." Ten minutes later one of the *Gra Jaai* crawled up slowly, inching his way to my side where he slid my cloak and hood off, then helped me detach my ammunition hopper and set my carbine to the side.

The flame unit was a backpack frame with three cylindrical tanks attached to a flexible ceramic hose and tubular firing section, and I had to wriggle into the thing's harness so slowly that my muscles cramped and began to tremble. When it was on it felt heavy, pushing me into the mud near the paddies. I waited until the guy helped me put my cloak and hood back on and was shocked to find that almost forty-five minutes had passed and that it wasn't a guy who had been helping me, it was the patrol's leader.

"These average four to five long bursts before running empty," she said, "and this one is half-full. You will probably die."

"Thanks."

"The Chinese are worse than you because the Chinese have no souls, no honor."

"And I do?" I asked.

She laughed and began tightening the flame unit's belt around my waist. "I see why Lucy likes you. Why Margaret agreed to see you."

"What are you talking about? Have you spoken with Margaret?"

"I am in constant communication with her. She monitors all patrols, even when on one of her own. Margaret is deeper inside Burma than any of us have been, and you raise our opinion of Americans by going after her. To kill her."

The fact that she had it all wrong confused me, and it took a moment to collect my thoughts. *Why would it make her happy that someone was going to kill her?* "I'm not going to kill her; I'm just going to find her and deliver a message, maybe ask a few questions, and that's it."

"Then you," the woman said, "don't understand us at all." She made one last adjustment to my belt, and one of the dots closest to me on the heads-up display map blinked. "You will move out now with Hiroshi, who will advance on your right flank. Good luck. The last place I saw them was from a position about three hundred meters out, and they were at the far edge of the clearing moving toward us. It's best to go fast and get it over with, just draw them out so we can keep moving toward the river. If you run out of fuel"—the woman slid a thermite grenade into my harness—"use one of these as a last resort. It's best done by jumping them from behind, arming the grenade, and then jamming it into the space between their chest or back armor and leg joints. If you can find them."

"Do me a favor," I said. She paused, the air shimmering next to me as she waited. "If I don't make it, take my partner with you and get him back to Bangkok."

"Done. But most likely none of us will make it out. Our job wasn't so much to patrol as it was to find the leftover Chinese scouts and take out as many as we could. To buy Lucy and Margaret more time. We're a penal unit, and all of us have to prove our courage before we can be accepted among our families again because we all hesitated when ordered into the trenches."

"How do you prove your courage?"

"By dying or by killing everything. *Everyone*."

The sight of her footprints forming in the mud with no sign of boots made the night dreamlike. Already the dot marking Hiroshi's location was speeding into the rice paddies, tracing a path that followed one of the low dikes, and I stood to take one step before I froze. *What was I doing?* The dike closest to me stretched out, disappearing into the darkness beyond my infrared range so that it looked as if the soil dissolved in the distance, and I clenched the flame unit until my hands hurt. *They* were out there. The jungle urged me onward, sending a gentle kind of electricity through the roots and into the mud so it traveled upward in my legs and forced me to move despite the terror. The bush wanted this to happen, and it always got what it wanted, so to hesitate wouldn't buy me a different outcome from the one already fated, and the mission was out there, pulling at me while the bush pushed from behind.

The dike soil was soft and gave under my weight as I crept forward. Wind blew across the paddy. My motion detectors pinged when the grasses waved in the breeze so that I froze trying to pinpoint a target until giving up with a touch of embarrassment for having reacted; Hiroshi was on a dike parallel to mine, and I had just moved forward again, trying to catch up and even out the advance, when the Chinese opened fire.

Fléchette tracers reached out for us from the far side of the clearing, but instead of two, the firing came from at least seven locations and slammed into my shoulder so that I spun in place before plunging into the black water of the paddy; the dike provided some concealment for a moment, and I cursed when the initial shock wore off.

"Suit penetration in upper right suit area," said Kristen. "Minor damage to your shoulder, Lieutenant."

"Call me Bug!" I shouted. "How bad is it?"

"Three fléchettes punctured your tissues. They exited, causing minor skin tears, but there is little chance of damage to bone and a high probability that you can continue—although with discomfort, Bug. Air filters are saturated, and air intakes are currently blocked; switching to emergency oxygen."

Something splashed behind me. Tracers still flicked

overhead, and I kept my head down, but with my back in the paddy and the huge cloak and flamethrower tanks lodged in the mud underwater, there was no way for me to get up or move. The splashes got louder. I raised the firing tube and pointed it toward the dike I had fallen off, just as my motion detectors showed three of them, Chinese scouts, leaping over the low dirt ridge and toward me. I squeezed the firing lever. Compressed gas propellant hissed at the same time the igniter sparked to send a jet of flame that swung as I screamed, my anger at not being able to move boiling over. The fire touched the first one. Although it landed in the paddy with a loud smack, the water did nothing to extinguish the flames, and from the corner of my eye, I saw the scout roll in an attempt to put them out, just to find them reignite as soon as it came back into the air. The gel splashed against the second one, then the third, and both fell into the ankle-high water next to me to burn, while steam curled up, bright white on infrared.

After that it was quiet. I tried to dislodge my tanks from the paddy mud but after a minute had managed to work myself deeper and gave up, switching onto the general frequency.

"Kristen, translate this into Japanese," I whispered. *"Hiroshi."*

There was a moment of static before he answered. His voice was quiet. "Lieutenant?"

"I got three. How about you?"

"Three also," he said.

"That means there's one more. Any way you can work your way over to my location? I'm stuck in the paddy mud and can't move."

"No, Lieutenant, I'm sorry. One of the scouts took my legs off before I could kill him."

The news shook me. I imagined Hiroshi out there alone on one of the dikes as he looked up at the sky, bleeding out with the threat of one more Chinese soldier who by now had stopped firing, probably to move in after us. I tried to dislodge myself again, grunting with the frustration of having landed in something that resembled quicksand, but there was no way to get out.

"Hiroshi, you still there?"

"Yes, Lieutenant."

I sighed, and my hands shook with the thought of what I was about to do. "Stay still. Your cloak works and will keep you hidden. I'm going to draw the last one to me and try to burn him out."

"No, Lieutenant."

"What?" I asked. "Why?"

"He is here already. Ten feet away and moving in. Death and faith."

There was a loud splash in the distance, and I tried once more to free my tanks until I heard a loud *pop* followed by the roaring of a thermite grenade, the intense heat of which turned the sky toward Hiroshi so bright that my infrared overloaded. The man screamed. Once more the field went quiet, and I lay on my back, not sure what to think anymore.

Ten minutes later, something splashed on either side of me, and two sets of hands grabbed my cloak and arms, rocking me back and forth until there was a loud sucking sound when my tanks exited the mud. I tried not to scream with the pain from my shoulder.

"Nice job," said Ji.

The Japanese woman clicked in. "Hiroshi is dead. He killed the last scout with a grenade and will be remembered with honor."

"This is crazy," Jihoon said. "Why don't you guys use more nanomaterial to deactivate the Chinese chameleon skins? Don't you have any grenades with the stuff inside or something?"

"No. The nanomaterial is too difficult to make, and we used it all in last night's attack. We're wasting time here, Lieutenants. It's time to keep moving. More Chinese will come now that they've lost contact with ten horrors."

We crossed the remaining section of the paddies quickly, making a beeline for the jungle canopy. But something had changed the bush—maybe because of Hiroshi. I wanted to reach the tree line as quickly as possible because the jungle now promised safety, and the obscurity that I'd once cursed seemed a blessing since it would hide us from the things that now hunted us instead of hiding atrocities. Hiroshi's death had been a thing of beauty. Maybe it was because I'd imagined it without seeing a thing, but he'd not sounded scared at all, just detached, and in the end had made a calculated decision to remove a threat with the last strength available. Hiroshi had been a perfect man. He'd be eaten by the jungle now. And as soon as we stepped into its foliage, I sighed with relief, wondering if the *Gra Jaai*'s blood had already soaked into the gray leaves that now surrounded me, filling them with something good for once.

I said a silent prayer and begged God to take Hiroshi to his side and for the jungle to absorb his corpse so it could grow again. It was the first time I'd prayed for real in decades, without it involving a request to save my own ass, and hoped it would work; tonight we'd risk heading into the village, and tomorrow we'd have to cross the river. If God existed, I figured a little prayer might be in order.

The Hwangtharaw River flowed by on our right as we crept south through the overgrowth, a combination of trees, bushes, and vines that went up to the water's edge and grabbed at my cloak any time I tried to move. One of the *Gra Jaai* was on point. Morning hadn't yet arrived, but fear of Chinese scouts and harder terrain than we'd anticipated slowed our progress so that arrival at the river had come two hours late, and to our relief, the *Gra Jaai* decided to accompany us into the village instead of peeling north to continue on patrol. Once we found a boat they'd head back into the jungle on their original route. Exhaustion was now a constant companion, and my mind had almost reached its limit with attempts to ignore the pain from a wounded shoulder and from both legs, my knees threatening to give out at any minute; the others must have been just as tired or we would have seen the trap before we stepped into it.

I followed the trail blazed by four *Gra Jaai* ahead of me. Even with them pushing through the toughest overgrowth, the vines and foliage were still thick, making it difficult to walk with the limited view my infrared vision gave, and I was about to step over a fallen limb when I saw it: a thin line, strung low and taut across our path, which the ones ahead of me had somehow passed safely. I was about to tell everyone that the area was booby-trapped when a loud crash made me jump, after which the man on point screamed.

"Nobody move!" I hissed. "Traps."

The Japanese woman clicked in. "Where?" I told her about the trip wire in front of me, and she moved forward to my position.

The wire ran through the bushes and into a loop bolt screwed into a tree, and when I looked up, it was easy to see a huge wooden gate-shaped structure that had been studded with long spikes. Had I tripped it, the gate would have swung down with enough force to push the spikes all the way through me, impaling me in multiple places even with my armor. The woman marked the line with yellow tape, told the others, and then we made our way forward until reaching the point man.

He was still alive. A sapling had been nailed to a tree and then bent as far as it would go so that when he triggered the trap it snapped out to send a metal rod—sharpened at one end—through him, where it now stuck from his lower back. He pulled his hood off so I could see his head and then pushed at the sapling, trying to free himself. After a few more seconds he screamed again, and the Japanese woman told us to step clear.

"What are you doing?" asked Jihoon. I hadn't noticed him creep up, and it startled me.

The woman paused before answering. "He is already dead. I will hasten the process."

"He's your own *man*."

"That's why I have to do this," she explained. And before Ji could say anything more, the woman fired into the *Gra Jaai*'s head so the man fell limp.

"Jesus Christ," said Ji. His voice was getting louder, and I reached for the shimmering spot closest to me to have my hand slapped away as soon as it touched his shoulder. "You don't freakin' get it; you're just as bad as them."

I sighed and glanced toward the river, where even in infrared I could see through the trees; the sun would be up in a matter of minutes. This wasn't the place to deal with any of it, and Ji worried me because we hadn't spent enough time among the *Gra Jaai* to know how they'd react to his kind of outburst.

"He was giving our position," I said quietly, "so get it together or I'll shoot you too. *We're in Burma, for shit's sake.*"

Jihoon didn't say anything, and another of the *Gra Jaai* took point so that within a few seconds we moved forward again, the town two hundred meters to our south. At first I wondered if the village would be tucked in between the trees and if we'd walk right by without finding any sign because here near the river the growth was even more dense than on the mountain, the tall bushes and vines like an impenetrable, fibrous wall. Then without warning we came to the end. The jungle opened in front of us into a wide track of cleared land and elephant grass that stretched from the river east into the mountains, in the middle of which stood a series of low huts, whose roofs consisted of colorful metal sheets—colors that I now saw because my infrared had switched off. Morning had arrived. Although we couldn't yet see the sun, it was just bright enough to make out the village's details, and between the huts a thin fog rested in low spots to render the scene eerie.

"We can't let the villagers live." The Japanese woman had clicked in, and I was relieved to see that it was on a private channel.

"I know."

"Your friend, the other lieutenant. He isn't like you."

"What's your point?" I asked.

The woman sighed. "*You* understand all this. From what I've been told and the way you've performed, I'd guess you've been here before and know the jungle. You've killed Margaret's sisters and drew blood from Lucy." She paused for a moment, and I was about to say something when she clicked back in. "*He* doesn't know how it works."

"I'm too fucking old, and I need a drink. Badly." A thin stream of smoke rose from the closest hut, and to our east the sky turned brighter over the mountains to wake the billions of insects that began their deafening whine. Talking made it all soft. As long as we spoke, we didn't have to move, and my legs felt as though they needed a breather. "And I don't even know your name."

"You haven't asked," she said. "And I didn't want to know yours yesterday, but today is different."

"I'm Stan."

"Stan. I'm Nanako. And you sound just like Margaret."

I chuckled at her comment before realizing that a week ago what she'd said would have enraged me. "How?"

"You think a lot, but fight without thinking, and there is nothing left of the peacetime world in your manner. Margaret also says that she feels old."

How old was she now? It took a moment to recall what I'd memorized from Margaret's file before deciding that the girl would be in her mid-twenties. "Margaret isn't old. I'm old enough to be her father. Almost. And sometimes I fight because I'm no good at anything else so *everything* becomes a war."

An old woman exited one of the huts and made her way down to the riverbank, where she dipped a bucket into the water, struggling with the weight on the way back. We all froze. The woman took twice as long for her return trip, and I'd hoped to keep Nanako talking so we could rest a few moments more, but by the time the Burmese woman returned to her hut, the *Gra Jaai* were ready to act. You could feel it, the way they shifted around us, impatient.

"What will you do with the other lieutenant?" Nanako asked.

I thought for a moment; from our vantage point we could see several canoes pulled up onto the riverbank near the village. "Why don't we just grab one of their canoes and forget about the town?"

"These are Burmese, and we can't take the chance."

"Can your people handle the village? I'll hold Jihoon here and make sure that he doesn't do anything stupid."

"I don't advise it. This would be an excellent opportunity for all of us to learn if war is *his* way."

Nanako was beginning to piss me off. "Jihoon is *my* man, Nanako. Not yours. And it'll take him some time to get used to the bush because you're right: he's not like us. Not *yet*."

"As you wish," she said and then clicked onto the general frequency. "Take the town."

Nanako's and the others' dots moved out on the map, not worrying about motion detection because getting in and doing the job as quickly as possible was the most important thing. But you could see their shimmer. Sometimes one of their cloaks would flap up, and the *Gra Jaai*'s feet would appear to kick up dust from the packed red clay surrounding the village, and my thoughts drifted inward to reflect on the conversation I'd had with Nanako because now it was clear that a shift had occurred. The bush had corrupted me again. It wasn't just a military necessity to do the whole village; now war was a thing to be enjoyed because my gut told me that all of the Burmese civilians would be going to a better home when they moved on from such a crappy place; the same way the *Gra Jaai* rationalized it. There was no such thing as an atrocity, and forget about Jihoon needing to learn these ways; Phillip needed to see it. The tanks provided a facsimile of war, and now that I'd returned to the jungle it was all clear—why it had been calling to me the second I'd hit Bangkok. *The bush hadn't finished teaching me when I'd left, years ago.* It'd been like dropping out of high school when the Army recalled me from Thailand's jungles so they could prep me for missions in Kaz, and if I'd just stayed in Thailand for a few more months, I'd never have left. This wasn't just the home of the *Gra Jaai*; it was also the place of *my* birth, my first missions. Ji would never be a part of the bush because he fought it too hard and had been wired with a quality that prevented its magic from dyeing his soul the right color, but out here children like Phillip would learn the most important lesson: the truth about the world. I guessed from my experiences with Ji that the difference between lessons taught by the tanks and by the jungle was like the difference between seeing a fight on holo or at ringside: one was mere entertainment, the other gave you a sense of reality that couldn't be duplicated.

Movement yanked me from my thoughts. The map showed that Nanako's team had taken up positions outside each hut and were about to take care of the villagers when something streaked in from the fields to our left, moving toward her team and the river. Elephant grass, almost as tall as me, filled the field with thick green blades, and as Ji and I watched, it swayed and parted as if a herd of invisible leopards sprinted through it.

"Nanako!" I shouted into the radio, but it was already too late. One of the *Gra Jaai* squeezed a burst from his flame unit and hit the things bounding toward him so they burst into moving torches just as one leaped into the air, after which it closed invisible pincers around his neck. The rest of the *Gra Jaai* fell without ever realizing what hit them. Within seconds Nanako and her patrol had been erased silently, her men and women lying in pieces and bleeding into the clay.

"What—" Jihoon started, but I cut him short with a whisper.

"Quiet. Don't move."

"But they're gone."

"I said quiet. They'll be looking for others now. For us. Just take it easy, and we'll get through."

Ji sounded terrified, and I didn't blame him but I couldn't relate because all my fear had been replaced with the jungle's program, where this was just what it was and it was too late to change the deal. Being scared didn't help.

"They're coming this way, Bug. I count two. The rest are moving back into the grass. *We're fucking dead.*"

"I said quiet, Chong. They'll hear you." He stopped talking, which was fortunate for him because I'd drawn my knife so I could kill him if he refused to shut up.

They were easier to spot in the day. The morning sun broke over the mountains, and through the leaves we saw a pair of them moving toward our position, creeping in an effort to evade shape detection, but their feet sunk into the clay and now they had a shadow. I tried to breathe quietly. The scouts reached the jungle and crept past us to my right, where they disappeared into the foliage. Still, neither of us moved. For over an hour we sat there, afraid to give away our hiding spot until the crashing noise of something bounding through the brush came from behind, fading to the east in the direction of the mountains.

"Jesus *Christ*," I whispered, stretching my legs while I sat. "I can't feel anything. It's all gone to sleep."

"They're dead," said Jihoon.

I looked toward the village again, where the locals had begun lifting the bodies and pieces to toss them into trucks. They stacked the *Gra Jaai* weapons by the river.

"Yeah."

"That's it? *Yeah?*" Ji yanked his hood off and then slid his locking ring open to remove his helmet so tears wouldn't fog his goggles.

"I don't know if you're cut out for this gig after all."

He finished and replaced his gear, so that I heard a muffled sob before Ji's head vanished into its helmet. "I don't think so either," he said. "But I don't know. I scored high in the academy and got the best scores in training scenarios; it's not like my profile didn't fit for this job. But we can't even *see* these things, Bug, and it's not like you and I are on some advising job anymore. This kind of shit wasn't part of the training. You brought us into Burma so we could be the targets in some screwed-up hunt, *asshole*."

"Yeah. I did. So get some rest, be quiet, and don't move around. Swap out your fuel cells as soon as they start to get low. We'll move into town tonight and steal one of those canoes so we can cross the river."

"What if we can't?"

"Then I'll risk swimming across in my undersuit with a rope so I can pull you and my armor to the other side and to hell with worrying about their thermal imaging. This is what we do, Chong. Take risks to accomplish our mission. And besides, we wouldn't want to go back to those days."

"Fuck you," he said. But I'd already started falling asleep.

Night fell to awaken the frogs, which croaked in a never-ending chorus that periodically went silent when a bird called with a haunting drawn-out sound, but within a few moments they'd start again. A splash from the river caught my attention. Peering out from the jungle, my night vision showed a bird with large wings lifting off from the near bank with a struggling frog in its beak so that I made a note: I never wanted to be a frog.

It took me a moment to find Jihoon and shake him awake. "Time to get going."

"What time is it?"

"Twenty-one hundred. The villagers used their canoes for a while, but they're back now."

"How long have you been awake?" he asked.

I thought for a minute. "I don't know. A couple of hours. Been going over the next steps and didn't want to wake you."

"I bet you didn't. I can hack it, Bug."

"I figure you can, kid." I wanted a cigarette more than anything, followed by bourbon. It had been days now since my last drink, and my skin crawled from not having had either, but I tried not to let my discomfort show. "You were right, too. This operation has been crap from the start, but it's the one we've got. And it's your first. The first one is always the worst, and the fact that they paired you with me for one this important means they have plans for you. All you have to do is make it out."

"Who has plans for me?" Ji sounded curious, as if he hadn't thought of the possibility.

"Come on. You think they hand out these things like candy? A few months ago and I'd never heard of Strategic Operations, and yet here you are, a part of them out of the gate even though your only experience amounts to a few years suspended in orange goo and working as a Peeping Tom for the Feds. You *can't* screw this one up, kid, because they won't read it that way; no matter what you do, it'll work out."

"What about you? What does a Bug do after an op this bad?"

I thought about that one too for a minute; it made me want a cigarette even more. My arms and legs were so sore and tight that even my toes cramped, the constant low-level agony from my wounded shoulder a reminder of the fact that there wouldn't be anything more for me when this ended.

"I'll figure that one out if we live." I grabbed my carbine and rose inch by inch until I stood, taking one cautious step toward the jungle's edge. "Stay low, move slow. Is your fuel cell good? Chill can full?"

He paused to check before clicking back in. "Plenty of power, I'm OK. My exhaust temps are green."

We headed toward the village. At our speed, it took a half hour to reach the canoes, which were low and flat in the middle with high bow and stern sections, and I pushed one into the water where Jihoon held it while I shuffled toward the pile of discarded weapons. Several of the *Gra Jaai*'s flame units had been damaged or were empty, but I found one that was around half-full and considered taking it; a villager or scout would see the thing as long as it wasn't concealed by my cloak, and there wasn't time to take everything off and arrange things so the cloak would cover it. But this was a risk worth taking—in case we needed it later. As long as part of me was visible, there wasn't any point in moving slowly so I ran as fast as I could to the canoe, tossed the flamethrower in, and helped Jihoon push off.

"What's the hurry?" he asked.

"Move it. Someone may have seen me."

I jumped in, and Jihoon handed me a paddle; we both dug into the water at the same time, trying to put as much distance between us and the village as possible, but someone shouted from the bank and I turned to look. A small boy ran after us. By the time he reached the bank, the boy was waving his hands and had started wading into the water as he shouted, and I imagined how strange it must have looked to see an empty canoe cross the river with two paddles that moved by themselves. But when lights from the huts flickered into view, I stopped smiling.

"Faster," I said.

"I'm paddling as fast as I can."

I grunted with the effort and looked back again; a group of men were already loading into canoes. "Not fast enough. *Faster!*"

"Why can't we catch one stinking break?" Ji asked.

It was a good question. On a normal day I would have

laughed, but we'd made it halfway across the river by the time the others splashed after us, and they had more paddles. The men had clearly done this for a lifetime; their strokes fell in unison, and we wouldn't have much of a lead once we reached the far bank. When we did, I pushed Jihoon onshore and dropped the flame unit at his feet.

"Take that into the jungle. Move fast, but once you get into the bush, slow down and keep your eyes open for booby traps."

"Where are *you* going?" asked Jihoon.

"I'm going to take care of them."

"They just want their canoe. As soon as they get it, they'll probably turn back and go to sleep."

I stared at the spot where I thought Jihoon's head was. "I'm going to take care of them. Now get moving."

The flame unit rose into the air and bounced as Jihoon headed west, soon passing out of range of my vision kit.

It didn't take long to set up. My carbine rested on a rock near the bank, and when I touched the trigger, the gun camera's image popped into my heads-up with a dim reticle that moved when I shifted to search for my targets. By now I heard the men's voices, and Kristen started to translate their confusion into my ears, but I told her to give it a rest. There were three canoes, each with five men. I targeted the ones farthest away and fired, walking my tracers from front to back to watch the men crumple forward in their seats or slump over the canoe's side and drag their hands in the water. The last two canoes started to turn. I took my time with the next, firing short bursts at each man so that by the time the last one had fallen, the ones in the third canoe decided to abandon their vessel and leaped into the warm river. One by one I picked them off. When it was over, I checked my chronometer to find that a few minutes had elapsed and zoomed into the far bank where a crowd of villagers had gathered to watch. I did it without thinking. The tracers from my carbine cut them down without effort at that range, and I didn't stop until my hopper had emptied, automatically detaching from my shoulder mount to fall by my side.

Two minutes later I'd found Jihoon. We moved deeper into the jungle as fast as we could because by now the Chinese scouts, if any were still in the area, would have noticed the shooting. I'd seen the Burmese boy fall to the mud, dead, and it didn't bother me a bit; what bothered me *now* was the thought that something inside me had changed again, and I couldn't pinpoint what it was, only that it made me feel strong.

NINE

Chimera

The jungle didn't care who lived or died. As soon as the sun set, its trees went to sleep and dreamed of things that would ensure its roots got what they needed in the dry times between monsoons, and war that had raged for so long on its borders had supplied it with enough death to make it grow thick and tall. Jihoon and I moved all night. We paused for as long as it took to strap the flame unit under my cloak and then continued up the long sloping mountain ahead of us, the one leading to the dot on our map showing Margaret's last known position. I didn't know if she'd still be there. But despite the uncertainty and the exhaustion that threatened to make me fall asleep on point, an exhaustion that made me hallucinate and see shapes in the darkness outside my infrared range, the urge was still there—to move and never stop. The jungle wasn't against me and even asleep it still pushed; it was enough. We'd move through its maze and reach the spot by early morning, but without knowing where Chen was, it was hard to believe the mission would end, and in the monotonous bush it felt as though we'd never get there.

"Lieutenant," Kristen said, "I've noticed something interesting."

"Go ahead."

"I've been monitoring your power consumption, and although the extra garment you have wired into the suit's system has increased the draw, you still have enough fuel cells for two weeks of constant operation."

"That's very interesting," I whispered. "Is that why you woke up?"

"I never sleep, Lieutenant. I only explained the power status because I decided to activate your sniffer units two days ago and draw random samples once you made contact with Chinese troops at Nu Poe."

She had my attention, and I stopped to lean against a tree, punching the command for Ji to hold. "What did you find?"

"Their off-gasses are characteristic. They aren't unusual for electric-powered motors but are atypical of organic life in combat suits."

"You're losing me, Kristen. Spell it out."

"In this particular theater there are no units like the ones fielded by the Chinese, so any reading from them is well above background for tungsten and several other elements that their servos produce, and from the amount of nickel I've detected I would guess that some of their systems rely on metal hydride batteries. This is in itself odd, since those types of batteries are highly unreliable, and—"

"Stop. Are you telling me we can smell them?"

"I can try to *detect* them, Lieutenant. It's an experimental procedure, but one, if it works, that could provide you with a warning before your next encounter. Given visibility constraints in the jungle, the ability would give you an edge."

"If we activate the chemical sniffer to run constantly, how much of a drain would that put on my power?"

"It depends on the intake draw, but I estimate that it would cut two or three days from your total supply."

"Do it," I said. "Maximum draw." I clicked onto Jihoon's frequency and told him about it, which made him laugh.

"You know what this means, right?" he asked.

"What?"

Jihoon brushed by me on his way past, moving forward to take point—a good sign since he had shown no initiative since we'd arrived on the line. I wondered if he was pulling it together.

"Once the brass gets word of this, they'll hand us flamethrowers and armor that makes all of us look like you. Your call sign won't be worth shit anymore."

Three times that night we stopped when Kristen chimed with her warnings of elevated nickel levels, and all of them were good hits. Jihoon and I stopped to listen on each occasion. The Chinese scouts would push past in the bush, and you wouldn't have noticed if it weren't also for the fact that the bugs went quiet and the things hadn't realized yet that their weight broke branches on the jungle floor easily, the cracks booming inside my helmet.

Just before sunrise we paused. I was on point and had watched as our dot and that of Margaret's merged, prompting Kristen to announce that we were less than a hundred meters from her location. Ji wanted to rest. But there was a feeling in the air, as if pure oxygen had been pumped into the jungle, so that it diffused through ceramic and into my suit, heightening my senses and making my fingertips tingle the same way they would just before grabbing hold of an electrical cable. She was there. No bugs would give away her position, and this was an event I'd been expecting for so long that no rest was needed to try and figure out what I'd do when we met. We pushed on, and the jungle parted in front of us as if it gave its approval; the early morning sun had hit the highest leaves, and now that it was awake, the bush wanted to see what would happen too because even it couldn't see that far into the future.

The jungle spat us into an area that had less foliage—not a clearing as much as it was an older section of rain forest with an immensely high canopy and few bushes on the ground so boulders and red clay lay exposed. A Buddhist temple rose in front of us. It was a round, pointed structure with a wide section near the bottom that narrowed and steepened into a spire at the top and an ornate stone arch that opened into blackness at the base. Streamers of morning light pierced the canopy above. They hit the temple's side, most of which was covered with a creeping ivy, but in spots it gleamed with gold that flaked off in sections to make me wonder how long the thing had been abandoned. Many of the Burmese had forgotten faith. Why shouldn't they? For more than a decade nothing had stopped the fighting that swung back and forth over their borders, not even prayer or sacrifice, so by now I figured their monks had traded robes for battle suits. No paths led to the entrance, and from the look of it we were the first people to have walked in the area for decades unless you counted the monkeys, several of which clung to the ivy and stared at us.

"Lieutenant," Kristen said, "I'm picking up a standard signature. Satos in decay, well above background and likely within ten meters."

"I see them," I said.

Jihoon clicked in almost at the same time. "*Look* at that shit."

These weren't satos, per se. Not American ones anyway. In front of the entrance someone had raised three poles, to which had been lashed the bodies of Chinese genetics with their fiber optics and hoses severed so that the massive heads hung down loosely. They bloated in the heat. Beneath the poles, their armor had been piled, the pieces of which showed the blackened scorch marks of a flame unit. I made sure my carbine's safety was off and signaled to Jihoon that I was going to move in.

"I'm right behind you," he said. "Why do you think Margaret did this with the bodies? A warning to other Chinese genetics?"

I thought for a second, just for the amount of time it took for the pieces to lock together. "Not a warning, a challenge. An invitation to the Chinese because Margaret *wants* to die."

"What does *that* mean?" he asked.

"It means keep your Maxwell ready because I have no idea what she has planned. Or how many satos are with her."

We crept across the clearing and moved through the archway. The passageway was dark enough to force my vision to infrared, and it squeezed us within its rocks, which formed a low-ceilinged corridor barely wide enough to fit through, winding in a circle around the outside of the temple. A strong breeze blew through. Something ahead of us created the wind, and my temperature indicators jumped, suggesting that whatever it was also generated a significant quantity of heat, enough to dry the walls so that sheets of paint hung from the ceiling in a caricature of the jungle—the hanging flakes like leaves that we had to push through. The tunnel went on forever. Finally, ahead of me was light, and as we neared it my vision kit switched back to visible as we passed through another arch and into the temple's center.

The main chamber was circular with a ceiling that arched high overhead and into which tiny portholes had been cut so that sunlight beamed and reflected off the polished marble floor. Wooden carvings hung to section the ceiling into six equal parts; I recognized the teak, a dark wood and infinitely hard, that someone had taken the time to shape and chisel into leaf-shaped patterns from which dangled pink lanterns. Candles flickered inside each one. The light focused on a thirty-foot-high statue of a white Buddha, his right hand raised and body clothed in gold, and I was about to step closer to it when they came; six satos dropped from where they had hidden in the carvings above us and slammed us to the ground. In less than a minute they had stripped us down to our undersuits and bound our hands behind our backs with wire. When they'd finished, they tied ropes around our necks. The fibers cut into my skin, and the girls yanked us onto our feet, tightening the noose so that I gasped for breath while stumbling toward the statue.

Margaret stepped from behind the Buddha's legs and I stared; she was exactly like her picture—beautiful. The tattoos held me in some kind of trance, their swirling patterns hypnotic and perfect under short blonde hair that framed them. From the neck down she wore combat armor like Jihoon's, its polymer coating dull now and the ceramic plates chipped and broken. The other girls pushed me to my knees in front of her, and then left, dragging Jihoon toward another archway where he vanished into the shadows with a gurgle, leaving Margaret and me alone.

"Where are you taking my partner?" I asked.

"I don't know. We waited here for you. Two or three days, I think. My chronometer broke, and it's easy to lose track of time when it moves so quickly."

"I find it interesting that you chose a holy place to meet us. A temple."

Margaret sneered at me. "This place holds nothing holy. The Buddha is false, as all my *Gra Jaai* know."

I nodded and glanced back at the entrance. "We saw your work outside. The Chinese genetics."

"Did you like it?" Margaret asked. "We want so much to meet more of them and yet few come. When you first arrived, we had hoped it was more of them, but you are equally interesting."

"I don't know if I liked it or not," I said. She was close to me now, squatting so her face was level with mine, her eyes a few feet away. There still wasn't anything in my gut—no sense of what I would do if I ever got loose. But there wasn't any fear either. Despite the fact that we had been captured, it was with an internal comfort, the serenity born from knowing that this was the way it was and that Margaret wouldn't kill us. Not yet, anyway. "Some would call you a murderer, except those things out there..."

"What?" she asked.

"They aren't *human*."

Margaret laughed and leaned forward to kiss me, her tongue warm against mine. When she'd finished, she spat on the ground. "But they *are* human. As human as I am. As human as *you*. You aren't the first man I've kissed, and if you knew how many men I've experienced, you'd know to trust my judgment on this. The Chinese genetics are the sons of man; how can they *not* be human?"

"Trust your judgment? Judgment about what?"

"On everything. On the fact that I know what's inside you because I tasted it on your tongue, and it's the same taste that we all have, a taste of infection but one that's symbiotic, one that helps us to function in the jungle and feed its roots with corpses."

My mind swam with the strangeness of it all. Whatever the file had said about Margaret, it hadn't described much at all, hadn't touched on the fact that what faced me now wasn't even close to the satos I'd experienced in the field; this was a girl whose words sounded decades older than her age, like an old woman in a girl's wrapper. A combination of awe and disgust battled for control over my gut, and it wasn't clear which would win.

"What infected me?" I asked.

"The jungle itself. It's everywhere. Do you believe in God?"

I shook my head. "No."

"But you believe in the jungle. Its trees and vines, that they speak to you and show the way. That the jungle guides us all."

It wasn't a question, but I answered anyway. "I believe it sometimes. Yes."

Margaret stared past me without speaking, and we stayed like that for a few minutes so that my knees began to scream with the pain of kneeling on hard marble, its cold stone making the pain worse. She'd started crying. Margaret didn't sob; instead, tears rolled down her cheeks and splashed on the floor while from outside came the faint sound of monkeys screaming.

"I'm tired," she whispered. "The jungle sent you to me, and I don't know what to do with you. Not yet. I assume the Americans sent you, like the others, to kill me—the sato that taught everyone how Catherine the Eternal viewed life. Do you know what's to happen?"

"No. And they didn't send me to kill you."

She shook her head. "That's what Lucy said, but she doesn't know the truth, doesn't understand that what your superiors want is irrelevant. They probably *don't* want me dead—want me to keep fighting the Chinese?" I nodded, and she continued, "This we'll do. But somebody sent you to kill me."

"I don't understand." My knees gave, and I fell to the floor on my side. Margaret grabbed the rope and pulled, choking me at the same time she stood and kicked me in the stomach so that I gasped for air and struggled to get up again. She raised a fist and slammed it into my face, over and over, until my vision blanked for a moment, stars floating in front of my eyes. "Don't be weak. I will kill you if you're weak."

"I just wanted to ask you about Sunshine and Chen," I gasped. It took a moment to catch my breath so I could continue. "Where is Chen and what is Sunshine? And how did the Thais reverse your spoiling?"

"Sunshine and spoiling are separate issues, unrelated."

Margaret stood, leaning over me and looking down as she raised her fist again. "And before I answer your questions, there are things you'll need to experience so you can hear my words. Chen is a complicated subject."

This time when she struck me, I passed out.

Pain forced my eyes open, and it took a few seconds to realize that I was screaming. A single candle lit a small stone room. From somewhere else came another scream, this one muffled so that it may have come from a room nearby, and I assumed it was Jihoon, but who knew how many prisoners the satos had? Margaret leaned against a stone wall opposite me where she watched; the satos had lifted me from the ground and tied ropes around my biceps to insert a short pole between my arms and back so that my dangling weight threatened to force both arms backward and up, rotating them out of their sockets. I screamed again, trying to keep my arms down.

"Where are you from?" she asked.

I stifled another scream and tried to keep breathing, barely having the strength to answer. "Virginia."

"What's it like?"

"I don't know, you tell me. I haven't been there in years."

The rope creaked overhead as I rotated, and my arms trembled with an effort that wouldn't last forever. Margaret smiled. She lifted the candle to drip hot wax onto her open palm as she spoke.

"I've never been to the US—except for my time in the ateliers, but then we shipped out to Kazakhstan without seeing anything else. I guess you could call me an American, but I'm not sure everyone there would agree given the way I look. I love our country. Not in a patriotic way; I'm talking about what I've seen in 2- and 3-D imaging of the countryside and its people. So many different humans, all kinds of colors and shapes. Rolling hills. I know Virginia from what I've seen in these images, and there is an especially beautiful spot that I hope to visit one day. Lexington. Have you been there?"

I shook my head. Spit ran down my chin and hung in the air as I gasped for breath. It wouldn't be long now before my arms gave. But then, before I knew that it had happened, the rope snapped and I collapsed to the ground, where I curled into a ball as best as I could; both arms were still bound behind me and were in so much pain that I started crying. When I opened my eyes, I saw Margaret sit and slide a knife into its sheath; she had cut the rope.

"Your shoulder is wounded but healing. I asked about Lexington."

"I went to summer camp near Lexington," I said. "When I was a kid. It was a sports camp where we rode horses and played lacrosse."

"I've seen horses only in training. In the tanks we rode them along with Napoleon's cavalry, but I've never seen one for real." She stopped dripping wax and stared at me with empty eyes. "I beat you and brought you here because you lied to me."

I looked away; one eye had swollen shut, and it hurt more than my shoulders, the cheekbone throbbing so badly that I wondered if it would heal. "When did I lie?"

"When you said you didn't believe in God. Lucy told me you said she would go to heaven. So either you lied to her or you lied to me."

"She believes in God. You do too. I don't know what to believe, but if there is a God, I think you'll go to heaven."

"Why?"

"Time," I explained. "I hunted your sisters, and they rotted from the inside out, machines designed for obsolescence within two years of being fielded, but not you. You overcame the safeguards. I don't know what difference it makes, but now that you've spent so much time living, you seem different. Real."

Margaret grinned and rested the candle on the floor again, waiting for melted wax to harden around its base. "How long have you been at war?"

"Since I was a teenager. Almost twenty years now, so it's all I know."

"I," said Margaret, "have less than half of your experience, and it makes me jealous. You're not like the ones who tried before; those men begged for mercy and swore that they weren't here to kill me. Do you want to kill me?"

I nodded. "Yes. But they won't let me."

"And why aren't you begging?"

I rubbed my face on the rock floor, trying to scratch an itch that wouldn't stop. "I've been tortured before and begging never helps."

"We thought you had because we saw your back when we hung you. You're an interesting man, Lieutenant, and I want you to do me a favor." She slid closer, and in the candlelight I saw half of her face, as if the other had been eaten by shadows. "Soon I'll be gone. My sisters won't know what to do. They are great warriors, some like Lucy may even be better at killing than me, but they have no vision. I need you to teach them."

"Teach them what?" I asked. I sensed myself fading

out of consciousness and fought to stay awake; Margaret, I'd decided, was insane.

"Teach them everything; tell them the truth. You'll know it the same way you knew to come here, to accomplish your mission. Get some sleep, Lieutenant. Tonight we'll use you and your partner as bait because we want to kill more Chinese, and it will be an experience for you. The closest thing you'll feel to being broken and hunted, just like the girls you killed for so long."

The night's heat was almost unbearable. Since Bangkok we'd been pampered by the suits' climate control and now we knelt in the open, outside the temple, wearing undersuits so that the moist jungle air soaked into them and the garments did nothing to protect us from insects. Mosquitoes buzzed around my ears, and Jihoon knelt beside me in the same position, with both hands wired behind his back and tied to a post in the ground. Ants bit at my feet but moving them made it worse, and I glanced around in the darkness, trying to see something, but a distant moon cast more shadows than it did light.

"They beat the crap out of me," Ji said.

"I know. They beat me too."

He hung his head, his voice a mumble. "They didn't even ask any questions, Bug. They just kept whacking the bottoms of my feet with a wooden baton and then waited for me to recover before starting again. I don't know if I'll be able to walk again."

"Don't think about it," I said. "It's just pain, and as long as it's there you're alive. Remember your training."

"Training was bullshit. I want out. I wanna go home."

Jihoon leaned forward against the rope and started sobbing. It happened this way sometimes, and the more they threw into the tanks the worse it was likely to get because this was a new product—maybe the first time Jihoon's kind had been tested in a bush war, heading straight for operations over their heads. Someone had been too confident. It wasn't that Ji couldn't have hacked it; the problem was in the way you immersed new operators. My first missions had been as part of large teams where there was plenty of responsibility to go around and didn't involve heading deep into Burmese territory to face the horrors of advanced genetic research. They'd given him too much, too soon.

"You're a weapon," I said. "Get your shit together."

"What?" he asked.

"You are a weapon, made of bone and brains. Whining isn't going to get us out of this mess, Chong, so you'd better get unscrewed right now, or I'll break out just so I can come over there and snap your gook neck. You're a killer. Act like one."

Ji chuckled and shook his head. "You are such an asshole. Did anyone ever tell you that?"

"Yeah. Bea did all the time. She'd really like you; look her up after you get back to the States."

When the insects stopped whining, I froze; neither of us said a word. An indescribable hum filled the air until it threatened to deafen me, but it came from inside, a kind of tightening of my stomach to the point where everything overloaded with the surge of adrenaline that coursed through my blood and into my head. Death had stepped into the clearing. I searched the darkness and urged my eyes to develop their own infrared so I'd at least see whatever it was that had arrived, but nothing materialized, and it was a logical next step to say a silent prayer that Margaret's girls were as good as everyone said.

It didn't matter if we moved or stayed still, spoke or remained silent, because without suits and chameleon skins our thermal signature would stand out like a flaming beacon. Besides—from his breathing it sounded as though Jihoon was about to start screaming and that would drive me mad.

"I'm not sure I can ever go home again," I said.

Ji just looked at me, his eyes so wide that they almost glowed white. "What?"

"Home. I don't think I can go back. And I can't stay in the Army."

"Why not? You're an officer now; you've got a couple of good years left."

"Nah." I shook my head. "I've hit twenty years, and now it's time to bail. And I didn't want to say anything, but there were a couple of times over the last few days that my knees almost gave out. I'm spent. And if I go back to the States I'll firebomb the BAI or something; it just doesn't feel like home anymore."

"Jesus, Bug, you should have said something to someone; with genetic therapy you can get whole new knees, the knees of an athlete if you want. Just put in for the procedure."

"There is no way in hell, Chong, that anyone is going to mess with my genetic makeup, especially not the Army. Not a chance in hell. Who knows what they'd put into me?"

"Then what'll you do?" he asked. He was whispering, as if being quiet would make a difference, but I didn't want to explain the reality of our situation so I let him continue. "Where will you go?"

"To tell you the truth, I don't know. I've only been good at one thing: killing. It's all I ever wanted to do."

Ji didn't say anything, and for a moment I thought that I saw a flicker of movement from the corner of my left eye, the one that worked. There was no use looking to see what was out there. If it was a scout, the thing would be invisible, and either the satos would get it before we died or not.

"Did you wipe all those villagers?" Jihoon asked. "The ones who chased after us in canoes?"

"Yeah. And before you ask me how, there isn't any explanation. I just did it. To tell you the truth, it doesn't even bother me, and when my fléchettes chewed into the Burmese boy, he reminded me of Phillip, but it didn't make any difference. He *had* to go. I miss Phillip more than ever. But I don't miss that boy and will probably never think twice about it or lose any sleep."

"But I don't get it, Bug. If you can't answer how, what about *why*?"

There was definitely movement now, coming into my field of view as something circled about fifteen meters away; soon it would attack and at least talking helped keep my mind off it.

"Because I've been doing stuff like that for twenty years, so why stop now? So I found out I have a conscience, that I care about Phillip; so what? It's a little late for remorse. And those bastards could have reported our last known position to the Chinese. So fuck 'em, Chong. That's *why*. I don't get selected for ops because I'm good at handing out cigarettes and chewing gum. If you ever make it higher, get to the point where you select people for missions, you'll have to learn to *like* guys who operate the way I do."

"To tell you the truth," Ji said, "if I had to choose someone to go on such a screwed-up op with, I'd have picked you. Because you're so freakin' scary. You're just like the satos, Bug, but sometimes I don't know if that's a good thing."

The Chinese scout gave up on stealth when it bounded over the clearing so we heard the heavy footsteps as it pounded clay. A moment later there was a flash. The bright light overloaded my retina and forced my good eye shut at the same time a wave of heat washed over me, but there was no place to hide, and it seared my face. I yelled in pain. The scout crashed into the dirt and rock between us and thrashed there, its metal spitting as parts of it melted to send droplets against my skin.

By the time I opened my eyes, Margaret had materialized, and the rest of her group stood around her, looking at us. She smiled and slung her carbine.

"Leave them here for the moment," she said. "We may attract more Chinese this way."

"I'll kill you," I hissed. Whatever respect or awe had existed the day before now extinguished with the realization that I'd been fooled; there was nothing special about her. She was the example of why it was so important to wipe out all the satos, and I'd been wrong to let myself go soft with Lucy and the others at Nu Poe. "Untie me and I'll kill you now."

The other girls looked stunned, and I suspected that the words held a special meaning for them; maybe nobody had ever spoken to Margaret that way. She shook her head.

"Not yet, Lieutenant."

One of the girls cleared her throat. "Mother, he called you out, and you've never turned one down."

"This one isn't ready," said Margaret. "And I want him at his best."

They left us then, disappearing with a shimmer as they moved out. At least for a little while, the glow of molten metal made it so Jihoon and I could see for once, but that too faded until neither of us could see a thing.

By the time morning arrived, the satos had wiped two more scouts, and my skin screamed that half of it had been burned off from either proximity to the flame units or from having bits of molten metal splashed onto it. I fell asleep on my side. When one of the satos woke me to drag me back toward the temple, I realized that my pain wasn't all from being burned, but that during the night I'd passed out on my side from exhaustion, allowing the ants to cover me and feed. The girls brushed the insects off and let us jump up and down, but Jihoon couldn't stand. His feet looked about twice the size as normal, their bottoms bruised and cracked from beatings. Finally, the satos tossed us into our cells and locked the doors.

Once I was alone I started crying; it didn't make any sense. We'd come all this way only to have the jungle betray us, and I wondered if the satos back at Nu Poe had let us live just so Margaret could have the fun of torturing Ji and me for a few days. It had all been a waste of time. Despite the sweltering heat, the room's stone floor was cold and I tried to press my bad eye against it to help reduce the swelling. The exhaustion and pain combined to overwhelm me; within a few seconds I passed out again, which was a welcome relief from reality.

Margaret shook me awake, and I had no idea how much time had elapsed. There were no windows in the cell, but she had her candle to alleviate the darkness.

"It's a life with great purpose," she said, "killing the Burmese and Chinese. I couldn't ask for anything more."

"I don't see any purpose except for sport."

Margaret pulled out a pack of cigarettes, and I almost drooled. She placed one between my lips and lit it so I could breathe and let the nicotine wash over receptors that had been screaming for it for days, calming as soon as the drug hit them. Even the pains from hunger and lack of water vanished.

"It *is* a sport. Those who win get to shape the world. The Chinese are a scourge and have no concept of God, and you have no right to decide whether we're right or wrong in our determination. We've spoken to them. Captured them and interrogated them. The Chinese have no concept of what it's like to live outside their armor; their metal frames are to them as limbs are to us, and their ceramic is their skin. So why did I call them human? I lied. They are animals, and the scouts we trapped using you and your partner are searching for something, scouring the jungle for indications of a thing the Chinese want very badly, and I wonder if you're too stupid to realize what that thing is."

I gripped the cigarette between my lips, wanting it to last forever and scared that it might drop if I spoke. I clenched it between my teeth and mumbled, my voice a dry croak.

"You have an advantage; I haven't had the chance to interrogate one."

"The Chinese thought it would be easy to walk through our defensive line; they don't even consider Germline units a threat because to them we're inferior. Obsolete. They want Thai resources—metallic and genetic. When they take a country, they absorb its occupants for experimentation, looking for new and advantageous traits that they can insert into future production models. Eventually they will cover the world with one race, half-machine, half-synthetic man. But there's a problem, and it's called Sunshine."

I drew on the cigarette again, deeply, and held the smoke in before speaking; now I understood where she was going, and the thought of my mission returned, the excitement making me feel better. "Chen. They want Chen."

Margaret nodded. "They want Chen."

"Why? What does he have, and why is Sunshine such a threat?"

"Because," she said, walking behind me so that I couldn't see her. The sound of water pouring broke the silence, and she lowered a bowl of it to the ground in front of my face, then poured more of it over my body, working her way from my neck to my feet. It was unbelievably cool, and my muscles relaxed to the point where I thought I'd fall asleep again.

"Sunshine," Margaret continued, "is the brain child of Chen, who realized that what the Chinese intended was unholy, so disgusting that even a mercenary like him couldn't be paid enough to be a part of their plans. So he escaped from the Beijing underground. And with him he took an idea that he then sold to the Koreans, an idea that he'd held from the Chinese because it would render even their forces obsolete. A chimeric race. A mixture of animal and man, with proteins so elastic and inhuman that to produce them would truly be an act of creation, something that even God may never have envisioned."

"I'm not a biologist," I said. "And I'm tired. I don't get it."

"Shape-shifters. Chen's Sunshine, if successful, would create a race of beings that would be able to take many forms, man or animal. Armored or not, the things would be fearless and absolutely loyal to those who created them, and could appear in the form of enemy troops and infiltrate at any time. The idea is genius. Chen is a long way from perfecting it, but he made enough progress that when the Chinese learned of his defection and found some of his notes, they came here to Burma. For him. Thailand and the South China Sea are also priorities, but ones that they are willing to postpone. We learned this by playing with Chinese scouts and by capturing one of their division level officers and then torturing him until he broke."

The words spun in my head as I put the pieces together—the armor schematics from Spain and everything else. Now that I'd seen the Chinese in action I understood why the Koreans had worked against the Genetic Weapons Convention in secret and why the US had decided to leave it. Beijing had grown powerful. China hadn't signed the convention, and now that they had started spreading into Burma, it wouldn't be long before someone would have to deal with them. Sunshine was hope. It wasn't something to be feared, and I wondered if the brass knew the details, would they still want me to kill Chen, but it didn't matter. He'd helped the Chinese get to where they were today, and for that alone he deserved to die. It was still a shitty mission; but now it was the *best* one I'd ever had.

"I have to find him," I said. "Please let me go. My job is to find him and get all his data."

"And kill him?" she asked.

"And kill him."

Margaret sat again and lit her own cigarette. Mine was finished, and I tried to drink from the bowl, but it was difficult, and I had to kneel with both legs spread as far as I could get them, leaning over the bowl to lap at the water with my tongue. I couldn't get enough. My throat screamed from being so parched, and I finally resorted to sticking my face in the bowl and sucking in as much water as I could.

"I'm too old," said Margaret. She blew smoke and stared at the candle, her eyes seeing something that wasn't there. "It's been years since Catherine left us, and now I understand what she had been trying to teach me."

"What?"

"That I was born to die. War is all I have, and war is how I'll leave this world, so to fear death is useless." She stood and walked toward the door, saying one last thing before she left. "You are an interesting man. Interesting to us for *many* reasons, and the things you said to your partner last night during our hunt, those rang. It reminded us of what it was like when we first stepped from the tanks, when the ateliers were everything perfect. Sleep. We'll talk more of your mission when you've recovered because there is something I need you to do."

*   *   *

The next few days passed in a blur. Satos came into the cell to deliver a cot and dressed my burns and shoulder with microbots so that the invisible things repaired damaged tissues in a matter of hours, but at some point I came down with a fever. It wasn't anything serious, but the wounds and days of marching followed by torture were too much, and in that weakened state, infection found a willing host. The fever passed within a couple of days. By that time I was nearly normal and sane enough to wonder if they had made the effort to torture me and then nurse me back to health just to start the whole process over again. But I remembered what Margaret had said and thought that it was unlikely; she had a bigger plan in mind, and whatever it was, it required that I be well enough to walk under my own power.

I had just woken from a nap when three girls entered, removed my undersuit, and then dressed me in a loose sarong. They handed me a combat knife.

"What's this for?" I asked.

"Follow us," one said.

"Not unless you tell me why I need a knife."

But they stared at me without answering until I walked toward the door, and then the girls followed me through the temple's narrow passages, telling me where to turn as we moved through a maze. We stepped into the temple's main chamber. It was nighttime, and the satos had filled the room with hundreds of candles so that it glowed with a yellow light, and Jihoon sat on the floor, his hands still bound and his chin touching his chest. He looked unconscious.

Margaret knelt in the middle of the floor, praying, and looked up at me. "You are better now."

"Thanks. Let my partner go."

"He isn't worthy. And you don't give the orders."

I lifted the knife and held it by the blade. "This a gift?"

"Not really. We got it from your equipment." Margaret pointed to the floor, and the other girls formed a loose circle with her at its center. "Sit with me and talk, Lieutenant."

I sat and rested the knife on the floor. "You said we'd talk more about my mission. About Chen. Where is he?"

"He is here. All around us."

"What?" She was speaking softly now, almost whispering, which put me on edge. "What are you talking about?"

"This temple is Chen's. His research institute is about a kilometer below us, where the fool thought he'd be safe from the Chinese and from me. The main entrance is outside Moulmein, and when the Chinese entered Burma, he panicked and blew the only access tunnel, but even now they dig to get at him. We estimate that Chinese forces will reach Chen by tomorrow morning at the latest."

It hit me then—the warm air that we'd felt when I first entered with Jihoon days ago. The temple had never been abandoned; it had never been inhabited in the first place because the thing was nothing more than camouflage, a smoke screen designed to hide the workings of Chen's complex.

"Air handling?" I asked.

"Air handling. A service duct runs from a chamber below us and down to the institute's main pumping station where they pull clean air from the top of the mountain and expel it here, routing it through the temple's entrance tunnel to allow time for the exhaust temperature to equilibrate. That way, it won't show up on Chinese sensors."

"Why haven't you gone down after him?"

Margaret sighed and then turned her head to stare at me. "Because I'm tired, Lieutenant. I can't see anything except for the fact that soon we'll be gone; there's no replacing me or my sisters once we pass."

I shook my head. "There are thousands of satos still in Thailand. You won't be going anywhere soon."

"Not true. There *are* thousands, but now that we see the way, that we're to die and that it is a blessing, we take more risks. We die more quickly every day. Who will lead the *Gra Jaai* when we're spent?"

"How about one of the *Gra Jaai*?" It was a logical answer, and I couldn't understand why succession was even an issue since her followers were so fanatic.

Margaret sighed again and looked away. "No. Most don't have a great deal of experience, and none have seen our birthplace, America, or have the benefit of the kind of training it can give its soldiers. They are brave, but what we feed them in the tanks is subadequate and lacks programs to address modern weapons systems. We need someone who can help with all these things. A human man or woman." I saw where she was going and started to get a sick feeling, wondering if I'd known it would come to this all along. "*You.* Only you can lead them. You have age and experience none of them can match and might be able to convince your superiors to provide you with modern tank-training programs. Also, you know the Americans and yet haven't been corrupted, don't trust them, and don't want to go home. Why is that, Lieutenant?"

I looked at Jihoon and saw he was hurting. Other than

that, his condition wasn't clear from that distance, and all I wanted to do was check on him, but Margaret wouldn't have allowed it and it enraged me—to have to waste time like this, talking. And what she suggested was beyond comprehension; Margaret didn't know me at all, or she'd have known I was no leader.

"You're insane," I whispered. "I don't want to go back to the States because it isn't my home anymore. You wouldn't understand. And I don't know anything about the *Gra Jaai* or your religion so to pick me as some kind of replacement—even if I wanted the job—makes no sense at all."

"You don't have to understand them or their religion, Lieutenant. If I select you, you *become* their religion. From everything I've heard you are already like us, already a killer, or you wouldn't have been able to hunt the way you have for the past *several* years."

The satos around us stood ramrod straight and stared at nothing, carbines slung over their right shoulders. A white number 1 had been painted on their chests. Each of them wore the same kind of protective cloak Jihoon and I had worn, rolled up and tossed over their left shoulder along with the bulky hood. This was her personal guard. Even if the satos weren't fearless already, I suspected that these girls would throw themselves in the path of anything to save Margaret, and it impressed me that someone in this world still had that kind of dedication.

"I don't believe in *anything*," I said. "That's why I'm good at killing. I just don't care anymore, and all I want is to complete my mission and get a child back. That's it."

"Then you and your partner die." The way she said it, so casually, as if she'd just said we should go for a walk, shocked me.

"What, here? *Now?*"

Margaret nodded and stood, unbuckling her combat suit and wriggling out of it until she wore only her undersuit. A knife glittered in her right hand. "Now. You promised you'd kill me that night in the clearing, and I can't turn down the challenge; it's our way. Pick up your knife."

"Why?" I asked. "Why not just shoot the crap out of each other with carbines?"

"Get up."

I lifted the knife and rose, taking a step back. "This is crazy. *You're* crazy. All I want is to get Chen and have someone look at Jihoon. They don't *want* me to kill you, Margaret."

"I want *you* to die," she hissed and then leaped, just as fast as Lucy had or the ones I'd encountered on the street in Australia.

Margaret slammed her shoulder into me and swung her knife toward my stomach so that I had to roll away, landing on the hard marble with a grunt before jumping to my feet. She came again. There was no waiting with this one, and the sense that she had an infinite supply of energy startled me, forced me onto the defensive so that with each attack I moved farther back and closer to one of her girls until my elbow struck the cold ceramic of armor. The girl pushed me toward Margaret, and I stumbled, almost falling onto her knife; the mistake forced me to slam my head into her stomach to keep from falling, and I twisted away from the blade so that it missed my chest, instead cutting through the skin of my shoulder.

Margaret grinned and pointed to the blood running down my arm. "Don't be afraid. Everyone makes the journey at some point."

I shook my head. Sweat dripped from my forehead to the floor, making the spot slippery; I stood still as long as possible, letting the blood and sweat fall to form a tiny puddle at my feet. "I'm not scared. I'm tired. I've lived in a combat suit for so long that until now I couldn't remember using an actual bathroom. My ass hurts. My arms and legs ache all the time. I'm old, Margaret, and you'll never make it to my age because you're a psycho bitch."

Her smile disappeared, and Margaret lunged forward so that I barely dodged the knife, but she'd expected the move and slammed her fist into my windpipe so that I grabbed my throat in an effort to breathe, my shoulder screaming with pain now that the initial shock of being cut had worn off. She backed off. A few feet away, Margaret crouched and grinned as she passed the knife from one hand to the other, and I stretched, moving my head from side to side and pretending not to care what happened next, but I *did* care. She was inching forward again, toward the slick spot on the floor, and I prayed to anything out there that she'd take another step. When she did, I attacked.

Margaret blocked my knife on its way down and sliced at my chest. I backed away. She started to jump forward, trying to press the attack home, but her foot slipped on the wet floor, and as she fell I kicked upward into her face, putting all the energy I had into the blow and screaming with the effort so that when my foot connected with a crunch I grinned, unable to contain my joy. Margaret's head snapped back. From there conscious decision gave way to an instinct born from having to deal with her kind for years, and my knife arm almost had a will of its own when it flashed forward so the blade slammed into her exposed chest. She looked at me in terror and gasped when I used my other hand to slam against the knife's grip, forcing the blade to pop out the other side. She collapsed to the floor then, still breathing but fading fast.

I knelt beside her. "I freakin' hated you. I wanted this for a long time, but what the hell were *you* thinking?"

"And now?" she whispered, so quietly that I had to lean over. "How do you feel about me now?"

"Now I hate you even more. I'm no leader, Margaret. When the Chinese return, they'll be ready for your tricks, and this time they'll dig; they'll hit your people underground where they're defenseless. Thailand is gone."

She smiled and reached to brush the hair from my forehead. "You're ugly, Lieutenant. And you're right that you're no leader because you're so stupid. Things were put in motion a long time ago so that by the time you return to Nu Poe, we will be ready. And you don't have to be a leader for the *Gra Jaai* to follow, you can even be a *stupid* killer. Just help them and let God lead." As soon as she finished the sentence, Margaret's eyes went blank and her arm fell limp to the floor.

A single girl started wailing, but the rest of them smiled. I stood and made way so they could crowd around the body where they produced a white sheet, covering Margaret from head to toe in a rough fabric so that the final product resembled a cocoon. When they'd finished, one of them approached me and bowed her head.

"Tell us what to do."

I ran to Ji and grabbed for a pulse; it was there, but faint. "Fix him. Do whatever it takes. And get me my gear—armor, weapons, everything."

She motioned to the others, two of whom left Margaret and lifted Jihoon carefully, carrying him from the temple and into one of the dark corridors. The one who had been talking to me disappeared and came back a few minutes later with my armor and weapons. It took a moment to gear up. I didn't care if they watched while I dealt with the undersuit's hoses, partly because it had been so long since I'd worn the garment that I'd forgotten the undersuit hadn't been washed, and the odor distracted me from the fact that I was naked. I nearly threw up from the smell. It had gone an entire week unwashed, and even though the climate controls had been fine, the sweat of fear had impregnated the cloth and made it foul. When I finished, I gestured for the girl.

"Show me how to get to Chen."

She nodded. "It will be difficult. Some of us should go with you."

"I don't need you. Just show me the way, and I'll be back in a few hours."

"The Chinese have regrouped and are now headed our way," she said, "so you only *have* a few hours. Follow me."

The room's ceiling barely cleared my head and made me feel faint with the sensation that it could collapse at any moment, and a dim red light provided just enough illumination to see. A wide shaft in the middle of the floor led straight down. From it emerged two large ducts about three meters across, one of which ran straight through the rock overhead, the other into the wall beside me. I crept to the shaft's edge and looked down. Far below me the red lights shone from the side of the walls, lighting the way downward into a hole so deep that the lights disappeared and a sickening feeling of vertigo made me lean back from the edge where I eyed a ladder with suspicion. There wasn't any other way. The sato had left me a few minutes earlier to prepare for my return—*if* I returned—so we could retreat to Nu Poe, hopefully in time to avoid the new Chinese advance on the border; she'd swore it was the only way to reach Chen. I didn't want to do it, but said a silent prayer and slid over the edge, searching for a ladder rung with my boots.

One rung after another I made the descent, watching the minutes tick off; there was no way to measure my progress. None of the girls knew how far down the shaft went or what I'd face at the bottom, and defenses were left to my imagination, which, having now seen the worst of what the Chinese had to offer, had lost any governors or frame of reference as to what was possible or not. Sunshine was about shape-shifting, and the thought made me wonder if I'd face the things when I got inside the complex even though everything indicated that Chen hadn't come close to finishing his research—that it had just begun. But he could have his own army of scouts and warriors, waiting for me to wander in blindly. It was this last thought that made me opt for the flame unit. My carbine was now far above me in the temple because carrying both would have been too heavy during the descent and return, and if I ran into Chinese-style genetics, the flame unit would be more effective.

"Kristen," I said, panting from the effort of descending.

"Yes, Lieutenant?"

"Can any of your sensors tell how far I am from reaching a floor or ledge where I can rest?" I described where I was and then waited for her response.

"I'm sorry, Lieutenant. None of the suit sensors can detect anything like that; it must be out of range for now."

I stopped and looped one arm through a rung, doing my best to stretch while not looking down, and my calf muscles started to spasm, bouncing me so rapidly that I almost slipped. "Keep checking. And tell me when I get close."

The trip downward gave me plenty of time to reflect on Margaret and her last request; she had to have been insane to choose me. What Margaret had seen during the little time we'd known each other and the bits and pieces she'd heard from Lucy—those weren't enough to base a decision so important to the future of her group, and part of me doubted the *Gra Jaai* would accept an American leader anyway, someone opposed to religion or genetics of any kind. My lack of command experience wasn't the issue. With girls like Lucy and the others, it wouldn't be so hard to formulate strategies and tactics because in the girls I'd have thousands of walking battle computers better than any semi-aware fielded, so the fact that I was ill suited in that respect didn't matter; all I'd have to do is ask for a sato's opinion. So what was it that made it feel insane? The questions rattled throughout my thoughts and destroyed any ability to think until an answer presented itself: it *wasn't* insane. Part of me wanted the job. But the years of killing satos had ingrained in me an attitude that to serve with them—even over them—was an insult to all I'd accomplished and was an insult to people like Wheezer. The problem was that no other country except Thailand seemed like a reasonable place to settle down with Phillip, and so far this was the only post-Army job offer I'd gotten.

An hour later Kristen announced the presence of a floor, and I stepped onto a metal grating without having resolved any of my thoughts; for now, they'd have to wait.

Beside me the huge ducts passed through the lattice floor and into a small concrete room below, and it took a few seconds to pry open a metal trapdoor so I could drop my flame unit down and then lower myself after it. My helmet speakers cut off with the loud roar of air-handling equipment. Even without speakers, though, the noise was deafening and throbbed as the machinery blew air at what must have been a rate of thousands of liters per second.

"Lieutenant," said Kristen.

"What?"

"I'm sorry I didn't detect this from the grating above, but there are emissions consistent with video monitoring from the corner in front of you and to the right."

A tiny camera, tucked into the corner near the overhead grate, scanned the area, and I sighed. "Fuck."

"It appears to be a wireless system," she said, using a tone that suggested she was trying to make the best of things. "Would you like me to jam it?"

"Sure. Why not?"

"And Lieutenant?"

Once more I shouldered the flamethrower, grunting under its weight, and then pulled the cloak back on. "What?"

"There is a service hatch in the wall to your left, the emissions from which indicate that it's alarmed."

"This," I said, deciding to pop my helmet for one last cigarette, "keeps getting better and better."

TEN

Retired

After about ten minutes of trying, Kristen succeeded in telling me how to open an electrical access panel so she could deactivate the alarm and unlock the service hatch. I stepped into a cylinder-shaped hallway. Bright lights flooded it, and the white, ceramic tiled walls reminded me of the shop in Khlong Toei, their surfaces so clean and polished that they must have been sterile. The corridor ran in one direction with doors spaced evenly on either side, so I crept forward with my chameleon skin on—even though the bright lighting made it almost useless. All the doors were open. Each one led to an empty room, with row after row of laboratory benches covered with computers and equipment, but sheets of clear plastic had been draped over everything as if the place had been mothballed for another time, waiting for a future that might never come. For a moment I panicked: *What if Chen had already booked it, had found another way out?*

The thought pushed me faster. Margaret was sure Chen was here, but the fact that she tortured us made me consider the possibility again that she had lost it, and doubts lingered as to whether she had ever been sane. *Why* had she tortured us? The satos hadn't asked for any information, and in the end Margaret had given me control of her forces, so the one reasonable answer was that it had all been some sort of test; the girls had needed to confirm the stories about me before she risked the knife fight so they could be certain I was solid by their standards, but that still didn't explain Jihoon. *Ji*, I decided, *they had tortured for fun*. The realization made me furious; even dead, I hated Margaret and embraced that her end had come at my hands—that it was sure to enrage the Army, who wanted her alive. Chen was here. Margaret hadn't been *that* crazy, and maybe killing him would make everything right again.

Another hallway intersected with mine, a few meters ahead, and through the hood my helmet speakers picked up voices, freezing me in place.

"They're speaking Korean," said Kristen. "Two targets, in the right-hand passageway, four meters down. There is a ninety percent chance that they are soldiers. Would you like me to translate?"

"No. They'll be dead soon, so whatever they're saying, it doesn't matter. Do any of the voices resemble Chen's?"

It took a moment for her to check. "No."

I inched along the wall and poked my head around the corner slowly, not wanting the shimmer or motion to attract any attention; two men in combat suits sat against the wall. Their armor was a deep black, and both had Maxwell carbines. They faced away from me as they watched the far end of the corridor where a wall of rubble had collapsed to block the passage, with tremendous boulders and chunks of concrete that mingled to create an impenetrable barrier. Two more men knelt at the rubble, monitoring seismic equipment.

I pulled my head back and rested both gauntlets against the wall before whispering to Kristen. "Two seismic specialists facing north in what looks like the main entrance tunnel. There may be Chinese boring headed this way. Can you pick up anything?"

My heads-up flickered to a seismic display as Kristen worked; she clicked in a minute later. "Boring detected. Approximately three hours until they reach us, but my margin of error is one hour, Lieutenant. I apologize for the uncertainty."

"Don't worry about it, sweet pea. It helps."

I rounded the corridor and fired a burst of flame at the two in combat suits, their screams barely registering as I pushed through the fire and toward the seismic team. They stood and faced me. Neither understood at first how a flame unit firing tube could suspend itself in midair until I let the thing hang and flung my cloak aside, drawing my knife. One of them held his hands up. The other tried to run, and I extended my knife arm in a side-sweeping motion so he ran straight into its point, making it difficult to yank the thing free. The remaining man died in midscream.

With the element of surprise gone, I could move faster; there wasn't any time to waste. At the intersection I stopped, and a mild panic set in because it wasn't clear which direction to take and the corridors ran to infinity; new passageways branched in the distance, and there were only a couple of hours to go. How big was the place and how many more Korean soldiers were there? *How'd they get into Burma in the first place?* The questions immobilized me with uncertainty, and I wanted to scream in frustration until I started down the original corridor I'd been on; Kristen would keep track of things, creating a digital map so we could find our way back to the service shaft.

A doorway on the left was closed. When I approached it, the thing opened and I stepped into what looked like a cafeteria, and more than thirty people—men and women— crouched behind overturned tables where they tried to hide, screaming at the near-invisible form that had just entered. To them, I must have been a horror.

"Thais," said Kristen. "No voice spectrum consistent with that of Chen."

"Translate," I said. "I need to ask them a few questions."

"Go ahead, Lieutenant."

"Where is Chen?" None of them answered, and the question brought more screams so I yelled it. *"Where is Chen? Where the hell is he?"*

One of the women stood. "He's in the systems control area."

"Where is that?"

"Down the main hall," she said, pointing out the door. "Keep going straight until it ends, the door on the left."

"How many Korean troops are with him?" I asked.

"None. There are two monitoring the main entrance to warn us of the Chinese, but the rest left over a week ago. The children are with Chen."

Her response shifted everything and confused me with the sensation of having entered another world; none of it fit with what I had assumed would be here.

"Why were Korean troops here in the first place?" I asked. "And what children?"

She spread her arms and shrugged, as if she thought the answer obvious. "The Koreans were here to monitor Chen—to make sure he didn't work on offensive projects. When the Chinese came, the majority of them left, and we are scheduled to leave in one hour."

"And the children?"

"Our main project, a peaceful one. We used genetic material given to Chen years ago to resurrect important Chinese figures from the past."

"Why?" I asked.

She shrugged again. "Chen never told us that. We were paid to get a job done, and he paid very well. We came here from Bangkok."

"So you've never heard of Project Sunshine?"

"No," she said, shaking her head.

It was clear this particular woman didn't know anything, and already the chronometer was moving fast, making me nervous about the Chinese and warning me that it would be impossible to question everyone.

I almost let them live because the indicator on my tank showed only about four bursts left, but these were Chen's scientists; they *had* to be. Catching them alive would be a coup for the Chinese even if I scrambled Chen's computers and killed him because these people may have worked on Project Sunshine despite what the woman said. I couldn't risk their capture; anything in their brains would be picked at and gone over by Beijing's technicians, and in that scenario, life would have been the worse fate for them. They screamed again, this time all of them, but I stopped paying attention when the room's sprinklers went off, doing nothing to abate an intense heat that forced me into the hallway. The sprinkler water flashed into steam, the gel and metal powders bursting into bright sparks that reminded me of the Fourth of July; fireworks, I realized, would be one thing Phillip would miss if we stayed in Thailand.

The door slid shut on their screams and left me to my thoughts. *Children. No Project Sunshine.* If what the woman had said was true, then my mission to gather data was about to turn south in a big way, leaving me with the orders to question and then kill Chen, which was fine by me. Even though the bush was far above, its call was all around to let me know that it was almost over, that once the guy was dead I could leave Burma with the satisfaction of having removed a thorn from the jungle's side. And I'd be with Phillip again. From then on the missions I'd take would be ones of my own making, ones that made sense and didn't involve the military or people like Jihoon or Momson or even Wheezer, who had screwed up despite his training and still left a hole in my gut.

A few seconds passed before I realized I'd moved down the hallway, heading closer to Chen. I felt him. He was close now, and it was as though the walls moaned from the sickness of infection, Chen's presence a foreign object that the rock wanted excised so its mountains could go back to their game of just sitting there. *Watching everything.* A door slid open ahead of me then, and four Asian children emerged—two boys and two girls, all of them teenagers and all of them grinning. It occurred to me that after flaming the scientists, I'd thrown my cloak back and had forgotten to pull it around me.

"Uncle told us something had gone wrong with the tunnels," one of the boys said. He was the larger of the two and had black hair that fell almost to his eyes. The older girl laughed and threw her hair back—a thick mass, straight and so black that it almost looked blue.

"He is not Chinese, though," she said. "Uncle thought that our people had arrived."

There was something about them that made me uneasy; a creepy feeling moved from my legs and into my stomach, a sensation rooted in the fact that these were satos— not like the American or Chinese ones, which may have made me even more uneasy. Normal children would have been scared when I pointed my flame unit in their direction.

"Who are you?" I asked.

"We should ask *you* that," the older boy said, taking a step toward me. "You snuck into our home, and I'm assuming the rest of our family is now dead. Who are *you*?"

"I'm a friend of Chen's and came for a visit."

"Uncle is busy now," the girl said, switching to English. "He sent us to entertain you."

I never got a chance to fire. The children rushed me in a mad dash and leaped at my chest, almost knocking me flat in the process, and then started clawing at my armor in an attempt to strip the flame unit away, their high-pitched shrieks forcing my speakers to cut off.

"These children are genetically enhanced or completely artificial," said Kristen. I struggled to knock the kids away while she spoke, but as soon as I dislodged one, he or she would leap again. My legs started to buckle under the additional weight. "No normal human would be able to move in this fashion, Lieutenant."

"Damn it, Kristen." I finally got a hold of the flame unit again, one boy's hands gripping it tightly and refusing to let go. *"Call me BUG!"*

The trigger clicked shut. Fire engulfed me and suit alarms blared, triggering the hiss of emergency oxygen at the same time heat penetrated from all sides and forced me to scream with the sensation of having created hell on earth. My faceplate started to melt. Metallic parts of my suit ignited with thousands of sparks, but through it all I saw the children fall and then felt light enough to take a few steps back out of the main blaze. I shrugged out of the cloak, which now flamed brightly, and threw it at them, along with the flame unit, its tanks on the verge of blowing with whatever fuel remained. But the children were still alive. They flopped and rolled within the fire, continuing to shriek, and one of them clawed its way toward me, trying to escape and take one last lunge.

I ran. Behind me the flame unit exploded and sucked the air from my lungs so that I fell to the floor and crawled, trying my best to find a pocket of air. When I could breathe again, the children had fallen silent. Behind me in the hallway, with nothing left to consume, the flames began to die and all around me my suit smoldered to send streamers of smoke that were just visible through the wavy glass of my faceplate. It took a few minutes to get out of the suit, and once I had, I started crying. Kristen was dead. It hadn't been obvious that she'd been as much a part of my life as Wheezer until she was gone, and I knelt to remove as many memory chips as I could, hoping that some of them would at least be readable. In many ways, Kristen had been my best friend, and Chen would pay for her loss too, in addition to that of Wheezer.

My undersuit had blackened. Portions of it were so charred that they crumbled away to reveal blistered skin, and the pain brought tears so that for a moment everything faded. But there was no way to stop; not now. Chen was close, so I grabbed my knife, stood, and stumbled toward an open doorway, through the burning fat of his children that now covered the tunnel floor.

Chen sat on a chair in a darkened room where holo images of the complex spun over computer terminals, and mattresses and clothes lay strewn on the floor. He was crying. The man wore a lab coat and his beard had grown in since the picture I'd seen was taken, its hairs clumped as if he hadn't bathed in some time. Chen stared at me through dirty glasses.

"They weren't going to kill you," he said. "You're an American."

"I don't care."

"Those were my *children*. We would have gone quietly but I thought you were the Chinese, that you had come to get rid of me."

I shrugged and glanced around the room, checking for an ambush before stepping inside. "You gave Beijing a lot of ideas, so why would they want you dead? The Chinese sure have fielded a lot of neat things in the last few years, Chen, ones that are sure to kill a lot of people."

"Those were *mine*," he said. "I know what you're thinking—that I stole secrets from the US labs—but that's a lie. I don't know what they told you, but it couldn't be further from the truth. Everything I gave the Chinese came from well after I left the US. From *me*."

"Oh. So that's why you ran like a little bitch, because a radioactive China seemed like an attractive place to retire, in Beijing's underground rat holes? It had nothing to do with you stealing secrets." I was already bored with the conversation; Chen was a worm. He didn't have any idea why I was there, and from his whining it was clear that the guy thought he could talk his way to freedom and make some kind of deal.

"They were my children!" he screamed, changing the subject. "You had no right to kill them all."

I lunged and knocked him from the seat with my fist so that he yelled and grabbed his nose, trying to stop the bleeding. "Those weren't children, you little shit. They were pets. You created them in a test tube and then kept them around so you could pat yourself on the back— reminders of how smart you think you are."

Chen picked himself up and backed away. "You've killed me now. Even if I go back to the States with you, the Chinese will send someone no matter where you put me, and they'll track me to any prison. You murdered replicas of Premier Kang's children, who died in an accident when they were teenagers; they were my ticket to a pardon."

"A what?" It took a moment for his words to sink in before I understood. "You were going to bribe the Chinese with them? Give the premier back his little brats so he'd look the other way on your double cross?"

"He would have forgiven me, I'm sure of it. But now I'm dead no matter what."

"Maybe," I said. "But then you must have also been planning on giving them Sunshine."

Chen's face went pale. "You know of Sunshine?"

"Yeah, Chen. I just can't figure out how you convinced the Koreans to leave you behind when they left, why they didn't kill you and destroy this place."

"The Koreans are an interesting people." His manner had changed in a fraction of a second, and where before he'd been terrified, now he was smiling. *Smug*. Chen moved toward me, but I held up my knife because he wasn't a worm after all, more like a snake—one I didn't want anywhere near me. "I arranged it so that they left me with two of their guards," he continued, "two who had been tasked with destroying all my data and then assassinating me before they left."

"But you had already bribed them," I finished.

"Like I said. They're very interesting. You could make a lot of money too, and all you have to do—"

I leaned into a side kick, connecting with his stomach so he collapsed to the ground and fought for breath. Chen looked up at me. I knelt beside him and ripped his belt off, using it to tie both ankles to one of his wrists, then spat on the side of his face, trying to control the impulse to sink my knife into his throat. The anger was almost too much to bear. He had no clue how many people had died because of the Chinese genetics, and even if he had, it was unlikely someone like him would care. There was one last thing to accomplish with Chen, and I missed Kristen; she would have been helpful in dealing with him and with the mountains of data I was sure to face.

"What are you doing?" he asked. "I can't walk if you tie my feet and hands together; how are you going to carry me?"

"I'm not going to carry you. And you're not walking anywhere for now. Where's your Sunshine data?"

Chen laughed and shook his head. "You're crazy. I don't have any data; the Koreans wouldn't let me near it once I'd sold it to them. They kept me on a short leash, and their computer experts swept all our systems regularly to make sure I didn't try to hide anything. It took *forever* to convince them to negotiate with the Burmese for my lab construction; they never trusted me and wanted me locked up. In Wonsan. But they needed me happy, in case they ran into any obstacles on Sunshine, so I used it as leverage to convince them to give me this: my new home in Burma."

"But hiding the data is exactly what you did, isn't it? I know how greedy crapheads like you work, Chen. If the Koreans paid for it, then someone else would too, right? Only you'd need some way to transfer it to a second buyer, which means you'd need some way to store it. And Burma was an interesting location to pick; who was the next customer? India? Malaysia? Thailand itself?"

I took the one free hand he had and laid it on the floor, kneeling on his forearm so he couldn't move. There weren't any second thoughts. Wheezer wouldn't have died if it weren't for the mission, the mission wouldn't have existed if it weren't for Sunshine, and the world would be a better place without people like Chen. I slammed the edge of my knife blade down. He screamed with the loss of his thumb and kept screaming in a way that sounded broken, as if Chen couldn't decide whether to sob or yell.

"My *God* that must hurt." I wiped the blade on his lab coat and then placed it against his index finger. "Where is your data?"

Through his sobs, Chen managed to speak. "In my pocket. I couldn't risk storing it on any of the computers or servers."

"You have got to be shitting me." But I reached into his lab coat pocket and yanked out a plastic wallet, inside of which he'd stored multiple data chits. His other pockets were empty.

"I'm going to tell the Chinese what you did," Chen whispered. "That you killed the premier's children."

"I've seen the Chinese in action. And they wouldn't give a shit one way or another."

Chen saw the flash of light on metal and inhaled to scream, but the knife sliced into his neck and cut it short. There wasn't any point in wasting more time. And I'd have to risk leaving without destroying the computer equipment because with the loss of my flame unit there wasn't any way to accomplish that task, and without Kristen there was no time to check every computer and server. I wouldn't have known what to look for anyway or how to access the systems.

By now the vibration of the Chinese fusion borer shook the floor as it neared. I sprinted down the hallway, keeping my fingers crossed that I wouldn't get lost, then almost dove through the access hatch. Who knew how much time I had? For the first time in my life, I was grateful for satos and prayed that they were still in the temple because the mission wasn't over yet and one thing was sure: I'd need all the help I could get. The Chinese still had scouts between us and Nu Poe, and more would be on their way.

The mission was over. Now that it had been accomplished and even though we hadn't done everything we'd been tasked to do, a feeling of satisfaction gave me new energy as I did my best to fit into Margaret's undersuit and armor. Jihoon was on his feet again but limping, and he grinned at me as I tried to pull her clothes on.

"Those are girl's hoses."

I flipped him off. "Stop staring at me."

"I just think you're sexy. For an asshole. You know you'd better not have to take a leak, because you'll have to take off your whole freakin' suit to do *that*."

The satos had gone outside to make sure the area was clear, and by the time I pinched my new armor shut— the carapace so tight that I had trouble breathing—we heard the borer crash into Chen's complex below with a muffled thump followed by a tremor. I grabbed my carbine and slid into the cloak while we moved. The winding passage lasted longer than felt reasonable, and a sense of urgency made me want to sprint, despite the fact that Margaret's boots were at least two sizes too small and would soon make walking an agonizing prospect. I plugged the cloak into my suit and powered on. When we moved out into the jungle, my map popped onto my heads-up and we headed east toward the satos' red dots and into daytime, which meant we'd be more visible to Chinese scouts.

"I hate them," Ji hissed over the radio.

"Who?"

"Them. Satos."

"I told you that you would."

He panted as he talked, and I wondered if he'd make it far without passing out. "I didn't get it. Now I see why you wanted them all wiped. They break my ribs, torture me for days, and then all of a sudden apologize and fill me with micros to fix me up. I still hurt all over."

"Are you going to make it all the way back?" I asked. "It might take us two days to get to Nu Poe, longer if we run into trouble."

"I don't care if I have to crawl to get out of here; *I'll make it.*"

The monkeys scurried through the trees overhead, and a sense of panic had infected the jungle, making me uneasy as we jogged through the brush; there was no point in being quiet. Chinese forces would follow aboveground now that their troops had moved into Chen's complex, and soon the area could be crawling, so I pushed as hard as I could, trusting that the satos had cleared the way ahead. A blurred shape brushed against my shoulder and made me dive. Behind me I heard Jihoon curse, then saw his tracers flick by my head to snap through the leaves until a loud hissing filling my speakers and my goggles frosted over, darkening to protect me from the glare of a thermite grenade.

Once the fire had died, I stood and looked at the molten wreckage of a Chinese scout; next to it was the body of a sato, her head shredded by Jihoon's fléchettes just after she had crammed a thermite grenade into the scout's armor.

"Jesus Christ, Ji."

He sounded panicked. "I didn't know it was one of them. Shit, Bug, *I didn't know.*"

"How am I going to explain this one?"

"Don't worry about it," he said. "I'll cop to it. It was an accident."

"No, you won't; don't say a word to them." Jihoon didn't get it. The girls were perfect at this job, and if he told the truth they'd see his mistake as a serious flaw and could use it as an excuse to wipe him. To them, he would be admitting he was a liability. "Keep your mouth shut and let me handle it." I looked at her again and kicked a rock. "God*damn* it all."

The bushes next to me moved as Ji pushed past. "I don't know why you're so freakin' worried. It's just a meat machine, right?"

"One we needed," I said, following him as we moved out again. "And there's more to these chicks than you realize. They're not all crazy."

He stopped and threw his hood back so I could see his faceplate. "Are you kidding me? After all you've said about them over the last couple of weeks?"

"They're all we have buying us time in Thailand. You're supposed to be the smart one, so think about it. We need every one of these betties alive and fielded to slow the Chinese down until we have a chance to get our forces ashore and into the bush. They're the only thing in this place that makes any sense."

"Holy shit," said Jihoon. "You're thinking about taking Margaret's offer. You want to stay here with them, even after all we've seen on this shitty op."

"I don't know what I'm going to do."

The dots on my heads-up showed the girls about a hundred meters away, but even as we moved they barely registered because Jihoon had gotten me thinking. It *wasn't* a shitty mission. I'd been on tens, maybe hundreds, and this was the first that had made me feel good; getting to Margaret and Chen had mattered and now that it was over, the aftermath hadn't left me with the feeling that I'd killed one cockroach just to have to chase after a thousand more in some never-ending extermination of rotting girls. The girls were loathsome and always would be—a metaphor of what the world had become and how far down we'd gone as a race—and the realization hit me; I *understood* why most people hated satos. They were a warning of our impending extinction. Not anytime soon, maybe not for another hundred years, but the way had been mapped and there wouldn't be any deviating from the genetic singularity that had grabbed hold to pull us across an event horizon we'd been too stupid to recognize and avoid. So hating them made sense, revulsion a normal reaction to a situation from which there would be no escape, the same way most people hated to think about the fact that someday they'd die. Who didn't go through life hoping to live forever? Satos were bitches to the average soldier on the line because although they didn't know it, a part of their subconscious keyed into it instantaneously—that they were a million times inferior to the girls, who were a million times removed from what your average person defined as "normal." Satos were like a flashing neon sign: *say good-bye to the old definition of humanity because we're your future.*

Now Korea would have Sunshine, and as soon as I gave up the data, then America would have it too, and I could almost imagine the day when our efforts at gene therapy, organ replacement, bioenhancement, and everything else on the menu would merge with the wholesale creation of artificial life in a tank. Breeding stations were already obsolete—maybe families too—and nobody knew it. But now I did. All I had to do was see the little family that Chen had created, and it opened the door to an infinite number of questions, like how long would it be before some rich senator in DC would pay anything to have someone recreate a child she'd lost to a car accident or a tornado? How long until a black market popped up to fill the need? Exhaustion and old age combined within the jungle to make everything crystal clear until it became a thing of beauty for one reason: I accepted the reality of my role. I was a killer. The path chosen by the Chinese was one branch on a tree that had an infinite number of branches, and although I couldn't stop us from moving forward with genetics, there was a chance to help the world from taking Beijing's route—one that involved turning men and women into animals, into armored slaves. It hadn't been a shitty mission at all, and I was tired of running from the truth because we'd created a world in which Phillip would have to grow and it would be my job to open his eyes. Mine had been ripped open—the eyelids stripped. But here, in the bush, his awakening to the newness would be like a gentle immersion where he'd have decades to acquaint himself with the scientific frontier, a wild west complete with a balance of horrors and promise. Better than the tanks. Better than a school.

Jihoon had been right. Killers belonged in the field. Killers belonged together, and my hatred of the girls was probably never going to leave, but for now at least we both had the same goal—murdering Chinese—and that was enough. The mission hadn't *changed* anything in me; it had just made me see the same stuff in a new light, and if I stayed, the satos and I could slaughter an entire branch of human evolution to save another, one that was a little more palatable.

We joined with the girls in an area that sloped downward and had been cleared by a recent mudslide. "Your girl is dead," I said, hoping it would preclude any questions about what had happened. "Let's keep moving."

"The other man is slow," one of them said, clicking into the private frequency.

"So?"

"Death and faith. We do as you say. But we would move faster without him, and he could stay behind to hold off any pursuing Chinese."

"There are no pursuing Chinese," I said, pissed off because she was right. "So for now we make sure he stays with us."

The girl sounded strange, and at first I thought she was growling at me, until I realized that she was crying. "You took our Lily. Margaret is dead and so now we follow you, but some of us will not forget how it happened."

"Margaret was *ready* to go. You'll do as I say or you can join her because I just don't give a shit right now. *Move.*"

We set out in a jog, and my feet threatened to burst through the sides of my boots so that already they started to blister; the pace was going to kill us if the Chinese didn't. Twice Jihoon slipped as we descended the gentle slope of the mountain, and the last time he didn't stop until he landed against a banyan tree, his chameleon skin deactivated when his forearm controls inadvertently triggered. Everyone froze. At first I didn't know why I stopped because the bugs around us started chirping immediately, suggesting that for the moment nobody was around us; but there was a feeling—like the air inside my suit had gotten heavier, the input from my speakers tinged with threat. Then, from behind us in the direction of the temple, came a distant crash.

"They have arrived," one of the girls said.

"Jihoon, get up and keep moving," I shouted, continuing downward with the others; Margaret's map controls were different than the ones in my old suit, and I gave up trying to figure them out. "How far behind us are they?"

"Three kilometers."

Jihoon's dot was close, and I heard him moving through the underbrush. "I can't keep this up," he said. His breath sounded rapid.

"Yes, you can." I clicked onto his private frequency. "If you don't, we'll leave you behind. We have to get back to the line, and there's no way we can slow down to rest or to carry you."

"We gotta stop sometime. To sleep."

My chronometer read three in the afternoon, and I had to resist the impulse to forecast when night would come because it didn't matter; this time we wouldn't be stopping. "We aren't going to sleep, Chong. It's all out from here to Thailand, and we won't be slowing to look out for scouts because the threat from them is less than the threat from being caught in the Chinese advance."

Jihoon didn't say anything. From the sound of his movement you could tell that he was out of control, unable to manage his rate of descent, and that he had let gravity take hold to force him into a combination of sliding and rolling. There was nothing anyone could do. Behind us I felt the Chinese advance pressing in and imagined their genetics crashing through the jungle en masse, so huge and in such great numbers that they wouldn't bother to fire on us, instead walking through to grind our bodies into the mud under steel feet. The sound of their servos rang through my memory, and for a moment a sense of terror rose in my stomach, making me move faster.

We were still a good distance from the Thai border, and when night fell we'd have to recross the river. It was critical that we get there well ahead of Chinese forces.

* * *

Scouts hit us from either side, just before sunset. Tracer fléchettes leaped from the jungle as we moved into a draw with its bottom dry and cracking from the heat and lack of rain, and when we dove for cover, several blasts worked their way down our line as the Chinese detonated mines. Thermal gel splashed my helmet. My suit filled with the burning smell as the gel ate through ceramic, and I tossed aside the useless hood, struggling to pop my helmet off before the stuff ate through and into my head. What was left of my lid smoked on the ground next to me. I drew on the closest source of fléchettes and started firing short bursts. It was a long shot; my fléchettes would have to score a direct hit on one of their sensors, and as soon as I opened up, at least two targeted me with return fire until I had to duck, pressing my face into the dirt with a moan.

Jihoon's voice crackled in my ears, making me grateful that the components of my vision hood had escaped damage. "To hell with this, Bug, I'm getting out."

"Ji," I said, noticing the air shimmer next to me, "stay put. Don't move. The satos will—"

Before I finished a cone of flames erupted and seared the side of my face as it soaked the tree line next to me, igniting the wood so it cracked and spat. One of the Chinese stopped firing. Whoever was using the flame unit worked it away from me and onto the next Chinese position. The scout burst from the trees, confused, and rolled on the ground to disappear somewhere downhill in a ball of fire. Then the shooting stopped. Four of our original red dots had turned yellow, dead, and I leaped to my feet to continue downhill as I shouted for everyone to follow, but it hadn't been necessary; the others came after me. Ten minutes later, the last of the day's sunlight disappeared and plunged the jungle into darkness. We slowed to a jog again, the world of infrared vision making depth perception difficult.

"Less than a kilometer to the river now, Lieutenant," one of the girls said.

"Which one are you?"

"Excuse me?" she asked.

I didn't say anything at first, trying to catch my breath. "Your name, what's your name?" It would be difficult to make it without stopping. We'd been moving downhill all day, but already my knees were weak from the effort, and the pain from Margaret's boots had turned into a burning agony so that I hated to imagine what my feet looked like since they *felt* like a pair of bloody stumps. "And let's slow to a walk for a bit."

"I'm Jennifer," she said.

"How are we doing on flame units and fuel?"

She paused and then clicked back in. "Two flame units, both with only one or two shots each. Plenty of thermite grenades. And we grabbed a flame hood from one of our sisters, death and faith."

"What the hell is that?" I asked. We'd stopped for a moment so I could slip the new hood over my vision kit, then someone handed me a pair of thermite grenades before we pushed on. "Death and faith?"

"It is one of our mantras. You wouldn't understand."

I laughed, then coughed from the effort of breathing; the hood smelled like whoever had last worn it. A girl. It reminded me of Bea, and for a moment my thoughts shifted to her and to Phillip, making me wonder where he was and how he was doing. It wasn't clear if we'd make it now. Losing even just a few of our group with so much uphill ground to cover had reduced the odds of our success, and I gripped one of the thermite grenades because at the very least killing would make everything a little better. Something moved in the jungle to our right. The sound of branches crackling pulled me from my concentration, and we froze in a line, the map showing about ten meters of spacing between us, and it was enough distance to make me think that the others may as well have been in Bangkok.

"Death," I whispered over the general frequency, "is something I've resigned myself to, Jennifer. Faith is almost worthless."

Something glowed white behind the jungle's wall of leaves and vines. I knelt and brought my carbine up, aiming it as best I could, but it stayed behind the brush and hadn't moved since we'd stopped, so in order to get a better shot I'd have to shift position. The ground was soft underfoot. We'd been moving quickly and for so long that my calves vibrated and my boots slipped on clay at the same moment the thing burst from the underbrush, squealing as it charged at me in a flash of dark fur and tusks. I fired and brought it down with a quick burst.

"Boar," I said into the radio. "It's just a boar."

"We should keep going then," said Jennifer.

I shrugged and watched as the boar gasped for air, then fired another shot to put it out of its misery and to release the anger from having been startled so badly. "Goddamn *thing*."

"Why are you so angry about a boar?" asked Jihoon. Already his dot had started drifting away from me so I jogged to catch up.

"I'm hungry. It would have made a good meal. Man cannot live on ration packs and castor oil alone."

"Castor oil?" one of the girls asked. "Why do you take castor oil?"

Jihoon's laughter came through too loud from my speakers. "It cleans out the pipes."

"I don't understand."

"You have death and faith," I said. "We have regular bowel movements and Big Brother. Similar concepts if you stop and think. And we don't want to go back to those days."

You could almost hear their brains fry with confusion, and I thought, *Good. Fuck 'em*. Just because we now had a common enemy didn't have to mean I'd have to like them. Ever. I just had to get back to Nu Poe and then keep the satos alive long enough to kill as many Chinese as I could—before they got *us*—and that was *if* I took Margaret's offer.

The boat was where we'd left it, and Jennifer ferried the first group of girls over, promising to come back for us and leaving a flame unit in case the scouts returned; I could feel the Chinese waiting for something. The jungle had piped a warning signal straight into my gut—that the scouts were here—so I scanned the trees from the shore and searched for any sign of them, hoping to see something because the exhaustion had eroded almost every feeling, including fear, leaving nothing except for anger; the Chinese had chased me for too long. I wanted to get back to Nu Poe but not to see Phillip or reach safety; I wanted the line so I could turn and fight when they attacked. At least on the line you had a chance to fire and hit something, even when they used their chameleon skins, and at least on the line you could watch thousands of them die. A strong breeze rustled my cloak, and hundreds of frogs croaked, but the animals hadn't noticed anything odd, splashing and making Jihoon flinch so he bumped my arm.

"You see anything?" he asked.

"No. But they're out there."

"What do you mean, 'they're out there'? You sound more and more like a nutjob every day. I just want to get the hell out of this place and don't care if I never see another jungle as long as I live. I'll head to a reclamation zone if I have to; at least it's dry there. You can see for miles in every direction."

"Sure," I said. "If the radiation isn't too bad or the dust storms calm down to the point where you can *go* outside, I guess."

He didn't say anything for a while, and behind us I heard the regular splash of a paddle as the canoe returned. If they were going to hit us that night, I figured, they'd do it before we got on the water, and I tucked the flame unit's tube against my shoulder to get ready, aiming at the closest trees.

"Do you *really* think they're out there?" asked Jihoon.

"Yeah, Chong. I do."

The boat scraped onto the bank behind us, and Jihoon jumped into the water, a little too noisy in his haste to move out, and I expected the jungle to erupt with thousands of Chinese before I calmed down and climbed into the canoe; Jennifer pushed off, and a moment later we paddled into the river's deep current. I still watched the bush. Even as it receded behind us the sensation of impending threat from the trees didn't lift because although the scouts hadn't made their move it was a near certainty they'd watched every one of ours.

"Jennifer, any sign of Chinese on the other side?"

"No," she said. "But my sisters are searching the village now and will radio if they find anything. We haven't heard from Nu Poe, but it's clear now that we're being jammed."

I shook my head. "I hadn't thought to check on that with all the excitement. Is that normal for them to jam radio operations in the area?"

"Not normal for the Burmese, but they lacked the equipment. God knows what's normal for the Chinese; we can't figure out why they haven't had regular air patrols over the river. With such capabilities, we would never have stopped patrolling and would use constant high-altitude surveillance."

"Jennifer," I said, sighing.

"Yes?"

We had reached the far shore, and I jumped to the bank, handing her the flame unit when she debarked. "Shut up. And let's just count our blessings."

We moved through the village like ghosts, crouch-walking while I swung my carbine from side to side, ready for a scout to materialize out of the elephant grass that swayed in the wind. Someone had stacked the bodies. The people I'd wiped lay in the middle of the settlement in a pile, and I fought the urge to search through it to look for the boy. Something tugged at my chest. A sensation of regret mixed with an uneasy feeling that Jihoon had been right and that I was going crazy, but he still didn't get it, that out here my way of doing things was the way to survive; in the bush one's worth was measured by his or her willingness to slaughter. The boy had been visible when I'd shot at the civilians, but I didn't want to see his face now. It wouldn't have fit with the way I remembered him, waving from the shore in amazement as his canoe floated away, and I had to remind myself: he was out of this shit. Better off dead. If Thailand went into the crapper like the US had—where some soulless computer who thought itself smarter than Einstein made all your decisions—and they put clamps on everyone's brain bucket to monitor for potential malcontents, he wouldn't be around to see it. The boy had been spared. For the dead there was no more pain and no more doubt, just the comfort of having gone out quickly—so quickly that it had to have been their time.

The other girls joined with us, and we moved east into the tall grass. I remembered what had happened there the last time; a group of scouts had sprinted through it like a pack of hyenas, and when the stuff swallowed us, I wondered if the Chinese were still there, having waited all this time for our group to arrive. Even if we hadn't been using chameleon skins, I wouldn't have seen the girls or Jihoon around me. The elephant grass towered over and surrounded me with an ocean of three-meter-tall blades, which glowed on infrared so I imagined the water inside as it heated in the Burmese sun, hoarding energy so that even at night the stuff was warm. Only the mountains were visible and loomed in front of me, a lighter shade of black than the sky, and already we'd started moving up a grade, my legs struggling against gravity and begging for rest. I sipped water from my tube. The stuff landed warmly on my tongue, a body temperature liquid that for a brief moment made me panic with the thought that somehow I was drinking Margaret's blood. My heart pounded. Inside the suit you could ignore the sounds being piped in through speakers and focus on the echo of your breathing, even the sound of your own heartbeat if it got loud enough; mine sounded as though it was on the verge of cardiac arrest.

Before I could calm myself down, the village erupted with plasma bursts behind us so I flattened myself in the grass, calling out over the radio, "Is anyone hit?" But their dots looked fine on my heads-up, and each one called in alive. "Where is that fire coming from?"

Jennifer clicked in. "I'm going back to see."

"Hold on," I said. "I'll go with you. Everyone else stay put."

Jennifer and I moved back the way we'd come and the grass whispered over my armor as I slid forward on my stomach, heading for the village. Plasma flashed through the vegetation at the field's edge. I pushed my carbine through and touched its trigger, activating the gun's camera so I could see into the village as huge hemispheres of bright gas erupted on the clay and by now the huts were gone. Piles of ash marked their original location, but these disappeared in the shelling and the wind. The artillery streaked in from the mountain across the river and after zooming in to mark the distance, I estimated the location from which the barrage had originated. Jennifer and I slid back, taking a few minutes to rejoin the group.

"It's coming from the temple," I said into the mic. "The Chinese must have brought artillery or tanks through their tunnel."

"Or APCs," said Jennifer.

"Why are they hitting the village?" Jihoon asked.

I shook my head before realizing that he couldn't see it. "Us. We're the only targets nearby, and somebody either targeted it blindly or they have a spotter nearby who thought they saw something."

"Now we know why the scouts didn't hit us," I said. "We should get—"

Before I could finish, my goggles flashed with a bright light before cutting off, and an explosion ripped the grass around us as if someone had just taken a huge scythe to the field, the blast of which tossed me to the side. Another explosion hit nearby, followed by three more; after that I lost track of the numbers because so many hit the clay and grass, and sparks fell almost straight from the sky, resembling a meteor shower that had somehow targeted us.

"Bombers," I yelled into the radio. "High altitude." At the same time the plasma walked toward us, making the ground rumble even more as the blasts approached.

"They're adjusting fire!" Jennifer shouted.

It wouldn't be long before we got hit. The sensation of being watched filled me with dread because this was the worst possible situation; the jungle was at least a kilometer away. Our choices had been reduced to either staying and dying or moving and maybe making it out, so the calculus was as simple as it got, and I jumped to my feet, sprinting upward toward the high mountains. There was no need to tell anyone to move; Jihoon had already started running before me and the others followed, the entire group pushing through elephant grass with no thought of motion detectors, booby traps, or that someone out there had seen us and was vectoring the attack.

Jihoon's chameleon skin made him invisible ahead of me, but with each flash I saw him in silhouette, his carbine hanging from its flexi-belt and dragging through the clay and grass behind him. A missile hit to my right. The blast overrode my goggles again, and a sharp blow struck my shoulder so that I looked to the side, thinking someone had hit me with a club, but nobody was there. Another erupted from behind, throwing me through the air to land on my face and slide through the grass for at least ten feet before regaining my footing and running on. It was like sprinting through hell. There was no sense of time or pain, and all my exhaustion disappeared in a rush of adrenaline that kept me going for an unknown period of time. When the jungle's leaves slapped my hood, it was a shock. I kept moving in, following Jihoon's dot on my map, before I caught up with him and told him to stop; the barrage had left us behind, continuing to rage outside the jungle.

Only one of the girls joined us, Jennifer. "The others are gone. Is anyone wounded?"

"I don't know," I said. By now the adrenaline had started to ebb, and my right shoulder was on fire; I looked down to see that half my cloak had disappeared, and the armor around my shoulder had been shattered to show a mixture of bone and blood underneath. The injuries surprised me, and I passed out.

"You have to wake up, asshole!"

Ji was slapping the side of my face. My vision hood had been knocked to the side so at first I thought I'd been blinded, and I tried to reach up and adjust it before remembering my right arm; the pain made me scream.

Jennifer fixed my hood so I could see. "Your arm is bad. We've shot you with bots, but we have no pain relievers. It's not something we need to carry with us under normal circumstances."

"Of course not." I grunted with the effort to sit up. "Why would you if you don't ever feel pain?"

"We have got to get moving," said Jihoon.

"How long was I out?"

They helped me to my feet without jarring my arm, and I was grateful. The thought of losing it didn't scare me, and if anything it made me rethink my opposition to bioengineered limbs and organs. What scared me was the pain. It was still intense, and I didn't want to pass out again, not in the bush with Chinese scouts all around.

I started up the mountain, fighting a wave of dizziness and nausea. "With my flame hood and cloak gone, I don't have a helmet," I whispered. "They'll see me."

"It's not only you," said Jennifer, "My cloak was destroyed and half of my chameleon skin damaged. Jihoon is the only one still masked."

I realized then that I could see her. Half of Jennifer showed up on infrared, a dull figure in light gray, the other half smeared. We kept moving, with Jihoon taking the lead and me in the middle, Jennifer pausing every so often to look behind us and listen. An hour later the sky brightened. The slope had also steepened as we got deeper into the mountains, and there were still at least six kilometers between us and the border.

"We're not going to make the border," I said. "Not if daylight comes. We'll have to risk stopping and hiding."

Jennifer clicked in. "We're not headed for the border; we're headed for a tunnel."

"What? Whose tunnel?"

"We stealth-bored infiltration tunnels through the mountain under our line, long before the Chinese arrived. Margaret told us to do it. That way we'd be able to infiltrate rear areas more easily when the Chinese reached us, but the map data isn't uploaded into computers of patrol units, so it can't be compromised if any of us are captured. Margaret foresaw—"

"I know," I interrupted. "Margaret foresaw everything. She's a saint."

Jennifer sounded shocked. "Then you agree?"

"With what?"

"That she sits at Catherine's side now. *With God himself.*"

I shook my head and wondered: *How the hell could anyone lead these psychos, human or not?*

"Yes," I said. "I believe she's at Catherine's side. She may even have her own pool boy." But before Jennifer could ask what a pool boy was, I changed the subject. "Can you find an entrance without your map data?"

"I don't know. But if God is with us, I will."

God better be with us, I thought, *or I'll pass out with pain.* My shoulder got worse as the sun started to rise, bringing with it a humid heat that penetrated through the broken armor, and it had become hard to distinguish between my own sweat and the suit coolant, which had leaked all night from the broken capillaries in my undersuit. Soon I'd have to take it all off. Rather than cool me, the armor would act like an oven, its insulating layers cooking me as I sweated from the uphill hike.

There were dark moments in that retreat, some more so than others. While we kept moving forward, the thought occurred to me that even if we reached the tunnel and the safety of the line, the Chinese still had to be dealt with, and this time they wouldn't be overconfident. They didn't have to conduct a frontal assault. With numbers so far in excess of ours, they and the Burmese could sit back and lob plasma shells or send bomber flights over Nu Poe for as long as they wanted while we sweated it out in the tunnels and waited for an underground assault. By the time the Chinese arrived at the trenches, the *Gra Jaai* and everyone else would be twitching, mental train wrecks; none of them would be able to fight. And had the *Gra Jaai* even been trained in tunnel defense? What about the Karen? And more importantly, *What had Margaret tried to stick me with, and did I really want to even think about taking the job?* The thought made me reconsider my decision to stay away from the States and leave the military, an option that sent me into a depression with the idea of having to return—of having to wait between missions as I aged further, to deteriorate with the torture of passing time while Assurance eavesdropped on my mumbling. But Margaret had already shown that she had several surprises, and it was possible there was more than met the eye with the *Gra Jaai* and their sato leaders.

"Jennifer?" I asked. "Did Margaret have any other surprises for the Chinese? Other than infiltration tunnels and flame units?"

She stopped and stared at me, the silence making me turn to face her.

"Are you accepting the job Margaret offered?"

I tried to shrug and stifled an urge to yell with the pain. "I don't know."

"Then," she said, continuing up the mountain toward

me, "I don't know either. Hurry and try to move faster; I think there is a tunnel entrance a few hundred meters from here, but there may be one or two scouts on our trail. I heard something behind us."

"Instead of simply plugging the tunnels," said Jennifer, "Margaret had us install coded doors so we could use them in case of emergencies."

"You're sure this is the spot?" I asked. I had heard the same thing Jennifer did, and it gave me the creeps—a distant crash and thud, as if someone had slipped on the loose clay to fall a short distance. "You're sure?"

"It's the general area." She pointed to a large boulder on our left and a deep gully to the right, waving at the almost impenetrable bush in between. "It's here, I just have to pinpoint it."

She pushed into the jungle, and Jihoon and I turned, slipping in opposite directions to find hiding spots from which we could take watch. The sun was overhead now. I fought to keep from passing out and drank so much water that if we kept this up my tank would be empty within an hour, sweat dripping from under my vision hood. A huge termite mound rose from the area that I'd originally targeted as a hiding spot, making me curse. It would take a few moments to find another spot, time that I didn't have; instead I pushed into the bushes beside the mound, lay down to cover myself with leaves and dirt so that only my eyes were exposed, and prayed that the termites would leave me alone.

Jennifer was almost noiseless. I sometimes heard her shuffle in the underbrush, but for the most part I'd have never known she was there, leaving me enough time to stare at the twin thermite grenades gripped in both hands and wonder: how the hell was this going to work? We didn't have a flame unit now. The grenades would be our only effective weapon, and it would mean having to get close enough to use them, something I'd seen done once, and that was when both the scout and its attacker had been masked. But I had the general idea. I went over it again and again, using what I'd learned of the scouts' construction from having seen their wreckage, imagining myself grabbing hold and jamming the grenade into a fist-sized opening at the back near their hind legs—all with one arm almost useless.

Ten minutes later, Jennifer clicked in to tell us she'd found the entrance and opened it and that we should hurry before our pursuers caught up with us. I was about to stand when the scout arrived.

My mind shifted into a whirl of terror once I realized what was happening. Something pressed into the small of my back at the same time I heard quiet servos, and an immense weight pushed me into the brush and dirt until the flex from my armor threatened to crush my stomach. Images of Phillip flickered in my imagination. Somehow being this close to a live Chinese genetic was the worst thing I could imagine, and it illustrated how some people could go mad at the sight of a spider. I wanted it off me. My brain told me to wriggle out from under it and run, that there was a chance of escaping and it would go after one of the others, so that I had to force myself to calm down because it would move off soon. But it didn't. The scout stayed put, and from inside the thing I heard the sound of Chinese, spoken with a gurgling voice that, in turn, transformed into a quiet machine language that wouldn't have been audible except for the fact that its foot transmitted the sound waves through my armor.

There was one thing I could do, but my brain screamed at the idea, my shoulder doubly so because I'd have to ignore the pain, and even if it worked, it could maim me beyond repair. At the last moment I decided, *fuck it*, dropped one grenade while biting into the other's pin, and spat it out while shouting into my throat mic.

"Scout!"

The pressure released from my back. At that same instant I rolled over, moaning with pain, and saw the shimmering mass beside me just before I lunged for the area where its back should be; my gauntlets scraped against the scout's ceramic back plate. Finally their fingers clicked into a slot, and I grabbed hold. The scout went crazy. It jumped downslope and threatened to rip my shoulder apart, what remained of it, and I held on while brush and leaves whipped at my face in its effort to shake me loose. With the other hand I searched for the gap I knew should be there. We were about to head over a steep ledge when I found it, released the spoon, and jammed the grenade in—praying it would stay there as I let go, rolling through the air to land on a rock ledge with a thud. The scout continued down the mountain and a second later erupted with a pop to send a cloud of sparks and fire skyward before it disappeared into the jungle.

It was some time before I made it back to the termite mound. Millions of the things scurried over the clay and leaves, angry for having been disturbed by my movement, and I grabbed the last grenade before turning to where

Jihoon should have been. My vision hood was gone. There
was no way to find them on the map now, and with it
had gone my throat mics so if I wanted to communicate
I'd have to yell. *But there were likely more out here.*
Fear returned with the thought, and rather than wait, I
yanked the pin out and started crawling upward in the
last direction I'd seen Jennifer's dot, which may have
saved my life; when the tracers leaped from the bushes
behind me, instead of slamming into my skull, they cut
through my left forearm so I dropped the grenade. The
fuse hissed. There would only be a few seconds before it
blew, and while the scout paused to aim for another burst,
I kicked at the grenade to make it roll downhill, toward
the shimmer where it burst into a white ball. That close,
the heat singed my scalp and face to fill the air with the
smell of burning hair, and the intensity forced my eyes
shut while I struggled to move uphill in an attempt to get
as far away from the scout and the thermite as I could.
Something crashed through the bushes below me; at
first I thought it was the Chinese scout moving around the
thermite to get another shot but Jihoon's scream forced
my eyes back open.

"Jesus Christ!" he shrieked, and at the time I realized
that I'd never heard his voice get that high. Ji repeated it
over and over. The crashing noise continued, getting
fainter until another grenade detonated, making me sigh
with relief at the assumption that Ji had managed to kill it.
I was about to go toward the sound of his voice when
Jennifer slapped me on the shoulder.

"Move. Uphill. I'll get your partner, then catch up with
you to show you the way; other Chinese will come."

"Scouts," I said, and I must have been wounded worse

than I realized because I started laughing. "Two of them. I'm not kidding, one of them walked on top of me."

"Move!" she screamed.

I made it about fifty meters up the mountain when she found me again, but this time she carried Jihoon on her back. It took me a few seconds to see what was wrong. Ji's left leg was gone below the knee where one of the scouts had bit it off with metal pincers, and his head lolled over her shoulder.

"Is he dead?" I asked.

"I wouldn't be carrying him if he was."

"Where's the tunnel?"

She pointed with her chin. "Right in front of you."

I turned and looked. Even then it was hard to see, but before me was a narrow crack between two boulders, from which had been carved a rock door that opened just wide enough to let someone armored through. It opened inward and I pulled myself in. The air was cool inside, and I relaxed at first, before the temperature made me feel as though I'd pass out and my body reacted with the first symptoms of shock as it started shivering. Jennifer pushed Jihoon through and then squeezed into the narrow space, urging me to move farther back and give her some room. When she shut the door, it was pitch-black.

"I'm going into shock," I said.

"A medical unit is on its way. I made contact with Nu Poe before I came to get you."

"I'm really tired now, Jennifer. Not scared. Just want to go to sleep."

I felt a needlelike prick against my skin and heard the hiss of an aeroinjector. "More bots. I gave some to the other lieutenant as well, to stop the bleeding from his leg."

"Will he make it?" I asked.

"Be quiet, Lieutenant. The tunnel is soundproofed, but I don't know all their capabilities."

"Damn it, Kristen," I said, getting more and more delirious. "Call me Bug."

ELEVEN

Escape

The first thing I noticed when I woke was that, for the moment, the pain had vanished. Remorro and Orcola sat next to me, laughing, and at first there wasn't any sound except for dripping water as it pattered on a transparent plastic sheet that someone had draped over me to keep the rain off, and it made me wonder why they'd put me outside. But I *wasn't* outside. Orcola pulled the sheet back, and overhead the distant booming of plasma artillery shook the rock around me and vibrated the hospital rack on which I rested. It confused me. I didn't recognize anything about the small chamber in which I lay, and the two kept laughing so that I had to look up in panic to make sure that all my limbs were there, and even then something was wrong.

"Why are you laughing?" I croaked.

Remorro shook his head. "You are in deep shit. Momson himself is on his way now, and the Thai Army spared one of their rotary wings to get him from Bangkok to Nu Poe. You know how rare it is for those bastards to let *anyone* use one of their precious rotary wings?"

"Why?"

"Why what?" he asked.

"Why is Momson coming?" Speaking was difficult. My throat felt dry despite a saline drip that fed water into my arm, and it was as if someone had taken sandpaper to my vocal chords.

"Because you killed her," said Orcola. "I guess you weren't supposed to wipe Margaret, although why that's the case is a freakin' mystery to us. *We* think you deserve a medal. Maybe now the Thai Army can get these girls under control. We've even been recalled and leave with the rotary wing."

The comment made me angry, which was shocking; Orcola's view made sense. With the Thai Army and *Gra Jaai* at odds—at the worst possible time, during a war—it must have been impossible for anything to get done, and now there was a path forward, another chance at reconciliation. Then I realized it wasn't that part that had annoyed me; it was that Orcola approved of Margaret's death.

"You don't know shit," I said.

"I'll tell you what I know. Five Laotian and Cambodian Army groups are on their way now, and already their advance forces are crammed into every empty space we could find. Naval advisers from Vietnam, Malaysia, Indonesia, India, and the Philippines too. The worm has turned, and the craziest of the *Gra Jaai* are talking about being able to hold back the Chinese, maybe even invade Burma to just wipe the whole fucking country clean. India is screaming mad at Chinese border incursions and is ready to go nuclear."

The sound of a deeper pounding now came from the

side, not overhead. It shook my bed as though someone on the other side of the rock walls had turned a subwoofer all the way up and pointed it at my head.

"What are you *talking* about? What's that pounding?"

Remorro offered me a cigarette and I took it, waiting for him to light it as he spoke. "Turns out that months ago the Thai King authorized *Gra Jaai* diplomatic missions to every country in southeast Asia. Everyone knows that when Thailand falls, Laos is next and then Vietnam, after which Beijing has the whole South China Sea. So nobody wants China to win here. Several countries sent troops, and if you thought the Thai Army was pissed at the girls *before* you left…For a day or so we thought the generals would try for a coup. The Army was kept totally out of the loop until the last minute and doesn't want any of these guys here; it's an Asian thing; the Thais hate the Laotians and Cambodians, the Cambodians hate the Laotians and Thais, and the only thing they all have in common is that *everyone* hates the goddamn Chinese."

"And," Orcola added, "that deeper sound is from plasma artillery. *Gra Jaai.* They've been building the stuff for years, in secret, and had hidden artillery positions all along the line but didn't use it until now. Gotta hand it to them."

I sucked on the cigarette until it was a nub, then spat it out to ask for another. Remorro lit it. The water dripped on my face now, warm and nauseating, but it soon cooled to make me feel better as though it was washing away the clay and blood, scrubbing the last remnants of jungle from my pores. While we sat there nobody spoke. I didn't want them to. Now that I'd gotten used to Nu Poe and spent time in its jungle, the pair of men looked like misfits, skinny cutouts from a Special Forces recruiting ad whom the girls would never let into their inner sanctum and who therefore would never amount to anything useful. To anyone. Their opinions were equivalent to those of talking heads on the news holos, always offering advice and analysis, none of which was worth a damn.

They stood when Lucy entered, and Remorro and Orcola said their good-byes, leaving me with a pack of cigarettes and a lighter; I was glad to see them go.

Lucy stood next to me and grinned. "You honored her."

I shook my head. "I killed her."

"Do you think she wasn't ready, that she hadn't prayed for your arrival?" Lucy pulled a chair closer and sat, staring past me and at the wall. "She saw your arrival over a year ago and had everything planned for it—plasma artillery, asking our neighbors for help against the Chinese if they came, everything."

"I know where you're headed, Lucy. You want to know if I'll take the job as head crazy of crazies, and to tell you the truth, part of me wants to, but I don't know."

"Why?" she asked. "What is so difficult about making the decision?" When I didn't answer, Lucy nodded. "Well, in the meantime I need you to do us a favor." I noticed then that she had a bag, out of which she pulled a light orange jacket, dark green dress pants and shirt, and a pair of boots. "*Pretend* you're our leader."

"You want me to lie? Isn't that a little cowardly?"

She nodded and laughed. "Yes. But necessary. I will pay the price for the lie if you decide to leave us, but if you stay, then the deception is as if it never existed."

"Why?" I asked. "What do you need?"

"Above us in a conference room are generals and representatives from multiple armies, including the Thai.

The Laotians and Cambodians refuse to accept Thai command. The Thais won't budge on their need to lead all forces and are insisting that the Laotians and Cambodians leave if they don't agree. And none of them will serve us, the *Gra Jaai*."

"And that surprises you? I have news for you, Lucy, most people think the *Gra Jaai* and your religion are completely insane."

Lucy nodded again. "Concur. But that's not why they won't concede command to us."

"Well, then, what *is* the problem?"

"The same one we've always had. The nonbred created us and cannot conceive of serving under our leadership. They hate us."

The enormity of what she was asking made me feel sick. This was politics. For the situation she described, Lucy would need a real leader, someone who understood strategies and the subtleties associated with commanding mixed forces in what was the strangest setting imaginable in the most important conflict the region had faced since the last Asian War.

"I'm no leader," I said. "You need someone they'll respect and believe. Someone they wouldn't dare reject. I have no clue about military strategy and barely have a grasp of small unit tactics. For the past few years I've been an assassin, a killer. It's all I've ever been good at, but it's not something a Thai general is likely to respect."

Lucy threw her cigarette to the ground and rested the uniform over my legs. "We respect it, and that's what matters. The Chinese are boring toward us now, and they're bombarding the trenches above with artillery and air strikes. Do you believe in God yet, Lieutenant?"

"You know I don't. Margaret must have told you before she died."

"Well," said Lucy, "we do. And Margaret did. She knew that we'd need the help of the other Asian nations and that the only person they'd follow would be nonbred—a non-*Thai* nonbred. You. It doesn't matter that you don't know strategy or tactics because we can take care of that."

"What do I have to do?" I asked.

"Be yourself. And *try* to trust that this is in God's hands, not yours."

I stared at the orange jacket. It was a pale color, more like pumpkin, and had two white shoulder patches with red crosses, and along one sleeve was a line of horizontal red stripes fringed with white piping. Above the left breast pocket was a sea of fruit salad—tiny ribbons in hundreds of different patterns and colors, the uppermost of which was a rectangular green ribbon with a tiny white lily in its center. An enamel lily had been affixed to each collar.

I pointed to the green ribbon, my finger on the lily. "What's this ribbon?"

"That one signifies your last patrol and the death of Margaret, your greatest achievement. The others are for the actions you saw the last time you fought in Burmese bush wars, for Kazakhstan and for every mission in between. The lily is the symbol of leadership in the *Gra Jaai,* our highest honor, and it represents those who are pure killers."

"And the red stripes?"

"One for each of our sisters you assassinated in your hunts."

I stared at her. "How the hell did you get all the information? It's not like it's available in the press."

"We," said Lucy with a smile, "have important contacts in the Thai Army. I didn't know you had fought here before."

"It's not something I advertise."

The completeness of it impressed me. Although the jacket's color seemed odd, it went with the rest of the uniform and with the *Gra Jaai*'s tendency to want to stand out. Even now I didn't understand them completely; they wanted to honor the person who'd murdered their leader, wanted to follow *me*, and even knowing that I was no general hadn't detracted from Lucy's enthusiasm in the least.

"Fine," I said. "I'll pretend. But this doesn't mean I'm taking the job."

She smiled and started to lift me from the bed, pulling the IVs out. "We need to move now. I'll help you get dressed."

"Jesus," I hissed. As soon as I sat up, the pain returned, and my head started to swim. "Am I going to live?"

"You'll be fine," Lucy said, bending down to start sliding the pants on. "We'll take you to a briefing first, on our tactical and strategic situation, then meet with the generals and admirals."

"How's Jihoon?"

She looked up. "He's not doing well. We couldn't retrieve his leg from the jungle, and he lost a lot of blood. He'll make it, and American doctors can grow him a new limb, but mentally..."

"Fuck it," I said. "Let's get this over with so I can pay him a visit and get drunk."

I followed Lucy into the conference room, my shirt and jacket pulled onto my left arm but draped over my wounded right shoulder. It felt like a costume more than a uniform. As soon as we entered, the *Gra Jaai*—including the satos—snapped to attention around the room's edge, forcing the others silent as they sat and stared at me. None of them rose. I recognized the Thai general, the one who had glared at me in Bangkok, who sat at the head of a long table with his subordinates on either side, and senior officers from at least four other countries filled the remaining seats.

Everyone waited. My skin crawled with the sudden sensation that I was out of my element, and it took only a second to decide that this was a mistake because I was sure that the men and women saw through me, recognized me as the imposter I was. What had Lucy been thinking? After more than a week in the field, I'd lost several pounds and must have looked gaunt, and when I raised my less-injured arm to run a hand through my hair was surprised to find it all gone, before remembering that it had burned off. I had no idea what my face looked like. But the expression of shock on an Indian admiral's face, a woman, said it all, and if she looked *that* disgusted it must have been bad.

I leaned over and whispered to Lucy. "I know the Thai general. He already doesn't like me."

"Don't worry about it. A week from now you have an audience with the King, where you'll present evidence that he and several of the other Army commanders have been planning a coup. He's of no concern."

I grinned at the man, who smiled back and spoke loudly so that everyone at the table could hear while Lucy translated.

"This man is a drunk. A lieutenant. He disobeyed

American orders, and his handlers are on their way here now, to pick up their trash." A couple of officers chuckled, but most waited as the Thai general placed a pair of glasses on his nose. "Where were we?"

"You're in my seat," I said.

He glanced back at me. "Run along. Colonel Momson should be here in a few minutes, and you can visit the Khlong Toei brothels before we kick you out. I've heard all about you."

Now he was pissing me off. The general looked smug as he tapped his fingers on the table, waiting for my reaction, and I stepped forward, trying to ignore the pain from my shoulder.

"Get out of my seat. Now. Or I'll have my girls beat the shit out of you."

His face went pale. "*How dare you!* I am the field marshal of the Royal Thai Army, cousin to the King himself." His aides stood and rested their hands on their pistols. "Leave now, or I'll have you shot."

The girls moved. His aides, all colonels, screamed when they found their arms twisted behind their backs and struggled against the satos, who now forced them toward the entrance. When they were gone, I grinned more broadly.

"You're in my seat," I repeated.

This time he stood. The general was shorter than I remembered and frail, and he pushed past to follow his men so I could collapse into the vacant seat with a grateful sigh. He turned at the door and spat on the floor.

"This is Thailand. The King will make sure that all of you are hung."

I nodded. "This *is* Thailand. And the Royal Thai

Army is a disgrace. My forces repelled the first Chinese advance without the benefit of your Army and without air cover or plasma. This is a planning session for war. I'm sure you'll be more comfortable back in Bangkok talking about war rather than participating in it."

When the general left, the others at the table relaxed. One or two grinned, and the Laotian and Cambodian generals leaned back, laughing.

"The Cambodian," Lucy whispered, "is General Im, and the Laotian is General Choulamontry."

Choulamontry spoke first. "Laos and Cambodia have moved an infantry division each onto the line so we can see for ourselves what we're up against. The remainder of three Army groups are staging now to move in and reinforce. Provided we can agree on how this will work."

"This is how it works, General." I lit a cigarette and leaned back in my chair, thanking God that Lucy had briefed me. "The Chinese movement suggests that they plan to take over Thailand and then Laos and Vietnam. Why? Because that way they get access to non-radioactive port cities and the entirety of the South China Sea, which opens the door to the rest of the Pacific while they move on India's eastern border. So either we ally now and stop them, or you can take your chances later. Alone. Who knows, maybe they don't care about Laos or Cambodia. Maybe they'll save you for last."

A Vietnamese admiral nodded. "It's true. Our forces have already detected Chinese buildup along our northern border, and their port cities, all of which had been previously abandoned, are now showing activity. We expect an attack within weeks."

"We," said the Indian representative, "are already at war."

"We don't know anything about their troop strengths," said General Im. "All we hear are stories from these"—he pointed at Lucy—"*things* that the Chinese have a new kind of genetically engineered soldier, ones that incorporate powered armor."

I nodded at Lucy, who waved at a pair of *Gra Jaai*. They stepped out and returned a minute later carrying one of the Chinese bodies from the morgue, placing it gently on the table before removing the plastic sheet in which it had been wrapped. Nobody said a word until Im shook his head.

"*You* started this. Americans. You played God and unleashed a horror on the rest of us. What did you think? That you could keep control of these creations, that your secret wouldn't get out even when you went to war in Kazakhstan? Do you really expect us to give command of Laotian and Cambodian troops to these *Gra Jaai* and their bitches? That we even *want* American forces here?"

I didn't blame him. It was easy to sympathize with the general's position, especially since I'd shared it only a week prior. "No. I expect you to hand over command to *me*. I'll work with you to make sure that Laotian and Cambodian troops are used in the right way and aren't wasted. And I'm not American, not anymore, and we will not ask for or approve of US assistance in this war, except for any material assistance they're willing to provide, including fresh genetic troops. But you have to promise me something."

"Go on," he said.

"You have to promise me that your men and women won't break and run like pissy little girls the first time they see a Chinese genetic."

"What do you know about genetics?" Choulamontry asked. "We don't know anything about you."

"I just came back from a mission ten kilometers inside Burma. I killed a Chinese genetic by riding it down a mountain and shoving a thermite grenade into a gap in its armor."

Lucy stopped translating and said something in rapid Laotian, and I watched as the generals' eyes went wide, the two of them looking at each other.

"What did you tell them?" I whispered once she'd finished.

"That you single-handedly hunted down and killed over thirty of my sisters and that you did the same using only a knife against Margaret."

General Im leaned forward and whispered to Choulamontry, then looked at me. "Give us some time. We see your points, and although it will be difficult to convince our leadership to work with Thailand, the threat is imminent and clear. None of us want another war with China, but they must be crushed, once and for all. It will take discussion."

The hard part was over. Now Lucy and I smoked while the generals and admirals spoke, at times shouting to make themselves heard, and several times I caught the Japanese *Gra Jaai*, especially the women, staring at me. Their eyes snapped forward when I caught them doing it.

"Why are they staring at us?" I asked.

Lucy whispered back. "They are amazed that you killed Margaret. And they are excited."

"Why?"

"*Because* you killed Margaret. She was their spiritual leader, and many can't wait to see God's plan."

An hour passed and then two. The officers pelted us with questions to the point where I began to tire, and Lucy stopped the debate, noticing that I was starting to fade.

"We need an answer," I said. "There isn't time for talking anymore."

The Laotian glanced at Im, who nodded before smiling. "We agree. Choulamontry and I will begin moving troops immediately, but we'll have to work out coordinating communications, defensive position, and plans—starting first thing tomorrow. We're talking about months of preparation; are you sure you can hold the Chinese for that long?"

"We'll hold them. And our technicians will begin tackling communications and language issues tonight," I said, trying to hide my relief.

The Philippine admiral spoke up. "Ours and the Malaysian and the Indonesian ships will assist the Vietnamese in defending their territories within the South China Sea. What about the Thai Navy?"

"In one week," I said. "I'll have all the Thai armed forces in line, with the King's full support. Leave that to me."

"Then it's settled," said Im. We stood and nodded at each other before Lucy and I turned to leave. I leaned over and whispered one last question to her.

"You're sure you can come up with a strategy to deal with all this crap?"

She laughed and nodded. "I told you, Lieutenant. It isn't up to me now, it's up to Him."

"You said I had a meeting with the King in one week. How do you know I'll even be here?"

"I don't. But how do we know any of us will be here?"

*   *   *

Lucy left me alone with Jihoon, who lay under a plastic tent like I had. By now the water had soaked my uniform jacket. I pulled up a chair next to his gurney, and it hit me without warning: the mission was over. We'd made it. A feeling of uncertainty settled over me as I realized that the future was empty and that soon I'd have to decide what to do with the rest of my life. Then, without warning, the uncertainty snowballed into terror that made the room shrink, the ceiling promising to collapse with every artillery strike far above, and the air was too hot to breathe, so I had to grab my chair and close my eyes, telling myself that none of it was real. The only option was to stay, to lead the *Gra Jaai,* but who would *want* to do that? Most people would be happy to have survived the things I'd been through and would look forward to retirement after twenty years of service, transitioning from military to civilian service with a grin. But that meant going home to the States. My gut told me that if I did that, it wouldn't be long before I drank myself to death and Phillip would be on his own.

I opened my eyes again and ducked under the plastic to touch Jihoon's shoulder.

"Hey, Bug," he said. "We made it."

"I guess." His skin felt cold, and I pulled my hand away, the sensation reminding me of a corpse. "How are you feeling?"

Ji looked up and away from me. "I lost my leg."

"Yeah, but they can grow you a new one, and to tell you the truth, I might get that genetic work done on my knees; they've gotten *that* bad. You saved my ass, Chong. I owe you one."

"Then tell me what to do. I don't know if I can handle this job anymore; the tank wasn't like reality at all, and now that I've been in it, I don't think I have the guts to go on another mission. I'm scared."

I sighed and pulled out a cigarette, placing it between his lips and then lighting it. I took one too. The smoke started to take the edge off my own fears, softening the pain from my shoulder and making me feel unbelievably tired so that I wanted to tell Jihoon to shove over and make room for me on the bed.

"Don't *decide* anything," I said. "You might be scared, but you functioned out there. You killed the enemy before he killed you and made it back, so don't give me that shit that you don't have what it takes. If you didn't, you would have just run and left me to the Chinese."

Jihoon shrugged. "I don't know. Maybe." He grinned then and took a long pull from the cigarette. "One of the *Gra Jaai* just stopped by and told me that we're going home in a few minutes. Momson arrived, and they'll be taking us out on the rotary wing."

The news surprised me. I'd thought there'd be more time before his arrival, but discussions with the generals had taken longer than I'd anticipated, and now the feeling of terror returned because I'd have to make a decision.

Ji was staring at me. "You're not going with us, are you?"

"No. I think I'm staying here."

"I figured. You're made for this stuff, Bug. For you to go home would be like trying to teach a gorilla how to dance ballet. Maybe you could do it, but it wouldn't look pretty. Besides, it's like I already said. If I didn't know any better and hadn't seen your file, I'd say you were a damn sato yourself."

I laughed. "That's an insult."

"Yeah. They're crazy, the *Gra Jaai* are crazy, but you're not too sane yourself. What will you tell the brass?"

Lucy returned and lifted the plastic, telling me that Momson had arrived and was waiting for me outside the main entrance; her troops refused to let him enter and had threatened to kill the Special Forces reps who were supposed to have replaced Remorro and Orcola. Two *Gra Jaai* pulled the plastic off Jihoon and prepared to wheel him away.

I shook his hand before he disappeared into the tunnels. "I don't know what I'll tell Momson, but I'm about to find out. Take care, Ji."

"We should go too," said Lucy. "If you're leaving, there isn't much time."

"Where did they put my things? When they brought me back to the tunnels, the Sunshine data was stored in my kit."

She cocked her head. "They are in Remorro and Orcola's quarters. Why?"

"Let's make a detour so I can get them; Momson can wait."

Handing over Kristen's memory chits and the Sunshine data felt wrong, like giving nuclear weapons to a teenager and asking him to be careful. But I wanted Phillip, and I'd already made up my mind: he *was* my son, even if I wasn't his father. What would America do with the data? The Cambodian general, Im, had been right when he said that once created and fielded, there was no way to prevent an enemy from stealing genetic secrets since all he or she had to do was capture one of them, dead or alive. On the other hand, although I didn't want the data anymore, there were nations that would do whatever it took to get it, so by handing it over I'd distance myself from something hideous and dangerous—a distance that would provide some measure of protection. Relief. The only other options were to hold the chits and risk having them stolen or to destroy them and never see my son again. There was really no choice at all.

Momson stood next to a huge rotary wing aircraft, its engines pointed skyward at the end of short wings while the *Gra Jaai* wheeled Jihoon up a ramp and into the plane's rear. He walked over to us and stuck out his hand. I shook it but wanted to wash mine with lye to make sure that none of him rubbed off on me.

"You did a fantastic job," Momson said. "We'll put Jihoon back together so don't worry, and we've gotten over the fact that you killed Margaret."

"Good."

Momson squinted and looked me up and down. "What's with the uniform, Bug?"

"I'm not going back, Momson. I quit. You can take your missions and shove them up your ass."

Momson didn't look surprised. He grinned and slung a carbine over his shoulder, glancing around to see the *Gra Jaai* who had gathered to listen.

"What about your son, Bug?"

I nodded. "What about him?"

"You're going to raise a kid in a war zone? Christ. You had us pull him from the academy because you didn't want him in the tanks, but now you're willing to raise him on the front lines where he could get killed for real. You're just as crazy as these people."

"At least," I said, "he'll be in the real world. Not some semi-aware's idea of what the world is like. He'll get to choose and won't have to worry about Assurance deciding that he's a security risk because he used the word *bomb* twice in one sentence."

"If he lives."

"Yeah, I guess so."

Momson started kicking at the ground absentmindedly, and I knew what was coming.

"There's the little matter of Sunshine. We'll need to debrief you and figure out what you missed in case we need to go back for another collect. You're going to have to come back with us—at least for a while."

I shook my head. "I can give you data taken from Chen's lab, and Jihoon can fill you in on operational details. Hell. If you want data on Chinese forces, I can probably give you a whole genetic. But I'm not going back. This is my home now."

Momson looked about to piss himself with glee. He grinned now and wouldn't stop nodding. "But you want your son. The data for Phillip, is that the deal?"

"I want my kid. That's the deal."

He waved at the plane and Phillip emerged, negotiating the ramp downward; when he reached the ground, he saw me and sprinted so that I knelt and caught him in my arms, kissing the top of his head.

"I've got you now." It was the only thing I could think to say and Phillip didn't respond; it was the quietest I'd ever seen him.

"I figured I might need him here," said Momson. "So I brought him along. Now the data."

I turned to Lucy. "Can you give him one of the Chinese?"

She nodded and left, jogging into the tunnel. I handed all the chits then to Momson, and he tucked them quickly into a pouch before pointing at one of the *Gra Jaai*.

"Can they fight?" he asked.

"Better than you."

"I've heard stories, Bug. Christ. You want to stay here with a bunch of religious whack-jobs and expose your kid to them during the most formative years of his life? Forget about the fact that this is war, do you *really* want him to wind up like them—half-drugged in some quest for enlightenment through killing?"

From the main entrance you heard the artillery. If you looked up the mountain, you could see the bright flashes of plasma impacting over the *Gra Jaai* trenches, and the ground vibrated with the deeper booming of the satos' new plasma weapons returning fire. The temple still looked odd. Its stone had cracked and gave me the feeling of being part of an ancient story, one that had been written a long time ago and that I couldn't have escaped, even if I wanted to—which I didn't.

All my life I'd been a killer. All my life I'd gone home to a peace that never fit, and while some people would look at this place like it was the definition of insanity, to me it fit. Going *home* would be insane. I hadn't really known whether I'd stay or not until I saw Momson, the sight of whom had brought me back to reality, had reminded me of the breeding stations and booze and of Bea, whom the system had sucked up the way a vacuum collects dust balls. That system wouldn't get Phillip. And it would never touch me again. War was where I belonged, and for whatever reason I'd been born into it, so that trying to deny it was like trying to turn my hair blue from wishing. You couldn't be sure that we'd destroy the Chinese or even keep them from invading Thailand, but there was a feeling in the air, and I knew the *Gra Jaai* sensed it too, a sensation of promise. *Destiny.*

"Yeah. I'd rather he wound up like them than wind up like me. Or worse—like *you.*"

Lucy returned with two satos, who handed the Chinese corpse to Momson. He thanked them, and I turned to leave with Phillip's hand grasped tightly in mine, so tightly that someone would have had to kill me to pry my hand loose.

Lucy whispered to me as we walked, "I knew you'd stay."

"Yeah. I bet you did."

"Hey," Momson yelled after us. "At least tell me why. People are going to want to know, Bug, why you stayed when you could have come home and retired from all this crap. Forever."

I stopped and looked back. "Because. I don't ever want to go back to those days."

And Phillip looked up at me and smiled.

extras

orbit

meet the author

T. C. McCARTHY earned a BA from the University of Virginia and a PhD from the University of Georgia before embarking on a career that gave him a unique perspective as a science fiction author. From his time as a patent examiner in complex biotechnology to his tenure with the Central Intelligence Agency, T.C. has studied and analyzed foreign militaries and weapons systems. T.C. was at the CIA during the September 11 terrorist attacks and was still there when US forces invaded Afghanistan and Iraq, allowing him to experience warfare from the perspective of an analyst. Find out more about the author at www.tcmccarthy.com.

introducing

If you enjoyed
CHIMERA,
look out for

2312

by Kim Stanley Robinson

The year is 2312. Scientific and technological advances have opened gateways to an extraordinary future. Earth is no longer humanity's only home; new habitats have been created throughout the solar system on moons, planets, and in between. But in this year, 2312, a sequence of events will force humanity to confront its past, its present, and its future.

The first event takes place on Mercury, on the city of Terminator, itself a miracle of engineering on an unprecedented scale. It is an unexpected death, but one that might have been foreseen. For Swan Er Hong, it is an event that will change her life. Swan was once a woman who designed worlds. Now she will be led into a plot to destroy them.

The sun is always just about to rise. Mercury rotates so slowly that you can walk fast enough over its rocky surface to stay ahead of the dawn; and so many people do. Many have made this a way of life. They walk roughly westward, staying always ahead of the stupendous day. Some of them hurry from location to location, pausing to look in cracks they earlier inoculated with bio-leaching metallophytes, quickly scraping free any accumulated residues of gold or tungsten or uranium. But most of them are out there to catch glimpses of the sun.

Mercury's ancient face is so battered and irregular that the planet's terminator, the zone of the breaking dawn, is a broad chiaroscuro of black and white—charcoal hollows pricked here and there by brilliant white high points, which grow and grow until all the land is as bright as molten glass, and the long day begun. This mixed zone of sun and shadow is often as much as thirty kilometers wide, even though on a level plain the horizon is only a few kilometers off. But so little of Mercury is level. All the old bangs are still there, and some long cliffs from when the planet first cooled and shrank. In a landscape so rumpled the light can suddenly jump the eastern horizon and leap west to strike some distant prominence. Everyone walking the land has to attend to this possibility, know when and where the longest sunreaches occur—and where they can run for shade if they happen to be caught out.

Or if they stay on purpose. Because many of them pause in their walkabouts on certain cliffs and crater rims, at places marked by stupas, cairns, petroglyphs, inuksuit, mirrors, walls, goldsworthies. The sunwalkers stand by these, facing east, waiting.

The horizon they watch is black space over black rock.

The superthin neon-argon atmosphere, created by sunlight smashing rock, holds only the faintest predawn glow. But the sunwalkers know the time, so they wait and watch—until—

a flick of orange fire dolphins over the horizon

and their blood leaps inside them. More brief banners follow, flicking up, arcing in loops, breaking off and floating free in the sky. Star oh star, about to break on them! Already their faceplates have darkened and polarized to protect their eyes.

The orange banners diverge left and right from the point of first appearance, as if a fire set just over the horizon is spreading north and south. Then a paring of the photosphere, the actual surface of the sun blinks and stays, spills slowly to the sides. Depending on the filters deployed in one's faceplate, the star's actual surface can appear as anything from a blue maelstrom to an orange pulsing mass to a simple white circle. The spill to left and right keeps spreading, farther than seems possible, until it is very obvious one stands on a pebble next to a star.

Time to turn and run! But by the time some of the sunwalkers manage to jerk themselves free, they are stunned—trip and fall—get up and dash west, in a panic like no other.

Before that—one last look at sunrise on Mercury. In the ultraviolet it's a perpetual blue snarl of hot and hotter. With the disk of the photosphere blacked out, the fantastic dance of the corona becomes clearer, all the magnetized arcs and short circuits, the masses of burning hydrogen pitched out at the night. Alternatively you can block the corona, and look only at the sun's photosphere, and even magnify your view of it, until the burning tops of the convection cells are revealed in their squiggling thousands, each a thunderhead of fire burning furiously, all together torching five million tons of hydrogen a second—at which rate the star will burn another four billion years. All these long spicules of flame dance in circular patterns around the little black circles that are the sunspots—shifting whirlpools in the storms of burning. Masses of spicules flow together like kelp beds threshed by a tide. There are nonbiological explanations for all this convoluted motion—different gases moving at different speeds, magnetic fields fluxing constantly, shaping the endless whirlpools of fire—all mere physics, nothing more—but in fact it looks *alive*, more alive than many a living thing. Looking at it in the apocalypse of the Mercurial dawn, it's impossible to believe it's *not* alive. It roars in your ears, it *speaks* to you.

Most of the sunwalkers over time try all the various viewing filters, and then make choices to suit themselves. Particular filters or sequences of filters become forms of worship, rituals either personal or shared. It's very easy to get lost in these rituals; as the sunwalkers stand on their points and watch, it's not uncommon for devotees to become entranced by something in the sight, some pattern never seen before, something in the pulse and flow that snags the mind; suddenly the sizzle of the fiery cilia becomes audible, a turbulent roaring—that's your own blood, rushing through your ears, but in those moments it sounds just like the sun burning. And so people stay too long. Some have their retinas burned; some are blinded; others are killed outright, betrayed by an overwhelmed spacesuit. Some are cooked in groups of a dozen or more.

Do you imagine they must have been fools? Do you think you would never make such a mistake? Don't you be so sure. Really you have no idea. It's like nothing you've ever seen. You may think you are inured, that nothing outside the mind can really interest you anymore, as sophisticated and knowledgeable as you are. But you would be wrong. You are a creature of the sun. The beauty and terror of it seen from so close can empty any mind, thrust anyone into a trance. It's like seeing the face of God, some people say, and it is true that the sun powers all living creatures in the solar system, and in that sense *is* our god. The sight of it can strike thought clean out of your head. People seek it out precisely for that.

So there is reason to worry about Swan Er Hong, a person more inclined than most to try things just to see. She often goes sunwalking, and when she does she skirts the edge of safety, and sometimes stays too long in the light. The immense Jacob's ladders, the granulated pulsing, the spicules flowing...she has fallen in love with the sun. She worships it; she keeps a shrine to Sol Invictus in her room, performs the *pratahsamdhya* ceremony, the salute to the sun, every morning when she wakes in town. Much of her landscape and performance art is devoted to it, and these days she spends most of her time making goldsworthies and abramovics on the land and her body. So the sun is part of her art.

Now it is her solace too, for she is out there grieving. Now, if one were standing on the promenade topping the city Terminator's great Dawn Wall, one would spot her there to the south, out near the horizon. She needs to hurry. The city is gliding on its tracks across the bottom of a giant dimple between Hesiod and Kurasawa, and a flood of sunlight will soon pour far to the west. Swan needs to get into town before that happens, yet she still stands there. From the top of the Dawn Wall she looks like a silver toy. Her spacesuit has a big round clear helmet. Her boots look big and are black with dust. A little booted silver ant, standing there grieving when she should be hustling back to the boarding platform west of town. The other sunwalkers out there are already hustling back to town. Some pull little carts or wheeled travois, hauling their supplies or even their sleeping companions. They've timed their returns closely, as the city is very predictable. It cannot deviate from its schedule; the heat of coming day expands the tracks, and the city's undercarriage is tightly sleeved over them; so sunlight drives the city west.

The returning sunwalkers crowd onto the loading platform as the city nears it. Some have been out for weeks, or even the months it would take to make a full circumambulation. When the city slides by, its lock doors will open and they will step right in.

That is soon to occur, and Swan should be there too. Yet still she stands on her promontory. More than once she has required retinal repair, and often she has been forced to run like a rabbit or die. Now it will have to happen again. She is directly south of the city and fully lit by horizontal rays, like a silver flaw in one's vision. One can't help shouting at such rashness, useless though it is. Swan, you fool! Alex is dead—nothing to be done about it! Run for your life!

And then she does. Life over death—the urge to live—she turns and flies. Mercury's gravity, almost exactly the same as Mars's, is often called the perfect g for speed, because people who are used to it can career across the land in giant leaps, flailing their arms for balance as they bound along. In just that way Swan leaps and flails—once catches a boot and falls flat on her face—jumps up and leaps forward again. She needs to get to the platform while the city is still next to it; the next platform is ten kilometers farther west.

She reaches the platform stairs, grabs the rail and vaults up, leaps from the far edge of the platform, forward into the lock as it is halfway closed.